IN HIS KEEPING

IN HIS KEEPING

A Slow Burn Novel

MAYA BANKS

AVON
An Imprint of HarperCollins*Publishers*

IN HIS KEEPING. Copyright © 2015 by Maya Banks. All rights reserved. Printed in the United States of America. No part of this book may be used or reproduced in any manner whatsoever without written permission except in the case of brief quotations embodied in critical articles and reviews. For information address HarperCollins Publishers, 195 Broadway, New York, NY 10007.

HarperCollins books may be purchased for educational, business, or sales promotional use. For information please e-mail the Special Markets Department at SPsales@harpercollins.com.

FIRST EDITION

Library of Congress Cataloging-in-Publication Data has been applied for.

ISBN 978-0-06-231248-8

15 16 17 18 19   DIX/RRD   10 9 8 7 6 5 4 3 2

IN HIS KEEPING

GAVIN Rochester stood in the doorway of his enormous living room watching as his wife carefully examined a Christmas ornament before quietly replacing it in the box and tucking it back into the plastic basin they used to store Christmas decorations.

Her sadness instilled an ache inside his heart that made him physically rub his chest in an effort to alleviate the pain. But some wounds were simply too deep. Permanent and unable to heal. And her pain was unbearable to him because he couldn't fix this for her. His connections, money, power. None of it meant anything if he couldn't give his beloved wife what she wanted most. He felt her pain as keenly as if it were his own—and it *was*. Because he couldn't stand for her to be unhappy. He'd move mountains just to make her smile.

She'd changed him. Made him a better man. A man he never thought he could be—never wanted to be. But she changed everything—his world—his place in his world. Suddenly he'd *wanted* to be a better man. For *her*. Because it was what she deserved. And he would never place her in harm's way with his business practices. It was a new experience for him. Living clean. In the light. Having someone who *made* him want to feel . . . worthy.

Then she turned from her sad perusal of the lone ornament, and when she saw him, her face lit up, rosy from the shining Christmas lights strung around the tree. He marveled at how, whenever she smiled at him, it took his breath away. It was something that would never go away. His love for his wife was like nothing he'd ever experienced in his life. *Staggering.* Yet warm, like the flames in the fireplace. Unwavering. Without reservations, strings or conditions.

She loved *him*, and that knowledge still had the power to bring him to his knees.

"That's the last one," she said, her gaze drifting one last time to the sole ornament that hadn't been hung on the tree. Sorrow briefly chased the warmth from her eyes before she appeared to make a concerted effort to collect herself, and the grief filling her features slipped away, but he'd seen it. Knew it to be there no matter the effort she made not to let it show.

He crossed the room, no longer able to bear the distance between them. He pulled her into his arms and thrust his fingers into her long hair and then nuzzled the top of her head, inhaling her scent as his lips pressed to her glossy brunette strands.

"We'll try again," he murmured, trying to inject confidence and reassurance in his tone. And yet he knew he'd failed miserably. He sounded as dejected as he knew her to be. Not because she'd failed him. He could live his life with only her and never suffer a single regret. But he'd failed *her*. He was unable to give her a child he knew she wanted with every breath.

She wanted them to have a family. Love, laughter, to fill their house with warmth he'd never experienced before her. She knew all of that, knew what his life had been like and she was determined to change it. To give him a home. Not just a house. A home with a family and her unconditional love. He had no defense against her. His love defied boundaries or parameters. He knew he would never love another living soul the way he loved this woman.

She shook her head against his chest, and he carefully pulled her away, gutted by the sheen of tears in her brilliant brown eyes. Even in sorrow she was the most beautiful woman in the world to him. He couldn't *remember* his life before she entered it.

He held the single most precious thing to him in the world in his arms, and he was powerless to give her what she wanted most. A child.

"No more, Gavin," she said, her throat working up and down as if the words were painful to speak. "I can't take another loss. I *can't* do it anymore."

The utter despair in his beloved wife's voice was more than he could bear. He was precariously close to losing control over his own emotions. Only his vow to be an unyielding rock for his wife kept him in check.

She needed his strength. Not his weakness. And the hell of it was, he only had one weakness in his life.

Ginger. His wife, lover and absolute soul mate.

He would have laughed at the idea of fate and soul mates. The professor of his Human Resources and Development class had once said that the concept of there only being one person out there for you was utterly false. That you could fall in love—and love—many different people in your life.

He'd believed the exact same thing until one day a beautiful chestnut-headed, brown-eyed, adorably shy woman had walked into his life and his existence had been irrevocably changed. He'd known since the very first time she'd shyly accepted a dinner invitation with him that he was already in so deep that he had no hope of ever finding his way out. He hadn't *wanted* to.

Gavin was a man who was decisive, could handle any issue flung his way. He had the total package, or so women liked to tell him.

Good-looking, charismatic, dark and brooding and wealthy.

He was no naïve fool. The last attribute was his most compelling one. The women he'd been with hadn't likely given thought to anything beyond the tag that was solidly fixed on his forehead.

Billionaire.

He'd actually laid eyes on Ginger the very first time, ironically, when he'd been out with another woman. He'd had his entire evening planned, in fact. Nice dinner, intimate atmosphere, flirt with his date, whose name completely escaped him now, and then go back to her place to have sex before returning to his own apartment.

No one came to his home or invaded his private sanctuary. Sex was always at his date's place or in a hotel, and he always left afterward. To some women that made him a cold bastard, but he was hardly hypocrite enough to indulge in postcoital cuddle when he'd made it clear that there would be no emotional entanglements.

He hadn't stayed when he'd dropped his date off, much to her disappointment. His mind had been too occupied with the sweet, smiling waitress with big brown shy eyes who blushed when he stared at her for too long.

He wasn't normally so ill-mannered or lacking in social graces, but he'd been captivated by her from the moment he'd laid eyes on her, and so the next night, he'd gone back to the restaurant. Alone. He'd made certain he was seated in her section of tables and he'd proceeded to be the most demanding of customers, commanding her attention every few minutes for some trumped-up need.

It had taken three agonizingly long weeks before he'd been able to talk her into going out with him to dinner. Three weeks of self-induced celibacy because he'd known that she would be the last woman in his bed forever, so he hadn't minded the wait.

It had then taken him six more months of dating before he took things further than heated good-night kisses and feeling the warmth of her soft body against his while he held her.

It had been the best six months of his life.

The night he'd finally taken her to bed and very gently made her his, he'd proposed and she'd cried all over him.

It had taken him three more months of her practically living with him to talk her into accepting his marriage proposal, but once he'd gained her acceptance, his patience had fled. He'd hustled her in front of a judge at the very first opportunity and had claimed her for all time.

After a blissful year of having her entirely to himself—and he was extremely possessive and selfish of his time with her— she'd begun talking about having his child. He hadn't thought he could be happier than he was, but then he'd begun imagining sweet little girls who looked just like their mama and he'd been determined to fill their home with a dozen if that was what she wanted.

And that was where they'd hit a brick wall.

She'd gotten pregnant right away, to both their delight. Only for her to miscarry a few short weeks later. And so had begun their nightmare of endless hope and then dismay. The final straw had come when she'd become pregnant again earlier this year, after four miscarriages. She'd made it beyond the stage where her previous pregnancies had ended. They'd begun to become excited and hope bloomed that they'd finally, *finally* managed to make it happen.

At five months pregnant, after having learned that she was having what he wanted most—a little girl—and they'd bonded with the child, felt her first movements and had even begun to decorate the nursery, something they'd never allowed themselves to do before, tragedy had struck and she'd miscarried. The worst part was that she'd had to deliver the baby, a tiny, perfectly formed baby girl.

Ginger had been devastated. For months she'd been listless and adrift, and he'd never felt more helpless in his life. He loved her so much and he would have taken any amount of pain he could from her, but it had been hell for her, and after she'd healed physically, she'd never mentioned trying to have another child again.

Even now when he offered his gentle encouragement that they'd try again, she refused. He couldn't blame her, but he hated the idea of him not being able to fix this for her. In his world, nothing was impossible. Money, while not a cure-all, certainly made lots of things happen, but all the money in the world, all the power in the world didn't help his beautiful wife achieve her heart's desire.

As if sensing the dark direction of his thoughts, she reached up to cup the hard line of his jaw, her smile achingly sweet and eyes full of understanding.

"You're all I need. All I want," she said simply. "Swear you'll never leave me for someone who can give you children. Swear that to me and I'll never ask you for more."

He was genuinely shocked to his bones. He stared at her in absolute befuddlement, growing angrier by the second. Not at her. But at himself. Because if he'd made her feel as secure as she needed then she'd never question such a thing. That thought— fear—would *never* have entered her mind.

He framed her beautiful face in his hands and simply held her there, staring into the hypnotic brown of her soulful eyes.

"I only care that we can't have children because I know how much it hurts you," he said hoarsely. "I'd do anything at all to spare you this, Ginger. I'm so damn sorry I've failed you."

She put a finger to his lips. "Shhh. Gavin, you haven't failed me. You've given me child after child. It's me who's failed *you*, because I can't carry them. My body rejects them."

Her eyes closed as she said the last, and tears leaked silently down her cheeks.

"I couldn't bear it if you ever grew to resent me for that," she continued in a broken voice. "I never want you to look at me and see what I can't give you. Something another woman *could*."

He pulled her tightly into his arms, wrapping himself around her until she relaxed and melted against his body.

"There will never be another woman for me," he said gruffly.

"I'll never want for more than you can give me. I swear it on my very life, Ginger. My heart and soul belong to you. You own them—and me. And I hope to hell I own yours as well."

"I love you," she whispered. "Now do me a favor and put the angel up for me, and our tree will be complete."

But it wouldn't be and they both knew it. A simple ornament lay nestled in a box where the other ornaments were stored. *Baby's First Christmas* and the year engraved on the commemorative sterling silver baby spoon.

If all had gone as it should, she'd be delivering in a matter of days. A Christmas baby, she'd exclaimed in delight, when the doctor had given them the due date. Even now she would be swollen and heavy with his child, and he'd be rubbing her feet for her and holding her in his arms feeling their daughter kick and roll between them.

Ginger pulled away and carefully unwound the bubble wrap from the delicate porcelain angel tree topper. Using the step stool, Gavin reached up and carefully put the last decoration in place.

"It's perfect," she whispered, eyes bright with tears.

He kissed away every single tear and then pulled her into his side so they could stare at the tree she'd taken such painstaking measures to make beautiful. His wife loved Christmas. Their first holiday together would long stand out in Gavin's memory because, before her, Christmas had been just another day for him. An inconvenience since most places were closed for the holidays and people were out of town or simply unavailable.

But when Ginger came into his life, she'd forever changed him. She'd laughingly dragged him out of his Connecticut home to get the biggest, most glorious live tree they could find.

That was yet another change she'd wrought. Though he owned a grand house with rolling acreage and complete privacy, he'd always hated to stay in it alone. He'd spent most of his time in his Manhattan apartment. Until Ginger.

Now it was rare that he ever stayed over in his apartment and if he did, he ensured she was there too. He hadn't spent a night away from her since the very first time they'd made love. She'd turned his house in Connecticut into a . . . home. Warm, inviting, full of love and happiness.

"I love the tree," he said honestly. "You did a wonderful job, just as you do every year."

"Is it possible that I've turned the Grinch into Father Christmas?" she teased.

He chuckled. "What do you think? I didn't personally spend an entire day trying my best to kill myself by attaching lights to every exposed area of the outside of the house because I hate the holiday."

"You *do* hate the holiday. But you love me," she said cheekily.

He laughed. "I'm getting better. And I don't hate anything as long as you're a part of it."

Her entire expression softened and love warmed her eyes. She turned, tilting her head to receive his kiss when their doorbell rang.

They both frowned and Ginger drew away, her gaze flitting toward the foyer.

It was nearly 11 p.m. Who on earth would be at their door at this hour? For that matter, how would anyone have gotten through their security gate without their knowledge?

Gavin immediately grew serious. "You stay here and don't move. I'll see who it is."

"But . . ." she protested.

He silenced her with a quick squeeze and then reached into the drawer of the sofa table, drawing out his pistol. He tucked it out of view and then gave her another look that told her not to move and then strode toward the front door.

He frowned when he glanced through the speakeasy window that could be opened but was barred to prevent anyone on the outside from opening it. No one was standing there, but the motion light had been activated and still shone over the glistening snow-covered landscape.

Pulling the pistol from its hiding place, he eased the door open and stared into the still night. Cold air washed over him, the wind whistling in his ears. There was a full moon casting a glow over the white layer of snow. Only the sound of trees swaying and the crack of ice as branches broke disturbed the serenity.

He damn near tripped over the object at his feet. He took a hasty step back and glanced down, stunned to see what looked suspiciously like a . . . *baby carrier?*

He immediately dropped to his knees, carefully pulling back the blanket that covered something inside the carrier. When he lowered it enough to take in the contents, his breath escaped in a startled gasp.

"Gavin, what is it?"

Ginger's worried voice reached him and before he could tell her to stay back, the baby chose that exact moment to begin wailing, though it came out more of a whimper of distress than a true sob.

His wife gasped and crouched down beside him, reaching for the precious bundle before he could think to do the same.

"Oh dear God, Gavin! Someone left a baby out here to *freeze*?"

The horror in her voice was evident. He was still too flabbergasted to collect his scattered thoughts.

"Bring the carrier in," Ginger said crisply, as she hoisted the baby higher in her arms and rose from her kneeling position on the porch.

He followed her in but something told him he should be out there looking for the person who'd left the baby. They still had to be on the premises. He owned quite a bit of acreage and it would take several minutes to get off his land no matter which direction they'd come from.

But he was drawn to the picture of his wife standing by the fireplace, carefully unwrapping the baby and then tucking the downy head beneath her chin as she swayed in an effort to comfort the crying child.

"Is there a note?" she asked anxiously. "Anything at all to explain what in the world someone was thinking to do such a terrible thing? It's Christmas! You don't abandon a baby in this kind of weather at Christmastime!"

Distress radiated from her in tangible waves. He quickly tossed the contents of the carrier and indeed, an envelope fell to the floor next to the blankets and two tattered stuffed animals.

"Read it to me," she urged, though she never looked at him. Her gaze was solidly fastened on the baby in her arms and for a moment he couldn't breathe.

He was looking at what could never be for them. The pain was nearly overwhelming. Ginger looked at the baby with such tenderness and love as she rubbed her hand over the baby's back in an effort to soothe him or her. Hell, was it a boy or a girl?

He tore open the envelope with shaking hands and quickly scanned, fully prepared to spare his wife anything that could hurt her. But what he read shook him to the very core.

I can't take care of my baby. She would always be in danger with me. She needs someone to love and protect her. I'm counting on you to raise her as your own and never let anyone know the circumstances of her past. You likely think I'm the most horrible mother on earth to give my baby to complete strangers, but it's because I love my daughter that I give her into your care and keeping and ask you to love her as I would and raise her as your own. She can never know about me or her biological father. Swear to me you'll keep my secret. My heart is breaking, but only the knowledge that you'll provide for her as I cannot gives me the strength to do what is best for her. She was deeply loved. Please never doubt that. I only ask that you love her every bit as much as her father and I do.

When Gavin finished reading the letter, his hand was shaking noticeably and Ginger sank onto the couch, holding the baby tightly against her chest as she stared incredulously at her husband.

Then he quickly went to sit beside her on the couch, reinforcing her hold on the tiny bundle because she was shaking every bit as much as he was.

She pulled the blanket down to expose the baby's face and Gavin lost his heart on the spot. A beautiful baby girl stared back at him as Ginger gently stroked her finger down one soft cheek.

And as quickly as he'd lost his heart, he made a decision. A decision that would forever change the course of his and Ginger's lives. Calm descended even as his mind began working at incredible speed, swiftly calculating their options.

"I want you to pack a bag," he said, the betraying note of uncertainty leaving his voice and in its place implacable resolve. "We're leaving the country and we'll be gone for a while."

His wife's eyes widened. "What are we going to do, Gavin?"

His gaze was steady as he stared back at her. He curled his hand around her knee, not wanting to take her hand away from the baby.

"We're going to do as we were asked and raise her as our daughter."

TWO

GAVIN had always had an understanding for what money and power could achieve, but it wasn't until Arial, the name they'd chosen for their precious baby girl, that he fully appreciated or felt there was a *purpose* for the wealth he'd accumulated his entire adult life. As though he'd always been preparing for something so important. In the moment that innocent baby girl had arrived on their doorstep, he'd known that his wealth would *finally* serve a greater purpose.

It had all come down to this and to what he had been able to provide his wife—and now his daughter.

Ari was theirs. There was a paper trail he'd meticulously crafted documenting his wife's pregnancy and the fact that after so many miscarriages he'd taken her away and kept her in complete isolation and privacy to give birth to their daughter.

A birth certificate listing date of birth, his and Ginger's

names as the parents, even the small clinic he funded where she'd been "born."

Now, for the first time, they were returning to the United States with their daughter, assured that Ari's past was airtight. That all the *i*'s were dotted and *t*'s crossed. All they had to do was resume their lives, but even with the confidence that Ari's past was unshakable, Gavin wasn't fool enough to ever even think about relaxing his guard. Their lives would be forever altered, and he didn't have a single regret for the changing course of their destinies. He had all a man could ever hope for—wish for. It was all finally his, a fact he gave thanks for every single day since that snowy Christmas night when Ari had entered their lives.

He'd carefully explained to Ginger the changes to their lives that would occur, that they would have to exercise complete caution in every aspect of their day-to-day lives. He'd worried that Ginger would feel imprisoned, that she'd grow tired of living such an isolated existence, but he should have known that his wife—like him—would do anything at all to protect their daughter.

An unbreakable bond had been formed that night when Ari had been left on their doorstep. It was inexplicable and instantaneous, as if she'd always been meant to be theirs. And that bond had only strengthened until neither of them could remember their lives before Ari was a part of their family.

The very first thing Gavin had done in his preparation to return to the United States was to quietly sell his house in Connecticut, because he wanted no trace of their past before Ari. No chance of Ari's mother showing back up at the same place she'd left her baby, asking for her back.

He'd systematically worked during the months they were out of the country to remove them from the public eye. He'd sold off several of his businesses and invested the proceeds so that his family would always be secure.

He'd bought a huge home under a dummy corporation that could never be traced back to him and made sure that the security was impenetrable. And then he'd worked to turn it into Ginger's dream home. A place she would love and wouldn't be upset over being confined to so much.

She laughingly told him that she had everything she could possibly ever want. A husband she loved and a daughter she adored. No sacrifice was too great for her if it meant keeping her family.

Seeing Ginger so happy for these last months had given Gavin a sense of purpose he'd never before experienced. After so much sorrow and loss, the woman he loved sparkled with life, love and laughter. Every day she delighted in discovering something new about motherhood and their precious baby girl.

Gavin knew in his heart that there was nothing he wouldn't do to protect them both. No price was too high to pay. No, he hadn't done it cleanly or by the book. He should have notified the police and social services. And pursued adoption through the proper channels.

But he only had to look into his wife's eyes as she stared at that tiny baby girl and he knew he could never risk losing their daughter by doing things the "right" way. He could live with his conscience and even live with his soul forever being damned just as long as Ginger was happy. He'd brave the fires of hell and the devil himself before ever being the cause of her eyes losing their shine.

She looked at him as though he was a hero—*her* hero—when in fact he'd broken so many laws that years in prison spread ominously before him were it ever discovered all he'd done. And he'd made damn sure that Ginger was in no way touched by the decisions he'd made. That if it were ever discovered what he'd done, Ginger—and Ari—would be free.

Ginger laced her fingers through his, clenching them anxiously as she adjusted the fabric baby carrier that held Ari so she faced Ginger and was nestled against her mother's chest. They disembarked the small jet, Gavin being extremely careful that she not stumble or fall as they hurried toward the waiting car.

When he slid into the backseat beside her, she turned to look at him, her brow creased with tension.

"I don't know why I'm so nervous," Ginger said in a shaky, apologetic voice. "I trust you, Gavin. Please don't think I don't. It's just that for the last five months we've seemingly lived a world away from reality. Like we had our own little bubble where time stopped and no one but us existed. And now that we have to return to the real world, I'm so scared. I'm scared this has all been a dream and when I wake up tomorrow Ari will be gone."

Gavin curled his arm around her shoulders and pulled her and Ari into his embrace. He brushed the top of her head with his lips. He hated that she worried, that she feared the unknown, but he understood it. Knew it was impossible to completely allay her fears, or his own, for that matter.

Theirs would be a lifetime of always worrying about discovery. Of having their child torn from them. Maybe as more time passed their fears would ease, but right now with their move back to resume their lives as before, they were both understandably afraid of the worst.

"I will never let that happen," Gavin said in a grave tone.

He glanced out the window of the nondescript vehicle that had picked them up at the private landing strip.

"Will you be happy here?" he asked Ginger, voicing just one of his many fears. His wife's happiness overrode any other priority in his life.

He'd scaled back his many business ventures to just the one oil company that was headquartered in Houston, Texas. It was a city he was familiar with. In his past life, he'd done "business" with Franklin Devereaux and even planned to renew their acquaintance, because Franklin still had his fingers into the life Gavin formerly led, and he could be useful in aiding Gavin in his quest for complete anonymity and the birth of a completely new life.

It was a decision he'd grappled with, because by contacting Franklin, he risked a breach in the security he'd gone to great lengths to establish. But Franklin had connections that Gavin no longer had, so in the end, he'd decided to assume the risk. Even if he considered Franklin a fool for risking his greatest treasures.

Franklin had what Gavin—and Ginger—both craved. Or rather had craved in the *past*. A family. But now Gavin no longer felt envy when thinking of the Devereauxs. Because of Ari and the fact that she had completed him and Ginger, had solidified their relationship and had made a couple a family instead.

Ari awoke from her doze nestled against her mother's chest and lifted her head, gifting her father with a toothless smile that never failed to make his heart do a complete flip-flop.

"Well, hello, little one," Ginger said, extending her finger for Ari to clutch her fist around.

As usual, anything that touched Ari's hand went straight to

her mouth and she grinned and gurgled as she gnawed on her mother's finger.

"How long before we get there?" Ginger asked. "She needs a diaper change and she's going to be hungry now that she's awake."

"Ten minutes at the most," Gavin reassured.

"She'll be good until then," Ginger said, smiling and cooing nonsense at Ari.

Then she glanced up at Gavin, her eyes full of love and warmth.

"We're really a family," she whispered in awe. "This is *real*."

Gavin smiled and leaned over to kiss the top of Ari's downy curls, inhaling her sweet baby scent. Then he captured his wife's lips and kissed her thoroughly, savoring the private moment with his wife and child.

"Yes, sweetheart. This is our life now and it's real. No one will ever take it from us."

His was a quiet vow, but determined all the same. Nothing or no one would ever take from him what was his. And he would forever shield his wife and daughter from the harsh realities of life. No matter the cost.

THREE

FOUR MONTHS LATER . . .

GAVIN squealed to a halt outside his home and left his steel-reinforced, bulletproof Mercedes before his driver had come to a full stop. His gun was in his hand, fear pounding a vicious cadence in his head. Ginger had been hysterical. Had told him to come home immediately, that something was wrong.

It took all his strength not to ram through the door and burst inside, laying waste to whatever threat there was to his wife and child. Instead he reached over from the side of the door and flipped the handle, allowing the door to ease open and give him an unimpeded view into the living room.

Ginger was pacing the living room, distress radiating from her like a beacon. As if sensing his presence, her gaze flew to the door and she called out, "Gav? Is that you? Are you home?"

Gavin relaxed, the terror slowly subsiding. He managed to

put a shaky hand out to ward off his personal security men who'd converged the moment Gavin had called them. Even his driver was behind Gavin, gun up and drawn.

Not in a hurry, Gavin tucked his gun into his shoulder harness and slowly pushed himself to his feet, hoping he didn't humiliate himself by face-planting on his own doorstep.

Never had he been as afraid as he'd been for the last fifteen minutes when his wife's terrified voice had pleaded with him to come home.

Gavin didn't often leave his wife and child. Once a week, however, he left them both, a veritable army guarding their estate, and he went into downtown Houston to take care of business or items that required his attention. After today he was wondering if he'd ever be able to leave Ginger and Ari again.

The door flew further open and Ginger stood there, eyes huge with fright, her face pale and her entire body trembling. While she might be all right, Ari's safety was still in question, and if his daughter was okay, then what the hell had frightened his wife so badly?

"Gavin, you have to come!"

Then she took in the men in position and Gavin could see her grapple with what he'd been through. But her face didn't soften in apology or regret. Her cold hand slid over his and pulled him inside, quickly shutting the door behind him, cutting him off from his security.

"Something or someone has been in Ari's room," Ginger said, her breath hitching as she hurried up the stairs, dragging Gavin with her.

He went rigid and once more drew his weapon.

"There's no one there now," Ginger said in a whisper. "She's napping. Put the gun away!"

Reluctantly, he re-holstered his weapon and as soon as they were inside Ari's room and he could see her adorable little diapered behind pooched up with her knees tucked underneath her, thumb inside her mouth, he was finally able to breathe again.

"What the hell is going on, Ginger?" Gavin demanded, a bite to his voice.

She flinched and looked startled by his anger.

"You took fifteen years off my life. *Never* do that again."

"But someone has been in her room," Ginger hissed. "I am not crazy, Gav. The first couple of times I thought it was my forgetfulness. That I just hadn't remembered leaving the two stuffed animals in her crib. But then I started paying meticulous attention to where I put them when I put her down for a nap or for the night."

Gavin frowned because it wasn't at all like Ginger to be careless when it came to leaving a choking hazard in their daughter's crib. He didn't buy that she'd forgotten anything for a minute.

Ginger crept over to the crib and then thrust her fist in her mouth to silence her cry. She held up a shaking hand to point. "Gavin, I took them out fifteen minutes ago. When I called you. I put them on top of the chest of drawers. And now they're back. Someone *is coming in here.*"

Gavin pulled Ginger into his arms and pressed a kiss to her forehead. "Shhh, darling. I'll take care of it immediately. It's quite simple, really. From now on her crib will be in our bedroom instead of the adjoining bedroom and when she naps, put her in her portable bassinet and make sure she's wherever you are. We'll get to the bottom of this. I can pull surveillance footage, because if anyone was in here, I'll know it."

Gavin stared at the video footage of his daughter's bedroom still unsure of what exactly he was seeing. It wasn't *possible*. And yet he had tangible proof that said otherwise. There wasn't *someone* in his daughter's room but rather *something*.

No matter how many times he replayed the footage, it remained the same. The two lovies, as Ginger called their daughter's favorite cuddle toys—and the only reminder of how Ari had come into their lives, a secret tribute to the woman who'd left her baby on their doorstep—would move from wherever Ginger had left them and float across the room before dropping into Ari's crib.

Logic was something embedded in Gavin. He simply couldn't wrap his mind around something so . . . *illogical*.

And directly behind the realization that logic clearly wasn't prevailing, was fear that chilled him to the bone. Was something evil shadowing their daughter? He'd never believed in spirits or ghosts. They didn't fit into his logical, well-ordered worldview. But *something* was causing those toys to float across the room and land in his daughter's crib.

What the hell was he supposed to tell Ginger without scaring her to death? He'd go to the ends of the earth to protect his wife and their daughter. If he could shield her from any fear, any hurt, then he'd damn well do it and suffer no remorse whatsoever.

He quietly gave the order to his head of security to move Ari's crib into his and Ginger's bedroom but instructed him to leave everything else untouched in the nursery.

• • •

THE NEXT MORNING

Gavin was roused from sleep the instant he heard Ginger's startled exclamation. He hurried from bed to where Ginger stood at Ari's crib, a baffled expression on her face.

The two lovies were in the crib with Ari and she was awake, one of the lovies in her chubby little fists as she gnawed on the ear. She smiled up at her parents, her legs waving and kicking as if to say she was wide awake and ready to be out of her crib.

Gavin's sharp gaze went to the door to their bedroom, the door he'd made certain was not only closed, but *locked* before they'd gone to bed. It was now ajar and the two lovies that had been left behind in the nursery were in Ari's crib, much to Ari's obvious delight.

He knew in that moment that he couldn't hide the video footage from Ginger. There was something seriously *wrong* here.

Ginger reached down to pick Ari up, the lovie falling from his daughter's grasp. The loss elicited an instant wail of displeasure and only when Ginger picked up the stuffed animal and allowed Ari to reach for it did the cry finally cease.

There were tears of genuine fear in his wife's eyes as she turned her pleading expression to him. She was wordlessly asking him to make everything okay. To make whatever was happening go away. And it gutted him, because he was utterly clueless, with no idea of *what* to do.

He'd never failed to supply his wife or daughter with *anything* they needed or wanted. His only purpose was to protect his family, to ensure their safety, happiness and well-being. And yet he didn't have the answer for the inexplicable.

"Feed and change her and then meet me in the video surveillance room," Gavin said in a low voice, keeping it calm and steady so Ari didn't pick up either his or Ginger's distress.

"What's happening, Gav?" Ginger whispered.

"I don't know," he said honestly. "But I intend to find out. Take care of Ari and then we'll sort this out."

Ginger silently walked from the bedroom but tension emanated from her in a nearly tangible wave. He hated that she was scared. Damn it, *he* was scared. Nothing in his life had prepared him for something like this. How did you defend the indefensible?

He wasn't a spiritual man, but in this moment he found himself whispering a prayer to God to remove whatever evil spirit had invaded their home.

Gavin went to the door after Ginger disappeared down the stairs en route to the kitchen, where she fed Ari. Carefully he examined the lock, looking for any sign of forced entry. To his discerning eye, there were none. No scratches, nothing at all to mar the paint, the bolt or the door handle itself. How the hell had the door been opened and the two stuffed toys end up in his daughter's crib without his knowledge?

He was a light sleeper. Always had been. But after Ari, he slept even lighter than ever, trained to hear any noise, any cry, any sign that something was wrong. And yet he'd slept the entire night, his arms wrapped securely around his wife, while Ari had slept in her crib mere feet from the bed. He'd purposely placed her crib against the far wall so his and Ginger's bed was between the crib and the door.

Shaking his head, he descended the stairs to see Ari in her high chair gurgling happily, clutching one of her lovies while Ginger prepared a bottle. He dropped a kiss on top of Ari's silky curls and was rewarded by a smile that never failed to melt his insides to molten lava.

What had their lives been like before Ari had come to them at a time when they'd thought a child would forever be lost to them? He couldn't remember. He and Ginger had been happy. He had the woman he loved more than life itself and thought himself complete.

Until Ari.

Ari was a true gift from the angels. She'd made him believe in the spirit of Christmas, of giving. And with her arrival, there was no more misery for Ginger to endure. No more doubts of whether Gavin would ever leave her for a woman who could give him something he didn't even want unless Ginger provided it.

Ginger finished prepping Ari's bottle but set it down on the counter when Gavin wrapped his arms around her and kissed her. Her kisses would never grow old. Would never lose their magic to make him completely forget himself and the world around him.

Ari, obviously impatient, dropped her lovie and made a banging noise on the tray of her high chair and said, "Mama-mama!" An obvious demand for her mother.

Ginger laughed softly as she broke away from Gavin's kiss.

"I think our daughter is hungry. I'll feed her in the video surveillance room. You did say you had something to show me?"

He hated the fear in her voice and her attempt at making light of it and the façade that she wasn't worried when he knew damn well she was.

"Gavin!" she said in a choked whisper. "Look!"

To both their astonishment, the fully prepared bottle simply lifted into the air and floated gently across the kitchen and right into Ari's outstretched hands.

Neither moved. Neither breathed. They merely stared in disbelief as Ari grasped the bottle with both hands, attempting to angle it enough that she could suck the nipple.

"Did that just *happen?*" Ginger whispered, her entire body trembling against Gavin's.

He was so shaken that he didn't—couldn't—form a response. First the stuffed animals that had inherently found their way to Ari despite a locked door. And now this?

For the first time he began to suspect that *Ari* was making these things happen. But she was a child—a baby! It was mindboggling to even consider she had the ability to move things she wanted into close proximity.

Jolted into action, Ginger hurried to the high chair where she always left Ari while she prepared her bottle and gently pried the bottle from Ari's grasp. Ari made a sound of displeasure and to Gavin's further shock, it appeared as though Ginger was in a tug-of-war as the bottle strained and tried to pull itself from her grasp.

Gavin immediately hurried over and slid back the tray before picking Ari up in an attempt to soothe her. As soon as Ginger handed him the bottle, Ari immediately settled and began sucking contentedly while cradled in her father's arms.

He lifted his gaze to Ginger, who was deathly pale, fear evident in her enormous eyes.

"What's happening, Gav?" she asked anxiously. "Is it possible *she* was the one who moved the stuffed animals? We can't refute what we just saw, no matter how illogical it may seem. We didn't both imagine it. How could we?"

Gavin wrapped his free arm around his wife, drawing her close so that his daughter and wife were next to him.

"It would seem that our daughter has some very unique abilities," Gavin murmured.

"What are we going to do?" Ginger asked, desperation creeping into her voice. "The very last thing we need is for anyone to find out. What if her birth parents come forward the instant it's revealed that she has . . . ?"

She closed her eyes a moment and laid her head against Gavin's chest, so close to Ari's forehead.

"What *does* she have, Gavin? I don't understand it, much less know whatever ability she has is called."

"The evidence points to telekinesis, but she's so young, just a baby. This may merely be the tip of her abilities. We have to prepare for anything. It's more important than ever that we never expose her to the public eye. She won't be able to attend school. At least not until we determine the depth of her powers and she learns to control them."

"That isn't the life I wanted for her," Ginger said brokenly.

Gavin could feel the warmth of her tears soaking through his thin T-shirt and his heart clenched. He squeezed her to him and kissed the top of her head.

"She'll have a good life," he assured. A vow. One he fully intended to see through. "She may not be able to do all the things normal kids her age do, but she will have a full and rich life. You and I will ensure it. Once she's old enough to understand the consequences of using her powers then she'll know never to do anything that draws unwanted attention to herself."

Ginger drew away, her smile trembling but a smile nonetheless. "I always knew she was special. A gift from God when I needed it most. Perhaps it was meant to be. We have the means to protect her, to give her an education and provide her with the necessary guidance and tools that she'll need as she grows up."

She hesitated a moment, biting her lip in consternation.

"I suppose my biggest fear, from the moment she appeared in our lives, is that someday someone may come looking for her and want her back."

Gavin slipped the bottle from Ari's grasp and then hoisted her to his shoulder so he could burp her. He looked Ginger squarely in the eye, because he wanted her to know he meant every single word he was about to say.

"Nothing or no one will *ever* take our daughter from us. As far as most of the world knows we've dropped off the map entirely. I made it known we had moved to Europe and even now reside there. This house can't be traced to me. The business I maintain here is owned by a handful of dummy corporations all belonging to me. It would take a lot of digging, a hell of a lot of red tape to wade through and a hefty dose of luck to ever link me to anything in the United States."

"I don't doubt you, Gav. Please don't think I do or that I don't have faith in you. But I suppose I'll always live with the fear of having her taken from me. Maybe in time it will diminish. Maybe one day I'll truly relax, but the mother in me realizes that I'll always worry for my baby girl no matter how old she is."

Gavin was utterly sincere in his response. "Me and you both, honey."

This time it came as no surprise when Ari's lovie floated from the floor where it had been dropped and hovered directly over Ari. Gavin plucked it from the air and turned Ari so she could take her stuffed animal.

"I guess she's ready for a nap already," Ginger said ruefully. "I don't suppose there's any point in keeping her lovies from her any longer."

Gavin's expression and tone were wry as he imagined the years ahead. "I think, my darling, that you and I are in for quite an adventure in raising our daughter."

FOUR

ARIAL Rochester sighed as she walked through the gate of the private academy where she taught English, a hint of sadness that always accompanied the end of the school year tugging at her.

But she shrugged off the momentary melancholy because soon she would be with her parents, and she'd spend the summer with them wherever her father chose to surprise her mother with this year.

She smiled as her thoughts drifted to her parents. So in love even after so many years of marriage. Her father was fiercely protective of her mother and in turn her mother and father were fiercely protective of *her*.

With good reason.

Never tell. Never let anyone know. Never use your powers.

It was a mantra her father had instilled in her since she was old enough to remember. She had grown up very sheltered, protected and extremely isolated. With good reason.

Her parents had done as much as they could to give her *some* sense of normalcy, but it wasn't possible because Ari *wasn't* normal. She was a freak of nature. Something from a cheesy sci-fi movie. People like her didn't exist. Except . . . she *did*. And there was no logical explanation as to why.

Her father was the epitome of logical. He had a brilliant, analytical mind, and even *he* seemed baffled over Ari's abilities. His greatest fear had been . . . discovery. That somehow Ari would be found out and taken away from her parents or exposed to danger from people seeking to harness her powers and use them for God only knew what. And so they'd hired tutors to homeschool her. She went nowhere without a security team.

But now, as an adult, graduated with honors from a small, private college, she'd stepped outside of the protective bubble created by her father so many years earlier.

He didn't like it. Neither did her mother. But they understood, thank God. All her father had asked was for her to never give anyone reason to believe she was any different from any other young woman in the world.

It was a promise she had no problem giving because normalcy was exactly what she wanted—*craved*. She didn't want to be "that freak." Her parents had raised her in constant fear of discovery, at least until she was old enough to understand not to ever use her powers and expose herself to the rest of the world. Only then had they relaxed somewhat and no longer lived in constant terror of Ari mistakenly revealing all that she could do.

Her parents had made great sacrifices for her. Their entire

lives had revolved around her protection. It was a fact Ari regretted with all her heart. That, because of her, none of them had been able to lead normal lives.

She dug into her purse for her keys as she walked briskly down the sidewalk of the busy street the school was on. The large brick building was surrounded by a wrought-iron fence with a gate that closed promptly after school started and opened just minutes before school let out. The teachers' parking lot was a half a block down from the gate and she was the last teacher to leave, judging by the vacant parking area.

Just as she was about to exit the sidewalk and cross the lot where her car was parked, she was shoved roughly to the ground, the pavement scraping her knees and palms as she planted her hands down to break her fall.

Shock splintered up her spine as she tried to comprehend what the hell had just happened!

"You fucking bitch! You think you're going to get away with failing *me*? If it weren't for you, I'd be going to college in the fall. Do you have any idea what my parents are going to do when they see my final grades?"

She recognized the voice as one of her students. Derek Cambridge. He came from a wealthy family and had a sense of entitlement a mile wide. He was arrogant and egotistical, but she would have never dreamed he would *attack* her for the grade he'd earned in her class.

She'd gone out of her way in an attempt to help him. She hadn't wanted to fail him, but he resisted her efforts at every turn, assuming in his arrogance that she would pass him regardless of his efforts—or lack thereof. Perhaps he thought his parents' wealth and social standing would allow him to glide through school and life.

When she looked up, her blood froze, because he was not alone. Two boys she assumed were his friends were with him and looked every bit as pissed as Derek. Were they crazy? Attacking a woman in broad daylight on a busy street in front of a school?

She glanced desperately around, looking for any source of help.

A kick to her side propelled her over onto her back, her purse now underneath her back as she gasped for breath.

What she saw when she looked up and met the furious gaze of Derek Cambridge chilled her to the bone.

This wasn't merely him roughing her up and blowing off some steam and rage. She saw death in his eyes. *Her* death. And his friends made no move to intervene on her behalf. They both wore smirks as if they firmly believed she was getting precisely what she deserved.

A flash of metal glinted in the sunlight. A knife.

Derek held it tightly in his fist, the blade pointed downward and she knew—she *knew*—he was going to kill her right there.

Though her powers had long lain dormant, though she had made a practice of suppressing them at all costs, they came roaring back, self-preservation overtaking all else.

It was instinctual. She didn't even have to force herself to concentrate. A cascade of stones suddenly pelted her attacker, sending him reeling backward, one hand covering his face protectively while the other hand still gripped the knife.

The wind kicked up in a fierce surge that rivaled a tropical storm. Now that there was adequate space between her and the teenager holding the knife, she searched the area for any possible weapon to use against him.

She glanced upward at the tree that lined one part of the sidewalk. A heavy branch cracked, the pop like a gunshot, and then propelled itself directly at the trio who posed a threat to her.

"What the fuck is going on, man?" one of Derek's friends shouted.

Ari didn't recognize the other two kids. She was ninety-nine percent certain they didn't attend school here because attendance wasn't as high as the public schools, and she was well acquainted with the faces and most of the names of the students who attended Grover Academy.

"Get the little bitch and hold her down so I can gut her like the pig she is," Derek snarled.

She'd done some damage. Blood was dripping from Derek's nose, and he didn't bother to wipe it away. His eyes glittered wildly, and Ari realized that, not only was he enraged over the failing grade he'd received, but he was also high as a kite on God only knew what.

This shit was about to get real.

She scrambled upward, using their momentary hesitation to her advantage. She needed leverage. She needed to be able to see what resources were available to her.

The brick planters that lined the front of the school where neatly trimmed hedges grew began to shake and tremble as though an earthquake was occurring. The boys felt it too, because unease spread rapidly over the two friends' faces. Derek was too hyped up on whatever drug he was on to notice anything but his determination to make her pay.

The bricks shook loose, falling one by one from their neat

formation. And then one flew through the air, striking Derek in the back of the head.

He dropped like a stone, the knife falling from his hand and clattering on the pavement.

The two friends watched in stupefaction as more bricks hovered in the air, spinning and changing direction when the kids took several steps back.

"Holy shit!" one of them exclaimed. "She's a fucking witch. I bet she's a Satan worshipper!"

Now that the knife lay on the ground a foot from where Derek had fallen, she summoned it. It floated effortlessly to her and she opened her hand as the handle pressed gently into her palm.

"Get away from me," she hissed.

At the moment she didn't care what they thought she was. If their belief that she was Satan himself aided her then let them believe it.

The bricks flew toward them, stopping mere inches from their heads. They already had their hands up to protect their faces, eyes closed, cringing, braced for impact. When nothing happened, they carefully opened their eyes and panic spread like wildfire over their faces.

When they hastily took several steps back, the bricks shot toward them again. Evidently deciding to leave their "friend" to his fate, they turned and fled as if the hounds of hell were nipping at their heels.

The bricks dropped to the pavement, one of them chipping at the corner. Ari stood there, trembling in the aftermath of her brush with death.

And then realization struck her that she'd done the unthinkable. No matter that she'd *had* to act to save her life, she'd just used telekinesis in front of three witnesses. But the witnesses weren't what concerned her the most. Most likely if they went to the police with such an insane story they'd be laughed out of the precinct. But the parking lot, as well as the entire school and all it encompassed, was monitored by surveillance cameras.

There would be tangible proof of her inexplicable powers.

She began to shake violently, the knife dropping from her hand with a clatter as it skittered across the uneven pavement. Paying no heed to her bleeding knees and palms or the pain in her side from the vicious kick, she yanked opened her bag, digging desperately for her phone.

It took three attempts before she managed to punch the right button to bring up her father's contact and connect the call.

"Ari," her father greeted in an affectionate tone. "How was your last day of school?"

"D-d-dad," she stammered. "I'm in trouble."

Her father's tone immediately changed. She could feel the tension vibrating through the phone as if she were standing right in front of him. She could well imagine how swiftly he'd shifted gears from thinking this was a casual call to knowing his daughter was in danger.

"Tell me," he clipped out. "Are you all right? Are you hurt? Where are you?"

She took a breath and related the events in as concise a manner as she could, knowing that time was of the essence. And then a horrible thought occurred to her because Derek still lay unconscious on the ground in front of her. Had she killed him?

Holding the phone to her ear with one hand, she bent down, nearly moaning with the effort it took, and pressed her fingers into his neck to feel for a pulse. Relief coursed through her veins when she felt a strong, steady pulse against her fingertips.

"Get in your car. Lock the doors. I'll be there in five minutes," her father said tersely. "If anyone and I mean *anyone* approaches you or you feel threatened in any manner, you get the hell out of there."

"Okay," she whispered. "But Dad, what about Derek? Should I call an ambulance? I can't just leave him here. Even if it was self-defense, I can't leave him to *die*."

Her father's voice was implacable, steel laced in his words. "Do as I said. I'll be there in five minutes and I'll take care of everything."

The call ended and Ari swiveled in all directions, looking to see if anyone was watching or had witnessed what had happened. Mercifully for her, Derek and his friends had hidden behind the stone enclosure that connected the parking lot to the fence surrounding the school grounds. Derek lay out of sight to anyone walking by on the sidewalk, but Ari herself was in plain view.

Her father was right. She needed to get into her car before someone saw her standing there bleeding and came closer to investigate.

Even though he'd tried to kill her, regret for what she'd done lay heavy on her. It went against every personal moral code to just leave him there. What if he'd suffered a serious head injury? What if he died because he wasn't promptly taken to a hospital? No matter the kind of person he was, he didn't deserve to die in the parking lot, alone and abandoned by his friends.

Confident in her father's ability to take care of the matter as he'd said he would, she shakily dialed 911 and then, in a low voice, she identified herself as a teacher at Grover Academy and reported a student lying unconscious in the teachers' parking lot.

Exactly four minutes later, her father's Escalade roared into the parking lot and came to an abrupt halt beside Ari's car. He was out and striding around to the driver's seat of her vehicle before she could even open her door.

When she stepped out and couldn't control the wince when her ribs protested, her father's face became stormy, his eyes like stone, his jaw clenched and ticking with agitation.

"I called 911," she said in a low voice, knowing her father wouldn't be pleased that she hadn't heeded his instructions. "I couldn't just leave him there."

"The little bastard is fortunate he's still out," her father said coldly. "I'd kill him for what he did to you." Then he put a gentle hand on her shoulder and squeezed comfortingly. "Are you all right? Are you in pain?"

"I hurt," she admitted. "I'm scraped up, but the kick to the ribs is what's bothering me the most."

Her father's gaze became glacial, but he bit back whatever response was burning on his lips.

"Get in your car and follow me. If you called 911, an ambulance will be here soon and probably the police as well. I want you as far away as possible when that happens."

"Dad, the school has security cameras," she said, her voice trembling.

He leaned forward and kissed her forehead. "I'm already on it, honey. Now get in your car. We need to leave now."

She breathed out in relief. Her father would handle it. He would protect her just as he'd always protected her. She turned and hurriedly slid back into the driver's seat, ignoring her body's protest. They likely only had minutes until medical personnel and the authorities converged on the parking lot.

There would be questions. She'd made the call to 911 and then left the scene. Most people would have remained, rendering aid or at least ensuring the safety of the victim until medical help arrived. And she'd have to answer for why she hadn't done just that.

But she had absolute faith in her father. He'd never failed her.

She took off with a jerk as she hit the accelerator to follow her dad as he roared from the lot.

Her father set a determined pace through traffic and she realized they were heading home—one of the many places they called home—but the place they stayed mostly during the year when she taught and her father managed his business.

They zoomed through the security gate and it swiftly closed behind them. As soon as she pulled into the garage, her mother appeared in the doorway and she rushed over to open Ari's door, her face a wreath of concern.

"Be careful, darling," her father told her mother gently. "She's hurt."

"Oh Ari, what happened, sweetheart? Do you need to go to the hospital?" She turned anxiously to her husband. "Shouldn't you have taken her straight to the hospital?"

Gavin Rochester put a reassuring hand on his wife's shoulder before leaning in to help Ari from the car. This time Ari was more disciplined and didn't let her discomfort show because her mother was already verging on panic and Ari didn't want to add to her worry.

"There wasn't time, Ginger. We have problems that needed to be addressed quickly. I've already put a call into Doctor Winstead and he's on his way over. If he feels Ari needs to be hospitalized or that she's seriously injured, we'll do so discreetly in his outpatient clinic, where privacy and anonymity can be assured."

Ginger wrapped her arm gently around her daughter and Ari could feel her shaking in fear and agitation. In turn, she wrapped her arm around her mother's slender frame and hugged her as tightly as the discomfort in her ribs would allow.

"I'm okay, Mom. We have bigger problems than my injuries. I messed up."

As she spoke, she glanced apologetically up to her father, regret for letting him down flooding her heart.

His expression immediately became fierce. He framed her face in his hands, turning her away from her mother, forcing her gaze to his.

"Don't you *ever* apologize or feel you've let me or your mother down for doing *whatever* it takes to protect yourself. You could have died today, Ari. If you hadn't done what you did, your mother and I would be planning your funeral right now. This is one time I thank God for your extraordinary abilities, and for the first time, I believe there is a genuine purpose—some higher reason—for your *gift*. Today that gift saved the life of someone very precious to me."

Tears welled in Ari's eyes at the sincerity brimming in her father's.

"Now let's get you inside," he said, urging her carefully toward the door. "I have some phone calls to make and Doctor Winstead should be here soon. Let your mother fuss over you like she's dying to do and don't worry about this, baby. I promise you, I'll take care of it."

"I know you will, Dad," she said in a low voice.

FIVE

ARI settled with a sigh into her bedroom her parents still kept for her, even though she had her own apartment—in one of the buildings her father owned, of course. It had been hard enough for her parents to let go, but her father's tolerance only ran so far. He'd insisted she move into his building that housed upscale apartments not far from where she taught, because security was tight and he could be assured of her safety.

It wouldn't at all surprise her if he had a full security detail also housed in the apartment building just to keep an eye on her.

Her mother had stood anxiously over Doctor Winstead as he examined Ari, almost as if she were afraid he'd miss something in his diagnosis. But other than the scrapes on her hands and knees, all she had suffered was severe bruising to her ribs; nothing was broken.

She'd be sore and stiff for a few days, and he'd advised her to take it easy and not to overdo it, something her mother had firmly said would *not* be an issue, and then he'd written prescrip-

tions for muscle relaxers and pain medication that her mother
had promptly sent out to be filled and delivered within the hour.

Talk of where they'd spend the summer hadn't even been
broached. Her father had spent the afternoon on the phone
making quiet calls and she'd purposely not listened in because
she didn't *want* to know. Guilt still assailed her because she
wasn't a violent person. It went against her every instinct to willingly hurt another human being.

Her father had always worried that she was too soft—like
her mother—but he hadn't worried overly much, because her
mother's sweetness was what had drawn her father to her in the
first place. Her father was a hard man. Unyielding. He could be
scary when crossed and yet with her mother? He was a completely different man.

The idea of her quiet, delicate, softhearted mother being able
to tame the ultimate bad boy had always been a source of amusement for Ari. And he'd often said that he thanked God that Ari
hadn't inherited any of *his* qualities. He didn't believe himself a
good man when in fact he was the very best sort of man.

But Ginger brought out the best in him and who could fault
a man for doing whatever it took to protect his wife and daughter from the harsh realities of life?

Her mother had hinted on a few occasions that her father
had not always been the most law-abiding man in the world but
that after meeting her he vowed to change. He wanted to be better. For her. He wanted to be worthy. Of her.

Ari thought it was terribly romantic, but at the same time
her parents' marriage had ruined her for ninety-nine percent of
the male population, because she wanted what her mother had.
A man who'd go to the wall for her. Who'd move heaven and

earth to make her happy. To put her needs and desires above his own and to remove any threat to her.

Which explained her lack of a social life. Her actual dates could be counted on one hand. Two hadn't measured up to her father's very extensive background check and weren't men he— or she—wanted to become involved with. The others? There just wasn't that . . . spark. The spark she saw every time her father laid eyes on his wife. How his face softened with so much love that it made her very soul ache.

She wanted that. And she refused to settle for less even if it meant spending the rest of her life alone. Not to mention she couldn't imagine many men who would be understanding or tolerant of her special "gift." Hell, they'd probably run as far and as fast away as possible while making the sign of the cross.

Who could she trust with her secrets anyway? And she refused to have a relationship steeped in secrecy and lies—even ones of omission. If she ever married, her husband would know the full truth about her and he'd accept it without reservation. Which didn't leave her with many options.

Not wanting to depress herself even further, she flipped on the TV as she snuggled further into bed, the effects of the medication starting to take hold and remove some of the nagging discomfort in her battered body.

But thirty seconds later, she wished she had just gone to sleep when she saw the lead story on the local news, which would no doubt be picked up by bigger networks and by the morning would be on the major media outlets like CNN and Fox News.

She watched in horror as a video, obviously filmed from a phone, replayed the entire confrontation in the parking lot.

Damn it, but there must have been someone passing by that stopped and captured the entire whole damning scene.

The anchor's words were sensationalistic—of course. How one young woman, a teacher at Grover Academy, and God, they even identified her by name, had managed to fend off three attackers in the parking lot of the school.

She knew from her father that he'd arranged for the video monitoring system for the school to be hacked into and to show the actual attack on Ari so there was no question of self-defense but the footage had cut off—an inexplicable "glitch"—when her powers became evident.

Whoever shot this video caught the entire thing from beginning to end.

Panic surged. Her pulse shot up and her throat closed in as anxiety viciously gripped her entire body. The medication that had eased the pain and tension was rendered useless, because the nagging ache was back with a vengeance.

And then the anchor's next words sent her right over the edge. The video had gone viral, with already a million YouTube hits and countless Facebook shares, and it was being picked up by the AP as everyone expressed shock and awe at what they'd witnessed.

Everything her parents had worked so hard for in the last twenty-four years was wiped out in a single unguarded moment. She was exposed and vulnerable. Her life would be forever changed because of one self-entitled asshole who thought his parents' money and status would allow him to coast through life unscathed.

She scrambled out of bed, ignoring the sluggish effects of the medication and the pain that shot through her rib cage. She hurried down the hall and quietly knocked on her parents' bedroom door. When she heard her father's summons, she opened the door and entered, her hands shaking, her face bloodless. and Her stark fear must have shown on her face, because her mother immediately got up and hugged her and then urged her down on the end of the bed where her mother and father had been sitting up against the headboard.

"Dad, you have to come see," she said, wringing her hands in agitation. "I can replay it with the DVR. It's bad. I don't know how we can fix this now."

"We saw," her father said quietly. "We leave as soon as we can get a bag packed. Tonight. We're going to another of our residences here as a precaution since Doctor Winstead was just here just earlier. We can't afford to be hasty in our decision, but neither do I want you exposed to the media feeding frenzy that will surely ensue. They identified you by name, and the school employees, students—past and recent—will be flooded with questions and requests for interviews by the media and even the police. Administration is going to be all over you and, honey, you need to prepare for the worst-case scenario."

"They'll fire me," Ari whispered. "I messed up. I'm so sorry, Dad. And you too, Mama. This will ruin your summer trip. It will change *all* our lives."

Her mom's eyes filled with such staggering love that tears welled in Ari's and she had to swallow back the knot of emotion nearly choking her. Then her mom gently wrapped her arms around her, pulling her head down to her breast as she stroked her hair as she'd done when Ari was just a little girl.

"Baby, you *are* our life. You've always been the heart and soul of us both. Since the day you entered our lives. Never apologize for who you are. You did what you had to do. If I had been there, that little bastard would be dead right now instead of dealing with a headache," she muttered.

Her father tried to suppress his grin as he looked at his wife and daughter, love shining like a beacon in his eyes.

Then he said to her mother, "Honey, go pack her a bag. She's in no shape to do so. She's shaking like a leaf and she took her medicine not long ago. We need to go. I'll take care of what you and I need. Let Ari sit here and you go get her things together."

Her father waited until his wife left the room and then he slid out of bed, pulling on a T-shirt he'd discarded by the bed. Then he sat next to Ari on the edge of the bed and pulled her into his arms.

"I know you're scared, baby, but one thing you need to understand is that you and your mother are the two most important people in my world. The only people who *exist* in my world as far as I'm concerned and there is nothing, *nothing* that I won't do to protect either of you."

He tipped up her chin so she looked him in the eye and could see the utter sincerity radiating from his expression.

"We've always known this was a possibility. We tried to protect you your entire life from just this sort of thing, but it was inevitable at some point because it's who you *are*. And I can only imagine how hard it's been for you to suppress something so integral to who you are out of fear. Fear of discovery and fear of somehow disappointing me and your mother. Let me correct something right here before this goes any further. We could not be prouder of you and who you are. And there is nothing you could ever do to disappoint us or make us love you any less. You are our only child. A blessing when we thought we'd never have a child, much less one as loving, kind and special and beautiful inside and out, as you are. So trust me to do what's best not only for you but for me and your mother. Because you two come first with me. Always. And that will never change."

"I love you, Dad," she whispered.

He brushed a kiss over her forehead and gave her a gentle squeeze. "And I love you, baby girl. Now let me pack your mother and I a quick bag. We can always get what else we need later."

SIX

BEAU Devereaux hit the pause button for the television after he'd replayed the evening news segment from the night before for his brother, Caleb, and the assembled members of their security specialist team.

They'd lost good men to a madman who'd put Caleb and his now wife, Ramie, through hell, and they realized they needed better than what they'd considered the best in the beginning. After a thorough vetting, more men had been hired, and the new recruits had gone through extensive training headed by Dane Elliot, their head of security. He was a former Navy SEAL and all-around tough-as-nails warrior. He was partnered with Eliza Cummings, a badass in her own right. The two had been instrumental in hunting down the fucker who had tormented Ramie, though it had been Caleb who'd taken the bastard down for good.

Zack was perhaps their most interesting addition. Beau had been drawn to him because he and Zack were alike in many ways. Quiet. Cynical. They were both content to sit back and observe, taking in their surroundings, studying quietly all the while gaining information. And neither were glory seekers. They simply got the job done.

He wasn't the typical recruit. Most of their men were ex-military or former government agents. FBI, DEA and a few organizations that didn't officially exist. When they were first getting off the ground in the hasty year following their sister's abduction and subsequent rescue, he and Caleb had done the best they could to hire capable security experts. They were in fact working trial by fire. But in the aftermath of losing men, Caleb's wife's near death and Caleb's own, they'd knuckled down, learned from their past mistakes and spared no expense in getting the best. Only the best. If the old adage was true and you got what you paid for, then they were getting top-notch operatives because they did not come cheap.

Zack, however, was a different story. Superstar college football player on a full ride. Drafted by the NFL in the first round as a starting quarterback. But after only two years, an injury had taken him out of football forever. For most people this would have been a setback they never recovered from. He'd shrugged it off, did his rehab and then followed in his father's footsteps and entered law enforcement, excelling and quickly moving up the ranks.

He'd been heavily recruited by a government agency, but Beau had been quick to snatch him up, his gut telling him it was the right decision. There was a ruthlessness and darkness to Zack that Beau sensed more than saw outright. His gaze missed nothing, always calculating, taking note and processing at lightning speed. For some this might be a warning sign. A reason *not* to hire him on. But Beau had witnessed the difference in Zack when it came to victims and the people they hunted.

He was infinitely gentle with the innocent, but was ice-cold when it came to taking down the monsters who preyed on the innocent. He was perfect for Devereaux security and their expanding network.

Caleb leaned back, his expression speculative as he eyed his brother. "So why are we looking at this exactly?"

The others assembled had similar questioning looks. Zack's was hard, though. Beau could feel the same anger that simmered in his own veins radiating through Zack.

"It doesn't bother you that a defenseless woman could have been killed?" Beau asked mildly.

Even as he spoke, his attention went back to the frame that was frozen over Arial Rochester's delicate, terrified features. He couldn't explain why he was more bothered by this attack than he was about others. And in their business, they'd seen a lot, even in the short time they'd been in business.

"I'm more interested in the 'freak' windstorm and the flying bricks," Eliza murmured. "Since posted on YouTube, this video has gone viral with over ten million views in twenty-four hours. News networks across the company have picked it up. Speculation is running rampant as to how she managed to fend off three attackers without so much as a weapon."

"Stranger things have happened," Dane said in his calm, implacable tone.

Eliza snorted, knowing full well he spoke the truth. In light of all that had happened with Caleb and Ramie, this looked like simple child's play.

Beau continued to study the wide, frightened eyes of the

small woman. Her arms were wrapped protectively around herself and there was panic evident in her every feature. *After* the threat to her had been eliminated.

Wouldn't she have been relieved? Some hint of relief or even upset? Reaction to her close brush with death. Instead she looked even *more* terrified than she had when confronted with the arrogant little assholes.

There was something about the entire thing that bothered him, but he couldn't put his finger on it. But the surge of anger over the attack of such a small, vulnerable-looking woman pissed him off. He usually approached his job impassively, never letting his emotions rule him or get in the way of his actions. Protection required absolutely no room for error. No mistakes. No letting emotion result in hasty, stupid decisions that could get someone killed.

"So do you think she has psychic abilities?" Caleb asked, addressing the obvious elephant in the room.

Beau shrugged. "Maybe. It's possible. She certainly caused a stir and the evidence is pretty inexplicable. But then again, it could very well simply be a freak occurrence and maybe she was scared because even she didn't understand what was going on."

"Or maybe she was worried about discovery," Zack said, speaking up for the first time in his gruff voice.

Beau had had the same thought.

"Well, if she was worried about discovery then I'd say she's a hell of a lot more worried now," Eliza said grimly.

The Devereauxs were intimately acquainted with the fear of discovery. Their younger sister, Tori, had psychic ability and they'd shielded her from public scrutiny her entire life. Caleb's wife was also psychic, her "gift" more of a curse than a blessing.

And while her abilities were known, Caleb went to great lengths to keep her out of the public eye and he made damn sure that the many requests for Ramie's help were filtered through the security firm and never reached Ramie.

Ramie still hadn't fully recovered from her brush with death. Neither had Caleb. Beau wasn't certain Ramie would ever be able to use her talents again. She'd seen far too much death, experienced too much pain and devastation and had barely survived with her sanity intact. Caleb was well aware of that fact, and he'd do whatever it took to ensure his wife was never at risk again.

"We need to focus on other matters—business matters," Caleb said pointedly. "While this is a subject of interest, that's all it is. We aren't involved in the case. We have clients who deserve our undivided attention."

With that, the meeting shifted its focus to their current client load and assignments. Planning and organizing, deciding who headed what as well as reviewing new requests that had recently come in.

Beau couldn't quite shake the incident from his mind and he wasn't sure why. But it bothered him. It bothered him a hell of a *lot*.

SEVEN

ARIAL knew she couldn't wait a moment longer. Fear and anxiety ran uncontrollably through her heart, freezing blood as it pumped furiously to keep up with the stringent demands of her chaotic mind and thoughts.

We'll be an hour, two at the most, baby.

It was what her father had said right before escorting her mother to a vehicle discreetly parked with easy access to at least three exit points from the large house owned by one of the many dummy corporations her father had funneled most of his properties and assets through.

Her father hadn't been thrilled, an understatement for sure, when her mom insisted on going with him. He'd wanted both women under constant guard. Her mother wasn't leaving the shopping for Ari's necessities to her husband and neither of her parents would even consider exposing Ari to the public eye.

Ari had very recognizable features and would most certainly be identified because not only were the local news and media in a frenzy over the anonymous video but the rest of the country as well. It was only after her mother had threatened to go alone to shop for her baby that her father had grudgingly capitulated, because there was no way in hell he was allowing his wife—or his daughter—to go anywhere without him.

Oddly enough, her mother was perfectly content to allow her husband to pick out *her* clothing. She'd said more than once over the years that her husband knew what looked good on her better than she did and he loved spoiling his wife. Wearing clothes chosen by him seemed to represent a tangible sign to him of his possession.

When it came to Ari, however, her mom was adamant about shopping for *her* baby. It was something special she liked to do for her daughter. And it was her way of spoiling Ari since her husband shamelessly spoiled them both.

But why weren't they back yet? Why hadn't she heard from them? In her heart she knew that something terrible had to have happened for them to stay gone so long and for them not to contact her. She was sick with worry, the possibilities endless as to why they hadn't returned, and she was torturing herself with every single one of them.

It was now long past time stores stayed open and she knew her father would have hurried her mother through the process and be anxious to return home to Ari, where he could be assured of both his wife's and daughter's safety.

Her father—or her mother—would never cause Ari stress or fear. She knew that for the absolute truth it was. And they wouldn't have wanted to be gone long from her. Especially her father, because he was most at ease when he could see his "girls" and know they were safe.

So something terrible had to have happened. It was the only reasonable explanation and she was utterly paralyzed by terror and grief because she couldn't lose them. She couldn't! They were her lifeline. Her support system. Her anchor, her rock.

It might seem ridiculous for a twenty-four-year-old woman to still be so dependent on her parents, but it was what they wanted—what she wanted. In an uncertain world and living every day in fear of discovery, her parents were her only sanctuary.

Yes, she'd spread her wings, gone out on her own after graduating with her teaching degree. She even had her own apartment, though it was in her father's building. She shopped for herself, went to her favorite restaurants and constructed a façade of an ordinary day-to-day life.

She was highly intelligent, excelling in her studies. She had a photographic memory and could store data in her brain much like a computer did. And yet with her superior intelligence and her psychic powers that she hadn't truly tested to see just how powerful she was, she was still fragile and vulnerable. She knew it. She hated it. But she accepted it, because it was who she was and she couldn't change it no matter how much she wanted to.

She wanted to be strong. She wanted to live life without forever looking over her shoulder and suppressing her true self. It was no way to live even if her parents surrounded her with their love, always protecting her. At some point she had to step from her parents' shadow and take on the world herself.

She sighed, closing her eyes after checking her watch for the hundredth time.

The two hours her father had assured her they'd be back in had turned into three and then four and five until every minute seemed an eternity. At first Ari hadn't been concerned, because above all else her father was lethal and fiercely protective of her mother. He'd never allow harm to come to either his wife or his daughter.

He'd left a security detail with Ari, surrounding her, the house. She didn't see them but she sensed their presence. Their watchful eyes. It should have reassured her, but with every passing hour that her parents remained gone, her anxiety mounted until she was literally paralyzed with fear. And indecision.

She was exhausted, unable to sleep with her parents gone and her not knowing if they were dead or alive. Now dawn crept across the sky, bathing her room in pale shades of lavender. She'd tried to call her father countless times. Her mother too. And each time both attempts had gone straight to voice mail.

She knew she had to do something. But what? She didn't even know where her father had taken her mother to shop, so tracing their route was impossible.

What if they'd been in an accident? Wouldn't someone at least check their cell phones, see all the missed calls and at least contact her to let her know if they were in the hospital? Or . . . dead?

Frigid cold gripped her insides. Her chest tightened to the point of pain, and she struggled to squeeze air into her burning lungs.

They couldn't be dead. And if they'd been in an accident, one of them would have called her. Unless they were *incapable* of making a call. Unconscious. Fighting for their lives?

Her knotted fist went to her mouth, her teeth sinking into her knuckles. Oh God. She couldn't imagine her world without her parents in it. They had to be okay. They *had* to.

She couldn't stand it another minute. She'd go find one of the men keeping silent watch over her. Her father had brought two of his detail with him and her mother. Wouldn't the men have known if something awful had happened? And if they knew, then why the hell hadn't they informed her and, better yet, taken her to wherever her parents were?

She dressed hurriedly, packing a light bag in case she needed to immediately rush to her parents' side. She took only what was absolutely necessary and threw everything into an oversized tote before slinging the strap over her shoulder.

Then she headed for the front entrance.

Ari stepped past the front door, shutting it firmly behind her. She clutched her bag and glanced furtively around as she moved farther down the walkway to where another vehicle was parked. Thank God her father had ensured that she had keys to every vehicle they owned in case she ever needed to use one of them.

Her gaze skimmed over the grounds, carefully observing for any sign of the men posted around the perimeter. The wind blew, ruffling her long hair, and she reached up with her hand to shove it from her face and tuck it behind her ear.

"Hello!" she called loudly. "I know you're there. I need your help. Please."

Only silence greeted her. No answering call. No one striding from nowhere to suddenly appear at her side. Maybe they'd been called away because her parents had needed them?

She tried once more, louder this time, until her voice cracked. And once again, there was no response. With an aching sigh, she trudged farther down the pathway, resigning herself to the fact she was flying blind.

She took the inside curve of the sidewalk that skated outward to where the other vehicles were parked. Dismay made her freeze momentarily because while she had several keys on her key ring, she wasn't at all sure what key went to which vehicle.

She paused, shimmying the strap of her tote bag down so she could reach in to retrieve the heavy clump of keys lying in one of the pockets. When she looked up again she let out a startled gasp and instinctively took a step backward.

There was a tall man dressed in fatigues and a white form-fitting T-shirt. His hair was cut short and he wore combat boots. Combat boots? And his eyes were completely shielded by dark sunglasses, but even so she could feel the heavy weight of his stare.

Something about him made her extremely nervous but then her nerves were already shot so he likely wasn't to blame. He had to be a part of the security detail her father employed. He could very well know where her parents were or have heard from the detail her father had taken with him and her mother. Someone had answered her summons after all.

"Have you heard anything about my parents?" she asked anxiously, though she still kept her distance. "They should have been home *hours* ago."

"They're fine," he said calmly, not so much as a flicker in his expression.

Relief made her unsteady. Her knees wobbled and shook and she let out a hard whoosh of air as it burst free from her lungs.

Before she could react or ask how he knew they were fine,

her face exploded with pain and she went flying backward, landing on the pavement. Her already bruised and tender ribs screamed their protest and her entire face throbbed. The son of a bitch had hit her!

She tasted blood but ignored it, focusing instead on the man bearing down on her. She caught the barest glint of something in his left hand and it was enough to have her on her feet in a fraction of a second, prepared to fight with everything she had.

Thank God, her father had taught her self-defense moves from the time she was a child. He'd always worried about her protection not only because she was his only child and he openly adored her, but because he never wanted her in a vulnerable position without a way of defending herself.

The attack in the school parking lot had caught her so unaware that her first instinct had been to use her powers.

And then dread pooled deep in her stomach, spreading its poison through her body as realization hit.

He intended to drug her so she *couldn't* use her powers.

Which meant not only did her father have a traitor in his ranks, but who knew how many others were involved? Were all of them bad? Her mother and father had fallen off the map when her father had a taken a security escort. They should have been able to protect him and for that matter her father was very capable of kicking some serious ass.

Unless . . . Perhaps they'd drugged her parents like they intended to drug her.

There were a million questions surging in waves through her mind, but she shoved them down and instead focused on her attacker, who was now only a few feet away and making no effort to hide the syringe in his hand.

She did a quick assessment and knew there was no way to physically overcome this man. He was a fighter. Looked ex-military. Still wore the clothing of an enlisted man with ease and confidence that told her he hadn't been out long.

The resolve in his features frightened her more than his obvious physical strength. He had a mission, one that would be completed at all costs.

But if he planned to drug her and hadn't killed her outright, which he certainly could have done, then his orders were obviously to bring her in alive.

She narrowed her focus and the rest of the world simply fell away. Sweat beaded her forehead as she concentrated on the hand holding the syringe. His arm lifted, as though he were a puppet on strings. Jerky, him fighting it the whole way.

He lunged at her, reaching for her with his free hand, and she dodged out of the way, her concentration momentarily broken. She had to get to one of the vehicles and the only way to do that was to impair him enough to give her that window of opportunity. She doubted he was alone, but perhaps they'd expected her to hole up in her room like a scared, defenseless child until they came for her.

She forced every bit of her mental energy on that syringe until it took on a life of its own, wrenching free of his grasp and hovering in the air, looking suddenly like a menacing wasp. The man cursed and ducked and dodged as the syringe stabbed forward, his sunglasses falling to the ground so his eyes were revealed. The entire time, he inched his way in Ari's direction, but she kept sidestepping, never taking her gaze from the syringe.

If it had been capable of incapacitating her, then it should do the same for him.

Impatience simmered in her consciousness. Things she used to do with ease that felt natural now seemed like such a long time ago. A lifetime. She'd grown so used to not using her powers that they seemed alien to her, not an integral part of her, as they should have been.

It required every ounce of discipline her father had instilled in her to push her panic and terror down and focus only on that syringe. She began to recognize the pattern in which he danced his intricate path to avoid being stuck by the needle.

She plunged the syringe toward him but at the last moment pulled it up sharply and then thrust with speed and accuracy exactly where she anticipated he'd be.

It struck him in the throat and she gave the plunger a strong mental push so it emptied the contents of the syringe into his body.

His expression was murderous as he reached up and yanked the needle from his neck, tossing it away in fury. But already his eyes were glazed, his movements sluggish. He staggered and collapsed to his knees but in a last rush of strength, he lifted his head, looking at her with a mixture of hatred and . . . respect?

"Don't think this is the end," he said, his words slurring. "We'll come after you. You aren't safe anywhere. There is nowhere we can't find you. I underestimated you this time. I won't make that mistake again. And if you ever want to see your precious mommy and daddy you'll do just what we want. Not that they're really your parents."

The last words slipped nearly unintelligibly from his lips as a goofy-looking smile that was completely incongruous given the situation curved one side of his mouth upward. There was a look of triumph in his glazed eyes, and then the sedative took full effect and he rocked over to the side, hitting the paved sidewalk with an indelicate thud.

"What?" she demanded. "What did you say?"

She ran over to him and kicked him in the side, trying to rouse him, though she knew he'd be out for quite a while. It was what he'd intended for her to be. Bastard.

Had she heard him correctly?

She shook her head and turned, pissed that she'd spent those extra precious few seconds worrying over something stupid her attacker had said when he was in the grip of a strong sedative. The whole thing was crazy and in a world where she couldn't be certain about much, the one thing she did know with certainty was that her parents loved her. She was their only child. She'd seen her birth certificate and had dual nationality since she was born outside the United States.

She was not going to give in and react to his words, because that would be precisely what he wanted. He wanted to plant a seed of doubt. He wanted to scare her. Well, he'd certainly succeeded in scaring her, because it was obvious he knew where her parents were and that it was Ari they wanted.

As she fumbled through her key set looking for the telltale symbol on the key fob that told her what key went to which vehicle, she decided on taking the biggest, toughest vehicle in her father's arsenal of vehicles.

She knew for a fact that the bulky SUV had a reinforced steel frame, was bulletproof with shatter-proof windows and would take a beating. And if another vehicle tangled with it, there was absolutely no way for her to come away the loser unless she was flattened by an eighteen-wheeler and even then it was a coin flip as to who would come out worse for the wear.

She unlocked the vehicle, slid behind the wheel and quickly revved the engine, leaving tire marks on the pavement as she began putting as much distance as was possible between her and the people she now knew couldn't be trusted.

EIGHT

ARI pulled her oversized purse closer to her body and walked at a fast pace toward the entrance of the building that housed Devereaux Security Services. She was dressed in a manner to indicate wealth and elegance. Designer clothing, diamond earrings and designer sunglasses with an Hermès scarf covering her head as if to protect her hair from the wind when in fact the sunglasses and scarf were to hide her distinctive hair and eyes, not to mention the bruises that colorfully adorned her face.

The car she'd parked curbside where she wasn't boxed in by cars front and back was a sleek BMW M6 convertible that comfortably fit the image she was trying to project. And it had the added benefit of being fast. Five hundred and eighty horses under the hood. She remembered every single detail her father had shared with her on every vehicle in his possession. The M6 was faster, more powerful, than a Mustang, a Camaro—even the ZL1—and the Corvette, though it would likely be a tight race with the latter.

While before she'd wanted an impenetrable moving fortress, now she wanted something easier to navigate and a vehicle capable of outrunning most others. If nothing else, her father had drummed into her the importance of advance thinking and planning.

She'd carefully considered her options when she'd gone to retrieve the contents of a safe-deposit box her father held at one of the local banks. He'd set it up so that if she were ever in trouble or need, she could access cash and alternate identity, including driver's licenses and passports—three total in all.

It had never occurred to her to question her father as to why the thought had even crossed his mind that she'd need such things. She knew well how protective he was of her and so she'd shrugged off his actions as him being paranoid and *over*protective. But perhaps he'd been all too right in preparing for the worst, because that was now what she was facing, and she was grateful for her father's foresight. She'd lived her life in a protective bubble, and now, for the first time, she didn't have her father to fall back on and have fix all her problems. It was up to her to get herself out of the mess she was in.

The people pursuing her would likely suspect her to do just the opposite of what she'd done. They would *expect* her to dress in an unassuming manner, try *not* to look like the daughter of a wealthy man rather than boldly going out in public with a car and clothing that would attract attention. In essence, Ari was hiding in plain sight, hoping that she was right about them looking for someone trying to hide the trappings of money and prestige. And if they'd been watching her, which she assumed had to be the case, or at the very least had done their homework, then they'd know she normally dressed casually, preferring jeans and a T-shirt to designer clothing. More at home in flip-flops than the elegant heels she wore right now. And well, she had no qualms about ditching the heels and fleeing barefoot if it came to that.

Her stride was brisk and confident, her chin slightly lifted so she had an unobscured view of her surroundings at all times. She took in everything, searching for any sign of threat. Anything that looked ... dangerous, though she wasn't sure how someone *saw* imminent danger. If everyone wore a warning sign screaming danger, then no one would ever be caught off guard, so the notion was silly that she could somehow spot a threat in the steady stream of people bustling down the sidewalk.

She breathed a sigh of relief when she entered the building, glad to be off the busy street and out of view of anyone watching. She signed in at the security desk, using one of the aliases she'd retrieved from the safe-deposit box, making sure she didn't appear nervous and agitated when both had their vicious claws firmly entrenched in her chest. After receiving her badge to get through the turnstile to the elevators, she hurried through, her anxiety mounting with every breath.

Her father had told her on more than one occasion that if something were to happen to him, or if Ari needed help, she was to go to Caleb or Beau Devereaux, preferably Caleb, as he was the oldest. He hadn't explained his relationship with the Devereauxs, but he'd been adamant that she trust only them and no one else. And just as she hadn't questioned the need for cash and aliases stashed in a safe-deposit box, neither had she queried him about his relationship with the Devereauxs, although she found it odd that she'd never met the men he'd told her to turn to if necessary.

She just hoped her father was right. Already, they'd been betrayed by men her father trusted. Who was to say the Devereauxs were any different? But what choice did she have?

She had none. Her lips formed a grim line as she stepped from the elevator on the floor Devereaux Security Services occupied. She had no choice but to trust the men her father evidently trusted and pray she hadn't made a huge mistake in going to them for help.

Beau glanced up from his desk when the silent alarm triggered a flash of light to his office, notifying him that someone had just come into the lobby of their firm. His office was strategically placed with a two-way reflecting mirror so he could monitor and form an impression of a potential client. People often gave themselves away when they didn't think they could be seen or heard.

A petite woman walked hesitantly toward their receptionist, Anita, and from his vantage point he could see her hands tremble, though she tried valiantly to hide that fact. He frowned, taking in the fact that she neither removed her sunglasses nor her scarf and instead remained hidden. Disguised, no doubt.

He pressed the intercom button that would allow him to listen in on the conversation between the woman and Anita, his interest piqued. He found himself leaning forward as though it gave him the advantage of being closer, though the glass separated them.

At one point, the woman, still silent, glanced sideways, her gaze resting on the glass wall. Since he couldn't see her eyes, he had no idea what she was thinking or if she suspected someone was watching her. But he got the uneasy feeling she knew exactly what the glass really was.

"Miss?" Anita prompted the woman again. "Is there something I can help you with? Do you have an appointment?"

"No," the woman said in a soft, quivering voice. "I mean yes." She took a deep breath and visibly let her shoulders sag as though she were gathering the courage to give her reason for being here. Beau could readily picture her closing her eyes in that moment of desperation.

"I don't have an appointment I meant," she said quietly. "But yes, you can help me. God, I hope you can. I need to speak with Caleb or Beau Devereaux, preferably Caleb if he's available. It's . . . important," she added, more desperation creeping into her voice.

Beau's eyebrows immediately rose. He was certain he'd never met this woman and the way she'd called them out told him she at least knew *of* them, because it wasn't widely publicized that either Beau or Caleb was actively involved in the actual running of Devereaux Security Services.

Dane was the front man. The face of DSS. Anytime interviews were granted, any police involved, et cetera, Dane handled it while Beau and Caleb stayed in the background. Though ever since marrying Ramie, his brother had turned more responsibility for the operation of DSS to Beau and their younger brother Quinn.

Quinn handled all the financial shit as well as the background checks, not only for potential operatives, but also on the people who wanted to hire DSS. Things Beau didn't have the patience for. Beau conferred with Dane on which clients they took on and which were referred elsewhere. Because many of the so-called clients were actually people who wanted to get to Ramie—and her powers. And over Caleb's dead body would that ever happen.

Beau pressed a button next to the intercom to send a signal only visible to Anita or anyone behind her desk. There were only two colors the light flashed. Red or green. Red meant for Anita to tell the prospective client that no one was available and to gently herd them away. Green meant to show the person back to one of the offices. In this case, Beau's.

Anita never missed a beat, her gaze not betraying the fact that the light had indicated her next move.

"I'm sorry to say that Caleb is unavailable."

Before she could finish, the woman's hand fluttered to her mouth and then clenched into a tight ball against her lips. Beau could practically feel the panic that radiated from her in waves.

"Beau is in, however, and will see you immediately," Anita continued quickly. She too had picked up on the woman's reaction and now she hastened to calm the woman.

The woman's entire body sagged. Beau feared her legs would give out. He frowned because she might not be able to make the walk to his office. She was shaking like a leaf.

He was up and on his feet in a split second and quickly opened his office door. He strode into the lobby, hoping his presence would soothe rather than freak the woman out.

She turned, obviously startled to see him there so close to her. It was then that he saw what she'd obviously tried hard to conceal, and would have if the light hadn't hit her face just right. There was a bruise on the side of her chin and evidence of a crack in the corner of her mouth. It would appear that someone had struck her.

There could be a million other reasons why the woman wore a bruise, but one, he'd seen the worst life had to offer and the terrible things people did to other people so his first instinct was to always think the worst. And two, if the bruise was innocent in nature—an accident of sorts—then why would she go to such extremes to hide it?

She took a tentative step back and he didn't move. He simply stood there, allowing her perusal without interruption. It was apparent she was sizing him up. Perhaps deciding if she could trust him.

"You wanted to see me?" Beau asked in a neutral tone.

Her fingers twisted together in a ball at her stomach. She sucked her bottom lip inward and then winced as though she'd forgotten the injury to her lip. She started to lift a hand to it, but then as if realizing that by doing so she'd only draw unwanted attention to the bruise, she let her hand fall back to her side.

"Yes," she said, nodding. "I need your help."

Beau glanced in Anita's direction and she gave him a quick dip of her head, knowing what he wanted. She would hold all calls and take care of anything that cropped up while he was with the woman so nothing disturbed them.

Beau gestured for the woman to proceed toward his office but she hesitated. Slowly, he put his hand on her forearm. Nothing alarming or sudden and he kept his touch infinitely gentle.

"Come," he said, nudging her forward.

Her shoulders squared and she looked resolutely ahead as if shaking off her earlier trepidation. At his door, she took the initiative and walked inside, leaving him to follow. He shut the door behind them and then turned to face his mystery woman who'd asked for him by name.

Her gaze was on the two-way mirror, a frown on her lips.

"I could feel you watching me," she said in a low, accusing tone.

"Not that it did me any good," he said mildly.

He went to sit behind his desk in his chair so he wouldn't appear threatening to her. He was well acquainted with the look of an abuse victim. God knows they'd seen more than a few. So he knew his size and demeanor could be intimidating and come across in a menacing manner to a woman already wary of men.

But he was also blunt, and on more than one occasion people had been put off by his straightforward manner. It was who he was, and he knew he would never change. So he couldn't be any other way now, when perhaps a lighter touch was called for.

"Before we get to what you has you scared to death, take off the glasses and lose the scarf."

She went rigid, staring at him behind the dark lenses. He could feel her gaze on him, studying him, the prickle of awareness at his nape.

"Is it the bruises you're trying to hide? Or is it *you* who needs to be hidden?"

Her hand went automatically to her face, but she didn't touch the bruise on the side of her chin. It went to cover one of the lenses of the glasses. It was his automatic reaction to scowl at the thought that there was more than one bruise. And as soon as she took in the look on his face, she stirred, turning toward the door.

"You're safe here," Beau said gently. "But I need to know

everything so that I can help you and that begins by you shedding the glasses and scarf and then you telling me what kind of trouble brings you to me and my brother. By name," he added.

She must be holding her breath because she was so utterly still that he couldn't detect the rise and fall of her chest. Then she let the air from her lungs escape in a long exhale. She swayed wearily and then put her hand down to find the arm of one of the chairs in front of Beau's desk.

Slowly, she reached up and tugged at the scarf. Evidently her hair had been pinned to the scarf, because when she pulled the scarf free, a silken mass came tumbling down her shoulders and arms. The color was unique. He could understand why she'd gone to such pains to disguise it. It was various shades of blond but contained silvery highlights intertwined with warm brown strands. There were at least six different shades reflected in the light of his office.

Her hand shaking, she grasped the sunglasses and pulled them away, casting her gaze downward so he didn't see her right away. But when she finally lifted her chin so that their eyes met, his widened in recognition. Her eyes, just like her hair, were distinctive. He was fascinated by how they seemed to change color when she moved even a little and light caught glittering specks of aqua and gold. If asked, he couldn't actually state what color her eyes were. How did one explain a turbulent mixture of the ocean, the sun and the brightest jewels?

And as he'd suspected, there were other bruises. One eye was swollen and had turned a dark purple. Only a slit allowed him to see the eye on that side.

Even with the swelling in one eye there was something decidedly electric in her gaze. He wondered if she was indeed psychic. There were suddenly a dozen questions he wanted to ask her, but he refrained because she was wearing bruises when none of the three punks who'd gone after her had been rough with her, no doubt, but hadn't touched her face. Someone else had hurt her and it pissed him off. And there was also the fact that she was here, in his office, having asked for him by name, and she was clearly scared to death. That kind of fear couldn't be faked unless she was a damn good actress, and he couldn't think of a reason why she'd lie to him.

His questions could wait. For now he focused on whatever threat had sent her running to him and Caleb. He needed to make her feel safe so that she would open up to him about whatever trouble she was in. Which meant patience on his part. Not one of his better traits to be sure. But he tamped down his impatience and desire to know everything right this minute and allowed her to settle and feel more at ease. If such a thing were possible.

"You're the woman on the news," he murmured. "The one everyone is talking about."

She nodded and then closed her eyes as pain and sorrow flickered across her face.

"I was stupid," she said hoarsely. "And now my parents are likely paying the price. I need your help, Mr. Devereaux. I'm so scared of what has happened to them. My father told me if I was ever in trouble, if I ever needed help and he wasn't there, to come here. To you or your brother."

Beau's eyebrow lifted in question. "And who is your father?"

"Gavin Rochester. I'm Arial—Ari—his daughter. Do you know him?"

Beau frowned. The name rang a bell with him. It had been

years, when his parents were still alive, but he was almost certain that Gavin Rochester had either been a friend or a business associate of his father's. And given the fact that his parents had died under suspicious circumstances, it made him uneasy that someone who'd associated with them had sent his daughter to him and Caleb.

Caleb had shed any and all connections to their parents' lives, associates, friends, everyone. They couldn't be sure who to trust, if anyone at all, and so they'd simply withdrawn, gone off the grid and started over. Clean. Whereas when his parents were still alive, they reveled in their lifestyle and enjoyed all the perks of having wealth and power, Caleb had gone the opposite way entirely. He hadn't wanted for his siblings the life their parents led. A life that had led to their demise.

"No, I don't know him," Beau said truthfully. "It's possible he knew my father. But my parents died many years ago. So perhaps that is why he told you to come to one of us if you were ever in trouble."

"I wish I could go back and undo it all," she said, grief choking her so the words came out choppy and sporadic. "I made a mistake. I was never supposed to reveal myself as I did that day, but I reacted on instinct. I *knew* he was going to kill me. I could see it in his eyes. And while I am versed in self-defense—my father insisted—there was simply no way for a woman of my size to take on three men."

"What exactly did you do?" Beau asked quietly.

She went silent, chewing on her bottom lip in consternation. He could tell she was waging one hell of an internal battle. Deciding how much she should tell him, if anything at all.

"Ari. Do you prefer Ari or Arial?"

"Ari," she said in a husky voice. "Everyone calls me Ari."

"All right, Ari. You came to me because on some level you knew that if your father trusted us then so could you. And if I'm going to help you I have to know everything. You can't leave a single thing out because I have to know what I'm dealing with. If you're worried about privacy, we have a very strict policy of client confidentiality. We don't even keep hard copies and our computer system is impenetrable. We hire the very best and we take our business—and our clients—very seriously."

"Does that mean you're going to help me?" she asked anxiously. "If it's payment you're worried about, I assure you I have the money."

Even as she spoke, she began digging out ten-thousand-dollar wraps and placing them on his desk in agitation.

"Just tell me how much. I can pay it. If the cash isn't enough I can get more."

Beau reached across the desk and captured one small hand, holding her still before she could go back to her purse again. He rubbed his thumb over her satiny soft skin in an effort to soothe her.

"We'll discuss money later," he said gently. "Right now I need information from you so we know what we're up against and so we know where to start looking. You said your parents disappeared? Or that they're in danger?"

Tears shimmered in those electric, almost neon eyes, making them even more vibrant. They practically glowed, making her eyes seem much larger against her delicate bone structure.

His gaze found her swollen eye again and he ground his teeth together because it pissed him off to imagine someone striking such a small woman hard enough to put that kind of bruise on her. She was lucky nothing was broken. But then how did he know there wasn't? It wasn't like she could just pop into the local ER to get X-rays.

He made a mental note to have a doctor come to see her once he got her settled somewhere safe.

She twisted her hands in agitation and then reached up, pushing her fingers into her temples as if to relieve pain and tension. It was all he could do not to take over the task himself and remain behind his desk as an impartial third party. Someone she wanted to hire.

"Why don't you let me ask questions," he prompted. "It may be easier for you to focus if you only have to answer instead of struggling with how to tell your story and decide whether you can trust me or not."

Guilt flashed in her eyes, telling him that he'd hit the mark and that she was indeed battling with herself over whether to trust him. Then her lips firmed and she straightened, looking directly at him as if she'd come to a decision.

"My father trusted you," she said softly. "So I do as well. He wouldn't have ever told me to come to you if he hadn't known with absolute certainty that you were a good man and that you would help me. You're all I've got, Mr. Devereaux. And beggars can't be choosers. Especially when it comes to my parents' lives."

"Please, call me Beau," he said. "Mr. Devereaux makes me feel like an old fart and I hope to hell that's not what I look like."

Her face flushed pink and a tiny smile tugged at the corners of her mouth. He was astonished by the change in her eyes during that one moment she'd let her guard down. He was mesmerized by the kaleidoscope of shimmering colors contained in those small orbs.

"You certainly aren't an old fart, so Beau it is," she said lightly.

He could sense her relaxing just a bit, some of the awful tension starting to leave her body.

"Would you like some coffee or tea? Perhaps soda?"

She shook her head and glanced down at her watch. "I've wasted too much time as it is. It could already be too late for them."

Pain and distress immediately flooded her eyes once more and desolation cast dark shadows over her features.

"When did they disappear?" Beau asked, deciding to take the bull by the horns and discontinue this delicate dance to try to make her feel at ease.

"Yesterday. Yesterday afternoon," she said, blowing out a deep breath. "I know it sounds silly to be worried when they've been gone less than twenty-four hours, but you have to understand. After what happened, they would never have left me for that long. They had only gone out to do some quick shopping. For me. We were moving to one of my father's undisclosed residences so I would be shielded from the media and any other nutcase out there who might possibly come after me."

Beau's eyebrow lifted at the "undisclosed residence" part, but then judging by the expensive clothing Ari wore and the several 10k wraps she'd dug out of her oversized purse, not to mention the obvious security measures her father took, her family must be wealthy. He made a mental note to dig up everything he could find on Gavin Rochester as soon as he could get word to Quinn. For now, he put it aside so he could focus on the rest, but at the first opportunity, without alerting her to the fact, he would have Quinn do some discreet, but thorough, checking

The name bothered him because he was certain there was a connection to his parents and he and his brothers were suspicious of anyone associated with his parents before their "untimely" deaths.

It was possible, given Caleb was the oldest, that he might even remember Gavin or perhaps might have even met him on occasion. Their parents had moved in wealthy circles, openly flaunting their wealth and making important—and wealthy—friends. Their father hadn't been discreet in mixing business and personal matters and had often, as Caleb had told Beau, entertained business associates in their home, allowing them to meet and mingle with the Devereaux children, though Caleb had always shadowed their younger sister, Tori, cautious about the people their parents associated with.

It was a sad testament to the fact that even at a young age Caleb hadn't trusted his own parents. Beau only had vague memories, not specifics, and Quinn and Tori had no memory of them at all.

"They didn't call," Ari continued. "They didn't let me know why they were late and all my calls to them went straight to voice mail, which tells me their phones are either turned off or have no charge left. They literally disappeared and they would never do anything to cause me worry, nor would they leave me alone on a whim. So I *know* something has happened to them."

"Tell me as much as you know," Beau encouraged. "Don't leave anything out, no matter how insignificant it might seem. We need all the information you can supply so we at least have a starting point."

She went still, holding her breath, her nostrils quivering as she stared back at him. "Does that mean you'll take the job?"

"I need to hear all the facts, but yes, DSS will help you."

Her nostrils flared with sudden exhalation and her shoulders visibly sagged.

"Thank God," she whispered. "I didn't know what else to do, who else to turn to. The men my father hired can't be trusted. I can't afford to trust *anyone*. But my father obviously had faith in you and your brother so I have to go with his judgment."

"Why do you say the men your father hired can't be trusted?" he asked, though he had a very good idea now that the puzzle pieces were coming together. Those bruises didn't get there by accident.

"My father only took two of his security detail with him and my mother. My father is very capable of defending himself and my mother, but he took two and left the rest of the detail with me at the house.

"When I realized that they weren't coming back, I went outside, hoping to get their attention. I knew they were there, but I couldn't see them. They weren't inside with me."

Beau frowned. Why the hell wouldn't her father have made certain that the house was every bit as guarded on the inside as the outside?

"After I got no response when I called out for help, I dug through my purse for the keys to the vehicles my father owns. When I looked up, one of the men was there. He told me my parents were 'fine' and then before I could react, he *hit* me."

Her hand went to her face though he doubted she was conscious of the act. Fury left a foul taste in his mouth at the idea of this young woman, so delicate, would be brutalized by a much larger man. A man who was supposed to *protect* her.

"When I looked up from where I was sprawled, he was

coming toward me and I saw a syringe in his hand. I knew he intended to drug me. And that he obviously wanted me alive, otherwise he could have just killed me as soon as I walked out of the house."

Beau nodded his agreement with her assessment but remained silent so she would continue, without distraction.

"I knew I could never physically fight him off. He was twice my size and he just screamed military. That look, you know? He was absolutely cold and methodical. I also knew that while he may have had orders to keep me alive, it didn't mean that he wouldn't hurt me in the process."

She trailed off for a moment and her lips formed a tight, white line. She'd grown pale and her respirations were much more shallow and rapid. She stared at him, her gaze penetrating as she studied him. As though she were at a crucial point in deciding whether to fully trust him or to censor some of the information so he wouldn't know all of it.

But he waited, not offering argument, nor did he try to compel her to trust him. It was a decision she had to make on her own, one he wouldn't bully her into making. If he was going to help her, he needed one hundred percent of her trust. Which meant telling him everything.

"You obviously saw the video," she said, her voice trembling. "You've had to have seen the speculation and drawn your own conclusions about who and what I am."

"I'd rather hear it directly from you," he said calmly. "I don't form an opinion without all the facts."

She flashed him a grateful look and then once more squared her shoulders resolutely.

"I have special . . . powers," she said hesitantly. "Telekinesis. I don't know if it's my only power because all my life my parents have tried to hide me—and my abilities—from the public eye. So I never used them. Not since I was a young child and didn't know better. So it was blind instinct to use them when I was attacked. I wasn't rational enough to simply try and escape without using my powers. And now everyone knows or suspects and God only knows what else they think or assume about me."

Her gaze was wary as she studied him intently, waiting for his reaction. He refused to give her one, though it was what she expected.

"I know it sounds crazy," she said in a low voice.

"You'd be surprised by what I don't find crazy," he said calmly.

She relaxed even more, some of the doubt and fear evaporating from her eyes.

"I called my father to tell him what happened and he told me to get in my car and he'd be there shortly. I'm almost certain he somehow manipulated the security camera footage so that it would be obvious that I was acting in self-defense but at the same time not showing how I defended myself. We never dreamed someone not only witnessed the incident but videoed it as well. And now it's everywhere."

She closed her eyes, her face suddenly showing signs of stress and fatigue.

"I don't know what else to tell you that would be helpful. I wasn't involved in my father's business matters. All I know is that he and my mother left after saying they'd be gone no longer than two hours and that's the last I've heard from them."

"And your attacker told you they were fine."

She nodded. "How do I know he was telling the truth?"

Then she sighed again and rubbed absently at her forehead. "I should have just let him take me. Why bother sedating someone if you want them dead? He could have shot me on sight and gotten away with it. I should have just let him drug me so that maybe he'd take me to wherever my parents are or perhaps even free them since it's obvious that it's me they want."

Beau's face drew into a scowl before he could call it back. "That is *not* the answer. If they want you so badly then they'll use your parents as bargaining chips because if they kill them, you'll never cooperate with them. They'll try to contact you. They'll likely want to arrange for a trade. You for them."

She nodded.

"That's never going to happen, Ari," he said, his tone brooking no argument.

Her eyes widened in surprise. "What other choice do I have?"

"You *chose* to come to me. *That* was your choice. Because deep down where fear isn't fueling your irrational thoughts, you know I'm right and that if you surrender yourself to them, you'll be signing your parents' death warrant."

NINE

ARI stared at Beau Devereaux seated in the chair across the desk from her. He looked relaxed and at ease but there was something in his eyes. Something dark and formidable. He was an imposing, intimidating man. Tall and muscular with strong features and bone structure.

He wasn't pretty by a long shot. There was nothing polished or refined about him, though she knew he and his brothers were wealthy. He had a rough edge to him that would always give people pause and, if they were smart, make them wary of ever crossing him.

She was hiring him, and she should be the one who held the power and yet he thoroughly intimidated her. He looked . . . hard. Like nothing ever unnerved him. And perhaps that was a good thing. She needed hard and ruthless if her parents were going to be found.

"Do you have somewhere safe to stay?" Beau queried as he studied her.

She tried to push the sudden panic down, but it nipped persistently at her nape and she knew she'd utterly failed to keep it from her expression. She'd never been adept at hiding her emotions. Her father had tried to teach her to be unreadable, but it was a futile effort. She just wasn't wired that way. And she knew, judging by Beau's expression, that she'd failed miserably in keeping the dismay from her eyes.

"I don't know," she admitted. "My father's security detail would most likely know the locations of all his residences. *I* don't know about all of them. I'll have to check into a hotel under an alias. My father provided ID and passports as well as cash in the safe-deposit box."

Once again, Beau's eyebrow lifted and she could only imagine what he was thinking. It *did* sound like her father was some sort of crime lord, because he shrouded himself in secrecy and security. She'd honestly never given it a thought. It was the way her father had been since she was old enough to remember, so she accepted it as normal, never considering how others would view his extreme security measures.

She assumed all he did was in protection of her. So that her powers would never be scrutinized by the public. And she'd failed him and her mother. Everything they'd done for the last twenty-four years had been washed away in a single moment of panic.

"I understand that your first concern is your parents and their safety," Beau said gently. "But *you* are in danger as well. You can't think only of them."

"Tell me what I should do then," she said, trying to keep the helplessness from her voice. She was an adult woman still emotionally dependent on her parents. She didn't like the fact that she had no idea what to do, what action to take, now that her father wasn't there guiding her with a gentle hand. It embarrassed and shamed her.

"For now, you come home with me," Beau said. "Security is extremely tight, and I can be assured of your safety until we figure out our next step. Do you know who Ramie St. Claire is?"

Her brows knitted at the sudden change of subject.

"Yes, of course. Who doesn't?"

Ramie St. Claire had been all over the news in the last year. She was a psychic who possessed extraordinary abilities to locate kidnap victims.

Ari's breath caught in her throat. Of course! Why hadn't she thought of it sooner? If Ramie could track victims, perhaps she could find her parents.

But as soon as the thought hit her, she sagged, momentarily deflated. How could she possibly contact the young psychic when she'd completely disappeared from the public eye?

"She's married to Caleb," Beau continued. "I can't promise you that she'll help. Caleb is very protective of her and her gift comes at a very high price because she experiences everything the victim does. But if you have something—an object—that was a particular favorite of your mother or father, or something they used frequently, it's possible she could locate them using that object."

Ari's heart leapt and her pulse stuttered, causing her breath to hitch uncomfortably.

"Cover your hair back up as you had it before and put your sunglasses back on. I'll summon our driver to meet us in front. Usually I drive myself, but I'm not parked close and I don't want you exposed or alone in the time it takes me to go get it and pick you up."

Ari blinked, wondering how they'd gotten from her wanting to hire him to her going home with him and him taking over completely. But even as she found herself questioning him, she obeyed without hesitation, redoing her disguise.

When she was finished, Beau picked up the phone and dialed a number. She listened while he tersely informed the driver to pick them up directly in front of the entrance to the building. When he finished the call to his driver, he inquired as to how she'd gotten here, and when she explained about the BMW parked curbside not far from the entrance to the building, he shook his head, frowning, then placed yet another call and instructed someone to pick it up and deliver it to Beau's home.

While she'd certainly hoped he'd agree to help her, she hadn't quite expected this kind of reaction. It felt as though her entire world had been upended and she wasn't in control of any aspect.

It wasn't a pleasant feeling. But then when had she truly ever been in absolute control of her life?

As Beau rose from his chair, she did the same, suddenly nervous and unsure of herself. But, as she'd already acknowledged, she had no other choice. She knew she couldn't trust any of her father's men, even if they weren't all traitors. The safest course was to assume they were *all* after her for whatever reason.

Which left the men—man—her father had always told her to seek out. If her father had placed his trust and her well-being into Beau Devereaux's hands, then surely she could do the same. She'd never questioned her father's judgment before and she wasn't about to start now.

With a deep breath, she allowed Beau to herd her out of his office and into the lobby area where their receptionist was stationed.

"Let Quinn know he's covering the office today, and let him know I'll check in with him later to give him the rundown."

Anita nodded. "Yes, sir. I'll call him now."

Ari gasped in shock when Beau actually growled at his receptionist and sent her a scowl. Before she could think better of herself, she elbowed Beau in the ribs, frowning at him in reprimand.

"Did you just *growl* at her?" Ari whispered in astonishment.

To her additional surprise, instead of looking chastened, Anita burst into laughter and smiled at Ari.

"Don't mind him. He hates that I call him sir and Mr. Devereaux. He's convinced it makes him sound like an old fart and he doesn't take it well that a woman older than him addresses him as sir. He insists that he call me ma'am, but I'm not to reciprocate and give him that same respect."

Her eyes twinkled merrily as Beau's scowl grew darker.

"He has good southern gentlemen manners, for sure," Anita continued. "They don't make them like they used to and Beau is definitely a throwback. But I call him sir and Mr. Devereaux just to needle him. Especially when he gets too serious. Which is pretty much all the time," she said blithely, unruffled by Beau's reaction.

A smile hovered on Ari's lips despite the fact that her situation was dire and she was frantic over the disappearance of her parents.

"So you're saying I should drive him crazy by calling him sir or Mr. Devereaux?" Ari asked in an innocent voice.

"Yep," Anita said, still grinning unrepentantly.

Beau's fingers curled firmly around Ari's wrist and he all but dragged her from the suite of offices to the elevator.

"My father always said I wasn't serious enough," Ari said lightly as they descended. "That my heart was too soft and I was too gullible and naïve for my own good. It appears you go too far in the opposite direction so perhaps we'll balance one another out."

He shot her a look, his eyebrows rising, and she immediately blushed, heat burning her cheeks as she realized how what she'd said sounded.

"I didn't mean it like that," she said hastily, nearly groaning over sticking her foot in her mouth. Yet another thing her father said she did frequently.

"Like what?" Beau asked in a mild tone.

She was sure she turned even redder. "Like we have some sort of a relationship. You know, yin and yang, that sort of thing. It was a stupid thing for me to say. But my mouth often gets ahead of my brain."

"So which one of us is Yin and which is Yang?"

It took her a moment to realize he was joking. He was *teasing* her.

She laughed, shaking her head. "And your receptionist accuses you of being too serious. Maybe she's never experienced your sense of humor?"

"I don't *have* a sense of humor," he muttered. "Ask anyone. They'll tell you I'm the grumpy bastard of the Devereaux clan."

"Hmmm. I guess I'll have to wait and create an informed opinion. Where are we going?"

The abrupt change in subject had Beau looking at her in confusion.

She sighed. "I do that too, unfortunately. You'll experience it soon enough. But I tend to blurt out whatever happens to cross my mind at the time. My parents are adept at following my train of thought but others? Not so much."

He smiled, the action completely transforming his grim features. He suddenly looked . . . approachable. Not at all the intimidating figure he'd been in his office.

The elevator doors slid open and they exited to pass the security desk where Ari returned her badge.

Beau's eyebrows lifted when his gaze skimmed over the pass.

"You weren't exaggerating when you said you had multiple aliases."

Ari shot him a serious look so he'd know she wasn't in the least exaggerating. "Yes, I have three sets of identification. Driver's license and passports for all three names. My father always told me that if I had need of them it was best to switch them around so that no one ever caught on to one and was able to track me. It sounded paranoid at the time and I just put it down to my father's overprotectiveness because that certainly wasn't anything new to me or my mother. But I honestly never thought I'd actually *need* them. Obviously I was wrong and should have paid more attention to the measures my father went to in order to secure my safety. It's almost as if he knew that I'd need them one day. I just don't know *why*."

Her voice trailed off as Beau pulled her into the rotating door. She hastily felt for her scarf and glasses, ensuring they were covering what they should. She was glad for the sunglasses, because the sun was particularly bright today and she would have been momentarily blinded by the sudden wash of light.

She saw the car parked directly in front of the building, blocking one lane of traffic, and knew it had to be Beau's vehicle.

But when they started forward, someone bumped into Beau, knocking him slightly off balance for a moment.

At the same time, the glass shattered behind them and screams went up. Ari found herself shoved painfully to the cracked pavement, Beau's body covering hers completely.

She heard his violent curse and felt him fumbling for something. She turned her head, trying to see what had happened, and terror clenched her insides when she saw Beau had pulled a gun she hadn't even realized he carried.

"Stay down," he said harshly. "Do *not* make a single move until I tell you."

She nodded, not trusting her voice to even work. Her throat was paralyzed and fear was fast closing off her airway.

At this point there wasn't much more damage Ari could do that hadn't already been done by the video of her using her powers and so she focused on two metal waste bins that lined the sidewalk further down.

They hovered in the air and then streaked toward her and Beau before coming to rest in front of them, giving them some cover at least. When Beau realized what she'd done, he cursed again.

But if he thought to reprimand her, he didn't take the time. She was suddenly hauled to her feet and shoved between Beau and what she assumed was his driver and they dove toward the car.

Ari landed in the backseat and cracked her head on the opposite door handle. Her already bruised body was taking yet another beating. She could feel every single one of those bruises and sore ribs screaming their protests.

"Go, go, go!" Beau barked. "Get us the hell out of here."

The car took off, tires squealing as it shot into traffic. She scrambled up so she could look out the back, trying to make sense of what had just happened. The street was empty of pedestrians. They'd all taken cover the moment a shot was fired.

Beau yanked her down roughly so her head was below the windows.

"Stay down, damn it! Are you just *trying* to get yourself killed?"

Her eyes were wide as she stared over at him to where he too was crouched low in the seat.

"What happened, Beau?"

"Sniper," he clipped out.

Dismay and confusion swirled in Ari's chaotic mind. It was simply too much to take it all in. Too much had happened in a very short span of time, turning her world completely upside down. Her life as she knew it had undergone a drastic change.

"I don't understand," she said, trying to shake the cobwebs from her brain. "It seemed so important that they *not* kill me. They tried to drug me when, if he'd wanted, he could have killed me on the spot. So why would they try to kill me *now?*"

"They weren't shooting at you," Beau said, his expression grim.

She shot him a puzzled look, her confusion growing by the minute.

"They were shooting at *me.*"

TEN

ARI was eerily silent on the drive to Beau's residence. She was pale, obviously shaken, and worse, guilt shadowed her eyes. He knew she was beating herself up for placing him in danger and that just pissed him off.

So when she shifted restlessly and turned her gaze on him, he knew before she ever spoke precisely what she was going to say.

"I shouldn't have involved you," she said in a low voice. "I had no idea this was so serious. I don't understand *any* of it. But I couldn't live with myself if someone was killed because they were helping me. I think the only reasonable thing to do is give them what they want. Me."

"Shut up and stop being a goddamn martyr," he said rudely.

He knew he was being belligerent when he should be more understanding and compassionate with her. She was clearly at her rope's end and was on the verge of collapsing and she didn't need him being a surly asshole to her. But it angered him to think of such a vulnerable, innocent woman in the clutches of some son of a bitch out there who planned God only knew what to do to her.

She flinched at the reprimand and he felt instant guilt when he saw the flash of hurt in her eyes. She masked it quickly, but not before he saw that his words had struck her like a dart.

"I'm not trying to be a martyr or overly dramatic," she said in a low voice.

Sadness clung not only to her features, but to her words, and swamped her vibrant eyes, turning them from the nearly neon, electric natural glow to a more dull, sedate blue-green.

"I just don't know what else to do. My parents are *everything* to me. My only family. They've given up so much for me my entire life. My powers impacted their lives even more than mine because they always made sure I was happy and safe and it wasn't until I was much older that I understood the sacrifices they'd made for me.

"My mother calls me their miracle child. After my parents married they tried, unsuccessfully, to have a child. My mother was young, though, and my father wasn't in a hurry. He would have been happy with just my mother if it ever came to that. But she desperately wanted to have a child.

"After countless miscarriages and my mother deciding to stop trying because the grief grew harder to bear with each child they lost, she got pregnant with me. I'm their only child. My mother was never able to have another. I wanted to be the perfect daughter, to somehow make up for the fact that my mother couldn't have what she most wanted. A house full of children, love, laughter and happiness.

"They've always, *always* protected me. Sheltered me from the harsh realities of life. Maybe they didn't do me any favors. Maybe they sheltered me too much. But I'll always be grateful for what they've given me. Their love and their willingness to do anything to ensure my well-being and happiness.

"So now, when it's them who need me, I feel utterly helpless. I don't have the knowledge or skills to even know where to begin looking for them. So when I say that I feel like my only option is to surrender to these people, whoever they are, I'm not being dramatic and I'm not being a martyr. I'm a woman who loves her parents more than life and will do *whatever* it takes to have them back. Safe. Even if it means my own life."

Sincerity rang in her words. Her utter conviction was evident in every single feature. Her eyes glowed once more but with purpose. Determination.

She didn't deserve his censure. It was clear that Arial had never had to face the harsher realities of life, as she'd said moments earlier. She simply couldn't comprehend that her parents would be used to get to her and it was obvious that she absolutely meant what she said when she'd firmly stated that she would do whatever it took, even if it meant trading her life for the lives of her mother and father.

That kind of selflessness rarely existed anymore. Beau was used to seeing the worst in people, not the good. His sister and sister-in-law had suffered the unspeakable at the hands of sick, twisted monsters. Evil was prevalent everywhere. In every walk of life. In those no one would ever suspect. Yet evil, the capacity for evil, existed in most everyone. True goodness, the kind that went soul deep, was a rarity. Most people wouldn't be as selfless as Ari appeared to be, and he didn't doubt her sincerity even for a second. She was utterly serious and that was going to make his job that much harder to keep her out of harm's way while he and his men tracked down her parents.

"I apologize," Beau said, hoping his words were every bit as sincere as hers. "It just enrages me that you'd value your life so little that you'd literally surrender yourself into their hands. It doesn't have to come to that. I need you to trust me. Your father evidently trusted me and Caleb. Enough that he told you to seek us out if you were ever in trouble and he couldn't provide help himself. So trust me not only to find your parents, but to protect you as well. And promise me you won't do anything hasty because, Ari, you have to understand, even if you had allowed yourself to be taken, they would likely kill your parents once they had what they wanted."

Ari paled, all the color leaching from her face until it was chalky white.

"I know this is hard to hear," he said, lowering his voice to a more soothing note. "But you have to face reality. Whoever these people are, they clearly mean business and just as obviously think nothing about killing anyone who gets in their way, as evidenced by the fact a sniper tried to put a bullet through my head just a few minutes ago."

"Do you think they're even still alive?" she whispered, choked with emotion.

She looked so lost and terrified that it was instinct to pull her across the seat and into his arms. He hugged her, feeling the rapid pattering of her pulse against his chest. Her respirations were shallow and just as rapid as her pulse.

The irony of the situation wasn't lost on Beau. He wasn't a hugger nor was he one who usually offered comfort. He was the arrogant asshole of the family, the one who always said what no one wanted to hear but needed to hear nonetheless. Such was the case with Ari right now.

She needed to know what she was up against and that the minute she lost her bargaining power—herself—her parents would almost certainly be eliminated.

"I think they're alive," Beau said, wincing inwardly as he made his statement. He hoped to hell he wasn't lying to her. He was the one usually counted on to speak the truth, no matter how hard it was. But he found himself wanting to offer Ari at least a glimmer of hope, because if she truly thought her parents were dead she'd likely snap.

He needed her to have hope so that she used sound judgment and adhered to whatever plan Beau and his team came up with. The last thing they needed was a wild card and for Ari to go off on her own. Powers or not, she was extremely vulnerable.

And even if her parents weren't killed the moment Ari was in her attackers' possession, they would most likely be used to control her. The attackers would threaten her with her parents' death to ensure her full cooperation and would forever have a stranglehold on her because she would do anything if it meant keeping two people she loved from dying.

"As long as you stay out of their reach, I think your parents will be safe," he said. Again, hoping he wasn't setting her up for horrific shock and disappointment. But it was the logical conclusion to arrive at since they hadn't killed Ari and seemed determined to bring her under control. Their control, whoever the hell "they" were.

"They'll use your parents as bargaining tools, at least for a short while. It will buy us some time to start our investigation and hopefully find them before their kidnappers grow impatient and start using more drastic measures to 'persuade' you."

She shuddered against him as if his words solidly planted a very unpleasant image in her mind. He regretted that too but again, it was information she needed to know. To understand. He couldn't—wouldn't—sugarcoat it for her.

The smell of her hair wafted through his nostrils, and he frowned, immediately setting her away from him, back onto her side of the vehicle. When he started noticing things about the way a woman smelled—a *client* smelled—then it was time to gain some perspective—and distance—between him and his "client."

He'd made a serious professional breach as it was by hugging her, even if it was only to soothe her frayed nerves. The problem was that he'd enjoyed it far too much, and what had started as an impersonal offering of comfort had immediately changed as he became aware of certain things. Like how she smelled. How her body felt curled into his. How petite and delicate her bone structure was. And how damn kissable her mouth was.

Jesus. He was losing it. If he had any sense whatsoever, he'd turn Ari over to Dane and Eliza's very capable hands and bow out. Let them do their job—a job they were damn good at.

But at the same time he completely balked at the thought of foisting her on someone else. Her father had told her to trust him and Caleb. No one else. If he handed her over to Dane and Eliza—or anyone else employed by DSS—she'd likely tuck tail and run.

She was already as skittish as a newborn colt and he could tell it was difficult and weighing heavily on her to place her trust in him as it was. And only because her father had instructed her to. Otherwise he doubted she'd trust anyone right now. He couldn't blame her for that. But his impression of her was that she was one of those "nice" people who gave their trust easily and always saw the good in others. If he was right, then this was her first experience with betrayal and realizing just how the world around her worked.

Her parents had obviously kept her cocooned her entire life and they hadn't done her any favors by doing so. But it wasn't his business or his concern. She was a client and his job was twofold. Find and recover her parents. And keep her safe and alive.

"Hold on tight!" the driver shouted. "We're in for trouble."

Beau barely had time to securely wrap his arms around Arial before the entire vehicle jolted, whipping both their necks forward and then lashing back.

"What the fuck?" Beau roared.

"Got a tail. Hang on. I'm going to get us the hell out of here," Brent, his driver, said in a grim voice.

"A tail?" Ari squeaked. "You don't call someone who just tried to run you off the road a tail!"

"Shit!"

Beau didn't like that muttered curse from Brent. It took a lot to ruffle the driver. He could handle himself in any situation. Not only was he a former race-car driver, but he was also ex-military and he'd been hired for more than just his driving ability.

Beau glanced up to stare through the windshield only to see two vehicles barreling down the wrong side of the freeway, on a crash course with them. They were caught in the middle of an inevitable collision. Which was pretty stupid if they were so intent on keeping Ari alive. How could they be certain she would escape unscathed?

Unless their objective had changed. It was hard to speculate when he had no idea what the source of the threat was. He was already well behind, had no starting point until he could question Ari at length and start investigating her parents—especially her father.

A low whimper tore through Ari's throat and then her eyes glazed over, tiny flecks of gold that sparkled like glitter in the oceanic pools as she stared through the windshield at the vehicles bearing down on them.

Her features tightened as though she were in pain. Her fingers bunched into tight fists, her knuckles white from the fierce grip. Then her entire body quivered, as though the electricity reflected in her eyes now surged through her veins.

He could feel the power emanating from her in waves. It was like nothing he'd ever experienced before. And it wasn't as though he were new to psychic powers or even a skeptic. He'd witnessed firsthand unusual psychic phenomena.

But when one of the cars bearing down on them from the front suddenly lifted into the air, turned on its side and slammed into the guardrail, Beau's mouth dropped open. His gaze shot between Ari's strained features to the wreck they were bearing down on closer and closer.

Blood suddenly dripped from Ari's nose. It slid silently from her ears and her body trembled as if in the grips of something terrible and all-consuming. And then she was suddenly pitched forward. She slammed against him, rocking them both forward. He barely had time to wrap his arms protectively around her and roll her underneath him when the entire world went upside down.

Pain splintered through one of his legs and his shoulders. The sound of metal crunching, the terrible scraping sound of an overturned car still sliding along asphalt freeway. Beau was only conscious of the small woman in his arms and his worry that he'd utterly failed to protect her as he'd promised.

ELEVEN

PAIN surfaced and with it the knowledge that Beau was alive. He cautiously moved first his arms and then his legs, relieved when all seemed in operating condition with only a few twinges that signaled bruising but not breaks. At least he hoped so, because they were still in great peril.

He reached automatically for Ari, opening his eyes to examine the turmoil of their surroundings. Ari was climbing awkwardly into the front seat, her hands going to Brent to gently shake him to ascertain whether he was conscious or not.

"My leg is trapped," Brent reported grimly to Ari. "But my hands are perfectly capable of working. Grab the gun from my holster and hand it to me. There's another in the center console. You need to keep it on you at all times. Be careful, they're loaded. Don't hesitate to shoot if one of those bastards gets near you. The Devereauxs will ensure that none of this falls back on you or that you're even remotely involved. Your first priority has to be protecting yourself. At any cost."

"Ari, you stay put," Beau bit out, voicing his directive as a harsh command.

She glanced back, relief stark in her eyes as her gaze swept over him. As if she'd been afraid that he'd been seriously injured or killed.

"They're coming," she said quietly. "I need to get out so I can draw them away. They'll kill you and Brent. You know that."

It did funny things to his chest—things he didn't like—that she seemed so concerned for him. It was his goddamn job to protect her. Not for her to protect *him*.

Brent's curses mixed with Beau's own. Beau's orders to her to remain here where he could protect her went unheeded as she slithered through the shattered passenger side window, gun in her hand.

Beau fumbled around for his phone, latching on to it when he found it lying just inches from his hand. He punched in Zack's number, knowing he would be able to get here faster than Dane or Eliza.

"Brent and I are down," Beau said with no preamble. "We need extrication stat. I have a client with me and she's vulnerable. They want her alive. Everyone else, not so much."

"On my way," Zack clipped out and then the connection went silent.

There was little point in wasting time giving Zack their exact location. All of the vehicles owned and driven by DSS had GPS that enabled any of the operatives to know where they were at any given time. And Zack was solid. Dependable. Yes, Beau probably should have contacted Dane, since Dane was over the recruits and he answered only to Caleb and Beau. But Beau trusted Zack completely and knew that he'd waste no time getting here as soon as humanly possible. And well, there were times when Beau wondered if Zack *was* human. He seemed to operate with ruthlessness and a cool head at all times. Nothing much fazed him. He took it all in stride and did his job effortlessly. He was precisely the kind of men that DSS needed to fill their ranks with.

Beau awkwardly made his way from the back to the front, his large body not fitting between the crumpled hood and seats as easily as Ari's much smaller frame had done. But the hell he'd leave her alone to face the bastards after her.

"How bad is it?" Beau demanded as he squeezed himself the last bit.

"I don't think anything is broken," Brent said through gritted teeth that told Beau regardless of what the other man admitted, Brent was in pain.

"I'll cover you," Beau said. "Just stay put and don't move. You may have sustained spinal injuries so wait until an ambulance arrives."

"How the hell you going to explain this one?" Brent asked. "You saw what happened as clearly as I did. I know I didn't imagine it."

"No, you didn't," Beau admitted. "It was Ari. She saved our asses and is *still* trying to save our asses. I'm getting out of here so she isn't facing those assholes alone."

Beau winced when some of the jagged glass cut into his skin as he shimmied his way out and onto the concrete freeway. He immediately looked for Ari and saw her a few feet away, taking cover behind their overturned SUV, a gun that seemed far too large for her small hands gripped tightly in her palm.

The vehicle that had hit them from behind had flown by

the wreckage and even now was doing a quick U-turn, uncaring of the oncoming traffic. The other vehicle that had approached from the front had skidded to a halt a hundred feet away and both driver and passenger side doors were open, men taking cover but with weapons drawn and aimed in the direction of Beau and Ari. And Brent.

Goddamn it. Brent was a sitting duck.

Ari turned, her eyes cold and ruthless. He could feel her fury. It crackled between them like an electrical current. She tossed the gun to him and he caught it on reflex.

"Cover me," she said softly.

Before he could open his mouth to protest and tell her to stay her ass right where she was, she stood, presenting an open target to their pursuers.

"Goddamn it, Ari! Stay down!"

"They want me alive," she said softly. "They won't shoot me. You and Brent on the other hand they probably don't give a shit about and I'm not going to just let them take you out because you were protecting me. Not when I have the power to at least slow them down even if I don't completely stop them."

Ignoring his further protests, she locked her gaze on the threat in front of her. Again, he saw blood drip from her nose, seep from her ears and her fingers curled into tight, bloodless fists at her side. Her entire body was rigid and he could only imagine the awful strain she was experiencing. She'd told him that until recently she hadn't used her powers at all. That she'd tried to blend in, be average, nothing special. As if a woman like her, whether she had psychic powers or not, could ever blend in. Not with her beauty and distinctive features.

More blood slid down her neck as the guns trained on them

wrenched themselves free from the men's grasps. They floated effortlessly through the air, one landing right beside the driver's side door where Brent could reach it, the other dropping harmlessly to the ground in front of Beau.

The vehicle that had executed the U-turn barreled forward, on a direct collision course with the already mangled vehicle with Brent trapped inside. Beau watched helplessly, because there was nothing he could do to prevent his man from being more seriously injured and likely killed. The sons of bitches after Ari meant business and they'd eliminate anyone who stood in the way of their goal.

Every vein distended in Ari's arms, her neck, even her forehead as if she was experiencing crippling pain as she focused on the speeding vehicle. And indeed, her features were marred with agony, a nearly silent moan escaping her tightly pursed lips. But as with the other vehicle she'd taken out single-handedly, it suddenly lifted into the air and turned on its side before crashing heavily onto the freeway. It skidded the last fifty yards to come to rest a mere car length in front of the downed vehicle Beau and Ari had taken cover behind.

To further ensure they wouldn't be able to get out, her face contorted once more and the unscathed doors facing upward simply crumpled inward, making it impossible for anyone to escape.

Her power was incredible—like nothing he'd ever witnessed before—but he knew it was costing her dearly. He'd seen psychic bleeds before. Knew they were caused by intense focus and concentration. The blood—and obvious strain on her features—concerned Beau greatly. She could easily suffer a stroke or incur a massive brain bleed as a result.

"Ari," he said in a gentle tone, reaching up to run his hand soothingly down her arm. "Honey, you need to calm down. Slow your breathing. You're bleeding. You've taken out two of their vehicles. I can handle the rest. You need to get down and out of sight until my people get here."

Either she didn't hear or she chose to ignore him. The two men taking cover behind the doors of the vehicle quickly scrambled back inside, reversing at great speed before performing a screeching turn and roaring away, for now, retreating.

Beau sighed in relief and then carefully circled her slender arm with his fingers, drawing her back toward the relative safety of their overturned vehicle.

She blinked in obvious confusion and then she frowned when she stared at the carnage around her. Traffic had slowed considerably as it had to navigate through three wrecked vehicles. Though there was plenty of rubbernecking, no one actually stopped to offer help, something Beau was grateful for. The very last thing they needed was more attention. He willed Zack to get there quickly so they could move Ari somewhere safe and under constant guard.

The police would most certainly be involved, although the vehicle Brent had been driving wasn't traceable. He doubted the other vehicles would net the authorities any more information than his would. The authorities would likely assume gang-related activity or drug trafficking. It didn't matter to him as long as Ari didn't suffer even more exposure as a result of her unleashing her powers.

When no movement was forthcoming from the two wrecked vehicles that had pursued them, Beau instructed Ari to stay down and then he crawled back into the interior of the vehicle to determine the level of injury Brent had endured.

"I'm okay," Brent muttered. "Damn leg is just trapped by the dashboard. When Zack gets here, take Ari and leave me. The police and ambulance will be on scene shortly. They'll have to pull me out and the last thing Ari needs is more media attention. Better for you—and her—to be as far away from this as possible. It's obvious who was at fault here and I doubt those idiots are going to volunteer much information to the police. I have enough contacts with HPD that I won't have an issue."

"Damn it," Beau swore. "You know that's not the way we operate. We don't leave a man down."

Brent's piercing gaze sought Beau's. "And you know this is the way it has to go down. You and Ari can't be involved in this. You have to get her away from here before the cops show up as well as the media if it's suspected or discovered you have any link to her."

Brent made a solid point but that didn't mean Beau had to like it.

Before he could argue, though he knew his arguments would fall on deaf ears because Brent, as well as most of the DSS operatives, were headstrong, stubborn as hell and tended to do things their own way, he heard a vehicle roar up and brake hard behind the wreckage of their vehicle.

He sighed because those under him always managed to get the job done, and he had left them largely alone and had instructed Dane and Eliza to do the same.

Zack stalked up, anger smoldering in his deep green eyes.

"Sitrep," he demanded.

Beau quickly brought him up to speed even as they hustled Ari into Zack's waiting vehicle. They didn't have time to stand around while Beau gave Zack the rundown from start to finish.

Suddenly Ari shoved both men aside, catching them off

guard so that they stumbled. Beau watched in horror as one of the men crawled from the wreckage Ari had caused and pointed a gun in their direction.

"No!" he roared, his shout immediately echoed by Zack as they both lunged for Ari, trying to cover her.

A shot rang out and the two men stared in bewilderment as the bullet slowed, enough that they could *see* it whizzing in Ari's direction. Even as much as she was able to slow it, and direct it away from the men, it clipped her side and she sank to her knees, her hand going to the wound that was already seeping blood.

Beau was furious. He was pissed that Ari had taken a bullet meant for him or Zack. He was pissed that he was supposed to be protecting *her* and yet she'd stood in the way while he and Zack had been shoved out of the line of fire.

Ari was bent over, pale, blood streaming from her nose, mouth and ears and now her side where the bullet had grazed her.

He and Zack immediately formed a protective barrier around her and Beau scooped Ari up and all but threw her into Zack's armored car, where no more bullets could penetrate the vehicle and especially *her*. His mind was a haze of fury. He wanted to take those sons of bitches out right here and now.

But in the distance, the wail of sirens could be heard. As much as it ate at him to leave Brent, his driver was armed and capable of defending himself and the ones capable of fleeing had already left the scene. With police and rescue en route, he doubted the idiot who'd shot Ari would chance another shot, and if he did, Brent's aim was deadly, even if he was trapped in the wrecked vehicle.

Beau settled Ari in the backseat and slid in next to her. He fumbled underneath the seat and dug out a first aid kit. He needed to clean the blood from her face and ears. She looked as if someone had beaten the hell out of her, with the older bruises and the fresh blood. But his first priority was seeing how much damage the bullet had caused. He hoped to hell it was only the graze it appeared to be.

"What the hell happened back there?" Zack demanded as he glanced in his rearview mirror. "Do I need to take her straight to the hospital? She's bleeding from more than the gunshot."

Ari was vehemently shaking her head even as Beau vetoed the idea.

"Psychic bleed," he explained to Zack. "She'll need to be monitored to ensure she didn't do permanent damage to her brain or if there was a severe hemorrhage."

Zack scowled, his expression causing Ari to scoot even closer to Beau as if she were afraid of the other man. Beau instantly put his arm around her like it was the most natural reaction in the world.

"Psychic bleed?" Zack questioned. "Is she psychic then? Is that what happened to those other vehicles who tried to run you off the road?"

Ari stiffened, going rigid in Beau's arms. Her respirations were shallow and he didn't know if it was from blood loss, fear or a combination of both.

"He can be trusted," Beau whispered against her ear. "He works for me and there's no one I trust more than my brothers."

She gave a short nod, but she still regarded Zack warily as they drove as fast as they could without gaining the notice or attention of a cop setting a speed trap.

"You going to fill me in on what the hell is going on and who our new client is?" Zack asked impatiently.

One corner of Beau's mouth quirked upward. How like Zack to automatically insert himself right into the thick of things. His hands were wrapped firmly around the steering wheel, his knuckles white as he performed swift lane changes to weave in and out of the busy traffic on the 610 loop.

"Later," Beau said shortly. "Right now I need to get her to safety and make sure she's okay. And I'll need you to get on the horn and figure out who's free to help out on this assignment. I know Dane and Eliza are tied up with another job at the moment."

"I'll handle it," Zack said simply.

"Where are we going?" Arial asked in a quiet voice.

She seemed in shock, the blood a stark contrast to the paleness of her features. Beau fished in the first aid kit and then slowly lifted her blood-soaked shirt so as not to alarm her.

In answer to the unspoken question and the wariness in her eyes, he soothed her as best as he could. He wasn't a smooth-talking guy. He was too blunt and abrasive to know how to calm a woman's fears. Especially a woman he was currently stripping free of her shirt.

"I need to see how bad this is," he said with calm he didn't feel.

Inside he was a seething caldron of fire, furious that she'd deliberately put herself in the line of fire to protect him and Zack. That was his job. To protect her. Not the other goddamn way around and it pissed him off no end that she'd put herself at such risk. It would not happen again, and as soon as he was assured she was all right they were going to have a serious come-to-Jesus meeting about the way things would be going forward.

She winced when he carefully prodded the two-inch-long gash in her side. But what pissed him off further were the purple bruises that were already present on her rib cage. Evidence of her last run-in with the bastards after her.

"It's not too bad," he murmured. "It needs stitching, but we can take care of that when we get to a safe place."

Her eyebrow rose in question.

"When you have more money than God, as is the case with Caleb, doctors come to him, not the other way around," Beau said with a shrug.

"And not you?" she queried. "Don't you share in the Devereaux fortune?"

He shrugged again, uncomfortable with discussing his financial status. Most of the Devereaux fortune was tainted money. Inherited from their parents, who had most certainly been involved in shady dealings. At least his father had. He had no way of knowing whether his mother had knowledge of his father's dealings or was directly involved herself.

They'd put the money to good use and had made their fortune the old-fashioned way. By earning it through hard work and smart investing. People no doubt thought all their money had been inherited when, in fact, their parents hadn't left them much, considering their net worth when they'd been murdered.

"Where are we going?" she asked, more firmly this time as if she'd shaken some of the numbness she'd experienced up to now.

"Someplace safe," Beau said grimly. "Somewhere I can be sure of your safety so you don't go off half-cocked in search of your parents. You hired me to do a job and that's precisely what I intend to do. But you're staying put where I stash you. The last thing I need is to have to worry about you when we're trying to track your parents' whereabouts."

"I won't get in the way," she said softly. "If you believe you can find my parents, then you have my full cooperation."

Satisfied with her promise, he carefully began cleaning the blood from Ari's nose, face and ears. Some had even slithered in long trails down the sides of her necks to her shoulders and even lower onto her chest.

He did his best to preserve her modesty, leaving her bra on even as bloody as it was. The last thing he wanted was to embarrass her or make her self-conscious.

"I've never bled before," she said in obvious confusion. "I don't understand. You called it a psychic bleed. How could you possibly know what that is?"

Beau gently scrubbed the last of the blood from her face and inspected her to see if she'd incurred more bruising. He frowned when he saw thin cuts to her arms and hands, no doubt received when she'd crawled out of the overturned vehicle.

He set to work cleaning and then putting antiseptic on the cuts before covering them in light bandages.

"I've had experience with people with psychic abilities," he said calmly. "The bleeds seem to occur when the psychic is concentrating very hard on an object or mental thread. It can be overwhelming. Sometimes it can seriously harm them."

She shivered, her arms going around her body in a measure of self-protection. He nearly drew her back into his arms, like she'd been before, but he forced himself to maintain a professional distance. Chill bumps danced over her skin either from shock or worse. With the mental strain she'd undergone, her brain might be temporarily unable to regulate her body temperature. It firmed his resolve that as soon as they had her safely tucked away he was going to have her thoroughly checked out by a physician he trusted. One who had experience with psychic bleeds.

"I've never used my powers like that," she admitted. "I had no idea if I could do something of that magnitude. In the past I've floated objects. Small things. My parents said that from the time I was an infant I would summon my two favorite stuffed animals to my crib. It freaked my mother out until they realized it was me doing it and not someone in the room with me without their knowledge. I was told never to use my powers and so I didn't. It's been years. And then the incident at the school. I didn't think about it. It just came naturally. Automatic almost, as though I'd been using and honing my skills my entire life. And just now. Did you see those cars flip?"

There was incredulity in her question as if she didn't quite believe it herself.

Beau nodded. "Indeed I did. Very impressive."

"I had no idea," she said in a grave tone. "I have to find a way to control it now that it seems to come so naturally to me. I don't want to hurt someone or, God forbid, kill someone by using my powers."

Beau tucked his hand underneath her chin and turned her face so she looked him in the eye. "You'll get it under control. What you did today seemed very controlled to me. You didn't blow up anything. You just made it so they were incapacitated."

Her face wrinkled in silent question. Then she flashed those mesmerizing eyes as she looked up at him.

"Do you think I could blow something up? I mean if I pictured it in my mind?"

Beau was hesitant to answer. Ari on a mission could be a serious wild card and impossible for DSS to do their jobs if she chose to go out on her own, confident in her ability to do anything. And maybe she could. But he'd be damned if she went after the bastards who held her parents alone.

"Is that how you caused them to flip and crash?" he asked calmly. "By picturing it in your mind?"

She slowly nodded. "It was hard, because I had to hold the image and focus solely on it. I couldn't allow any distraction; otherwise I wouldn't have been able to flip the car like I did. I haven't practiced, haven't used my powers since I was a child. So I'm not entirely certain what I'm capable of. Simply because I've never had the chance to measure my abilities in a controlled environment."

"I'd say you're pretty damn powerful, especially for someone who has barely used her talents and only when you were a child. I'm thinking if you practice any more then the world had better watch out."

He said the last with a quirk of his mouth, a hint of a smile hovering on his lips.

"You forget I saved our asses," she said tartly.

"Yes, you did, and I certainly thank you for it, but in the future, if you ever pull a stunt like that again, I'll spank your ass and tie you to a chair so you can't go anywhere. And I'll make damn sure that there is nothing in the room for you to use to free yourself. Are we clear?"

She blinked in surprise. "Why on earth would you want me not to use telekinesis when we rescue my parents?"

He took note of the fact that she said when, not if, they rescued her parents. While he wanted her to have hope, at the same time he didn't think he could bear her grief were she to discover they were already dead. It was obvious that she was extremely close to her parents and that they, in turn, loved her just as much.

"There is no *we*. I don't want you involved, Ari," he said bluntly. "Your father sent you to me for a reason. Because we're the best at what we do. You'd be a liability because our focus would be split between protecting you and ensuring they don't get their hands on you and rescuing your parents. Trust me to do my job and be patient. We—meaning me and my men—*will* find them."

Relief was stark in her eyes, as if she'd shouldered a heavy burden for some time and now found it suddenly lifted.

"I believe you," she said honestly. "And yes, I'll stay out of your way unless you fail to find them soon. Then we do it my way and I turn myself over to them for the safe return of my mother and father. That's all I can and am willing to promise."

TWELVE

AFTER the initial surge of adrenaline wore off, pain snaked through Ari's head and her side where the bullet had grazed her. She clenched her jaw, determined not to make a sound or allow Beau to know how much pain she was in. He had his own injuries from the wreck and the last thing he needed was to have to babysit and coddle her.

She'd been pampered, catered to and sheltered her entire life and it was time to take control of her own destiny, be proactive and grow a spine. It was time to become the independent woman she'd planned to become when she'd taken the first step in her bid to remove herself from the bubble her parents had surrounded her with, by taking a teaching job.

It was a job she loved but now she faced a very uncertain future since she'd been attacked by a student and defended herself using telekinesis.

She let out a soft sigh and then promptly sucked in her breath and held herself completely still, hoping she hadn't betrayed herself to Beau. She should have realized he'd pick up on the slightest noise.

He instantly glanced her way, his eyes narrowing in concern. His gaze raked up and down her body almost as though he could see right through her clothing to the bruises, scrapes and cuts.

"We're almost there," he said, surprising her by not commenting on her condition.

She appreciated the fact that he was all business and treated her like a real . . . person. Not some helpless, useless little doll who would break if touched.

Mentally, she reprimanded herself because she sounded ungrateful and resentful of the care her parents had taken with her. The lengths they'd gone to in order for her to lead a somewhat normal life.

She had no regrets for the way she was raised. She loved her mother and father dearly and wouldn't trade those years or their closeness for anything. It was merely time for her to step out of the shadow of her parents and lead her own life. Make her own choices. Face her own consequences. Most people did so long before the age of twenty-four.

There had never been any consequences for Ari, because her father had always ensured that any issue she encountered simply disappeared. It was who he was, but now she had to be who *she* was. Powers or not, she had to enter the world and face her problems head-on.

They turned into a winding driveway that snaked over terrain that sloped gently toward a heavily wooded area surrounding the house on all sides. She blinked because she hadn't even processed them driving out of the metropolitan area. She'd been too absorbed in her thoughts, worries and trying to keep Beau from seeing how much pain she was in.

Zack pulled to a stop and instantly got out, opening the door on Ari's side. Beau started to get out and then stopped, suddenly moving slower as he gripped the door. She glanced at him in alarm, but his expression was unreadable.

He walked around as Ari began to scramble from where she was seemingly rooted to the seat. She couldn't contain her wince and instantly closed her eyes when agony shot straight down her spine and ricocheted back up to the base of her skull, causing her neck to spasm.

She slid her feet down to the paved carport and her knees instantly buckled. Beau and Zack both made a grab for her and caught her just before she face-planted on the cement.

Zack simply hooked his arm underneath her knees and hoisted her up, cradling her against his chest. Beau looked as though he were going to protest, but Zack leveled a hard stare at him.

"You both look like shit," he said bluntly. "You'll be lucky to get *yourself* inside much less her."

"I'm fine," Beau bit out.

But he didn't argue further, and heat crowded Ari's cheeks as Zack strode purposefully into the house. It humiliated her that she had to be carried like an invalid. She hadn't been prepared for her body's reaction when she'd tried to move.

Even now the dull throb that had persisted the entire ride home had blown into jagged pain, like shards of glass scraping the inside of her skull. Thankfully Zack had picked her up so that the injured side of her faced outward and wasn't pressed against his body. But he'd probably been cognizant of that. He didn't seem like a man who missed the smallest details.

The wash of cool air raised chill bumps over her skin as soon as Zack carried her through the door. She began to shake in his arms and she had to clamp her jaw shut to prevent her teeth from chattering.

Zack looked down at her and then at Beau, frowning.

"She's in shock. You need to get a doctor here to see to the both of you."

"I said I'm fine," Beau snapped. "Ari is the one who needs medical attention. She bled from her nose and ears and then she was shot. All I got was a few bruises from being knocked around in the accident."

Zack shrugged, his expression indifferent.

"Where you want me to put her?" Zack asked.

She hadn't thought it possible to be more embarrassed than she was already, but having the two men blithely discuss where to "put" her, like she was some inanimate object, just made her feel even more helpless and damn it, she was tired of feeling that way. She was tired of being so dependent on others. She wanted to be self-sufficient. But the fates were obviously working against her, because if she had any hope of seeing her parents alive and well and safe she had to depend on Beau's promise that he'd find them. Because she certainly didn't possess the skills to track down an unknown enemy or even find out why her parents had been taken and why someone wanted her badly enough to use her parents as leverage.

Was it her powers? It was the only plausible explanation. Before that damn video had gone viral, her existence had been peaceful. Sheltered, yes, but she'd finally spread her wings.

Her father had not been pleased when she'd refused his infusion of cash into her bank account. She'd gently but firmly told him that it was important to her to make her own way. To live as most other young women lived. A job, modest housing and an economical car. To her, those had all been signs of her achieving independence. It was a need that burned inside her, one that had bloomed and grown until it was all she could think about. It had become her sole focus and her goal. Not to run to her parents for every little thing. To do what most other adults did. Live within their means and make it work. Make life work. Meet normal people. Flirt, date, have a relationship without her father running a background check on any guy who so much as looked her way.

And now everything she'd worked to achieve had vanished because of one moment of panic when her survival instincts had taken over and all rational thought had fled. Not only was she paying the price, but her parents were paying dearly for her lapse in judgment. If they died because of what she'd done, she could never live with herself, could never forgive herself for doing the only thing her parents had ever asked of her. Never tell. Never use. Never reveal.

She closed her eyes against the sting of tears that had nothing to do with physical pain. Zack gently set her down on a plush sofa, propping pillows around her so she didn't fall sideways. And she would have, because she was utterly boneless and sagged into the softness of the couch, keeping her eyes closed and inhaling through her nose so she didn't give in to the urge to cry.

Crying did nothing to help her parents. They needed her to be strong. To have a level head and come through for them. Just as they'd come through for her time and time again. Always there when she needed them. Now they needed her and she'd be damned if she failed them.

"Ari, you're bleeding again."

Beau's softly spoken words jolted her to awareness. She opened her eyes and blinked to bring her surroundings into focus. Beau and Zack both stood directly in front of the couch where she sat, their features etched with concern.

She lifted a hand to her nose, and it came away stained with fresh blood. She frowned because she hadn't been using her powers. But she *had* been focusing very intently on her thoughts. Painful, terrifying thoughts.

Zack hurried away and Beau knelt on the floor so he was eye level with her. He reached up to thumb away more blood that trickled from her nose and then wiped his hand on his jeans.

"You need to calm your thoughts," he said. "Find a good memory or image and focus on that. Try to blank your mind to everything else."

Zack returned with a warm washcloth and Beau took it, gently wiping the fresh blood and then the remnants of her earlier bleed from her ears and neck, spots he'd missed in his haste to see to her injuries on the drive here. Wherever here was.

She glanced nervously at Zack, self-conscious that he was witnessing her at her weakest. It was bad enough Beau had to see her like this.

"I gave Caleb a quick call so he could get the doc headed this way," Zack interjected as if sensing Ari's discomfort. "You might want to put her in one of the bedrooms and let her lie down until he gets here. That way he can examine her in private."

Beau slowly stood, and despite his insistence that he wasn't hurt, she could see that he was at the very least bruised and stiff. When he reached down, obviously to pick her up, she put her hand out to ward him off.

"I can make it," she said quietly. "I'm a little shaky but if I hold on to your arm, I can walk just fine."

Beau's lips thinned in displeasure but he didn't argue or insist. Instead he slid his warm hand underneath her elbow and helped her get to her feet. She swayed slightly and just stood a moment, his fingers tightening around her arm as she got her bearings. She took a shaky step forward, Beau at her side.

Her hand automatically went to his shoulder to further steady herself and his hand dropped from her arm and he instead wrapped his arm around her waist, careful not to touch the gunshot wound. He anchored his arm underneath her shoulder and then glanced down at her.

"Okay?"

She nodded and then took another step, this time less hesitant because she was secure in the knowledge he wouldn't let her fall. She relaxed into his grasp, leaning into his side as they slowly navigated from the living room down a long hallway to a room at the end.

When they entered the bedroom, Beau assisted her to the bed and then instructed her to brace herself on the nightstand while he pulled back the covers and positioned the pillows to cushion her head.

"You'll hurt yourself more if you try to crawl up on the bed," he said gruffly.

Not awaiting a response, he simply lifted her, and her arms instinctively wrapped around his neck, clinging to his strength as he lowered her to the soft mattress. She immediately sighed, her eyes closing as she absorbed the pleasure and the comfort the bed brought to her battered body.

"I'm going to clean you up better before the doctor gets

here," he said, already heading toward what she assumed was the bathroom.

He returned a moment later with a damp washcloth, gauze and several bandages. First he carefully went back over the area he'd already tended to, her ears and then her nose, scrubbing gently at the dried blood. Then he lifted the hem of her shirt, which had a large rip where the bullet had seared through material and skin.

Thankfully the wound was just below the band of her bra and he made no attempt to remove it. She was certain her cheeks were flaming and she stared up at the ceiling, tempering her thoughts, telling herself not to be embarrassed. He was no different than the doctor who was coming to examine her. Or so she told herself.

A low growl emanated from his throat and she opened her eyes, her gaze darting to the ferocious scowl on his face. He was staring at the bullet wound and there was murder in his eyes. She shivered, unable to control her reaction to his obvious rage. In that moment she knew he was capable of great violence when it came to someone under his protection being threatened.

He ran his finger lightly over the crease in her skin, frowning harder as he examined the wound.

"This shouldn't have happened," he said in a low voice. "I promised to protect you and instead I got you shot."

"No—"

Her immediate denial broke off when his head lowered and to her shock, he pressed his mouth tenderly over the wound.

There was nothing sexual about the kiss. It was tender. Meant to comfort. *Exquisite.*

She stared down at his dark head, pleasure flooding her

veins, replacing the pain so evident just moments before. Such a simple gesture and yet it tightened her chest, emotion welling in her throat.

The brush of his lips was like touching the wings of a butterfly. Soft and infinitely gentle. A direct contrast to the seething caldron of rage he'd been just moments before.

She lay there, holding her breath, afraid to move, not wanting to break the spell that hovered. They were cloaked with intimacy and time seemed to stop. Everything else melted away and there was only her and him, and his lips pressed tenderly against her skin.

As abruptly as he'd leaned down to touch his mouth to her wound, he jerked upward, his eyes brimming with regret and self-condemnation. He stood, tossing the washcloth several feet away on the floor.

Not meeting her gaze he turned and walked toward the door.

"The doctor will be here soon," he said gruffly. "Rest until he arrives."

THIRTEEN

BEAU'S mood was black and he was filled with self-loathing for taking advantage of Ari when she was at her most vulnerable. What in the hell had he been thinking when he kissed her?

It didn't matter that it wasn't a passionate kiss or even a kiss to her mouth. Somehow the brush of his lips over her wound, as if he could somehow make it better, had seemed decidedly more intimate than if he *had* kissed her lips. How arrogant and what an asshole it made him to think he had the power to make her pain simply go away, even if that is exactly what he *wanted* to do.

He shook his head as he returned to where Zack waited in the living room.

"You got a plan?" Zack asked, cutting through Beau's thoughts and focusing them entirely on the situation at hand. At least one of them was thinking clearly, because Beau was still replaying the moment with Ari over and over in his mind until it was making him crazy.

Because what he really wanted to do was to charge back into

that bedroom so she wasn't alone. He'd been a dick to gruffly dismiss her and leave her just because he'd been thoroughly disgusted with his lack of self-control.

He wanted to hold her and simply offer her comfort. Precisely what she needed when her entire world had been upended and she was terrified that her parents were dead or terribly injured. Because of her.

It was a burden no one should have to bear and especially not this vulnerable, fragile woman who at her core had a thread of steel regardless of whether she realized it or not.

Beau sank onto the couch, allowing his stiff muscles a moment's respite. Then he eyed Zack. "No," he said honestly. "She walked into my office today with a rather incredible story and if I hadn't witnessed everything that happened after firsthand, I'd think she was either crazy or making it all up. But she's the real deal. And after hearing her story, it's very likely that her parents were taken as a way to manipulate Ari. To make her come to them as an exchange for her parents."

Zack made a derisive sound. "Like they're just going to let her parents walk away unscathed after they have their hands on Ari? Not likely."

"Yeah, that's what I've been trying to convince her of because she was prepared to go off half-cocked in her panic and surrender to them in order to get her parents back. I had to break it to her that they weren't simply going to let her parents go once they had their objective. And if they did keep her parents alive, it would be only so they could control Ari and use them and the threat of harm to them if she didn't comply with whatever the hell it is they want with her."

"Seems that needs to be our starting point," Zack said. "We

need to do a background check, starting with her parents and any potential enemies her father has. A man does *not* go to the lengths he did with security and keeping his family well off the grid unless there's a threat. Maybe we'll get lucky and there's something in either Ari's past or her father's that will give us a lead on who's after Ari now. And why."

"I can well imagine the why," Beau muttered. "After that damn video went viral, there are any number of nutcases out there who would see the value in being able to control Ari—and her powers."

"But no ordinary nutcase would have the resources these people evidently do," Zack argued. "And I doubt her father's security team, men he obviously trusted with his wife and daughter's lives, didn't just turn on him on a dime. This was likely planned well in advance and it may have taken them years to get the right men in place, with her father as careful as he was. That tells me the video had nothing to do with this particular threat, which makes it even more important to poke around her father's business—and personal—affairs. Because this looks to be a carefully orchestrated attack. Not one dreamed it up on the fly. It was too pat, too professional. The video may have simply moved their timeline up on a plan already in motion to get access to Ari."

"Which means someone knew of her powers *before* she was forced to defend herself and the video surfaced."

"Exactly," Zack said in a grim voice.

Beau scrubbed a hand through his hair. "We need information and we need it yesterday. Ari is only going to cooperate for so long. She's desperate to find her parents and thinks nothing of turning herself over even though it's the very *last* thing she should do, because then she loses the upper hand and any bargaining power she has."

Zack nodded his agreement. "You're going to have to sit on her, Beau. And keep her on a very tight leash. We can't do our job if we have to worry about protecting her at every turn."

"Tell me about it," Beau muttered.

He rubbed his hands over his face, suddenly weary as the events of the day caught up to him. Shot at, forced off the road, shot at again. Ari going down. For him. Ari using her powers. To protect him. He'd never felt so goddamn useless in his life. Even when Caleb had been utterly focused on Ramie's protection as well as his family, particularly Tori, who was still fragile and dealing with nightmares from her abduction well over a year ago, Beau had always maintained a steady hand, helping his brother through the unthinkable.

Yet one small slip of a woman, vulnerable and . . . good . . . had him shaken and unsteady, things he'd always possessed— needed. And she *was* good to the depths of her soul. He had uncanny instincts for discerning people's character, and it was evident, not only to him, but to anyone who came into contact with her. She wasn't right for, nor did she deserve someone like him, who saw in shades of gray and not black and white. The lines of right and wrong blurred for him when it came to those who mattered to him. He wasn't above bending the law when it suited his purposes. People like Ari only saw the *good* in others, and now suddenly she was witnessing a whole new side of the world and it was heartbreaking to see the veil of innocence gone from her eyes and the deep hurt and sorrow that had replaced it. Her entire existence, the carefully constructed protective barrier she'd always lived in, had been shattered in the space of one day. It was natural that she was bewildered, frantic and her thoughts in utter chaos, and yet she hadn't crumbled at the first sign of adversity. She'd faced down their attackers and unleashed a storm of fury and retribution and the hell of it was she very likely felt guilty for acting to save not only herself but him and Brent as well.

"Just so you know, when I called Caleb, he demanded to know what the hell was going on and he's on his way over. Knowing him, he'll probably beat the doctor," Zack said dryly.

Beau didn't know whether to be relieved or pissed that his older brother was inserting himself. Usually they worked as a team but for some inexplicable reason, he considered this mission . . . his. Only he, and those he chose as his team, most certainly headed by Zack—not Dane—would work this case.

Caleb had other concerns. He'd just finished construction on the house he'd built for Ramie after their old one had undergone extensive damage. Tori—for now—stayed with Caleb and Ramie while Beau had rebuilt on the same piece of land. The security breach that had led to the destruction had been taken care of permanently and Beau liked the isolation and the security of the original home. He understood why Caleb would want a fresh start with his wife, away from a place that had brought them both so much pain.

For the first time since their parents had died, the Devereaux siblings had split up, no longer living together under the same roof, where they could ensure the protection of their younger sister. Tori was safe with Caleb. Beau had chosen to remain here, in the rebuilt home that had been nearly destroyed, while Quinn had chosen a high-rise apartment close to the DSS headquarters in downtown Houston.

On cue, the front door burst open and Caleb strode inside, his features set in stone, but worry was reflected in his blue eyes. To Beau's surprise, Ramie accompanied him and Beau frowned. Had they left Tori alone?

His question must have been obvious on his face because Caleb immediately responded.

"Dane and Eliza are with Tori," he clipped out. "I'm more concerned with what the hell went on today. Why didn't you fill me in from the start?"

"Ari came to me," Beau said simply. "She came into the offices, scared to death. Her father had told her if she was ever in trouble to seek out either you or me. I was the one there so it was me. I saw no reason to bother you when I have things well in hand."

Caleb arched a brow. "I don't consider being shot at, run off the road and having three destroyed vehicles and you narrowly escaping with your life having things well in hand."

"I've got it handled," Beau said through gritted teeth.

"What happened, Beau?" Ramie asked softly as she took the seat next to him on the sofa.

He noted she was careful not to touch him and it was just as well, because she'd instantly be blasted with his rage and dark thoughts and that was the last thing he wanted for his sister-in-law. She'd had enough violence and evil in her young life. He'd be damned before ever being the cause of further pain.

Just then the buzz sounded from someone wanting to gain access through the security gate at the entrance to the long winding driveway. Zack strode over to the call box and briefly exchanged words with the doctor, all the while studying the video monitor carefully to make sure the physician was the sole occupant of the vehicle. He buzzed him in and Beau rose, unwilling to have this conversation with his brother until he was assured that Ari was all right.

"Zack can fill you in on what we know," Beau said. He narrowed his gaze at his older brother, staring intently, not looking away even for an instant. "But Caleb, this one is mine. Zack will work it with me and he'll handpick his team."

Caleb's eyebrows rose in surprise. "Dane is the head of security. Shouldn't the call be his?"

"I sign Dane's paychecks," Beau ground out impatiently. "He has a job going on and I'm not going to pull him off for this. Not when Zack and I are perfectly capable of handling this situation."

Caleb's frown deepened, and he looked at Zack in question, obvious impatient for a report on just what this case involved.

The door opened and the doctor, an old family friend, walked into the living room, carrying two medical bags. Beau went to greet him, ignoring the others as he led the doctor to Ari's room.

He knocked softly to alert Ari so she wouldn't be startled when he entered with a complete stranger. But he shouldn't have worried. When he quietly pushed the door open, Ari was curled into a protective ball, lying on her uninjured side, and he was struck by the image she portrayed.

Even in sleep, her features were marred by fear and exhaustion, as if her dreams were taking her straight into hell. Her forehead was wrinkled and furrowed as though she were in pain, and he cursed softly when he saw the slow trickle of blood seeping from her nose.

He went to the bed and eased on to the edge, reaching up to smooth her hair from her forehead, gently stroking the lines to ease her strain. She stirred and her eyelids fluttered open, her eyes droopy from fatigue, cloudy with confusion.

"Beau?"

"Yes, honey. It's me. I'm sorry to wake you but you're bleeding again and the doctor is here to see you."

She reached self-consciously to her nose, but before she could wipe it away with her hand, Beau caught her fingers and reached for the washcloth he'd discarded earlier. Carefully, he wiped the blood away and then turned so she could see the doctor standing a few feet away.

Her pulse leapt. He could feel the sudden surge of her heartbeat against the hand he now had against her neck.

"It's okay," he said soothingly. "He can be trusted."

"But I'm all right," she protested. "I don't need a doctor."

Doctor Carey moved forward in his brisk, no-nonsense fashion and set his bags down on the bed in front of Beau.

"Why don't you let me be the judge of that, young lady?" he said kindly.

He glanced sideways at Beau. "Would you like to step out while I examine her?"

Ari's respiration immediately sped up and she glanced in panic at Beau as if her were her lifeline.

"I'll stay," Beau said firmly.

Ari sagged in relief, her eyes closing briefly as she settled more comfortably on the pillows.

"My head hurts," she admitted. "Much more than my side. The bullet wound just stings a bit but my head is *killing* me."

Beau looked at the doctor in concern. "She had a serious psychic bleed. She was bleeding profusely from her ears and her nose. I'm concerned she could have incurred a brain hemorrhage or permanent damage."

Ari choked out an instant protest, looking frantically at Beau as if she couldn't believe he would betray her confidence.

Beau instantly put a reassuring hand to her cheek. "It's nothing he hasn't seen before. He can be trusted, Ari. I wouldn't put you at risk if I weren't certain of his trustworthiness and his complete and absolute discretion in this matter."

The doctor frowned. "That does sound serious indeed and is evidence of great strain on your brain. I'd like to do a scan just to make sure there is no bleed or that it's continuing to bleed. Left unattended, it could be life threatening. But first let me see your bullet wound and then we'll decide what's to be done about your head."

The doctor's brisk, efficient manner seemed to calm Ari's distress and she didn't protest when Beau carefully lifted her torn shirt to reveal the two-inch cut in her side. The doctor frowned and prodded gently, examining the depth of the injury.

"This really needs stitching. I can do it here, but as I said, I'd feel better if you brought her into the clinic so I can do a CT scan of her head. That way we can know exactly what we're dealing with. It won't take long. You'll be a priority case and I'll make sure there are no medical records to indicate you were ever a patient in my clinic."

Ari's gaze shot to Beau as if seeking his guidance. He nodded, agreeing with the doctor.

"You should be checked out," Beau said firmly. "If you're going to be of any help to your parents, we need you at one hundred percent and that's not negotiable. So either you give in gracefully and agree to go or I'll haul you in myself."

A small smile hovered on her lips. "Has anyone ever told you how demanding you can be?"

His smile was as small as hers, but he offered it to her in an effort to give her at least a small measure of reassurance because he sensed she was hanging on by a mere thread. "I've been told that a time or two, yes."

"Okay then, since you're leaving me no choice. Can I at least change into something that isn't bloody and torn? I look like a mess and I don't want to call even more attention to myself than necessary."

"I have some of Tori's clothing still here," Beau said. "I'll get you something to wear and then we're leaving immediately. I'm not going to stand down until I know you're all right. You come first, Ari. Then we'll go after the bastards who have your parents."

FOURTEEN

DESPITE Beau's threat for her to go willingly or be hauled out, he still insisted on carrying her out of the bedroom and no amount of protesting did her any good. He simply scooped her up and strode out, ignoring her assurances that she could certainly manage to walk.

As soon as he walked into the living room and Ari saw more people gathered, heat crawled up her cheeks. She was embarrassed that Beau was carrying her like she was an invalid, but he'd been adamant, stating that he didn't want her to incur any additional stress until they knew for certain the extent of her injuries.

She lowered her gaze, unable to bear the scrutiny from a gruff man who resembled Beau. She assumed that he must be Caleb, the other man her father had told her to seek out. In that instant, under his piercing and probing gaze, she was relieved that Beau had been the one in the office and not Caleb. Beau was an imposing figure to be sure, and at first she'd definitely been intimidated by him and extremely nervous. She'd almost changed her mind and fled his office. But despite his outward gruffness, he'd been nothing but exquisitely tender with her.

Caleb on the other hand? He looked hard and unyielding as his gaze raked over Ari in almost an accusing manner as if he didn't appreciate her intrusion into his family.

There was a young woman sitting next to Caleb on the sofa, and Ari once again made the assumption that she must be Ramie St. Claire. Or rather Ramie *Devereaux*, since she was now married to Caleb. The intimacy between the two was too obvious for the woman to be a business colleague. His fingers were laced with hers and he had her hand drawn over onto his lap, his thumb absently tracing a line along the outside of her index finger.

Ramie had been on and off the news over the years and Ari had followed the reports, often delving further into the stories than just one random article or news sound bite, because she was fascinated by what she considered a kindred spirit. Which was silly given she didn't even know the woman. But in a world where psychic powers supposedly didn't exist, it had given Ari a measure of comfort to know she *wasn't* a freak—or at least the *only* freak of nature. That there were others out there who shared her bizarre gift. Even if their gifts manifested themselves in different ways.

She peeked at Ramie from underneath her lashes, not wanting to be caught overtly staring. She had to bite her lip in order not to beg the other woman to help locate her parents. Ramie had a one hundred percent success record in locating kidnap victims, though two of the kidnappers had eluded authorities, well until last year, when one of them had finally been brought down by the combined forced of the Houston Police and Devereaux Security.

She unconsciously shivered, fear skating up her spine at the *idea* of someone having to track her parents' *killer*. She shut her eyes and huddled closer to Beau, seeking his strength and comfort because she couldn't—wouldn't—allow herself to think her parents could be lost to her forever. She held firmly to Beau's assurances—his vow—to find her parents and return them safely. It was all she had in a world where everything else was uncertain. She had to believe in *something* or she'd simply go crazy torturing herself with the what-ifs and the gruesome possibilities she conjured up every time she thought of her parents out there. Captive. Subjected to God only knew what.

In her worst nightmares, she imagined her mother alone. Separated from her husband, terrified and not knowing if he lived or died.

Beau's grasp on her tightened, his head lowering to the top of her head as if sensing the terrifying direction of her thoughts and he was shielding her in some small—but welcome—manner.

"I'd appreciate it if you and Ramie remained until we return," Beau said to his brother. "There's a lot we need to talk about, but first I have to ensure that Ari is okay and that she doesn't have a brain bleed."

Ramie's eyes widened and she glanced first at her husband and then at Beau, silent question in her expression.

"Psychic bleed. A bad one," Beau said shortly. "Much worse than what you and Caleb have suffered in the past."

Ari's forehead wrinkled in confusion. Did Caleb also possess psychic abilities? Was it something the Devereaux family shared and was that why her father had seemed to know so much about them?

Ramie's features immediately creased in concern but she remained silent, still studying Ari, who was firmly nestled in Beau's arms. She seemed to be much more interested in the fact that Beau was carrying Ari, which made Ari even more self-conscious. Her fingers curled into Beau's chest in a silent plea for them to go.

Beau simply turned and headed for the foyer. The doctor strode ahead of him to open the door and when Beau got to the opening, he paused briefly and turned his head to look over his shoulder, presenting his profile to Ari, his firm jaw and strong cheekbone. His teeth seemed clenched, whether in determination or worry. Perhaps a combination of the two.

"Start digging, Zack. We need all the info we can get like yesterday. I'll be back as soon as possible unless Ari requires hospitalization."

"On it," Zack said.

Ari made a strangled sound of protest even as Beau walked swiftly to the waiting vehicle.

"I don't need a hospital," she insisted as he settled her into the backseat. "What I need is to find my parents. *That* should be our priority."

He put a finger to her lips, effectively stanching any further protest.

"*You* come first," he stated, his tone brooking no argument. "Without you, we have no bargaining power, no leverage and you can kiss your parents goodbye. Because if you die then the people who abducted your parents no longer have any reason to keep them alive. You need to understand that. I know it's hard to hear but you have to face facts. You *matter*, Ari, and it's only going to piss me off if you say you don't. I am not willing to trade your life for your parents. Period. And I'm damn sure not going to let you do something rash, irrational or hasty. You came to me for help so we do things my way. Got it?"

Rage and helplessness bubbled up, singeing her nerve endings and ratcheting up her pulse. Her breaths were rapid and labored as she sought to control the overwhelming fury caused by his abrasive words and his thoughts regarding the two most important people in Ari's *life*.

"Goddamn it," Beau swore. "You're bleeding again. Ari, you have to get your thoughts under control and calm down. You can be pissed at me all you want, but I'm *going* to keep you alive and healthy, and I'm also going to get your parents back. You need to stop fighting me and *believe* in what I've promised you."

She swiped at her nose with the back of her hand, smearing blood on her cheek in the process. Her head pounded, the pain intensifying from an already unbearable level. She closed her eyes and put her palms to her temples, pressing inward.

Beau swore again, violently, but when he wiped at the blood on her face, his touch was infinitely gentle, a direct contradiction to his black mood and fury.

"Lie down and try to get comfortable. I'll make sure Doctor Carey gives you something for pain when you get to the clinic."

She nodded, the slight movement sending shards of pain splintering through her skull. Maybe she did need medical help. This was new territory for her and she had no idea if this was a normal result of using her powers or not because she'd never *tested* them.

"I hurt," she said quietly, conveying in those two words a wealth of emotion she could no longer suppress.

Beau cupped her face ever so gently in his palms and leaned in to press his forehead to hers. Like the kiss he'd pressed to her wound earlier, there was nothing sexual about the gesture and yet it was so intimate. Poignant. With those two touches, his mouth and now merely resting his forehead against hers and their breaths mingling, her heart swelled in her chest and she was nearly overcome with how reverent every touch, every action was that came from him.

"I know, honey," Beau said just as quietly. "I can't even imagine the pain you must be in and how exhausted, worried and sick at heart you must be. But do this for me. Take care of *you* first, okay? Let Doctor Carey at least ease your physical pain. The emotional pain will be much harder to bear, but you're strong, Ari. You have me. From this point forward, consider me your constant shadow. You will never be out of my eyesight unless I have men I absolutely trust surrounding you. You are *not* alone. And you *will* get through this."

Tears burned her eyelids and she blinked rapidly even though the slightest movement sent a jolt of pain through her head, echoing and re-echoing through her fragmented mind. Overcome and unable to possibly put to words what was in her heart, she instead curled her fingers around his hands cradling her face and she pulled them against her chest so he could feel the thud of her heartbeat. So he'd know the effect his solemn vow had on her.

He surprised her by brushing his lips, like the soft tip of a feather, over her brow and then drew back in a swift, jerky motion as if pulling himself back into awareness and the reality of the moment. He frowned but then seemed to make a concerted effort to school his features, but Ari couldn't help but feel as though he'd rejected her in some way.

She turned, as had he, so he couldn't see the flash of hurt in her eyes that she was sure was evident. Her parents had forever told her that her eyes always reflected her every emotion, her every thought. They'd laughingly told her she was utterly transparent and that it was a good thing she was inherently honest, because it was impossible for her to tell a lie and not be caught out.

She sighed, the flutter of warmth in her chest turning to a dull ache as she leaned over on her uninjured side across the backseat of the SUV. Frowning, she lifted her head when the door by her head opened and then gentle hands carefully lifted her head and a pillow was slid underneath her neck so she wasn't lying at an awkward angle.

Hot and cold. Beau Devereaux was a puzzle she couldn't decipher, and she wasn't sure she wanted to. One minute he was exceedingly tender, protective, *demanding* when it came to her care and well-being. The next he was stiff, withdrawn and looked as if he regretted so much as touching her.

She was too mentally and physically exhausted and drained to figure out the riddle of Beau's dual personality. She closed her eyes, reaching for something warm and comforting, anything to ward off the sharp pain and the dull roar in her ears and the constant fear and worry for her family.

It suddenly struck her, that without her parents, she was utterly alone in the world. Her parents had lost their parents at a relatively young age. Her mother had been working her way through college when she'd met Ari's father. He was ten years older, had already amassed a fortune and he'd swept her mother off her feet in a whirlwind romance that had resulted in their marriage in a matter of months.

She had no grandparents. No aunts, uncles, cousins. There was simply no one but her and her mother and father. It was why they were so close. Her father had always said that their family was all he could ever ask for, more than he'd ever hoped for, and considered his wife and his daughter the two most precious gifts in his life.

Her eyes squeezed shut even tighter as sadness overwhelmed her. Then she immediately castigated herself for the feeling of loss that had fallen over her. She wouldn't give up hope. Hope was all she had and when she gave that up, she was well and truly lost.

She clung tenaciously to the promise Beau had given her more than once. Her father had chosen him. To a man who trusted no one, it had to mean something that he would entrust his daughter's safety to the Devereauxs.

Had he known of Ramie's psychic powers? Had that been why he'd been certain that Ari would be well received by Beau or Caleb? But no, Ramie and Caleb hadn't been together that long. And her father had exacted her promise three years earlier, when she'd graduated from college an entire year early.

A frown tugged at the corners of her mouth even though her eyes remained closed. What was her father's connection to the Devereauxs? Beau didn't appear to know her father and if Caleb did, he hadn't acknowledged it in any way, nor had he looked at her with any sign of warmth, such as would surely be the case if her father was a friend or acquaintance of his. Unless Caleb had no liking for her father, but no, that couldn't be right either, because her father would never trust this man with her safety if there was any discord between them.

She sighed, her head hurting more as she sorted through her chaotic thoughts. A warm trickle slid over her lips and she immediately lifted her hand to wipe the blood away in hopes that Beau wouldn't see it. Her eyes fluttered open only to see, to her surprise, that Beau was in the passenger seat of the SUV and Doctor Carey was driving. And Beau was looking directly at her, a deep frown furrowing his forehead.

"What the hell are you torturing yourself with this time?" he demanded, though he kept his voice low, perhaps in deference to her headache.

"I was just trying to sort out everything," she murmured, sliding the sleeve of the thin T-shirt she wore once more over her nose to remove the remainder of the blood smear.

So much for changing into clothing that wasn't bloodied in an attempt not to draw attention to herself.

"That is for *me* to do," he said in a firm voice, fitting his piercing gaze to her as if willing her to yield to his unspoken command to let it go.

How could she simply "let it go"? How could she just stand idly by, hiding, while someone else—a stranger—headed the search for her parents? And why weren't they calling in the police? There were too many questions unanswered. Questions she hadn't asked Beau. Hadn't had time to ask, she acknowledged.

Everything had happened so quickly. Her visit to his office and then everything had gone to hell. Literally. They hadn't had a single moment to sit down and focus on the matter of her missing parents. Beau hadn't had the opportunity to question her or even ascertain simple facts like her parents' names, their address, any of their background and history.

What seemed an eternity to Ari was in fact only a few short hours, and furthermore less than twenty-four hours had elapsed since her parents simply disappeared.

God, had it only been yesterday? She automatically glanced at her wrist where her watch—a gift from her mother—had always been, but it was gone now, and Ari didn't even know when, where or how it had been wrenched from her wrist.

"What time is it?" Ari asked faintly, staring at Beau in question.

His brow furrowed, his expression blatantly questioning, as though he thought it the last question she'd ask. And maybe it did seem ridiculous when so much else was far more important. But for Ari, a lifetime had passed and suddenly it was all-important to know just how long it had been since she'd last seen her parents.

"It's almost three," Beau said in a gentle voice, as if speaking to a half-wit or someone who was poised to jump off a bridge and any wrong word would send her plummeting right over the edge.

God, her brains were scrambled. To have such idiotic, ridiculous thoughts when her situation—her parents' situation—was so dire was . . . insane. Maybe she *was* crazy. Perhaps she'd simply snapped when she'd unleashed her powers after them lying dormant for nearly a lifetime.

Maybe it had caused her brain to short-circuit and the nerve endings were simply fried.

She heard an odd noise, and to her further humiliation, she

realized it had been *her*. *Laughing*. A shaky hysterical-sounding shrill *giggle*, for God's sake.

Beau gave up any attempt not to look concerned. He turned to Doctor Carey, a grim expression on his face, and said, "Step on it. She needs care *now*."

"I'm okay," she said faintly. "I was just realizing that though it seems like a lifetime has passed, it's not even been twenty-four hours yet since I last saw my parents."

"You are *not* okay," he said in a tone that sounded suspiciously like a growl.

Did people actually growl? Oh God, there she went again. Ridiculous, random thoughts spiking through her mind, almost as if her brain was trying to protect her, wrap her in a protective bubble of mundane, senseless thoughts so she didn't have to dwell on the awful reality of her situation.

Her hand automatically went to her nose just to see if she was bleeding again. Beau, damn the man, never missed anything, and his gaze was sharp as he too looked to see if there was any sign of blood.

To her relief, her hand came away with only remnants of already dried blood from earlier and nothing fresh. Too bad the pain hadn't ebbed like the blood had. She put her palm to her forehead, pressing inward as if to someway ease the overwhelming pressure. The top of her head literally felt like someone was trying to pop it like a pimple and that at any moment it would simply give way and explode from the top.

"Tell me about your mother," Beau said softly. "Is she as beautiful as you are?"

She stared back at Beau in bewilderment for a moment before she realized what he was doing. He was distracting her from the chaos swirling in her mind and trying to center her thoughts on something good. And then his choice of words sank in, and something in her chest softened, warmth spreading soothingly through her veins.

Her smile was automatic, as it always was when she thought of her mom. For a brief second, an image of her mother, smiling and beautiful, flashed in her mind, temporarily giving her a respite from the pain and darkness that had seemed to permanently settle in the deepest recesses of her soul.

"She's the most beautiful woman in the world," Ari whispered. "Warm. Loving. Always smiling and happy. And the way my father looks at her. Like she lights up his entire world. And the way she smiles at him when he looks at her that way. Theirs is a love I thought only existed in romance novels, but I've lived with the reality of two people who love each other with all their heart and soul, who both love me. Unconditionally."

"Who do you get your eyes from? They're such an unusual color. Or rather colors plural," he amended. "I've never seen anyone with eyes like yours."

She stared at him, momentarily without words. Then she frowned, drawing on the image of her mother and her father. She sent Beau a puzzled look because she'd never considered where her eyes had come from or who she'd inherited the unusual kaleidoscope of colors from.

"Neither," she said honestly. "I assume perhaps one of my grandparents, but I don't know. They died—both sets—before my parents were even married. And they were both only children. No family. Kindred spirits, my father always said. Two halves of a whole, alone in the world until finally finding one another."

She ducked her head self-consciously because spoken aloud by her and not said in the reverent tone with which her father spoke of his wife, it seemed contrived. Something she'd made up or some lame attempt at poetry.

Beau surprised her. "That's a beautiful sentiment. It's too bad more people don't feel that way about the person they choose to spend their life with. Or at least a portion of it."

She frowned at the last part. "You don't believe in forever?"

He shrugged. "I guess I've just never met someone who made me *want* forever."

His matter-of-factness didn't surprise her. He was a man after all. They often didn't think in the same ways women thought. She shouldn't have even wasted a frown over his brisk, no-nonsense view of relationships. She had quickly learned that her father was . . . well, he was one of a kind and not because he was her father and she put him on a pedestal as some daddy's girls did.

She saw the adoration in his eyes every time he looked at his wife. Saw how openly affectionate he was with her when he was grim and cold to the rest of the world. She'd never realized how other people viewed her father until she was older and was more cognizant of the differences between her father, when he was home with his "girls," as he termed them affectionately, and when he was outside their sanctuary.

But he also didn't give one damn who knew that he was, in effect, at his wife's feet. While it might seem that he was the dominating force in their relationship, Ari knew for a fact that her mother held all the power and that everything her father did was for her mother. And for Ari.

"Feeling better?"

Her frown of concentration disappeared at Beau's question and her lips softened into a smile, one of thanks for even the brief memory of all the good things in her life. And in fact, the pain and pressure in her head had lessened. It was still there. Still quite painful, but it no longer felt like it would explode at any second or that she was a ticking time bomb primed to go off.

"Yes, thank you," she said in a husky voice, laced with emotion. "I needed that moment of happiness. It gave me a much-needed boost of hope. Because without hope, I have nothing."

To her surprise, the vehicle came to a stop. She hadn't even registered them slowing and turning into the parking lot of a one-story building that sported the name of a medical clinic.

Beau didn't move immediately, however. He focused his gaze on Ari, his entire being radiating seriousness and . . . sincerity.

"You do have something, Ari. And I don't want you to ever forget it. You have me now. And you have the full power and resources available to DSS."

Ari held her breath, his last words fading, unheard, because all she'd registered was the fact that he'd told her she had *him*. And she wondered if he really knew and comprehended what a statement like that meant to someone like her.

Someone who believed in miracles and happily ever afters, even in the face of seemingly hopeless obstacles.

Ever the optimist. She could literally hear her father's teasing voice and her mother scolding him for even suggesting such a trait wasn't a good one.

And then Beau was opening the door, and this time, she didn't utter a single protest when he protectively cradled her in his arms and swiftly took her into one of the side entrances marked "Employees Only."

Apparently the rules didn't apply to men like Beau. Her smile was rueful even as she shivered at the chill present in the medical clinic. She hated the smell. The sterile antiseptic odor and even the subtle smell of sickness and illness, death and desolation. This was a place of complete opposing factors. People who came here either got good news, or they received life-changing bad news. She couldn't help but feel sorrow for those who fell in the realm of the bad.

Beau carried her into a room where a CT scanner was centered in the middle, and she looked at it in panic, because it was for all practical purposes a tube, an enclosed tube into which they slid you in and where walls closed tightly around you.

Her respiration ratcheted up and she held her hand to her nose just in case her sudden bout of stress initiated another bleed. Beau was already freaked out enough over her. There was no reason to give him even more reason to be unreasonable.

The doctor directed Beau to lay Ari down on the table and position her just so. Then he kindly patted her on the arm.

"Would you prefer for Beau to stay with you? Some of my patients fear enclosed spaces and avoid claustrophobic situations. I can put a protective garment over him that will prevent any harm coming to him. Our first priority is ensuring your comfort and more importantly we need you to relax and obey our directives as we give them. Can you handle that?"

"No. Yes. I mean I'll be fine," Ari said quickly although she wanted nothing more than for Beau to remain. But she refused to put Beau at further risk because of her. He'd already been shot at—twice. Wrecked and forced off the freeway in an overturned vehicle. Enough was enough and it was time to put her big-girl panties on and act like the independent woman she'd worked so hard to become since graduating college and going out on her own in the workforce, not that her father was at all happy with her choices. But it had been her mother's gentle but steady hand that had caused her father to back down and allow Ari freedoms she hadn't been granted until the last few years.

"I can handle this. I'm okay. Really. I don't want to put Beau at any further risk. He's risked enough for me to day."

"And you're terrified of enclosed spaces," Beau said tersely. "I'm staying."

She looked at him astonishment. "How could you possibly know that?"

"Honey, you didn't see your absolute look of terror and utter discomfort the minute you laid eyes on the scanner. I'm not leaving you alone to endure it when it will be hell for you. So don't even try to argue. Because this is one argument you will *not* win."

"Fine," she grumbled. "But if you get radiation poisoning or whatever it is you get from these X-ray machines, it's your own damn fault and I refuse to feel guilty if you get cancer and die."

Beau's lips quirked into a smile. "Why, Ari, you're beginning to make me think you care," he teased.

Her expression went utterly solemn. "I do care, Beau. I care too much. I wish I could be selfish and do whatever it took to get my parents back no matter the cost to others' lives or the injuries they could sustain, but that's not who I am. It's not the kind of person I've ever been and it's not who I want to *become*."

It was becoming an increasing habit for him to press his lips anywhere but her mouth, almost as if he were guarding against the possibility of creating too much intimacy between him and a client, but in Ari's mind, those tender moments meant far more to her than if he *had* kissed her on the mouth.

She closed her eyes as he briefly feathered a kiss over her furrowed forehead.

"Now, we've wasted too much time on senseless arguing and we need to get you suited up and me as well, because as I said, I'm going to be here every step of the way. If you get scared just say my name. I'll be right here."

"Thank you, Beau. You know and I know you've gone above and beyond what you'd normally do for a client. So thank you. It means a lot to have your support, your promise to find my parents and your promise to protect me from the people who are after me."

"You've already thanked me and it was more than enough," he said softly. "Now let's get you checked out so Doctor Carey can ease my concerns over your condition."

FIFTEEN

BEAU shouldered his way into the house, carrying Ari's limp body firmly against his chest. As requested, Caleb and Ramie were still there, lounging in the living room, though Ramie looked to be asleep, nestled in the crook of Caleb's shoulder, her hair partially obscuring her face.

Beau cocked one inquisitive eyebrow in Caleb's direction. The brothers had always been masters at silent communication. It was if they were so in tune with one another that a simple look could convey a wealth of information. Or questions.

Which is likely why Caleb had seemed confused and even angry that Beau hadn't consulted him about Ari, not that Beau had been given the opportunity, given the speed in which Ari's situation—and the danger to her—had escalated.

"She's fine," Caleb murmured. "Late night last night. Tori had a bad dream. Ramie stayed up with her."

"Anything I should know about?" Beau inquired.

Caleb was silent a moment. "At the time, I wouldn't have thought so. But now? Yeah, I think you probably need to hear this." His gaze drifted over Ari's unconscious form. "How is she?"

"I'd say she has zero tolerance for painkillers," Beau said wryly. "Either that or she's just exhausted, which is likely given the events of the last twenty-four hours. Doctor Carey gave her the all clear on the CT scan, but gave her an injection because she was out of her mind with pain. She was out like a light in less than five minutes. I had to carry her out of the clinic and into the car I called for while waiting for the results of her scan."

"Put her to bed then," Caleb said quietly. "We have a hell of a lot to discuss. Zack's been doing a lot of digging. Despite you not wanting to involve Dane and Eliza, I did call upon Eliza's expertise in accessing data not readily available to the public. Zack's in the security room making some calls, but he'll know you're back, so I'd expect him here by the time you return from putting Ari down."

Something about Caleb's tone immediately raised Beau's hackles and his internal radar started beeping like hell. His brother's expression was grim and he radiated seriousness.

Cursing softly under his breath, he turned and carried Ari down the hall, but instead of putting her in the extra bedroom where she'd been before, he veered to the right, where the restructured master bedroom was located.

The original home had been two stories, but after having to escape from the second-floor window and climbing off the roof after a bomb had taken out most of the main floor, Beau had decided against rebuilding the home as a multilevel residence. He liked his escape options a hell of a lot better when he didn't have multiple stories to contend with.

He settled Ari onto his bed, telling himself that he didn't want her to wake alone and frightened, and that was his only reason for putting her in his room. Even as the defensive thought crept through his mind, he knew he was a damn liar.

Yes, he would sleep in the recliner in the corner of the room that faced the big flat-screen television mounted to the wall at the foot of the bed, but the simple fact was he wanted her in his space. He'd made her a promise, and perhaps he was using that solemn vow he'd made as an excuse to have her in his bed, but he was not going to leave her alone and unprotected, even for a second. That included when she slept.

He even tucked her in, for God's sake, carefully arranging the covers so nothing lay directly over the now stitched and bandaged wound. The doctor had unwittingly made it far easier to stitch Ari by giving her the injection as soon as the CT came back within normal limits.

It had indicated what the physician had called a slight "bruise" to an area of the brain that Beau couldn't recall the scientific name for. He'd been too concerned over the word "bruise" until the doctor had informed him that it was nothing to be concerned about. Unless she underwent further trauma.

Beau's relief had lasted only about three seconds before he began to worry about "further trauma." Did that mean if she incurred another bleed, the bruise could worsen? There were a thousand questions that in retrospect he should have asked, but he'd been too focused on Ari, and soothing the anxiety in her eyes.

And well, once she'd been administered the injection and

had quietly slipped into unconsciousness, Beau *had* been relieved then. Because her eyes were closed, which meant he couldn't see pain reflected in the mesmerizing depths. And he knew that she'd at least momentarily found respite from the physical *and* emotional hurts she'd endured.

The doctor had ruefully announced that he'd never had a patient fall so hard under the effects of the pain medication he'd administered, but he also acknowledged that it would make the task of numbing the area and stitching the wound much quicker and more efficient. And in fact, it had taken him little time at all to finish, write scripts in Beau's name and give him instructions on her care for the next several days.

Beau hadn't needed *those* instructions. Because he fully intended to make damn sure Ari encountered no stress, no pain, and if he could help it, no incessant worries. Which meant he had to work fast to try to unravel the mystery surrounding her parents' disappearance.

Something in his brother's expression had told him that what he discovered might not be good. If that was the case, he had to prepare for the worst and handle Ari with extreme care or risk her incurring a potentially fatal psychic bleed.

He fiddled with the covers a moment longer and then realized he was merely delaying the inevitable and that he was loath to leave Ari, even for the space of time it took for him and his brother and Zack to discuss their findings.

With a sigh of disgust for his lack of perspective when he was usually all business when it came to clients, he turned and stalked out the door, though he was careful to leave it slightly ajar so he could hear her if she displayed any sounds of distress. And he also flipped the switch for the video feed that would display the interior of his bedroom on monitors in the security room.

Caleb could damn well have his say in the security room with Beau and Zack so Beau could keep vigil over Ari via the video feed.

He returned to the living room to find that Ramie had awakened and Zack was leaning casually against the far wall, hands shoved into his pockets. It was a misleading stance, however, because Zack was always prepared, even when he *appeared* relaxed and at ease. There was a constant wariness about him that had always made Beau curious about the man's personal past and whether events in his past had led to his quiet, but lethal, manner in the present.

"We'll talk in the security room, where I can monitor Ari," Beau said shortly, not waiting for their responses.

He turned and walked back down the hall, in the opposite direction of his bedroom, leaving his brother and Zack to follow.

After punching in the security code to gain access to the room, Beau entered and took position in the chair from which, if turned, he could see and talk to the others and also view the monitor displaying his bedroom. The screen was just to the left of where Caleb and Zack would either sit or stand.

Zack ambled in, seemingly unhurried, though his expression was stony and somber. Caleb entered with Ramie, his fingers laced through his wife's. It was rare for Caleb to be near Ramie and not be touching her in some way. After the nightmarish events that had nearly torn them apart forever, Caleb still grappled with his demons and touching Ramie seemed to give him a measure of reassurance that she was well, whole and alive. The fact that *Caleb* had been the one who nearly killed her was never far from his mind. Beau knew that with certainty.

"So who's going to start and how much do we know?" Beau asked bluntly.

Caleb raked a hand through his hair. "Before we go any further, there's something you need to know regarding Ari Rochester's father, Gavin Rochester."

Beau lifted an eyebrow and simply waited as he watched the myriad of emotions play out on his brother's typically schooled and nonexpressive features.

"Gavin was unmarried at the time, but apparently he knew our parents."

Beau nodded, wondering why Caleb was stating the obvious. Why else would Ari's father instruct her to seek out Caleb or Beau when neither man had ever laid eyes on Gavin Rochester, much less made his acquaintance?

"He was also the last person to see our parents alive," Caleb said in an icy tone. "After his marriage and Ari's birth when Gavin made the move to Houston, effectively wiping all traces of his past from record."

Beau's eyes narrowed as he grappled with the possible ramifications. It was no secret between the three Devereaux brothers, although they'd always shielded Tori from the truth, that their parents, or at least their father, hadn't been clean. They weren't sure of all he was involved in, but he hadn't made his fortune entirely by inheriting old "oil" money.

Their parents had lived large and in the fast lane, openly flaunting their wealth and influence. Their children were little more than nuisances and a hindrance to the kind of lifestyle their parents—their mother—wanted to live.

Though a nanny had been hired, for all practical purposes Caleb had been the one to foster and raise his siblings. As a child he'd been solemn and serious, bearing the weight of so much responsibility on his young shoulders. But he'd never complained. And he'd damn well ensured that his siblings were kept as far away from the people their parents regularly mingled with as possible. As a result, he'd been forced to grow up way before his time, his childhood taken away by selfish, thoughtless parents.

Though young, both Caleb and Beau had been old enough to take their parents' indifference in stride, but Quinn and especially Tori, just a toddler, had been bewildered by the fact that they went largely unnoticed by their mother and father. It had infuriated Beau and he'd spent many a night consoling a crying Tori, or reading her bedtime stories because the nanny, while competent enough, wasn't a nurturer and she'd quickly learned that she didn't *need* to do much in order to satisfy her employer's "demands."

The only rules seemed to be to keep them out of the way and make sure they were never underfoot. The brothers had often remarked that they simply didn't understand why their parents had bothered to have children at all unless it was to cement the image of a wholesome family not involved in whatever his father's shady dealings had been. It was a well-known fact that being a family man was good for business.

Beau had never admitted it, even to Caleb, but it had been a relief when his parents had died. Or rather murdered. Their deaths had been ruled a murder/suicide, precipitated by his father, but Beau—and Caleb—knew better. Their parents enjoyed the trappings of their wealth and lifestyle far too much to ever willingly give it up. But the case had quickly been closed, never reopened and never questioned. Which added to Beau's suspicion of a cover-up even more.

"Just what was Gavin Rochester's relationship with our father?" Beau asked in a deadly quiet voice.

It ate at him that he'd been hired by an innocent-eyed temptress to find and rescue a man who could very well have had a hand in his father's death. Even if there was no love lost between him and his parents. And then he mentally castigated himself for making such a huge leap. He was naturally cynical—growing up as he did, he'd had no other choice but inherent cynicism—but to automatically make an assumption based on one event was *not* an inherent quality he possessed.

"That's the unknown factor at this point," Caleb admitted. "But certainly something to delve into. Do you not agree?"

"I can answer at least some of the questions regarding Gavin's relationship with your father," Zack said, pointedly excluding their mother from the equation.

Both Caleb and Beau glanced Zack's way in silent inquiry.

"They were business associates of sorts."

"Of sorts?" Caleb interrupted before Zack could continue. "How is one an 'associate of sorts'?"

A look of impatience simmered briefly in Zack's eyes, evidence of his displeasure over being cut short.

"Of sorts meaning there is—or if there is I have yet to find it—a clear-cut association between the two. But Gavin's name popped up frequently in regard to your father's various business enterprises."

The way Zack said "enterprises" immediately raised Beau's hackles, because it sounded very much like Zack knew or at least suspected what Beau *knew* to be true. It was one thing for Beau to know—to acknowledge—the truth about what and who his father was. It was quite another for someone not in the Devereaux family to think. Or speculate about.

It was evident that Caleb reacted to the way Zack had worded his statement as well, because his eyes grew cold and Ramie slid her hand from Caleb's, the overflow of his emotions likely unpleasant for her to bear. It was a testament to just how intently Caleb was focused on Zack's report that he didn't seem to notice the loss of Ramie's touch.

"What kind of enterprises?" Beau asked, his stare piercing as he gazed at Zack, trying to ascertain just how much the other man now knew about Franklin Devereaux.

"Most, from what I've been able to discern at first glance, were fictitious dummy corporations that were virtually untraceable, a veritable maze for anyone investigating him or his businesses. It's going to take some time for me to navigate through the mire to see where it all leads back to. It was very carefully—and thoughtfully—arranged. He covered his tracks very well."

There was no judgment, no condemnation in Zack's words or manner. He related the information in a matter-of-fact tone, as though he were discussing any DSS client.

His tone seemed to ease the tension radiating from Caleb. Caleb's expression softened, the lines disappearing from his forehead, and he automatically reached for Ramie, glancing down at her, his eyes faintly puzzled as if he'd only just now realized that her hand had escaped his grasp.

There was instant apology in his eyes and he tucked Ramie gently against him, anchoring her slim figure to his side. Then he turned his gaze back to Zack.

"Unless there is a direct correlation to Gavin Rochester then leave it alone," Caleb said flatly.

"I'll be the judge of that," Beau said, directing a terse look in his brother's direction. "Back off, Caleb. This is mine and Zack's. If you don't want to hear the information, fine. But I need to know everything I can about Gavin Rochester if I'm going to find him and his wife before their time runs out. And Ari's as well."

Caleb's jaw tightened and Ramie stirred beside him, instantly warding off any potential argument Caleb posed. His lips twisted into a grimace and then he sighed.

"Okay, it's yours. I get it. But I do want to know if he had anything to do with our father's death."

Beau nodded his agreement. "Now what about information Eliza uncovered?"

Zack looked pointedly at Caleb, a faint flicker of irritation in his eyes, as though he was pissed that Caleb encroached on a mission Beau had specifically said belonged to him and Zack. But it was gone so fast, he wondered if he'd only imagined it. It was unusual for Zack to express much emotion at all. He was curiously dispassionate, and until Ari, Beau would have said he himself was very similar to Zack, thus why he'd felt an instant kinship with his employee. But Ari seemed to have changed all the rules, effectively throwing them out the proverbial window for Beau.

He'd definitely lost objectivity, rare. He was invested on a personal—not completely professional—level, even *more* rare. And the hell of it was, he couldn't summon the will to remove himself from the case, which was what he *should* do. If anything he was adamant that he, and *only* he, would head up Ari's personal protection and he'd deliver on his promise to her, no matter what it took. He was willing to use the entirety of the DSS resources, and for that matter *any* other available means if it enabled him to achieve his primary objective, to track and recover Ari's parents and most important keep Ari out of harm's way. Even if her father did have a hand—directly or indirectly—in Beau's father's murder.

"She's working several angles," Caleb answered. "But the simple truth is, Gavin Rochester is—or was—mired in gray, never *caught* engaged in illegal activities, yet clearly working outside of the law. He had numerous connections and was untouchable. Friends in high places. Powerful and influential. Those who openly opposed him or challenged him suffered sudden and mysterious financial setbacks."

So far it sounded eerily similar to the way their own father operated. Beau could remember his father flying into a rage over some perceived or actual slight, insult or challenge from a competitor or simply an acquaintance. He knew for a fact his father retaliated but was careful to be as far removed from the fallout as possible. Beau had overheard him gloating to Beau's mother over his "victory" and how whoever the unfortunate victim was surely regretted ever crossing Franklin Devereaux.

"Now when it gets interesting is three years after his marriage to Ginger Crofton—now Rochester—who was a waitress working her way through college when she and Gavin met. He subsequently swept her off her feet and they were married within a year."

"Get to the interesting part," Beau said impatiently, because so far all Caleb was giving was a sterile recitation of facts that were likely public record, available to anyone with access to decent search tools.

"His wife suffered multiple miscarriages in a relatively short amount of time. Then suddenly they simply disappeared. Gavin liquidated most of his assets. Sold off his businesses—legitimate and not so legitimate—and they left the country. When they came back, they had a baby daughter. Ari."

"So? Maybe he took her away so she could recover, she got pregnant again and he made sure she was constantly monitored. I can well imagine if she suffered so many miscarriages that he would be extremely protective as well as determined that she would carry to term that time."

"The timeline doesn't add up," Caleb said impatiently, obviously annoyed with Beau's incessant interruptions. "Hear me out and just listen for a minute. They were only gone for five months and even before they returned, he sold off everything in New York and the East Coast and set up his base in Houston. His only connection to Houston was one legitimate business. And our father. To me that seems extremely presumptive and over-confident when I can't imagine, after so many failed attempts to have a child, he'd suddenly *know* that she would deliver this time."

Beau bit his lips, forcing himself to remain silent and wait for his brother to make his point. Whatever the hell point he was getting around to making.

"They came back with Ari, which means she would have to have been four months along, possibly three if she delivered prematurely. And according to classified records, she miscarried at five months during the time she would have been pregnant with *Ari*."

Beau frowned, mulling over the implications of his brother's findings.

"Is it possible he falsified records to make it *appear* she miscarried so they could drop out of sight for her to carry to full term with absolutely no stress in a place where perhaps she felt more at ease?"

Caleb shrugged, blatant skepticism written all over his face. "Possible but highly improbable. This is just a guess, but I think they may have adopted Ari and the fact that they left the country and he completely pulled out of everything connected to their lives pre-Ari makes me suspicious of the way in which they acquired a child."

Zack frowned, reacting for the first time to the report being given by Caleb. Beau was having his own bout of WTF as he grappled with why, how and . . . well, again *why*?

"She looks nothing like her mother or father. Eliza was able to pull photos of Gavin's deceased parents as well as Ginger's and there is no resemblance there either and both were only children. How do two people with dark hair and dark eyes and darker-toned skin produce offspring with at least ten different shades of blond, silver and gold, eyes that defy description and very fair complexion?"

A chill skittered up Beau's spine and on its heels, worry for Ari. She'd said nothing about adoption. She'd even spoken of having traits of her mother. And the fact that her powers had been revealed as a baby.

If Gavin and Ginger Rochester weren't her biological parents then who were? Had Ari's entire life been a *lie*?

Once again he was jumping the gun, but his gut was starting to churn and the discrepancies and coincidences were starting to pile up. He rubbed absently at his temple, his gaze drifting away from his brother for a moment. When he once again met Caleb's stare, he saw concern in his eyes.

"I'll have Eliza email you the full report so you can read the detailed information and draw your own conclusions," Caleb said quietly. "Ramie and I should go. We've been away from Tori too long as it is."

"He needs to know about Tori's dream," Ramie softly interjected, speaking for the first time.

Her expression was solemn and her smoky gray eyes were troubled as she glanced between the two brothers.

Caleb ran a hand through his hair, a sign of agitation. "I got so caught up in everything else, I momentarily forgot. And yeah, you need to hear about it."

Zack crossed his arms, his gaze piercing as he stared at Caleb with an air of expectancy. Beau too looked at Caleb, silently prompting him to get on with it.

"She dreamed about you," Caleb said in a low voice. "You were covered in blood. It scared her to death because the last time she dreamed about one of her brothers drenched in blood I damn near killed my wife. So she's understandably traumatized and scared as hell."

Beau blew out his breath. "That's easily explainable. I've already been covered in blood. Ari's blood. At the accident scene, she had a bad bleed. There was blood everywhere. So Tori was right—she usually is—but you can tell her there's nothing to worry about now. It's done with and I'm fine."

Ramie's troubled gaze settled on Beau, her features drawn in concern. "She didn't see Ari in her dream. Only you. And you were lying down. On your back, blood spreading over you. I think you need to take this more seriously, Beau. Please be careful."

Beau's tone softened, not wanting to take out his frustration and impatience on a woman who deserved neither.

"You weren't in the dream she had where Caleb was covered in blood. Your blood," he pointed out.

Caleb visibly flinched and Ramie paled, the color fleeing her cheeks.

"So it's probable that her dream was about the sequence of events that transpired after Ari and I left the DSS offices," Beau pressed, guilt nipping his heels for reminding his brother and sister-in-law of the darkest day of their life.

Ramie's eyes were cloudy with doubt, but she didn't argue further. She slid her hand into Caleb's almost as if she were trying to judge his innermost emotions. When she didn't withdraw her touch, Beau assumed that Caleb mustn't be too fierce with his thoughts.

Movement on the video monitor drew his attention and he honed in, watching as Ari stirred restlessly. He started to surge to his feet and leave the room to go to where she lay, but as quickly as she'd exhibited signs of stress, she quieted and went still once more.

Beau let his muscles relax and then turned his attention back to Caleb and Zack, who were both studying him intently. He shifted uncomfortably under their scrutiny and suddenly wanted to be away from all of it.

"Zack, get the report from Eliza," Beau directed crisply, ignoring their intent expressions. "See what pops up and what you can piece together between what you've found and what Eliza's found. Caleb, you and Ramie go back to Tori. I've got things under control here. I'll let you know if I need you."

He'd effectively dismissed them both. Zack had no issue and turned to walk out of the room, no doubt already focusing on his objective. Caleb, however, looked poised to argue. Beau held up a hand.

"Save it, Caleb," Beau said quietly. "I need you to back off on this."

It was the closest he'd come to asking his brother for what essentially amounted to him turning a blind eye to activities the brothers usually shared, worked on together, decided on. Caleb studied him in silence a moment and then seemed to reach a decision or at least heed Beau's request, which was issued more as a directive when Caleb was unused to answering or deferring to anyone.

Ramie let go of Caleb and crossed the short distance between them and bent slightly to kiss Beau on the cheek.

"Promise you'll be careful," she said in a low voice.

He offered her a reassuring smile. "Always."

SIXTEEN

BEAU roused instantly from sleep, his neck protesting as he straightened from his awkward position in the recliner where he'd drifted off keeping silent vigil over Ari. He blinked rapidly to bring the room into focus, adjusting quickly to the dim light radiating from the slightly ajar door of the bathroom.

Then he blinked again, unsure if he was seeing correctly or if he was having some bizarre hallucination.

Random objects floated haphazardly around the room. The lamp, which was turned off, bumped the wall and suddenly flickered on. The television remote hovered a foot off the floor beside his recliner. Novels that lined one of the shelves of his bookcase thumped and banged against one another before popping out from the shelf and then dropping suddenly to the floor in a cascade of motion.

Things he couldn't see, but could *hear*, rattled, knocked and clicked. It seemed the entire room was in motion. He automatically thumped his hands down on the arms of the recliner just to ensure that *it* wasn't moving, shaking or floating. Then he planted his feet solidly on the floor to regain his sense of equilibrium.

Suddenly realizing just what was going on, he yanked his gaze from the jittering objects to where Ari still lay curled up on his bed. Her brow was creased, deep furrows appearing in her forehead. Her mouth pursed and then opened, a whimper escaping. One arm flailed outward as if warding off an unseen attacker.

Realization was swift that she was in the throes of a nightmare and her power, now unchecked, was like an electric current in the room, zapping and moving objects with no rhyme or reason, reacting to the utter chaos of her current thought pattern.

He lunged to his feet, afraid she'd incur a serious psychic bleed if she continued as she was. Calling her name softly, he slid onto the bed, catching her flailing arm and trapping it against the hard wall of his chest.

"Ari, honey, wake up. You're all right. You're safe. It's me, Beau Devereaux. Open your eyes, sweetheart. Look at me. I'm right here."

He continued his soothing stream of babble, reaching with his free hand to rub up and down the curve of the arm secured against his chest. Not knowing what else to do, he leaned in, pressing his lips to the deep lines that marred her forehead, all the while murmuring soft reassurances and pleading with her to wake up.

He lifted his hand, brushing his thumb underneath her nose and then over her plump upper lip, emitting a huge sigh of relief that as of yet, she wasn't bleeding. Now if he could only pull her back from the vicious grasp of her dreams before she *did* start to bleed.

"Ari, please baby, you've got to wake up," he pleaded softly, his breath blowing warm over her chilled skin.

She shivered violently and he pulled away just as her eyes jerked open, the pupils dilated, nearly painting her vividly colored eyes black. Her respirations were rapid and erratic and as his hand lowered to her chest, he could feel her heart beating wildly against his palm.

"Beau?" she whispered.

Just that one word—his name—conveyed so much fear that his heart ached for her.

"Yes, honey, it's me. You were having a bad dream, but you're safe. I've got you. Do you remember where you are?"

Her nose wrinkled momentarily, and a faint puzzled look flashed in her eyes before she visibly calmed, and then she seemed to wilt before his very eyes.

"Oh God," she said, closing her eyes. "Please tell me that *this* is a dream. That none of *this* is happening. That my parents are at home—safe."

Utter helplessness gripped him, seizing his heart and mind, a sensation he wasn't at all accustomed to. Nor did he ever *want* to be accustomed to such weakness. It was the worst feeling in the world, knowing he had no power to fix this, to make it all go away for her.

"I can't tell you that. I'm sorry," he said, regret echoed in his every word. "I'd give anything to be able to tell you that, honey, but you're not dreaming *now*."

Her eyes flashed open again, her pupils more normal—and equal—one of the things Doctor Carey had told him was a warning sign of brain injury. Pin prick or uneven or unreactive pupils. It gave him some small measure of relief that despite having used her powers—unconsciously—she hadn't incurred another bleed, nor did she seem to be ill affected by the incident.

"Are you hurting?" he asked quietly. "Do you need the medicine the doctor prescribed?"

She shook her head in silent denial. She stared into his eyes, seeming to *absorb* him. Awareness slithered up his spine, despite his attempt to quell it. But she felt it too. He *knew* she did, because her eyes widened, and she focused in on him even more intently until he felt as though he were drowning in the pools of her eyes.

They were as two magnets, inexorably drawn to one another by a power that defied explanation or definition. It felt . . . right. So very right. More so than anything else he had ever experienced before.

Her pull was electric. His nerve endings were painfully aware. His skin suddenly felt too tight. Uncomfortable and yet . . . pleasurable. His thoughts were as chaotic as hers had been when she'd been firmly in the grasp of her dreams. Only, *this* dream was one he never wanted to awaken from.

Slowly, as if they *were* in a dream, she lifted her head, her hand sliding up his arm, over his shoulder, lightly caressing up the sensitive skin of his neck to finally come to rest against his jaw. Her lips were mere centimeters from his, her breath whispering softly against his mouth and chin.

Carefully, almost as if she feared rejection, she angled her head just a bit so that their mouths were perfectly aligned, and she pressed her warm, lush lips to his.

It was an electric surge, a jolt to his entire body. He held his breath, his muscles rigid and straining as she explored his mouth, tentatively at first, and then when she met with no resistance, she grew bolder, her tongue dancing over his lips, an invitation for him to open.

He complied with her silent request, relaxing his jaw and allowing her access. The feathery strokes of her tongue against his was driving him insane with want and need. So much need. Like nothing he'd ever felt in his life. With no other woman. Not this overwhelming urge to protect, to dominate, to possess, to cherish, to reassure her and make promises he had no way of knowing if he could keep but wanted to offer nonetheless.

Alarm seared through the haze of mindless pleasure her mouth offered. She was vulnerable. Fragile. In no condition to truly be cognizant of her actions. One of them had to be thinking clearly and at the moment, it wasn't him.

He couldn't do this. He couldn't—wouldn't—take advantage of her. Even as his body and mind roared in unison to take, to possess, to claim.

He hadn't understood Caleb's obsession with Ramie. How any man could be so wrapped up in a woman. To be completely without reason or rational thought. But now he realized, that if his brother had felt even a fraction of what Beau was currently feeling, then he understood. It was a nearly blinding moment of clarity, when everything clicked into place, and he experienced the sensation of rightness that only a *specific* woman could bring to a man.

It took every bit of his will and strength to break the kiss. To tear his lips from hers, his chest heaving as though he'd just ran a mile uphill. His heartbeat was every bit as thunderous as hers had been minutes ago when she'd just surfaced from the throes of a terrible dream. Only his was the *sweetest* of dreams, the kind one never wanted to be shaken from.

"Beau?" she whispered, hurt evident in her voice.

Her eyes immediately became shuttered, and she tried to turn her face away, so he couldn't see what his rejection had done.

Gently he cupped her cheek, forcing her gaze back to his. He forced control into his words, and he made himself look her in the eyes, hoping like hell that she could see the utter sincerity that surely had to be blazing from his.

"We can't do this, Ari."

He nearly choked on the words. Why couldn't he be the selfish bastard he'd always considered himself? Or the cold, blunt bastard he was well accustomed to being? Why now, of all times, did he discover a conscience that demanded he absolutely protect Ari when she was at her most vulnerable and not to, in any way, take advantage of her at her weakest.

When her eyes became glossy with unshed tears, he nearly lost it. Goddamn it, but he hadn't meant to hurt her. His tongue felt clumsy, thick in his mouth, when just seconds ago it was tasting the sweetest of pleasures. He grappled with the words— the *right* words—to ease the sting of his rejection.

Hell, he wasn't rejecting her. Far from it. He was rejecting *himself* and the idea of causing her further pain or anguish. And worse. *Regret.* Because it would damn near kill him to ever see disappointment *or* regret in her gaze after he'd just made love to her.

"I can't take *advantage* of you," he said in a husky voice. He stroked his thumb over her lips, even as he spoke, remembering the way they'd felt against his. "You're at your most vulnerable right now. You just awoke from a terrible dream, and you're shaky and confused. You feel lost. Alone. Your entire world has been rocked. The people you love the most are in danger. It would make me the worst sort of bastard if I made love to you right now."

She instantly frowned, and her eyes flashed with quick anger. Then her expression eased and she sighed, nuzzling her cheek against his palm.

"Would you consider me an intelligent, capable woman, Beau?"

He blinked, staring back at her, for a moment at a loss as to how to respond. The question came out of left field, but she was staring pointedly at him, waiting for him to answer.

"Of course," he said, mimicking her small frown. "Why on earth would you ask such a thing?"

She put her finger to his lips to silence him and he went utterly still at her touch. Reaching for that rush of pleasure cascading through his body at something so simple as her fingers against his mouth. Though, admittedly, it was a poor substitute for her mouth, her lips. Her tongue.

He mentally moaned at the torture he was subjecting himself to. He had to be a complete masochist.

"If an intelligent, capable woman is attracted to you. *Wants* you and wants you to make *love* to her, would you consider it taking *advantage* of her to give her what she *wants*? Unless, of course, you don't want *her*."

He nearly laughed. Instead he groaned, a sound of frustrated male desire. Then he simply took her hand from his face and lowered it, cupping her palm over his aching groin, where his dick was about to tear a hole in his jeans.

"Does this feel to you like I don't want you?" he demanded.

Her face was flushed. Not with embarrassment or shame. He could see the heat enter her eyes, her cheeks. Her lips unconsciously parted, emitting a breathy sound that made him hurt all the more.

"Me not wanting you is *not* the issue," he growled. "Me taking advantage of you *is*."

A soft smile curved her lips, her eyes glittering more boldly. A distinctly, *delicious* feminine spark of mischief fired in the depths of those expressive eyes. And he knew in that instant he was in trouble. The kind a man didn't necessarily mind.

Then she heaved an exaggerated sigh, as though she was sorely put upon, even as her eyes held the promise of tender retribution.

"Well, if you aren't going to take advantage of me, then I guess I'll just have to take advantage of *you*."

SEVENTEEN

DESPITE her teasing words and her brazen manner, Ari was terrified. She only hoped she could pull this off without giving herself completely away. Beau Devereaux was not a man women overlooked. And he likely never had to look far for sexual company, of that Ari was certain.

While not handsome in a sophisticated, pretty and polished manner, as some men of wealth were, Beau was . . . harder looking. Like he'd seen—endured—the other side of the sun. Where darkness and danger lurked. And his confidence was extremely attractive to a woman like Ari who didn't possess it, but craved it. She admired confidence in others, and one thing she'd noticed about all of the DSS employees or operatives or whatever they called themselves is that they wore confidence like skin. Perfectly fitted. That kind of assurance couldn't be faked. She ought to know, because she sucked at faking anything.

She applied just a little more pressure to his groin, where he'd placed her hand over his rigid erection. Even through the thick denim and the underwear he wore, she could feel his penis pulsing and straining eagerly toward her touch.

It seemed body and mind weren't in accord for Beau. His manner was reluctant, but his body wanted her. Even with as little sexual knowledge as she had, she recognized the signs of lust and desire, and it gave her an infusion of badly needed confidence.

She didn't know how to be a siren. A temptress out to seduce a man with body and words. But she was about to get a crash course, because there was no way she was passing up the opportunity to see Beau Devereaux naked, beautiful. And hers. At least for one night.

Her possessiveness surprised her. The fact that she wanted to lay claim to this man, put her brand on him so others would know to back the hell away or incur her wrath. Who knew she could be so jealously greedy? She quite liked this undiscovered side of herself.

More than her powers were now unleashed and operating at inhuman speeds. Her sexuality was unfurling like the petals of a flower in spring. Her body ached for this man. Her soul ached for him. The touching of two hearts, two spirits, becoming one.

A stuttered hiss escaped his lips and she glanced up to see his jaw tight and quivering, his eyes closed, head thrown back even as his pelvis lifted, arching into her touch greedily.

"*Do* you want me, Beau?" she whispered, the words catching in her breathy excitement. "Because I want you—*this*. I need *you*. Right here, right now." She paused for a microsecond, held her breath and then said, "Please."

It was too close to begging for her liking. Yes, she was pampered and spoiled. She readily admitted that. But she had pride.

And the truth was, she'd never had to beg for anything in her life. This was completely new and foreign and she was fraught with uncertainty even as her pulse raced in delicious anticipation of having Beau's body above hers, inside her, feeling the hardness currently filling her hand and nearly delirious with wondering how he would feel sliding into her most intimate recesses.

"God, yes I want you," he said through clenched teeth. "Have mercy, honey. You're killing me here. There is no need to ask me to give you what you want—what you need. If you're sure—if you are absolutely *positive* that I am what you want, then I am more than happy to comply with your sweetly worded request."

She moved her hand up his muscled body and curled it around his nape, pulling him down to her mouth, desperate to feel his lips on hers again. Then she shivered, imagining his mouth on other parts of body. Her breasts . . . the throbbing, clenching lips of her vagina.

It was simply too much to process all at once. Her mind was alive, brimming with erotic images of the two of them, tangled up, moving as one. Him coming inside her, on her, marking her as though he owned her.

Chill bumps erupted, doing a tantalizing dance over her skin. Her nipples puckered and her breasts were heavy and aching, swelling with need for his touch. She was suddenly impatient, wanting to be skin on skin, no barriers between them.

"Show me," she whispered. "Show me what to do. How to do. How to please you. I want to see you, Beau. Take your clothes off. Please."

This time the please wasn't her begging. It was a demand of lover to lover. She shivered delicately again. The word *lover* had never had such an impact on her, because she hadn't experienced the essence of having a lover. Of being someone else's lover.

Beau rose up from the bed, nearly tearing his clothing as he stripped down to his underwear. Then, as if sensing her heightened excitement, he took his time with his underwear, inching it downward to expose his thick, distended cock, inch by delicious inch.

He was a feast of pure alpha male and she wanted to touch and explore so much that she didn't even know where to start.

"Now you," he said in a gruff voice. "Sit up on the edge of the bed so I can help you. You aren't going to get so carried away that you hurt yourself. I must be insane for agreeing to this. You were *shot* for God's sake."

She was poised to launch an argument, but he leaned over her on the bed, his arms on either side of her body, his mouth just inches from hers, even as he slowly began divesting her of her clothing. Before she knew it, before she even acknowledged *how* he'd been able to do it so quickly without her registering the fact, she was naked, and he still loomed over her, his gaze raking over her, his expression absolutely intense.

"You may have instigated and you may have had to talk me into this, but that's the extent of your control. This is my show now and I'm going to take my sweet time showing you just how much I want you. Which means we do things my way. And you're going to lie there and not do a damn thing to put strain on your stitches while I do all the work."

Oh my . . . She swallowed hard, her heart nearly leaping up her throat. He nuzzled his mouth against her jaw and nibbled his way down to graze his teeth over the delicate skin just below her ear.

He nipped, followed it with a leisurely swipe of his tongue and then he fastened his mouth and sucked gently until her eyes nearly rolled back in her head. In fact he had to catch her as she swayed precariously and that had nothing to do with the pain medication rendered earlier. Beau was a hundred times more potent than any drug.

She leaned her forehead on his chest, the top of her head grazing the underside of his chin, and she inhaled deeply, absorbing his scent, enjoying the feel of her skin against his heart. She also got a prime view of his straining erection and she gasped softly.

Unable to stop herself, she pulled slightly away and let her fingers wander aimlessly down his midriff, trailing through the brisk whorl of hair at his groin. He went completely still when her hand brushed up the length of his cock. She was fascinated by the fact that he was utterly rigid and yet the skin, stretched so tightly, was like velvet over steel.

She pressed inward with her thumb, finding the plump vein that ran the length on the underside of his erection, and traced a path upward, surprised when moisture suddenly welled and beaded at the tip, slipping onto the tips of her fingers like silk.

Her hand left him and she lifted her index finger to her mouth, wanting to know what he tasted like. Beau let out a groan that sounded as though he was experiencing extreme pain, and yet when she looked into his eyes, they burned fiercely with pleasure and desire.

He looked like he was about to eat her up and devour her whole and she wanted it all and she wanted it now. She was simmering with impatience, wanting to experience everything she'd read about but had never gained firsthand knowledge of. This was like . . . a fantasy, a scene from the sexiest book, only it was *real*. And it was happening to her!

Sending him what she hoped was a sultry look of invitation, she slowly reclined back and stretched her arms over her head in a symbol of submission, hoping it would drive him as wild as he was driving her.

His eyes glittered dangerously, raking over her body like a blowtorch. Immense satisfaction marked his features at her acquiescence, her obedience to his demand that she lie back and allow him to do as he wanted.

He crawled slowly and deliberately onto the bed, over her, straddling her body with his own. When he'd slid to just below her waist, he dug his knees into the mattress and sat upward so he looked down on her, his beautiful, muscled body like a work of art draped over her skin.

He skimmed a hand over the bandage on her side, frowning slightly as he examined it. She was determined that he not change his mind and decide she was too "injured" for sex so she arched upward, deliberately drawing his attention to her breasts instead.

It worked because his gaze immediately smoldered and his hand moved from her side and over her breast. He added his other hand to the other side and pushed them toward one another before leaning down and running his tongue in a swirling motion around one nipple and then the other until they were rigid, straining peaks, begging for attention. His mouth. His lips. His tongue. She wanted him to suck, wanted to feel the delicious tug that she instinctively knew would blow her mind.

As if reading her thoughts or perhaps his restraint was wearing down, he tugged one puckered ridge between his teeth, gently grazing the ultrasensitive nub and then sucking the entire areola into his mouth.

She emitted a strangled cry, arching up, her hands flying to his head, holding him firmly against her so she didn't lose the exquisite suction. A growl rumbled through his throat, almost a purr of pleasure that gave her delicious satisfaction.

Her fingers dug through his hair, reveling in the sensation of so much skin-to-skin contact. Her senses were ablaze, consumed by fire. *His* fire.

He very quickly discovered her pleasure points, knew just how to make her insane with the need for release. He discovered places she hadn't realized were erogenous zones as he conducted a very thorough head-to-toe perusal with his hands, his mouth and his tongue. God, his tongue.

She was mindless, boneless, helplessly sliding further and further into sweet oblivion. So many times she'd thought she'd simply break apart and float away and yet he always seemed to know the exact moment to pull her back, preventing that free fall into space.

She was ready to scream, to beg him to give her relief from the ever-increasing tension, boiling, simmering, stoking and fanning until she was a seething cauldron of ecstasy. Just as she reached her breaking point and parted her lips, trying to draw in enough oxygen to voice her plea, he raised his head from his sensual exploration of her throbbing clitoris, dug his fingers into her hips, roughly nudging her thighs apart with a knee and thrust into her with one forceful lunge.

Her lungs caught fire as pain burned through her swollen passageway. Beau froze, his entire body going rigid as he stared down at her in shock. Her eyes were wide as she stared helplessly up at him as she processed the bombardment of conflicting sensations snaking through her body.

She didn't know how he managed it, but he leaned down, so carefully and tenderly, and leaned his sweat-beaded brow against her forehead.

"Ari. Honey. Why didn't you tell me?" he whispered.

"I didn't know," she whispered back, shock still reverberating through her body and mind.

His lips curved into a half smile. "You didn't know you were a virgin?"

Her hands wouldn't remain still. They glided up and down his arms and up the slope of his neck, her enjoying every bulge of muscle, each hard ridge.

"That's not what I mean," she said, giving her head a small shake.

He groaned. "I need you to be still, honey. I'm trying very hard to rein myself in, but if you keep that up, I'm not going to be able to hold back."

"I didn't think it would really hurt," she said, stilling her hands and body so she was in complete accord with his. "I mean in books it never hurts. It's always this glorious . . . thing. I honestly figured the whole hurting thing was a myth to discourage girls from having sex too young."

He feathered a kiss over her furrowed brow and let out a sigh. "I ripped in to you with all the finesse of a rutting bull. Of course it hurt."

She gave an experimental wiggle, gauging the now not so burning sensation. Or rather the burn was still present, but it was a *good* burn. She rubbed against him like a cat, locked her arms around his neck and then raised her legs to loop over the backs of his, solidly linking them, keeping their bodies connected so there was no question of him pulling out.

He was right where she wanted him to be and she wanted the edge back. That flying sensation, the about-to-catapult-right-over-the-edge free-falling spiral of need, want, lust and desire, all inexorably wound together in a seamless, never-ending chain.

"Okay now?" he asked, an edge to his voice that told him her movements had done to him precisely what he was doing to her. The wait was agonizing for them both.

"Yeah," she whispered against his neck, turning her mouth to nuzzle and inhale. She began to nibble at his throat and then ran her tongue over the slight bristle of his evening shadow as she worked her way upward to his jaw and then she licked and scraped her teeth on a path toward his ear and when she sucked the lobe into her mouth, he let out a long hiss and he finally, *finally* moved.

She let out an honest-to-God moan when he withdrew with agonizing slowness, but the genuine tenderness in his care of her was utterly heartwarming.

"Hold on to me," he husked out.

His hands slid down her curves, plumping and molding her breasts, weighing the slight swells in his palms before continuing their downward trek. They skimmed her sides, slid underneath her hips and then he cupped her behind and lifted her, adjusting the angle so that this time when he entered her, he went deeper, touching parts of her that caused her eyes to widen and her mouth to round into an O.

A really *big* O. Corny pun absolutely intended.

"I think I just figured out what a g-spot is," she said in wonder.

His chest rumbled with laughter and his teeth flashed as a grin widened his face.

"I feel like a virgin as well," he said in a rueful voice.

She reared back, planting her head deep into the pillow so she could look at him. "Not to completely mimic you but why on earth would you say a thing like that?"

He smiled again and playfully tugged at several thick strands of her hair, wrapping the tendrils around his fingers while squeezing her behind with his other hand, both gestures of obvious affection.

"Because this is the first time sex has been *fun*."

He sounded as confused as she was about sex, which was pretty hilarious given she had zero experience and he'd probably been around the ballpark more than once. Surely a man wasn't this great at sex without a lot of practice.

But she drew absurd pleasure from the fact that she was his first anything. However, realization dawned that he seemed baffled by the fun aspect.

"Sex isn't supposed to be fun?" she asked in puzzlement.

"Oh yeah. It is," he said, his voice laced with satisfaction. "You make a compelling argument for it being *very* fun. It's just that I've been called brooding and intense and supposedly chicks are into that. I can't say I've ever laughed while having sex. But you're so damn cute."

He chuckled as he said the last and nudged her chin affectionately and then pushed his hips, wedging himself deeper, momentarily rendering her speechless as euphoria swamped her. She danced along a razor's edge, the very thin line between pleasure and pain as his fullness invaded her, stretched her.

Her inner walls rippled and clutched greedily at him, trying to prevent him from withdrawing each time he began easing back. She no longer cared about the vague discomfort because the sensual haze surrounding her, whispering through her veins, was as potent as any drug ever manufactured.

"You undo me," he whispered as his lips brushed against her ears. Said so lightly that she wasn't sure whether she'd truly heard them or if she'd merely imagined them.

She clutched the back of his neck and pulled him to meet her mouth, sucking his tongue inward just like her body sucked his cock deeper and deeper with every thrust.

"Need to get you off," he said gruffly. "I want you there when I come. I want to watch you experience it all for the first time."

Finally.

He was going to give in to her desperate need. He was finally going to give her the relief she needed so badly. Her insides clenched in anticipation and he groaned, a raw, tormented sound of a man at his very limit.

"Tell me what you need," Beau demanded. "Let me get you there, honey."

"I don't know!" she cried. "Just don't stop. Please don't stop."

Every muscle, every nerve ending, every single cell in her body was taut, tension coiling about to ... almost ... oh God, it was happening.

She hurtled through the air, the rush so exhilarating that it was akin to a downhill ski race, slick like snow, out of control. Faster and faster. Higher and higher.

The room blurred around her. The bed shook. There was a faint thudding sound that grew louder and the bed vibrated beneath her while Beau thrust into her from above, driving her deeper into the bed, covering her like a blanket with himself. Skin to skin. No barriers. No separation. Just time standing still for one brief moment when everything else drifted away and nothing or no one could intrude, could break the tangible connection between heart, mind and soul.

He filled her. Not just her body. He completely and utterly filled her. Her heart. Her soul. He filled her with hope. With confidence. With the knowledge he wouldn't fail her. That he'd protect her from the outside world and would shelter her from the storms of life.

Her small hands pressed into his shoulders, her fingers curling and turning white at the tips as she held on for dear life. A painting that hung on the wall came sharply into focus and she stared because either it was a lot lower than it had been before or she was much higher.

It was then she realized the entire bed was levitating. Laughter escaped her.

"You're not supposed to laugh right after a man just gave you the best orgasm of your life," Beau said dryly.

His eyes gleamed with mischief, telling her he'd been intentionally arrogant in his assumption. But he was also right.

She grinned up at him. "I feel like we're in *The Exorcist*. You know, the whole bed levitating bit."

He kissed her, the soft smooching sound echoing softly through her ears.

"Or maybe we just rocked it so hard that our sexual energy was raising the roof. Literally."

Her shoulders shook and then she hugged him to her just as the bed settled gently back onto the floor, jarring them just enough that it shook her hold on him. Her smile was likely permanent now. Never in a million years had she imagined her first time to be so earth-shattering, and her expectations had been high. And wrong, for that matter.

So good fiction was apparently just that. Fiction. At first she'd felt extremely let down, and well, she'd felt stupid and naïve. But Beau hadn't laughed at her. He'd laughed because of her. Because she'd made sex fun for him. On a hotness scale, she wasn't sure where "fun" rated, but it did odd little things to her heart to know that she'd somehow been special to him. Not just another woman in what was undoubtedly a really long line. Men like Beau never had to worry about forced celibacy. If anything he likely had to beat them back with a stick. And yet he'd chosen her.

That falsification jolted her back to awareness and her "permanent" smile just went south. She glanced up at his passion-laced eyes, uncertainty, something definitely not new to her, crowding in and dimming the aftershocks of something truly wonderful.

Beau's body came down over her, concern flaring in his eyes. "Ari? Did I hurt you again? Was I too rough?"

"No," she hastened to assure him. "I was just being silly. It's nothing to worry over. It was wonderful."

She was absolutely sincere in that regard. But Beau continued to study her intently, his stare probing, looking beyond the denial she'd hurriedly issued.

He bore his weight with one arm pressed into the mattress so he wasn't too heavy and he had shifted his weight to her uninjured side so no pressure was exerted on the wound. With his free hand, he smoothed several wild strands of hair that lay haphazardly over her damp, flushed cheek.

"What were you thinking?" he softly prompted.

She sighed and made a face. "I'm not the most self-assured person and you're going to think me completely absurd. But I was thinking about the fact that I was actually something special or at least unique to you. Because you said I was the first you had fun with. Then the thought expanded to the idea that men like you never have to worry about enforced celibacy and in fact you likely have to beat back the women wanting to get with you."

She bit her lip, loathing having to admit the last. It was one thing to harbor secret thoughts. They were her own and she never had to worry that anyone would know her weaknesses. But Beau wanted access to those thoughts and the idea gave her hives.

His expression was still puzzled but he stared pointedly at her, obviously waiting for her response, and just as obviously *knowing* there was more.

"I got this really giddy feeling like a sixteen-year-old high school girl who just got asked to prom by the hottest guy in school. I thought to myself he could have his pick of women and he chose *me*. As soon as the thought came to me, I realized that you *didn't* choose me. I threw myself at you, all but begged you to have sex with me and then made you feel guilty for turning me down. Basically making this a pity fuck . . ."

She flinched at her choice of words. They sounded stark and crude and she was surprised by them. That she'd actually voiced the last bit. The expression had wafted through her mind just as she'd mentioned him turning her down and just spilled out before she could think better of using it, and now she was ashamed at her language because regardless of his reasons for making love to her, it had been beautiful, soul-stirring, and she'd reduced it to a crude euphemism.

"*Pity fuck?*"

The words sounded strangled. Anger radiated from him in strong surges and she immediately regretted blurting out her thoughts in a single unguarded moment, a mistake she couldn't take back and one that could very well completely wipe out an exquisite coming together of hearts and souls.

"Do you honestly not see yourself?" he asked incredulously.

He shocked the crap out of her by easing out of her aching, hypersensitive, swollen tissues and then simply scooped her up and carried her into the bathroom. Naked.

He gently set her down in front of the mirror and stood behind her, forcing her to look at her reflection. Color stained her cheeks as she took in her disheveled appearance.

She had the look of a woman who'd just been thoroughly made love to. Lips swollen. Eyes still glazed from the remnants of her mind-blowing orgasm and yet they glowed brightly, making them appear particularly brilliant in the lower lighting the bathroom cast.

He framed her body between his hands, one on either side of her, allowing his palms to roam freely up and down her and over her curves, to her breasts, holding them from underneath, thrusting them upward so there was no possible way not to see the puckered, taut crests, also swollen from his tender ministrations.

"You're beautiful," he said hoarsely. "But you're the *most* beautiful in a way you probably don't think. I'd say it's obvious you don't see yourself the way I do. The heart of you."

He laid his hand over her chest, splaying his fingers possessively.

"Let me tell you what *I* see."

She held her breath, yearning. So filled with hope and yet afraid to allow herself even a kernel of it when she could so easily be crushed by his rejection of her.

"I see a beautiful, loyal, brave young woman who places the people she loves before herself and her own safety. Not many people would be as selfless as you are. You gave me a gift, Ari. Do you realize how humbled and absolutely gutted I was that you chose *me* to be your first? And yet you don't think I chose *you*? That I gave you a goddamn *pity fuck*?"

She winced upon hearing her words thrown back at her again. Because now, in light of his reaction, and all that he was doing in an attempt to reassure her, it would look as though she'd been chasing compliments from him. Ultimate female manipulation. And it made her cringe, not to mention feel hugely embarrassed and if possible, even more self-conscious.

"Not only do you sell yourself short and do yourself a huge disservice, but you do the same to me to even suggest I'd use *my* body as an object of pity. That I would pour my *soul* into making love to you, as you *deserve* to be made love to. I get that you struggle with confidence. But do not ever show yourself such disrespect in my hearing—or any damn time for that matter. Because you'll just piss me the hell off."

She swallowed and slowly nodded just as he leaned in to nuzzle her neck. Even as ultrasensitive as she was after her orgasm, her body reacted violently to his touch. To the sizzling heat that erupted between them when they got into touching range.

He rained kisses down the entire curve of her neck until he got to the top of her shoulder and then he simply pulled her backward, her back flush against his chest, and he wrapped his arms securely around her.

Their reflection presented such an intimate, erotic, picture in the mirror that she instantly committed it to memory, never wanting this memory to fade, to always be able to bring it sharply back into focus. Because it was one she'd never forget. A night of so many firsts for her.

He rested his chin atop her head, staring directly at her in the mirror, his gaze seeking. Evidently satisfied by what he found or that at the very least he had found what it was he was looking for in her expression, he gave her one last squeeze and then turned her around so she faced him.

He cupped her chin, his thumb whispering over her cheek. There was no anger or judgment in his dark eyes. Just unwavering resolve. Comfort and warmth spread through her limbs, infused into her bloodstream and rapidly pumped to the rest of her body. Euphoria once again wrapped her in its intoxicating embrace and she relaxed in his hold, allowing her body to mold itself to his. A perfect fit.

"Look at the mirror, Ari," he murmured, his lips brushing the hair just behind the shell of her ear. "See how beautiful you are. Really see."

Reluctantly, she turned and complied with his gentle request and what she saw surprised her as she looked at herself through objective eyes, as though it weren't her, but another woman. It was as if it were the first time she saw herself without the self-imposed filter.

She looked . . . beautiful. More importantly, Beau made her feel beautiful. And desirable. Like a woman he chose, not someone he was "talked" into making love to. Now, away from that vulnerable moment when she'd been stripped bare and was so raw and exposed from the power of their lovemaking, she knew just how ridiculous her original thought—fear—had been.

Beau was not a man easily manipulated. For that matter manipulated at all—by anyone.

She wanted to apologize, but it would only make things worse and that the best thing she could do was simply acknowledge what he saw and what *she* now saw.

A beautiful, thoroughly made love to woman who'd just lost a piece of her heart to a man she'd only known for a very short amount of time. But at the same time, she felt as though she'd been waiting for this moment her entire life.

EIGHTEEN

BEAU quietly left the warmth of his bed the next morning, glancing at Ari every so often to ensure he didn't wake her. She needed rest, and well, he needed ... distance. Objectivity. Because the night before had permanently altered the course of his relationship— his supposedly objective, professional relationship— to a woman he damn well should have kept his hands—and various other parts of his body—off of. Maintained a strict level of professionalism. Not compromising his perspective and preserving the contractor/client strict level of impartiality.

Hell, who was he kidding, though. He might think he needed to distance himself, and he might acknowledge that's what he *should* do, but it sure as hell wasn't what he wanted, and he was at least honest enough with himself that he wouldn't make up excuses or try to rationalize his breach in the professional code of conduct he and Caleb insisted their security specialists maintain at all times.

He was a flaming hypocrite and he didn't give a flying fuck. Which meant he was in way over his head.

He hurriedly dressed and walked into the kitchen to prepare a cup of coffee, needing the infusion of caffeine to penetrate the haze of contented lethargy that fully encompassed him. What he wanted to do was remain in bed with Ari, his body solidly wrapped around hers so she awakened in his arms, warm and sleepy, that drowsy, contented look in those beautiful multi-colored eyes.

But he had work to do and a hell of a lot of catching up to do. The clock was ticking and they were working on a tight deadline. Every passing hour that Ari's parents remained missing heightened the chances of them not being safely recovered.

If it were him, and he was the sort of bastard who'd use a vulnerable woman's greatest weakness against her, he'd kill one of her parents, send her the evidence and then tell her if she didn't meet their demands she could kiss the remaining one goodbye, too. And he'd take out the father, since he'd be a greater threat than the mother.

It would destroy Ari. It was something she'd never recover from, and he'd bear the weight of that responsibility—his inability to follow through on his promises—for all time. Ari would never forgive him, and he'd never forgive himself.

As he stirred in a dash of sugar in the strong brew to cut the sharpness just enough to make it palatable, his cell phone rang. It was a ringtone assigned to a noncontact, and as he pulled up the phone to check the incoming call, he frowned when he saw "blocked" on the screen.

Normally he wouldn't answer an unidentified caller with at least some means of tracing the call but given the current status of his latest case, he couldn't afford to miss anything.

"Hello?" he clipped out, forgoing his usual greeting of "Beau Devereaux." No sense giving the caller any information he—or she—didn't already know, and if it was a wrong number, he hardly wanted to relate his name that now had his number attached to it and showed up in the caller's phone log.

"Mr. Devereaux, you have my daughter, and it's imperative you keep her safe and out of sight. The people after her will stop at nothing to get to her."

Beau's forehead wrinkled, anger nipping at his nape as he tightened his grip on the cell phone. "Gavin Rochester? What the hell? Do you have any idea how frantic your daughter is? What the hell is wrong with you? You're putting her through hell."

"I'm not Gavin Rochester," the caller said wearily. The man sounded fatigued and after Beau's initial anger, he caught the thread of fear in the other man's voice. "Ari Rochester is my biological daughter."

Beau was on full alert now, automatically turning to ensure Ari wasn't coming up behind him. After ensuring the coast was clear, he strode to the security room, gained access and then secured the door behind him.

The room was soundproof, and all the video feeds tying in the entire security field around—and inside—the house were displayed on the monitors. His main concern was Ari, so he made sure he was standing facing the image of her still curled contentedly in his bed.

"What do you mean her biological father?" Beau demanded, returning his attention solidly on the caller now that he was assured Ari was in his line of view. "Swear to God, if this is some crackpot call I'll track you down and feed your own testicles to you."

There was an uncomfortable silence as the other man seemed to be gathering courage—or at the very least the right words.

And then another thought occurred to Beau. How in the hell had this person, no matter his wild claims, gotten Beau's private cell phone number. A number that only a few people had. His brothers. Dane and Eliza. Zack. Not even Anita had access to this number. He had a work cell and a personal cell. His person cell rarely got used since most of his brothers' or the other single-digits people who had the number also happened to be co-workers, so usually it was just easier for them—and more natural—to punch in the number to a phone he'd answer no matter what he was doing or what time of the day the call was placed. Although last night? He'd have thrown it through the damn window if it had rung.

"How did you get this number?" Beau asked, his quick temper already displaying signs that his patience was waning. Fast.

The man also demonstrated his impatience with the flurry of questions from Beau. Ignoring them all, he simply plunged ahead.

"You're right in that Gavin Rochester is her father. It's a well-deserved title. He earned it. The last thing I want to do is to hurt Ari. I was young, cocky, arrogant. I'm sure you know the type." The man claiming to be Ari's father—bio father—cracked or rather his words did.

Indeed Beau did because he'd been that kid while in college, and he was pulled to others who displayed the same traits. While Beau had been saddled with a hell of a lot of responsibility at a very young age, college had been his form of rebellion even as he continued to shoulder a hell of a lot of responsibility for his family.

"Yeah," Beau said faintly. "I know the type."

The other man plunged ahead as if giving Beau no time to process much less question. And there were a lot of damn questions brimming in Beau's mind. Questions he wanted answers to because Ari damn well deserved those answers.

"She's in a lot of danger. You need to be aware that these people will stop at nothing to get their hands on Ari. They know what she can do. What she's capable of. And they're determined to use her, and it's not for good," he said quietly. "We—I—thought she would be safe with Gavin Rochester. He had a certain reputation for ruthlessness. It was the hardest thing I've ever had to do. To give up that baby girl. But I knew we couldn't keep her safe. That we didn't have the resources or the means to ensure she was never found."

"Just who is we?" Beau demanded.

There was a pause and when the man spoke again, sorrow was reflected in the soft words. "Her mother and I."

"There's a lot I don't understand," Beau cut in. "But we'll start with the most pertinent. How could these "people" as you call them—and we'll get to who they are in a moment—but how could they possibly know a mere infant could possess the kind of powers she would later exhibit? Her adopted parents didn't discover it until she was nearly a year old."

"Because she was an experiment," the man cut in. There was

suddenly a sense of urgency in his voice and he became more hushed. "Look, I don't have much time. So you need to know what sort of men you're up against. The whole reason they discovered Ari, and it was years ago, not just days ago, as you may think, given the media attention raised when she did use her powers."

Beau was nodding, though the other man couldn't see. Zack had pegged this one entirely. It had been a very thought out, methodical plot to infiltrate Gavin Rochester's ranks, gain his trust, and then when he least expected, strike and take Ari. But where and why?

"How did they find out?" Beau said, tired of this delicate dance between them.

"Ari's mother and I were selected to participate in a program for the development and research of psychic powers. We both possessed unusual talents. Ari's mother was dirt poor and struggling just to make ends meet. They hired her to be a surrogate mother, not really explaining that the baby wasn't going to an actual family. They posed as a legitimate adoption agency specializing in surrogacy. They played on her vulnerability and she agreed to carry a child because they offered her a lot of money, free housing, bills and expenses paid.

"I was the sperm donor. Same song, same dance. Only Ari's mother and I fell in love. And when we discovered, by accident, just what this organization really was and what their plans for our child was, we ran. And we kept running. Each brush was more difficult to escape than the last, and we knew when Ari was born, there was simply no way for us to be able to keep running when we had a baby to support. So we went to . . . your father for help, and he directed us to the Rochesters, who by all accounts were unable to have children of their own."

Beau's response—reaction—was explosive. "What the hell? What does my father have or rather what *did* he have to do with any of this? You better damn well explain yourself."

Beau was struggling to take it all in. It was like a bizarre science fiction movie, but it was chillingly real. All of it. It fit too well with the background information they already had on Ari and her parents. But now it was suggested that his father was in some way involved? And then he remembered Gavin Rochester's vague association with his father. His blood chilled in his veins. Gavin had been the last person—to their knowledge—to have seen their father alive. Had Gavin silenced him in order to protect Ari? Or had he done it to protect his own selfish interests?

To Beau's seething frustration, the other man completely ignored Beau's impassioned demand and continued as though he hadn't just dropped a bombshell.

"They found Ari, or rather found out who had Ari, because they caught up to us and took my wife." Pain radiated from the choked words. Grief was tangible through the phone connection and Beau automatically tightened his grip on the cell and glanced up at the monitor just to reassure himself that all was well with Ari. "They tortured her," he said hoarsely. "They did unspeakable things for three days until she finally broke and told them who she'd left our daughter with. Then they killed her and dumped her body where I'd find her with a note that this is what happens to people who cross them. So you need to know who you're dealing with, Mr. Devereaux. You need to know they mean business and they will not simply give up and go away. It was four years ago that they murdered my wife. And they systematically began to put the wheels in motion that would allow them access to Ari, and believe me when I say that them being thwarted just makes them all the more determined to succeed in their objective."

Shock echoed through Beau's mind as he grappled with the ramifications of what Ari's biological father had just revealed. God, if they'd done that to Ari's biological mother—a defenseless woman—then they certainly would do no less to Ari's adopted parents. He couldn't face Ari, if one of her parents appeared on their doorstep or in a place they knew the body would be discovered by DSS. They'd want Ari to see—to know—exactly how serious they were and it only made Beau that much more determined that they would never get their hands on her.

There was background noise and then the man spoke hurriedly. "I have to go."

"Wait!" Beau quickly spoke up. "How do I get in touch with you?" There was a damn lot more he wanted to know from this man, particularly how his own father was involved in this complete clusterfuck.

"You don't," the man said tersely.

And then the call ended just like that, leaving Beau frustrated, even more questions than ever vibrating through his mind.

"Goddamn it," Beau swore, flinging the phone toward one of the leather chairs in the security room, where it landed with a soft thud.

Once more he glanced up to the monitor, fear seizing him

as he watched Ari sleep the sleep of an innocent. Someone who didn't live in a world where women were tortured and then discarded like yesterday's trash.

The question was whether he should tell her what he now knew to be truth. Or at least what he'd been led to believe was truth. Because it seemed his—and her—lives had been a tangle of lies from the very start.

NINETEEN

"THE first thing I want to do is inject an undetectable tracking device on Ari as a precaution," Beau said to the gathered members of DSS who had been called in the moment Beau had gotten off the phone with Ari's "biological" father.

Ari had slept, very likely exhausted from the events of the last forty-eight hours, and only when his brother, Zack, Dane and Eliza had arrived on the heels of Beau's urgent request for their presence had she stirred. He had gone to the bedroom and told her to take a nice long bath and relax, that he'd call her when breakfast was ready.

He winced over the lie, but he wasn't ready to fill Ari in on things that may or may not be true and he needed time to go over all he'd discovered with his team before making any decisions with regard to her.

Ramie was in the kitchen, fixing the breakfast Beau had promised Ari, most likely deciding to opt out of what was likely to be a volatile meeting and difficult for her when she absorbed so much of the negative emotions in others. Beau knew for certain he didn't want to touch his sister-in-law and subject her to his seething thoughts of murder, revenge and utter ruthlessness if it came to that. He also had no intention whatsoever of divulging the potential role his own father had in this clusterfuck until he was certain of the facts. Caleb would be enraged and objectivity would fly right out the window, to Ari's detriment.

"Good idea. You can't be too careful," Dane acknowledged. "We can plan to the nth degree, but with the resources this group has and their utter ruthlessness we can't possibly cover all angles when we don't damn well know who and what they are and what their higher purpose is."

"It's obvious they have no problem torturing innocent women," Zack said darkly. "Caleb, I'd think you'd want to lock Ramie down and make damn sure she is under strict guard 24/7 because if these assholes have already made the connection between Ari and DSS, which is obvious given they were shot at coming out of the DSS building, then no one connected to DSS, particularly their loved ones, is safe."

Caleb's eyes became glacial, his features carved from granite. "You can be absolutely certain I *will* protect my wife," he said in a deadly quiet voice.

"Quinn and Tori both will be under mine and Eliza's constant guard," Dane said. "Though Quinn is pretty damn pissed and said he doesn't need a goddamn babysitter and that he's more than capable of taking care of himself."

Beau leveled a hard stare at Dane. "I don't give a fuck what Quinn says. You sit on him if you have to. Until this is resolved, no one in this family—or DSS—goes it alone. I expect you to inform all your guys, Dane."

"We're on it. We've got everyone on our end handled. You just worry about yourself," Eliza said softly. "I'm concerned that you and Zack are basically going it alone with Ari. And *she's* the primary objective. Not the rest of us."

"But they don't want to kill Ari," Zack argued. "She's got to be recovered at all costs, which means all of you are expendable. Ari is not. She's probably the safest of all of us."

Silence greeted Zack's blunt statement and then there was grudging acknowledgment that he'd scored a direct hit. They knew he was speaking the truth. And that the rest of them were in danger because they could and *would* be used to manipulate Ari.

This mysterious group reeked of fanaticism and yet they operated with patience and methodical coldness. If DSS was waiting for them to eventually fuck up and make a mistake, they were likely going to be waiting a damn long time.

"I'll take care of the tracking device," Dane said. "The rest of you should go. Cover your tracks and act as though you're being followed and monitored at all times. Lose your tails and then make damn sure you use a location that isn't linked to us in any way."

"We think it's a good idea for you to move Ari as well." Eliza spoke up, her gaze connecting unflinchingly with Beau's.

"I've already considered that," was Beau's quiet response. "I don't want to stay anywhere with her more than a few days at a time. I want to keep her on the move constantly, making it that much harder for anyone to follow a trail leading to her."

Ari grew impatient with waiting for Beau to come get her. Surely he didn't intend to carry her into the kitchen. Enough was enough. If she felt well enough to indulge in the sexual antics of the night before she could certainly manage walking on her own.

Warmth invaded her cheeks as her thoughts drifted to the night in question. She was deliciously, decadently sore in intimate places, the ache certainly enough to distract her from any discomfort she might feel from a lingering headache and the cut in her side that had stitches.

Funny but she hadn't given either a thought until now. She was more focused on those more intimate hurts. She frowned. Hurt wasn't an appropriate descriptor.

Aching awareness? Yeah, that pretty much nailed it. She was tantalizingly tender and only the lightest of brushes over her breasts, between her legs, even her mouth—swollen by his all-consuming kisses—was like an electrical charge, lighting her up and throwing her back to the moment when he'd finally taken her over the edge.

She could stay in bed reliving that experience the entire day and be sated and lazy and definitely wanting to do it all over again.

Her stomach growled when tantalizing smells wafted into the bedroom. Her mouth watered and she rubbed a hand over it. Who knew having sex worked up such an appetite? She wasn't normally much of a breakfast eater and in fact rarely ate before noon, but she was suddenly starving.

She was so tempted to play the wicked temptress and walk into the kitchen without a stitch of clothing on and see how long it took for Beau to take her *back* to bed. A satisfied smile curved her lips as she remembered how . . . freeing it had felt to actually play a part in a very mutual, very satisfying seduction. Who knew she had this total sex kitten inside her just waiting to come out and play. Instead of being embarrassed or ashamed she defiantly slammed the door on those two emotions.

Something that good, that heart-achingly beautiful was nothing to regret, to be embarrassed over, and definitely no shame should ever touch something so perfect.

And then two thoughts simultaneously burst her cloud of euphoria, evaporating it into a fine mist as reality hit her square in the face.

One, they very likely weren't alone for her to go parading through the house, butt-ass naked. And two, oh *God*. How could she just forget? How could she embark on an affair like her world *wasn't* upside down and like everything was in perfect harmony, balance and in accord, when in fact her life lay in shambles. Complete and utter ruin.

Shame, something she'd sworn not to feel, slammed so violently into her heart that she had to sit down on the edge of the bed or fall to her knees. And fear, her constant companion that she'd briefly been able to escape for a few stolen hours, was back with paralyzing vengeance.

While she'd been indulging in a night of complete abandon, a door to a brand-new, previously unexplored world opening wide for her to breeze through, arms stretched wide, like she was reaching for the sun, her parents' whereabouts were unknown. Their condition was unknown. Whether they were even still alive was unknown.

And she'd been happy. Deliriously happy. Smiling. Laughing. Having sex for the first time and finally understanding what all the fuss was about. Acting like she didn't have a care in the world when her parents *were* her world and without them in it, she faced a lonely, barren existence.

Tears stung her eyes and she hung her head. She instantly became aware of the warm slide and metallic smell from her nostrils. Blood dripped onto her lap. She touched it with a trembling finger, already feeling the echo of pain start at the base of her skull and spread out like a spiderweb over the rest of her skull.

"I love you, Mom and Dad," she whispered.

Why couldn't her psychic power be telepathy? So she could talk to her parents no matter where they were. There would never be any barrier she couldn't breach. No place where they could be hidden from her.

What was the use in being able to move objects with her mind? It seemed all she was capable of was chaos and violence. And a levitating bed during sex. Really big freaking deal. Who cared?

She could almost hear her mother saying in her soothing, gentle tone reserved only for her daughter and husband, *Stop being so hard on yourself, baby. You have nothing to prove to anyone. Certainly not to me or your father. We love you exactly the way you are and we wouldn't change a single thing about you. You are the proudest accomplishment in our lives. The most important. No one makes us happier than you do.*

She wiped a tear from the corner of her eye, smearing blood on her face. Then she sighed in disgust. She couldn't walk into the kitchen looking like something from a horror movie. Beau would freak.

Feeling the weight of so much sorrow and fear, she trudged into the bathroom and winced at the paleness of her skin and how stark the bright red blood looked against her colorless face.

She warmed the water and then soaked a washcloth, wringing it out and then burying her face in it, inhaling the heated, moist air. Tears seeped in to mingle with the dampness from the water from the faucet and she dropped the cloth, squared her shoulders and visibly pulled herself back together.

The last thing a man wanted was to see the woman he'd made love to the night before walk into his kitchen the next morning looking haggard and mournful. Not exactly good for his ego and she wanted to make damn sure he never thought she had a single regret. Because even though she was ashamed of the fact that she'd given her parents no thought during those precious hours, she couldn't bring herself to regret it.

It likely made her a terrible person, but she was at least honest. Most important, she was honest with herself. She wasn't going to be a flaming hypocrite on top of her other multiple sins.

But making love with Beau had been like touching the sun after weeks of rainy, drab days. He'd been the only light in her world since it had been irrevocably altered by her parents' disappearance. He was her anchor. The only thing she had that was real and solid, and she was clinging desperately because she had nothing—no one else—to lean on in her time of very real need.

If that made her weak and dependent, who cared? It—he— was what she needed, both to find her parents and ensure their safe return—and she trusted him to keep his word—and to be her rock, to hold her when she could no longer keep it together and fell apart.

She wished she could be a stronger person. More independent. She'd certainly taken steps to be just that. But in the end, she'd failed in even that regard, because at the first sign of adversity, she'd turned to her father. And then she'd been forced to turn to Beau.

Superwoman she wasn't, but she could live with that. She just hoped that Beau didn't wake up one day and look at her in disgust, wondering why he ever got involved in someone who was not even close to being his equal.

He was strong. He was a doer. She couldn't imagine him ever needing *anyone*.

But he wanted her. He'd chosen her. And he'd gotten very angry when she hinted that he'd done so out of misplaced obligation. And pity.

She clung to his fierce denial that he hadn't chosen her and that she hadn't forced him into anything he hadn't desperately wanted. It bolstered her spirits and gave her a much-needed boost when her spirits were flagging and she was at her lowest point.

With a sigh, she quit delaying the inevitable, and she refused to remain here, hiding, despite the fact he'd said he'd come for her when breakfast was ready. The least she could do was face him. Look him in the eye and tell him without words that she didn't have one single regret for the night she'd spent in his arms.

She only prayed that she didn't see disappointment or regret in *his* eyes.

Quickly completing her cleanup, she hastily arranged her hair in a messy bun, rummaging in his drawer to find a rubber band. Not the best thing to use in her hair, but she could hardly expect him to have actual ponytail holders. His bathroom was not remotely girly and had no accoutrements that signaled a woman had *ever* been in here.

It was a leap in logic to make that kind of assumption, but it gave her absurd pleasure, so she clung to it nevertheless.

Too bad she didn't have makeup to disguise her paleness and the shadows under her eyes. With a shrug, she pulled clothing on, leaving her feet bare, and she took a deep breath before leaving the sanctuary of his bedroom to face reality. To escape the bubble where all time had seemed to stop and suspend indefinitely. If only she could go back in time to before her parents had disappeared and beg them not to go.

She briefly closed her eyes to compose herself just before she turned out of the hallway, in the opposite direction of the living room, and stepped into the kitchen.

Her eyes widened and suddenly she felt self-conscious when she saw Ramie Devereaux spooning scrambled eggs from a skillet onto a serving platter. Ari paused in the doorway unsure of whether she should go in or not, and for that matter if she was welcome.

She hadn't gotten a good feel for Ramie—or Caleb—the day before and had no idea what their feelings were about the fact Beau had agreed to help her.

As if sensing her stare, Ramie looked up and smiled welcomingly.

"Good morning," Ramie said, setting the skillet into the sink. "You're just in time for breakfast. I just took up the bacon and all I have to do is pop the biscuits out of the oven. Unfortunately grits are a southern thing I've yet to master."

She wrinkled her nose as she mentioned grits and Ari couldn't help but smile at the other woman's easy charm and open manner.

"Don't feel bad. I've lived in Texas my entire life and I've never even tried grits. I've been told it's a hanging offense in some parts of the Deep South, but my parents were from the east coast and so they never caught on to the whole must-have southern staples."

Ramie wiped her hands on the dishtowel on the counter and then she walked purposely toward Ari, her hand extended in greeting.

"We weren't exactly properly introduced yesterday. I'm Ramie Devereaux."

Ari froze, dropping her hands and pressing her palms against her jeans, instinctively taking a step back.

"You shouldn't touch me," Ari said in a low, embarrassed tone.

Ramie's expression was puzzled.

"It would only hurt you," Ari explained. "I've read about you over the years. How you only feel negative emotion. I know it's silly of me, but I always imagined us kindred spirits of sorts. Sisters from a different mother and all that. You made me feel not quite so alone in the world."

"Why would you hurt me?" Ramie asked.

"Because I'm not having good thoughts right now," Ari said honestly.

Ramie smiled gently. "None of us are capable of never having a bad thought, Ari. My gift manifests itself rather uniquely. It's really more of a curse or a blessing but I guess that determination is better left to others, since they usually benefit from my gift while I . . . suffer."

"It's why I don't think you should touch me."

"What I was getting around to saying," Ramie said, paying Ari no heed as she herded Ari toward one of the bar stools in front of one of the plates, "is that I sense the true nature of a person. Whether they're *inherently* evil. Their sins. Not necessarily thoughts. I realize this may sound completely bizarre and it's confusing even to me at times. But you strike me as someone who is good to her soul. Just because you have dark thoughts—particularly at a time when you have every right to be thinking them—does *not* mean you're evil."

As if to prove her point, Ramie's hand slipped around Ari's, linking their hands so their palms pressed together.

For a moment Ramie fell silent and then a frown creased her forehead and Ari tried to yank her hand back, not wanting to cause the woman even a moment's pain. But Ramie tightened her grip, forcing Ari to remain there, hand still held solidly in Ramie's.

Then finally she let go, and a smile replaced her earlier frown.

"You're not evil, Ari. In fact, you have one of the sweetest hearts and souls I've encountered, and believe me when I say, I've seen inside many a heart and soul."

"Then why did you frown?" Ari asked, perplexed.

"Because I did sense your pain. Your sense of loss and your utter helplessness. And I know how that feels," Ramie said softly. "I frowned because it upsets me to see you in such distress. You must believe in Beau. He's a good man. My husband is a good man, though he'd dispute such a statement."

Her smile turned mischievous. "In fact, he still insists he's not good enough for me, but he's too selfish to let me go. I just tell him that's him being smart. Not selfish."

Ari laughed, relief filling her chest.

And then the magnitude of Ramie's gift hit her. Her breathing sped up as she recalled the countless news stories over the years. Her earlier conversation with Beau in his office, now seemingly a lifetime ago. About the possibility of Ramie being able to help locate her parents.

She bit into her lip, unsure of how to broach such a sensitive topic. Especially when it was a fact that Ramie suffered whatever the victims suffered. And if she did help, if she was able to ascertain exactly what was happening to her parents, Ari didn't know if she could face that terrible truth.

"What's wrong?" Ramie asked. "You have the most horrified look on your face, Ari."

Ramie stared at her, concern evident in her smoke-colored eyes.

Ari closed her eyes briefly, bolstering her courage, praying for strength. Praying that Ramie would agree and that Ari could bear knowing the truth.

"I know this is asking a lot," Ari said nervously. "But as you know, my parents are missing. They disappeared without a trace and I have no idea where to even start looking. Would you . . ." She sucked in a deep breath before plunging ahead. "Would you be willing to use your powers to try and find them?"

TWENTY

"*HELL* no!"

Ari jumped, so startled that she stumbled and had to throw her hand out to clutch the back of one of the bar stools to keep her knees from buckling and doing a face plant right on the kitchen floor. Her heart nearly exploded in her chest at the sheer vehemence of Caleb's outburst. She whirled anxiously, fear knotted in her throat, to see Caleb, Beau, Zack, Dane and Eliza had entered the kitchen just as Ari voiced her request. Her pulse had escalated so swiftly and jittered so erratically that she was lightheaded. She swayed precariously and suddenly Ramie was there, wrapping a steadying arm around her waist, holding her as she shot her husband a glare of reprimand.

Fury emanated from Caleb. His entire *body* bristled with rage, his eyes glittering, making him look . . . lethal. She took an instinctive step back, Ramie's arm falling away as Ari made her escape. But she bumped into the bar and then felt trapped with nowhere to escape Caleb's terrible wrath.

She swallowed, unable to articulate any sort of response, not even to apologize. She was utterly paralyzed, panic knotting her insides

"Where do you get off trying to emotionally *manipulate* my wife when you *know* damn well the hell she endures when she uses her powers to locate kidnapping victims?"

Ari clenched her fingers into tight balls, wishing she could take the words back, suddenly wishing she'd never walked into the DSS offices. Whereas just moments earlier she'd felt safe—comforted by the knowledge that Beau would protect her *and* find her parents—now she felt terrified and wanted to be as far away from this place as possible.

She skated sideways, eyeing her pathway to the hallway that led to the bedrooms. There was a doorway just outside the exit from the kitchen, on the left, that led into the living room. And escape. There were other security firms. She'd only sought out the Devereauxs because it was who her father had said to look up. She could even hire a private investigator or simply go to the police, which is what she should have done from the very start.

When she'd eased past the barrier of the bar stools just enough to make her bid for freedom, she lunged for the hallway, bolting like a spooked deer. A strong arm wrapped solidly around her waist, hauling her up short, and she turned, prepared to fight. Two of the bar stools simply lifted in the air, hurtling toward her unseen attacker.

"Damn it, Ari! It's me, Beau. Stop with the chairs. Those sons of bitches hurt!"

His voice infiltrated her utter panic and the overwhelming desire to be away. Anywhere but here. She went still and the chairs tumbled to the floor, lying on their sides. Beau had his arms solidly around her waist, facing her, his expression hard, fury so like his brother's a storm in his eyes.

Tears suddenly welled up in hers. He was angry with her *too*? When she and Beau had discussed the possibility during that first meeting? He had been the one to broach the subject. Not Ari!

A tear slid down her cheek, warm against the ice of her skin.

"*Why* are you so angry with me?" she choked out, it taking every ounce of her control to prevent the words from ending in a sob.

The rage in his eyes was simply too much for her to bear. She dropped her gaze, her head lowering in defeat, her hair falling like a curtain and obscuring her view. She was aware of more tears, blurring her vision, so she simply closed her eyes, shutting out everything around her.

Helpless anger bubbled up in her veins, replacing her utter despair. She wanted to bring the whole goddamn house down—and she could. Now more than ever, she was cognizant of just how much power she wielded. Never tested before a few short days ago, it was now like a second skin, always lurking just beneath the surface and for the first time she embraced it.

Because she had something her parents' kidnappers didn't. The ability, from a distance, to wreak complete and utter chaos. She'd already proved she could slow a bullet. Her only vulnerability was being drugged and someone would have to be close enough to her to be able to manually inject it into her. Because someone wielding a dart gun would be ineffective because not only could she slow its trajectory, but she knew—*knew*—she could redirect it right back at the shooter. Unless . . . She didn't *know* it was coming? Was she vulnerable to something similar to a sniper only in closer proximity and with a dart gun?

As soon as the thought occurred, she shook it off. The knowledge was there, buried in her subconscious. Certainly no one told her these things. Who would have told her? Her parents were as baffled as she was as to the how and why of her powers.

And yet she knew or maybe she sensed, but whatever the case, she was absolutely certain that she could deflect a threat to her, *even if she didn't know it was there.*

Just how extensive were her powers? To have such reflexes, such instincts was more than simple telekinesis that required concentration and focus. Walking down the street, being randomly shot at and yet still being able to deflect a bullet was something else entirely, even if she had no idea what, how or why.

She felt a surge of power, restless, edgy and eager to be unleashed. Set free to do what it had always been meant to do. Protect her. Protect the people who mattered. And these people, all standing there, angry, slinging hurtful words like arrows *didn't* matter.

Cabinet doors flew open. Glasses hurtled through the air in Caleb's direction. She turned just enough to see him in her periphery, cursing and dodging as glasses hit the floor, the wall behind him, even the ceiling. One scored a direct hit, glancing off his shoulder to then shatter on the floor.

She was careful to protect Ramie. She projected an invisible shield, constructing it carefully in her mind, silently commanding the objects doing her bidding not to come near her. Amazingly it worked. Ramie threw up a hand to protect her head but a plate met with resistance two feet away and literally bounced off, falling harmlessly to the floor where it broke in half.

Beau's hand curled around her shoulders, firmly holding her but careful not to hurt her. He turned her, and then simply crushed his mouth to hers, his kiss deep, demanding, powerful. If his intent was to distract her from the barrage of objects his brother and the others were currently dodging, it certainly worked.

He released her shoulders and gently cupped her cheeks, framing her face in his hands as he tenderly kissed away the remnants of her tears.

"I just want to go," she whispered brokenly as soon as his mouth allowed her to speak the words. "Please just let me go. I'll find them on my own. I'm used to being on my own with only my parents."

When he spoke, it was barely above a hushed whisper. "I was *not* angry at *you*, Ari. *Never* with you. I was *furious* at my dick of a brother, but you were about to bolt so I had to choose between laying his ass out or making sure you didn't disappear out of my life forever."

His eyes burned with sincerity, the edge of anger diminishing as he stared intently into her eyes.

"I chose *you*."

The words from the previous night weren't coincidental. They were meant to evoke the memory of their lovemaking and that he *had* chosen her.

The electrical current that had arced through the room, crackling with her power—and hurt and rage—dimmed, the shards of the glass, plates and other items ceased their vibration on the floor and the room went utterly silent.

She knew everyone was staring at her and Beau. She could feel Caleb's furious gaze, now even more so since her attack had been aimed at him.

"You protected her," Beau murmured, gesturing behind her to where Ramie stood.

Ari turned slightly, an unhappy frown curving her lips and marring the quiet, intimate exchange between her and Beau. Ramie's eyes were wide as she stared incredulously at Ari. The others wore similar expressions and Ari fidgeted under so much scrutiny. She felt like a freak show and it made her want to run all over again. Anything to escape the awkwardness of the situation.

"I'm sorry I asked, Ramie," Ari said quietly, tears evident in her voice. Then she turned back to Beau. "And yes, I protected her. She didn't deserve my anger."

Beau's fingers, now firmly entwined with hers, shook with silent rage.

"You erected an invisible barrier around me that protected me," Ramie said, awe reflected in her words and expression. "Ari, do you even realize how extraordinary your powers are?"

"I'd trade them for yours without hesitation," Ari said bitterly.

"You have *no* idea what you're talking about," Caleb said harshly.

It was as though Beau's tenuous grasp on his control snapped and he launched himself across the distance separating him and his brother. He bunched Caleb's shirt in his hands, forming tight fists and he slammed Caleb against the wall that so many of the glasses and plates had been shattered against.

The veins in his neck were distended and his face was red, his breaths coming in erratic puffs. His jaw was clenched so tightly it bulged out and ticked in supreme agitation.

"I've had *enough* of you abusing Ari," Beau spat. "Swear to God if you say one more goddamn word, I will take your fucking head off. This is the only warning you get, Caleb. You do *not* want to test me."

Ari glanced nervously between the brothers, the three other DSS operatives and finally Ramie, who looked furious. Ari couldn't blame her for being angry that her husband's brother had just slammed him against the wall and proceeded to threaten him in a menacing tone that sent a shiver down Ari's spine.

He sounded lethal, the words violent and passionate but most of all . . . convincing. In that moment Ari believed that if Caleb uttered another word aimed at Ari, Beau would enact violence on his brother.

"Beau!" Ari cried, finally spurred to action.

She sent a pleading look in Ramie's direction, silently asking for help in breaking up a potential disaster as she ran to where Beau still had Caleb pinned to the wall. Beau's forearm was pressed into Caleb's neck and Ari realized that he'd temporarily cut off Caleb's airway by pressing so hard on his neck. Caleb's face had reddened and was growing redder still as Beau exerted even more pressure.

Ari tugged uselessly at Beau's arm. "Beau, please," she begged. "Don't do this. He's your *brother*. I'll leave. No one should ever cause dissension in a family and that's obviously what I've done. You can't blame him for being angry. I had no right to ask Ramie what I did. I was just . . . desperate. Can you remember how you felt when your sister was missing?"

She directed the last more to Caleb, though she included both brothers in her question. She knew she scored a direct hit because guilt flashed in Caleb's eyes and they turned bleak. Despair crept in behind and she softly cursed because she'd inflected yet more pain. Poured more salt onto a wound.

She turned, knowing the best thing was to simply leave. Let the brothers come to terms after her departure. With the source of conflict gone, everything could go back to normal. Life would resume. But at least she'd have the memory of one beautiful night. That, she would never give up. Never give back. It was hers to keep. Nothing or no one would ever take it away.

Wanting to make a clean break, not wanting to linger simply because she was leaving her heart and part of her soul behind, she briskly made a beeline for the other exit, the one that led directly into the living room instead of the two connecting hallways Beau had just prevented her from taking.

She brushed past Dane and Eliza and leveled a glare at Zack when he simply stepped in front of her, barring her from leaving.

"Get out of my way or I'll make you move," she said in a menacing voice she would have never thought she possessed.

"I can't do that," Zack said quietly. "I lost someone once, Ari. I know what it feels like. And I know how Beau would feel if you walked out of his life and disappeared. I think you would feel it just as keenly. I'm not wrong, am I."

Though technically a question, the last was voiced as a statement. As if he could reach in and pluck out her thoughts, delve into the very heart of her and see the imprint of . . . Beau. See that Beau had already marked her. Permanently. There would always be a part of her that was reserved for him and the memory of their lovemaking.

"I'm very sorry for your loss," she said solemnly. "Perhaps then you can understand why I refuse to stand by and allow my parents to be taken from me when I'm doing nothing to get them back."

Frustration crept into her voice and was more pronounced by the time she finished.

Then familiar arms stole around her body and she was drawn against Beau's chest, though she was still facing Zack. She had no knowledge of what had occurred behind her. She'd only been focused on escape. If words had been exchanged, apologies acknowledged, she hadn't heard, but then she hadn't really been listening because she was mentally bracing herself as she recognized that this was goodbye.

Warm lips nuzzled into her hair just above her ear.

"Don't go, Ari," Beau whispered. "Just . . . don't go. *Please.*"

Shocked that he would ever beg anyone for anything, she swiftly turned in his arms, staring intently into his eyes to try to decipher just exactly *what* he was asking. He made his request sound so . . . *permanent.* It wasn't spoken as though he were simply trying to get her to stay until his mission was accomplished.

Actual vulnerability shadowed his eyes, astonishing her almost as much as the fact he'd begged. She had an instant image of him on his knees, staring up at her, sincerity burning in his beautiful, dark eyes. Sorrow filled her because never would she want this proud, arrogant man on his knees for *anyone.* Unless, of course, he was proposing marriage.

Whoa. Talk about jumping to major, far-fetched conclusions! She shook her head to rid herself of all the clutter that had seemed to accumulate. It was an unfortunate side effect of using her powers, one she, of course, had never been aware of since she'd refuse to *ever* test them.

And then she felt the betraying warm slide from her nose and she glanced up at Beau in dismay just as the dull throb in her head that had gone unnoticed until now, because she'd been concentrating so fiercely on everything else, made itself known in a jagged burst of pain as if it had been caged and suddenly burst free of constraints.

She bit into her lip to prevent a moan escaping, afraid that any sound would simply make her head explode. She lifted her hands to cover her ears and simply held them there. The roar in her ears grew louder and louder until she could bear it no longer. The room seemed to spin around her while she stood still, making her so dizzy she feared she'd be sick. She swayed, closing her eyes to make the constant motion stop.

Beau swore violently and she winced, nearly screaming as the sound, magnified a hundred times, speared through her head.

She let out a whimper, no longer able to control her sounds of distress. "Please," she whispered so softly she wasn't sure she'd even be heard, but to her it sounded like she'd screamed it. "Please don't talk. No sound. Beau, I'm going to be sick!"

"Nobody say a goddamn word," Beau bit out, turning away from her so she didn't feel the impact of his words directly.

When he turned, she wobbled precariously and suddenly a foreign set of hands clamped down around her shoulders, holding her steady. But even that didn't prevent her legs from giving out. She shot downward, cringing and bracing for impact, knowing the jarring would split her head wide open, or at least that's the way it would feel.

Before she hit the floor she was suddenly lifted and she immediately shut her eyes again as the room spun wildly out of control. Zack. She'd all but forgotten he was there, that he'd been the one who'd prevented her from leaving, the moment she'd turned away from him to face Beau.

"What the hell?" Beau murmured softly.

She cracked open one eye, wincing as the light seemed to

pierce her eyeball like a needle. Beau had turned back around, his dark eyes even darker with concern as he viewed her cradled in Zack's arms.

"She almost took a header," Zack said grimly.

In response to the softly worded explanation, Ari let out another low sound of distress.

Beau immediately closed the distance between them and very carefully took her from Zack's arms.

"Lay your head on my shoulder, honey," Beau whispered. "I'm going to take you back to bed and Zack is going to get your medicine. Everything is going to be all right. I promise. Try to relax and school your thoughts. Focus on something soothing and relaxing, something happy and mellow. Or just blank your mind completely if you can manage that."

The low cadence of his voice, while roaringly loud, was oddly soothing. Or perhaps it was the vibration, the low rumble from his chest that was a balm to her frayed nerves.

He carried her like she was the most precious, fragile thing in the world, like she ... *mattered*, careful not to jar her in any way. The covers were still in disarray and he laid her down onto the mattress and then pulled and straightened the sheets around her, pausing only briefly to ensure her bandage was still in place underneath her shirt.

She was barely aware when Zack entered and she turned her face into the pillow, trying to muffle the sound of the jangle of pills in the bottle as Zack shook two of them out and reached over to carefully put them to her lips.

"Open up, sweetheart," Zack murmured. "I brought you a little milk to take them with since you didn't eat breakfast."

She vaguely wondered why Beau wasn't administering the medication but then her unspoken inquiry was answered when Beau very gently lifted her head, just enough so she could open her mouth and allow the pills to be placed between her lips. She was astonished by the effort it took to simply roll them to the back of her throat with her tongue. Then Beau lifted her the barest of inches more and Zack held the glass to her mouth and tilted it, careful not to allow too much of it into her mouth. Which was good because the pain had made her so nauseated that she feared anything she swallowed would simply come right back up.

The task accomplished, Zack withdrew and Beau sat on the edge of the bed, running his hand down her hair, pushing it away from her face in a soothing motion.

"Hurt," Ari said. It was the only word she could muster. Something felt terribly wrong, but she couldn't articulate what or for that matter anything at all.

"I know, honey. I'm so sorry. I should have flattened the jack ass the minute he opened his mouth. He had no right to attack you that way," Beau said darkly.

"He's ... brother ..."

Her intended admonishment that Caleb was Beau's brother and nothing was more important than family had narrowed to the only two words she managed to form. But it was enough to get her message across.

Beau stroked her hair, not responding to her words. He acted as though he hadn't heard them. Or perhaps he simply chose to ignore them all together.

"After the medicine has had time to work, I'm going to get

you out of these clothes so you're more comfortable," Beau said, continuing the soothing caresses up and down her body. "Try to relax, honey. I know it's hard, but try for me."

"Asked . . . me . . ."

A brief look of confusion skittered across his forehead as he leaned in closer so he could hear her barely audible words.

"What did I ask you, Ari?"

"To . . . stay. What . . . did . . . mean?"

His expression softened and his hand went to her forehead, his thumb pressing into her brow and rubbing along the lines, applying just enough pressure that it was soothing.

"I don't want you to leave," he said simply.

"Why?"

Her eyelids were growing heavier and heavier and she didn't want to go under yet. She wanted to hear *why*. Sluggishly her eyelids fluttered, half closed, and then the room seemed to go dimmer and dimmer.

"Beau?" she asked fearfully, wondering why the room was going dark.

"I'm here," he said. "Medicine working yet?"

"Why?" she persisted, determined not to surrender to the pull of the medication until he answered her question.

He hesitated, seeming to wage an internal battle, almost as if he couldn't decide whether to tell her or not. She reached blindly, searching for his hand. Her anchor.

His hand closed around hers and immediately warmth spread up her arm and into her chest. He lifted her hand to his mouth and pressed his lips to her palm.

"Because you're mine," he said simply.

TWENTY-ONE

BEAU stalked out of the bedroom, his face set in stone. He knew the others had moved to the living room because he heard voices in that direction. He was so pissed he literally couldn't see straight. Rage formed a red haze that made his vision cloudy.

As soon as he strode into the living room Dane looked up and said, "Oh shit."

"Beau, man, let it go," Zack softly advised.

Ignoring them all he headed straight for where Caleb stood rubbing his throat from where Beau had pinned him to the wall, blocking his brother's airway. Caleb barely had time to look up before Beau flattened him with a punch to his jaw.

Pandemonium ensued. Beau followed Caleb down, intending to yank him up by the shirt to look him in the eye. But Caleb connected with a roundhouse kick from a supine position, knocking Beau back several feet as he stumbled to maintain his footing.

It gave Caleb enough time to bolt to his feet and he glared

at his younger brother, rubbing his jaw where Beau had landed the punch.

"That's the only one you get," Caleb warned.

"Says you," Beau said in a menacing soft voice.

"That's enough!" Ramie said sharply.

She shot across the room and stepped between the two men just as Beau advanced to close the distance between him and Caleb. Beau pulled up, not wanting his very petite, small-boned sister-in-law to take an inadvertent hit. If he accidentally hit *her* as hard as he'd punched his brother, he'd very likely break her jaw.

Instead he stood there, seething, fists down at his sides, his fingers flexing, curling and uncurling, itching to pound on his brother some more. He couldn't even look at Caleb without unfettered rage overwhelming all else.

"He was wrong, Beau," Ramie acknowledged quietly.

"The hell I was," Caleb said, a stubborn set to his jaw.

Ramie rounded on him, but not before Beau got a good look at her expression and it was positively murderous. He watched in surprise as Ramie dressed him down and informed him that he did not make decisions for her and that if she wanted to help Ari then she damn well would.

"Swear to God, if you cause so much as one moment of pain to my wife, I will take you apart," Caleb said, his face red, eyes blazing.

"You hypocritical son of a bitch," Beau said softly.

Ramie started to speak up but Beau gently put his hand on her shoulder but let it slide away quickly before she picked up on his utter fury. It was a motion for her to stand down, one she acknowledged with a short nod, but she remained solidly between the two men.

"Did you not see what you *did* to Ari?" Beau demanded. "That woman is desperate, terrified and alone. The only family she has vanished without a trace and you *attacked* her. Worse, you made her feel *unwanted*. What is *wrong* with you? And that wasn't enough for you. You kept poking at her, so that she felt completely defenseless and when she uses her powers it is debilitating for her. You ought to know all about psychic bleeds. Only yours weren't nearly as bad as the ones she suffers. And if that's not bad enough, the pain she suffers is horrific. She already had a brain bruise before you brutalized her tonight. I just put her to bed and she couldn't even say more than two words because she was so weak and even the lightest sound sent shards of glass through her head. And I had to sit there and watch because there's not a damn thing I can do to help her besides shove a pill down her throat and hope she gives in to oblivion quickly so she can escape her reality. Now, you fucking tell me, big brother. When did you become an asshole who verbally beats up on a fragile, vulnerable young woman? Oh wait. I remember. You've had plenty of experience given how you forced Ramie's compliance when she quite plainly told you no."

Ramie paled and the color leached from Caleb's cheeks as pain shadowed his features, shadows collecting in his eyes. Beau wished like hell Ramie wasn't in the middle of them. That his reminder to Caleb had to be stated in front of Ramie, who needed no reminder of the hell Caleb had unwittingly unleashed on her.

"Are you forgetting who her father is? That he was the last one to see our father alive?" Caleb asked hoarsely, though regret already simmered in his eyes. He cast a sorrowful look in his wife's direction, abject apology etched on his features, and it just pissed Beau off all the more that he could feel that kind of re-morse and be utterly appalled by what he'd put Ramie through, but he saw nothing wrong with brutalizing a complete innocent.

And in that instant, Beau knew he'd been right not to con-fide all the details of the phone call he'd received to his brother, because he would be completely ruthless and unstoppable when it came to Ari.

"So far as I can tell, Ari's only sin was being born," Beau said. "You're a fucking hypocrite if you think she should be judged and held accountable for the actions of the man she calls father. Because you and I both know that our father was no saint. And if you're going to make Ari answer for her father's sins then you better be fucking ready to own up to ours."

Caleb closed his eyes, but not before Beau saw that he'd scored a direct hit.

"God, I'm a dick," Caleb said wearily. He reached for his wife as if needing to touch her, as if by touching her he'd be clean again. But it wasn't Ramie he needed absolution from. She'd given him hers already by marrying the bastard.

"Yeah, you are. But that's nothing new," Beau said, a bite still to his voice.

He was still seeing Ari, hurt and then fear flashing in her eyes. Her hasty retreat from the heat of the words Caleb hurled at her like daggers. And worse . . . *defeat*. As though she had no one. No one who cared. No one to hold her. To tell her it would be okay.

And then her terror, fueling rage, the glasses and plates hurling through the air, lashing out because Caleb had hurt her and Beau hadn't had time to intervene. She'd thought he was as much against her as the other occupants of the room who stood back, allowing Caleb's words and actions to go unchecked.

Beau wanted to fucking fire every goddamn one of them in that moment. Where was Eliza's fury? She'd damn sure taken Caleb to task when it came to Ramie. Only Zack had been gentle with her, anger simmering in his gaze when he'd briefly glanced at Caleb before preventing Ari's escape.

Thank God for Zack. That someone in the room had some goddamn sense. He couldn't bear to picture Ari out there alone, unprotected . . . rejected by the very people sworn to protect her . . . without rage consuming him all over again.

He shook with it, his entire body vibrating with the raging need for retribution.

And then a small, gentle hand slid over his arm, and he turned, instinctively reining in his seething mass of emotions, because he didn't want to hurt Ramie. She didn't deserve it. She'd been nice to Ari and Ari, sensing just that, had ensured that no harm came to Ramie even amid a torrent of bewilderment at the source of such animosity emanating from Caleb. It would have been easy to just say to hell with all of them, shake the house down and walk from the wreckage and wash her hands of the whole lot of them.

"Even while you were ripping Ari to shreds, piece by painful piece, she protected Ramie. Your wife. Because she's good to her soul, and she doesn't deserve any of what she received tonight."

He turned, including Dane and Eliza in his condemnation.

"She didn't deserve it from any of us, and yet that's precisely what she got. And why? Because she's desperate to find the only family she has in this world? I don't give a flying fuck if the Rochesters are her blood relatives or not. To Ari, they're her entire world. So that makes them important, and it's not up to us to play judge and juror and condemn a man with evidence so flimsy even a fool could pick it apart."

"You have strong feelings for her," Ramie said in her sweet, gentle voice.

He stared at her in astonishment. "Why does a man have to have strong feelings for a woman in order to condemn the abuse of a woman by a man twice her size?"

He knew as soon as the words were out of his mouth that he sounded defensive. As though she'd struck a huge nerve. And hell, maybe she had. He was so fucked up over the entire situation that he didn't know which end was up. He felt like this was his first rodeo, like he was the virgin Ari had been.

The reminder that just the night before she'd so sweetly offered him her innocence sent another wave of fury rolling through his veins. He should be holding her. Offering her comfort. Ensuring that she felt no pain. Instead he was out here, outside the sanctuary of his bedroom, defending her against inexcusable abuse at the hands of his own damn brother when he should be with her so she didn't wake alone and think the worst.

Caleb scowled at Beau's response to Ramie but Beau sent him a withering look that challenged him to say one fucking word.

To Beau's surprise, Ramie reached for his hand, sandwiching it between her palms, and she smiled, her eyes sparkling as she looked up at him.

"I was telling you what I sensed," she said, seemingly battling laughter. Why the hell would she be laughing at a time like this?

She gave his hand a gentle squeeze and then leaned up on

tiptoe, brushing her lips across his cheek. "You're done for, Beau Devereaux," she whispered as her lips dropped away.

Still grinning she stepped back, shooting her husband a look of warning. It amused Beau that Caleb immediately took a step back and relaxed his stance, automatically obeying his wife's silent command. Caleb was as whipped as Ramie claimed Beau was. And it appeared neither brother gave one damn.

Then her expression became utterly serious, her smoky eyes somber and swirling with streaks of gray, reminding Beau of a summer thunderstorm.

"When Ari feels better, please tell her that I'll help her. But I can't guarantee anything." She said the last with a grimace. "Typically I use an item from the area where the abduction—or other violent act—occurred. Obviously that's not possible in this instance since Ari has no idea what time or where her parents disappeared."

Ignoring Caleb's instant protest, Beau turned to Ramie, focusing only on her as Zack took Ramie's place between the two brothers.

"Can you even do it then?" Beau asked, realizing he was holding his breath when his lungs started to burn.

"It's possible that I could if Ari could provide me with a favorite object or even a piece of clothing that they either touched or wore frequently. If she had something they shared, it would be even better," Ramie said, rubbing one hand up her opposing arm in a gesture of agitation. She was obviously fretting over the idea of somehow failing Ari.

Caleb moved and Zack immediately stiffened, shooting his employer a warning look. Caleb might be the older brother, but it was clear whom Zack's allegiance lined up with.

Beau got to Ramie first, wrapping his arm around her much smaller frame. And yet Ari was even smaller, though the two women shared very similar bone structure. Delicate features. They had a lot in common and not just their psychic abilities.

He brushed a kiss over the top of Ramie's head and gave her a gentle squeeze.

"Ari will understand. She's good and sweet to her very core. She'll be overwhelmingly grateful to you for simply trying. Offering your help. It will mean the world to her. Despite Caleb's ignorant assertion that Ari has no clue what you endure, how much your ability makes you suffer, she is very well aware and it's why she was so hesitant in asking you. It's why she didn't immediately ask you for help the first moment she laid eyes on you.

"We spoke about you the day she came into the office. She knows precisely who you are. She later confided that she always felt a kinship to you and followed all the stories that made any mention of you whatsoever. I think it embarrassed her a little because she feels it's presumptive of her to believe you and she are kindred spirits. You made her feel not quite as alone. You made her feel less of a freak, because she drew the conclusion that since the two of you possessed psychic ability it was a reasonable assertion that there were others out there as well."

Ramie wrapped her arms around Beau's waist and hugged him fiercely. "I know exactly how she feels. And it's not silly or presumptive to believe we're kindred souls. I quite like the idea that there are others out there like me as well. I'm not entirely certain why she or I find comfort in that knowledge, but it is reassuring on some level to think we aren't some accident of nature. An abomination of sorts."

"I once knew someone who could read minds," Zack said quietly, surprising the rest of them by speaking up. He was typically a silent observer to the goings-on around him. "She felt much the same as you and Ari."

Beau's eyebrows went up at the uncharacteristic outburst from his usually reserved and extremely private partner. It only added to his belief that something in Zack's past had shaped the man he was today. Now he wondered if Zack had endured the loss of someone who mattered to him. Mother? Sister? Woman he loved?

Caleb scowled and finally maneuvered past Zack when Zack's attention was momentarily not on him, instead a distant, faraway look in the other man's eyes. Caleb wrested his wife from Beau's grasp. Then he cupped her chin and tilted it upward so he gazed down into her eyes.

"You are *no* freak. You're a fucking *miracle*. *My* miracle. And I thank God for you every single day."

He glanced up at Beau, sincere apology brimming in his eyes before he returned his gentle gaze to his wife.

"And neither is Ari. She—like you—is a beautiful, giving woman who has a tender, generous, *selfless* heart and is extremely loyal to the people she loves. Beau's right. I'm a complete dick. And unlike you and Ari, I *am* selfish. I readily *admit* I'm a selfish bastard. But damn it, Ramie. I hate the idea of you experiencing something so horrific. *Again*. You've been through so much already. I just want to *protect* you. Can you understand that? I *love* you and I never want to see you hurt like that again," he said gruffly.

Beau's anger fled in that instant, and he too offered silent apology to his brother with a single look that was acknowledged by a flicker of a smile, though his eyes were still clouded with worry. And Beau couldn't fault him for that. The brothers were doing the same exact thing. Protecting their women from the horrors of evil and agony.

Their women . . .

With that acknowledgment, Beau had sealed his fate and forever altered the course of his life—his future. *Ari's* future. In actuality, he'd accepted what destiny had provided him the previous night in the most time-honored way a man proclaimed his possession. He'd marked her in the most primitive fashion a man could brand a woman.

She was his.

He'd even *said* those words to her an hour before, and yet it still hadn't quite registered. He hadn't openly acknowledged what his heart already knew.

The truth slammed into him with the force of a speeding train.

Did he love her? Because it sure as hell felt like love. Or at least what he perceived love to be. Surely something else couldn't be this powerful and all consuming. But it wasn't the time to make such a huge leap. There was too much to be resolved between them.

Ramie's lips formed a smirk and her look was triumphant. "I'd say I was quite correct right now, but that would make me smug, right? Dooonne for, Beau Devereaux. Stick-a-fork-in-you *done*," she said drawing out the last words for emphasis.

"That's exactly what it makes you," Beau grumbled.

Dane and Eliza, who'd discreetly backed away from the initial fracas, now stepped forward, both looking all business.

"This poses a huge security risk," Dane said. "And it can't be our only plan of action. Ramie herself isn't certain of her ability to locate her parents so we have to operate under the assumption we don't have her as our ace in the hole. And we can't have Ari jaunting off to collect some personal item for Ramie to use. The danger is too extreme."

Eliza nodded her agreement. "They'll most assuredly have her residence staked out."

Beau frowned. "She mentioned that her father has several residences and our records indicate when comparing the addresses Ari provided to the registered owner there's a paper trail about a mile long and then begins repeating."

"One does have to wonder why someone would go to such lengths to hide their whereabouts," Caleb murmured.

"Makes perfect sense to me," Zack said shortly. "If I had a daughter with powers like Ari, I'd do whatever it took to keep her out of the public eye and the risk factor to her low."

"Very true," Beau agreed. "However, I can't help but think there's more to it than that. Between the call from her supposed biological father to this mysterious faction who tortured a woman for information and then killed her when she finally caved."

"I find it interesting that her biological father *knows* his wife or partner or whatever they were to each other was tortured and killed and that he also happens to know what they wanted and that they were successful in gaining it from Ari's mother. That's a hell of a lot of information to know in such exacting detail unless he was present and witness to the event," Dane mused.

"And if he was present, how did he escape unscathed?" Eliza asked, tapping one blunt fingernail against her chin. "For that matter how the hell did he know where Ari is now and how did he get Beau's private cell number?"

Beau hadn't wanted to divulge all the gory details that had been provided him because he hadn't wanted to scare the hell out of Caleb, and this might well be the nail in Ari's coffin once Beau did reveal how Ari's biological father knew what he purportedly knew.

"He told me they dumped her body where he would find her," Beau said quietly. "It was bad. And they left him a message saying this was what happened to people who crossed him. Whether any of it is true is anyone's guess. I'm not naïve enough to believe in the coincidence of receiving a 'helpful' call at a time we need it the most."

Caleb's features froze, and fear registered starkly in his eyes. He drew Ramie close into the shelter of his body as if protecting her from the unknown or the possible repercussions of her involving herself in helping Ari.

Beau sighed, rubbing a hand wearily through his hair. A glance at the grandfather clock in the corner told him he ought to be getting back to Ari before the meds wore off enough and she awakened. This was the perfect opportunity for Dane to inject the tracking device underneath Ari's skin. With her already exhausted and under the influence of pain medication it would take mere seconds for Dane to make the insertion and then they had a way of finding her if the worst happened. And it would be the height of arrogance—and stupidity—to consider themselves invincible or impervious to such an attack. Beau certainly wasn't taking chances when it came to Ari's life.

He looked to Dane. "You have the chip ready? She's out so let's get it over with."

Beau knew he was being edgy and impatient, but he wanted to be there when she opened her eyes. He wanted to be the very first thing she saw. He fidgeted with impatience, knowing none of this mattered if they weren't able to locate Ari's parents. Biological or not, she loved them dearly, and it was equally evident by the way she spoke of their affection for her that she was dearly loved in return. And well, if the information Zack had collected was true, then Ginger Rochester had experienced her share of heartache trying unsuccessfully to carry a child to full term.

It just seemed highly coincidental—*too* coincidental—that mere months after miscarrying a fourth baby late in the second trimester, a newborn baby had been simply left on Gavin Rochester's doorstep right around the time his wife would have delivered her baby if she'd carried it to term.

More and more, Beau realized that the answer to *everything* was in discovering just where and *who* Ari came from. And what the hell *his* father had to do with the entire sordid affair.

TWENTY-TWO

ARI awoke to a dull throb at the base of her skull and her fore-head, but the pain had lessened to a much more tolerable level. She was deliciously warm, and she tried to stretch, to work the kinks out of her sore muscles when her elbow collided with a hard chest. Which certainly explained the cozy warmth.

Their two bodies under the covers formed a seal and the air surrounding them was heated, mainly by Beau, because it seemed after using her powers, when she was utterly vulner-able and defenseless, that the strain on her brain made it so her body temperature wasn't able to be regulated like normal. The result was that she always woke from the post-trauma, drug-induced fog with shivering cold permeating even her bones, and it seemed she was chilled on the inside, making it impossible for her to get warm.

Not so this time.

She instinctively snuggled deeper into Beau's body, twining her legs through his so that his heat surrounded her completely.

She nuzzled her cheek against his chest and then sighed in contentment as only a woman with the perfect man could do. The perfect man for *her*.

I chose you.

Those words, so powerful and heartrending, played over and over in her mind, soothing away the splintered fragments of pain, anger and violence.

Were there any three sweeter words to hear? She thought a moment and then acknowledged there was. Only one phrase that had more power than a man telling a woman that, out of the millions of women in the world, he chose only *one*. One! He chose *her*.

I love you.

Oh to hear those words from his lips, from his *heart*. To know that he meant them with every fiber of his being. She'd give anything in the *world* to have her heart's desire. Her parents alive, safe, *home*. And Beau Devereaux's love. If she ever were assured of those two things, she'd never ask for more.

By acknowledging the yearning from the deepest recesses of her soul, she was forced to acknowledge the depth of her *own* feelings. Her heart had literally been breaking apart, splintering, cracking. Piece by piece, chipped away as she'd walked—or rather tried to walk—away from him. To leave him the peace and strength of family that he deserved.

She knew how important family was. Her own family wasn't as large as Beau's, but it didn't mean it was any less strong. And perhaps it was *because* it had always been only her, her mother, and her father, that their bond was so indestructible.

In a world where divorce was common. Where children left home at an early age. Where husbands beat wives. Spouses cheated on one another. Children were abused. Ari's family had stood the test of time, and in fact, had strengthened—not weakened—with each passing year.

Her memories—so many wonderful, cherished memories—were so very dear to her and she prayed with all her heart that they would share many more memories to come. That she would one day give them grandchildren to protect and spoil every bit as much as they'd done with her.

Beau's children.

The thought whispered enticingly through her damaged mind. She automatically lifted her head, seeking the reassurance that looking at his strong facial features always gave her. Her lips parted in surprise when she realized he was fully awake—*had* been awake for a while, because there were no cloudy remnants of sleep lingering lazily in his eyes. They were alert and aware. And they were solidly focused on her.

It was apparent she wasn't the only one who'd been absorbed in a quiet moment of reflection. She only wished she was privy to his thoughts. She wanted so badly for her wants and desires, her hopes and dreams, to align with his. She wanted to share her *life*. With him. *Only* him.

Was she crazy to have fallen so hard and so inexplicably *fast*? Her brow furrowed momentarily as her perusal of Beau's beautiful face gave way to silent contemplation of just how long, or rather how short, a time they'd even been associated.

Her only knowledge of Beau Devereaux, until just a few short days ago, was by name only. And only when, in those rare moments when her father was in a serious mood, and she'd always gotten the uneasy feeling that he was . . . *afraid*. Of something. Or someone. Because it was when he was in those very rare moods that he seemed to further gather his wife and daughter to him and would only separate himself from them for a few moments at most.

It was those times that he'd, out of the blue, very somberly remind Ari that if she were ever in need, ever in danger and that he wasn't, for whatever reason, available, close or simply unable to see to his daughter's safety and well-being, she was to immediately contact Caleb or Beau Devereaux and only in person. Not over the phone. Never to give them the opportunity to give her the brush-off, think she was nuts, or say they were booked solid.

Her father—and mother—had laughingly told her many times over the years that no one had a chance upon laying eyes on Ari's sweet, beautiful features and that her eyes were capable of bewitching even the hardest of hearts.

She supposed that was why he'd wanted her to seek Beau out personally. Perhaps he'd been afraid that he wouldn't help her unless she pleaded her case in person. Whatever the reason, she offered silent thanks to her father. As a result of that extracted promise, not only did she have her best chance to save her parents, but she'd also met a man who made her want to dream. A man she wanted forever with.

"What on earth are you thinking, honey?" Beau asked softly, reaching out with one finger to gently caress away the lines creasing her forehead. "Are you worried about something? Are you hurting?" he demanded, as though the thought had just occurred to him.

He was already reaching for the medicine bottle on the nightstand when she issued a hasty denial. She placed her hand on his chest to stay his motion and he reluctantly turned back to her, concern burning brightly in his eyes.

"Are you certain?" he asked in a skeptical tone. "Ari, if you hurt, you need to control the pain or risk another bleed, or God forbid, a more serious *hemorrhage*."

She smiled, her heart warming to its very core over the depth of concern, both in his words and in his entire body language. She looped her arm as far around his broad chest as she was able and gave him a fierce squeeze, her attempt at a hug since they were both lying down, him on his back and her on her side nestled into the curve of his armpit.

"Hey," he queried softly. "Not that I'm complaining at all, but what was that for? What's going on, honey? You looked so puzzled and then worried. Your eyes were flashing as though you were processing half a dozen thoughts in that pretty head. And the very last thing you need is any kind of stress. So tell me so I can take care of it and make it better."

She wanted to say it so badly. The words burned on her lips, begging to be set free. Instead she licked them to ease the tingling sensation. Just the thought of offering him those three little words, the most important words in the world—in her world, at least—filled her with gut-wrenching terror. And offering someone your love should *never* be terrifying. It should be celebrated. Embraced. A memory to savor—and hold close to your heart—forever.

But she was scared. Of rejection. Of seeing discomfort or even dismay flicker in those dark eyes. Or the worst possible reaction of all. *Pity*.

The very last thing she ever wanted from this man was pity. She wanted his love. His commitment. His protection. She wanted the kind of love her parents shared, and oh but she could see it so clearly with Beau. Never before had she met a man who even made her wonder if he could possibly be a man who'd measure up to her father. That she could share with him all her mother and father shared.

Wistful yearning twisted her chest and brief sadness tugged at her heart, squeezing it gently as she imagined a love like that simply . . . disappearing.

The world was a better place with people like her parents. Everyone should want more—better—should *demand* it. Her parents were an example to be held up in esteem, an example of the testament of absolute love, loyalty, fidelity and selflessness.

"Okay, Ari, you're starting to worry me," Beau said firmly, reaching up to nudge her chin so her attention was forced to him once more. "I swear you keep drifting away to God only knows where. I only know you're not *here* with me."

"But that's exactly where I want to be," she said softly, her palm sliding over the wall of his chest, exploring every hard contour, the ripple of his abdominal muscles. Then she pressed a kiss just above his left nipple, enjoying the brush of her lips over his firm skin and even firmer pectorals.

"You can't possibly want it more than I do," he said, sliding his fingers up the length of her arm that was still flung across his body.

"Do you mean that?" she asked hesitantly, instantly searching his gaze for any sign of the veracity of his words.

He looked confused and then worried. He turned on his side, his hand wrapped around her arm so it stayed anchored around him when he moved. Then he reached to trace a line from her temple to her cheek, sending shivers of sheer contentment coursing through her veins.

"How can you doubt that?" he asked. And then faint alarm

registered in his eyes and he stared intently at her, as if doing the exact same thing she'd been doing to him. Trying to see into her thoughts, to understand or discover her thoughts, her feelings. And her fears.

"Ari, do you doubt that I want to be with you? That I want you with me? And not just temporarily. Not days. Not weeks. Not months."

"How long then?" she whispered, dodging his question of whether she doubted his words. She was much more interested in the last things he'd said.

Hope made her pulse flutter and then speed up. She held her breath for seemingly an eternity as she waited for . . . confirmation? Something more? Commitment?

Love?

Oh God, she couldn't go there. Could not set herself up for devastation. She had to learn to steel herself. Not to take so much to heart. To be able to shrug off the negative things and embrace the good.

His cheeks puffed as he blew out a long breath and his hand slid from her face to capture the arm lying over his chest. He took her hand, lacing their fingers, and then simply placed their joined hands over his heart.

"This is where you are, Ari. Here. And this is where you'll stay. And because you're here," he said, pressing her hand harder against the steady thud of his heartbeat. "That means that I *want* you here."

He gestured to the bed. And then swept his arm to encompass the room.

"Everywhere," he said softly. "Everywhere I am is where I want you to be."

He leaned forward, still keeping her hand trapped solidly between their bodies and he fused his mouth to hers in the sweetest of kisses. He was still treating her gently, as though he feared she would break or that he'd somehow cause her more pain.

"Forever," he whispered into her mouth, the word swallowed up as she inhaled the scent, the taste, the feel of him surrounding her. "I want forever."

And that one word, so simple but utterly sincere, gave her contentment such as she'd never known or experienced.

Love finds you when you least expect it. Under seemingly impossible circumstances, but it was there. Young and blooming still. Unwavering and constant.

Love truly did conquer all. Love required trust, unconditional faith in the face of adversity.

Some of the overwhelming fears of losing her family dimmed, because, in this moment, Ari knew without a doubt that Beau would find her parents and that Ari and Beau's love would be as steadfast and true as her mother and father's and that they too would withstand the test of time.

TWENTY-THREE

BEAU'S expression blackened and he emitted a soft curse when a firm knock sounded at his bedroom door. He rolled to his back with a groan and slapped his palm to his forehead in a signal of frustration.

"You've got to be fucking kidding me. Now? Someone's going to interrupt us now of all times? Swear to God, the house better be on fire."

Ari smothered a smile and tried to summon irritation equal to his, but he was too funny with his pouty sullen look of a boy who'd just been denied his favorite toy.

When the knock persisted, Beau rolled, sliding his feet to thump on the floor, and then rose to stalk to the door, yanking it open with enough force to rip it from its hinges.

"What?" he barked

Ari turned, curious as to whom would brave Beau's wrath to interrupt them so early in the morning. She frowned. Or at least she thought it was morning. Yesterday was a fog bank, and she had to struggle to part the veil of mist in order to remember all that had happened.

She shivered with the bone-deep cold that always assailed her after a psychic burst—a word she'd made up on the fly because, well . . . it was appropriate—because Beau was no longer there to warm her and the bed was suddenly chilly. She dug her feet deeper, seeking residual warmth from the imprint of his legs and feet.

At first she couldn't see who had knocked on Beau's door because Beau solidly filled the doorway and they were speaking in low tones. So she couldn't hear? Or out of deference to the fact she was always so sound sensitive. But she wasn't now, so it had to be that they didn't *want* her to hear.

She frowned, sitting up in bed, craning her neck to see around Beau, and was finally able to see enough of the intruder to recognize him. Zack. Only he wasn't alone. Caleb and Dane were both flanking Zack. She bit her lip in agitation. What on earth was going on? Why were all *three* men standing there wearing determined expressions? Except Caleb, whose eyes and face seemed locked in impenetrable stone. He neither frowned nor smiled. He was utterly unreadable—but obviously serious, and even so, he definitely intimidated her.

She unconsciously settled further back into the pillows, drawing the covers protectively to her chin as if by doing so she offered some kind of barrier between her and the daunting, cold figure Caleb represented.

What had made him so? Only when he was around his wife, or she entered the room, did his entire demeanor soften, and he seemed to light up, glowing from the inside out. Ari could see the immediate change—the difference—knew that he quite obviously adored the other woman and that he'd lay waste to any threat to her.

Surely a man who became utterly defenseless the minute his wife walked into the room couldn't be *all* bad. Her own father could be considered quite ruthless. Even cold and daunting, all the qualities she'd attributed to Caleb. But, like Caleb, he became a different man the moment his wife so much as smiled at him. And she knew for a fact that her father was a good man, despite appearances. So perhaps she wasn't being fair to Caleb. She'd jumped to some rather hasty conclusions fueled by her overwhelming fear. Something that now made her ashamed.

Beau spoke to the men a few more moments, but it didn't escape her that he ensured he was a solid barrier to the inside of the bedroom. Specifically the bed where Ari lay. Not that he needed to have concerned himself since she was currently buried in the bed and only her face peeked out from the covers.

Then he softly closed the door and returned to Ari, his features carefully schooled. Instead of crawling back into bed and under the covers with her as she'd hoped, he sat on the edge of the bed and simply held out his hand as if he needed that contact with her.

Or perhaps he thought *she* would need his touch after he told her what had prompted the early morning visit from his brother and their operatives.

She slipped her hand from beneath the covers and laid it over Beau's. He immediately curled his around hers, giving her hand a comforting squeeze.

"I need you to listen and hear me out," Beau said in a carefully measured tone.

Her heart skipped a beat before resuming regular rhythm,

but the one irregularity caused a momentary catch in her breath. He seemed perfectly in tune with her responses, her body language and reactions. He was perfectly in tune with *her*.

"Honey, this could be a *good* thing. So don't jump to hasty conclusions. I need you to be calm and rational."

Okay, so it wasn't horrible. She could deal with that. She made a concerted effort to regulate her breathing and to relax. After a moment when Beau seemed satisfied that she was ready to listen, he scooted a bit closer to her and held her hand in his lap.

"Ramie has agreed to help us. She's going to try to establish a link to one or both of your parents."

This time her pulse leapt in excitement, not dread. It took all her control not to literally bounce up and down on the bed like an excited child.

"She did?" Ari whispered, unable to keep the incredulity from her voice. "But Caleb . . . He was so *adamant*." And Beau did *not* miss her sudden shiver that she couldn't control when she remembered just how vehement Caleb's reaction had been.

Beau's eyes grew cold at the reminder of just how adamant his brother had been. But then he seemed to make a concerted effort to shake off his sudden anger and smiled at her hesitant yet hopeful question.

"Ramie is her own person, despite what Caleb may think or what he may make others think. He'd very much *like* to control every aspect of her life. Not because he's an overbearing asshole—although he certainly can be just that—but because he loves her dearly and he only seeks to protect her and I can't fault him for that. You have no idea the sheer horror they endured not so long ago. What Ramie has endured time and time again over the years. One day when I have the time and we aren't pressed for it, I'll tell you their story, but it's not a pretty one," he said in a grim tone.

"And since Ramie doesn't allow Caleb to run roughshod over her and exert the control he *wants*, Ramie pretty much told Caleb that he did *not* make decisions for her, and that if she chose to help you, then she was damn well going to do just that. She really likes you, Ari. You struck a chord with her. It may seem silly, but no sillier than your thought—your belief—that the two of you were somehow linked—kindred spirits, even sisters of sorts, though you'd never met—is precisely the way Ramie feels about you. And it breaks her very tender heart that you've lost your only family. Ramie grew up with *no* family. She never had one until us. We're her family now so she especially feels as though she can identify with the way you feel, and she wants to do whatever she can to try and help locate your parents."

"When?" Ari choked out. "Where? *Today*?" Oh God, let it be today. Please today. She didn't think she'd last even one more day without something—anything—to let her know her parents were alive.

Beau's hand tightened around hers. "Yes, today. But first you have to do something for us."

"Anything," Ari instantly vowed.

"Ramie is usually able to establish a link to the victim by touching an item at the scene of the abduction. Even a small piece. Sometimes the seemingly obscurest of things. But if the killer touched what the victim had touched, or if he was even close enough to it, and if he gives off particularly strong imprints, Ramie can use that as a pathway."

Ari frowned. "I sense a *but* coming."

Beau nodded. "We're in a bit of a quandary. The problem is we don't know where your parents went missing. We know nothing at all, so we don't even have a starting point. But Ramie seems to believe that if you can think of something that was a particular favorite of your parents, something they would have touched frequently and left strong mental impressions on as well as physical, that she *may* be able to open the pathway. But she wanted me to make it clear to you, that although she is going to try *everything* she can and exhaust all possibilities, she doesn't want you to get your hopes up and set yourself up for horrific disappointment and despair if this doesn't work."

Ari's mind was already working furiously, drifting momentarily away from Beau as she concentrated hard on possibilities. She ignored the last, because she wouldn't allow herself to contemplate, even for a moment, that Ramie would fail. She had to succeed. Or Ari truly *would* shatter, and she may never recover or be whole again. The only thing that was holding her sanity by the thinnest of threads was the hope of getting her parents back. If that was taken away from her . . . She physically shuddered, knowing that she would simply fall apart.

Beau's vehement swear filtered through her scattered thoughts and she glanced up, puzzled over what could be wrong. He got off the bed and stalked to the bathroom, returning a moment later with a soft, warm washcloth, and then carefully wiped at her nose and mouth.

When he pulled the washcloth away and she saw bright red blood, she frowned.

"But, Beau, I wasn't using my powers. Honest. I was merely thinking—concentrating hard—and trying to focus."

But guilt crept over her shoulders, gaining a tight hold

on her throat because she'd left out the more frightening turn her thoughts had taken, which was very likely the cause of her bleed.

"Apparently that's enough. You're in a very weakened state, Ari. You incurred what I believe *has* to be a psychic overload yesterday. I've never seen you that wrecked after using your powers. I imagine this is simply residual damage, not yet fully healed areas of your brain, and any overexertion of your mind could trigger a bleed, even a small one."

She shrugged as though she didn't care. And she didn't. She wanted to get back to her parents and the fact that Ramie had agreed to help.

But, in deference to Beau's concern, she did at least attempt to calmly sort through memories, mementos and any object that her parents would have both loved enough to touch often frequently.

It seemed there were simply too *many*. Pictures, photo albums, but none that really stood out. And she wanted to provide Ramie with something that offered the best opportunity to pick up a thread to her parents.

And then it simply came to her, slipping in with little fanfare. But it was so obvious that she berated herself for not having thought of it first.

"Oh my God," she whispered. "Of course!"

"What?" Beau asked urgently. "Did you think of something?"

"My lovies."

He gave her a look of confusion. "Your *lovies*?"

She smiled, once again leaving the here and now as she relived all the moments over the years. The sacred place her lovies occupied, because it was through those adored stuffed animals that her parents had first discovered her powers.

She'd kept them with her, though when she'd still lived with her parents they had a place of honor on one of the shelves in the living room and both parents often picked them up, soft smiles appearing on their faces as they lost themselves momentarily in those memories of so long ago.

"They were my favorite stuffed animals in the world. Even at just nine months old I was cognizant of them. They were my comfort items but my mother would never leave them in the crib with me because she worried they were a choking hazard. Apparently I was not pleased with this and was able, even as a baby, to summon them from across the room so they floated to my crib and dropped within my reach."

Beau shook his head. "That's incredible."

"Imagine my parents' shock," she said dryly. "They had to come to terms when I wasn't even a year old yet that I was different, and as such, I wouldn't be able to lead a 'normal' life. And it altered their lives as well. They made many sacrifices for me, adjusting their own lives to revolve around mine and my needs. I always came first with them, which is why I have to find them. I owe it to them. To myself. To do whatever is necessary, even if it means sacrificing my own life to get them back."

His expression immediately blackened, his hold on her hand nearly crushing.

"You will *not* die," he said harshly, but vulnerability had flashed in his eyes before he could call it back.

"I don't *want* to die," she said softly, to reassure him. "I have so much to live for. I'm only saying that if it ever came to that—and I trust you and DSS to ensure that it *never* comes to that—for me it is an easy choice. One I wouldn't have to ponder, consider or have to talk myself into. They're too important to me and I can't imagine my world without them in it."

"You need to realize that they feel the same about you. Imagine how they'd feel, knowing that you sacrificed your life so they could live. Do you think they'd be grateful? Do you think they could possibly live with themselves? It's not something they'd ever recover from and get over, Ari. It would devastate them."

There was a long pause, his breath coming in long bursts on the heels of his impassioned statement. Then he looked her directly in the eye.

"It would devastate *me*."

Her heart turned over in her chest. Love, so much love filled her until she was nearly bursting with it. With the need to tell him. To share that one piece of herself that she'd held back from him. But now simply wasn't the time. They had a task to complete. The single most important event in her life.

"We need to get those lovies," Ari said. "As quickly as possible. I don't want to wait. Not a single minute more than is absolutely necessary. If Ramie is willing—and is prepared—please ask her if we can do this today. As soon as we retrieve the stuffed animals."

"Whoa," he said, holding up his hand. "There is no *we* in this equation unless that *we* applies to me, Zack, Dane, Eliza and a number of other DSS recruits."

She frowned. "But you don't know where they are and I do. It just makes sense that I go with you to get them. If you have so many people lined up for this job then surely we'll be well protected. And you seem to forget that I'm pretty badass myself," she added with a twinkle in her eyes replacing her frown of disagreement.

Beau sighed. "Where are they, Ari? The house that was already compromised? Because they'll most certainly have it staked out just in case we're stupid enough—and it appears we are—to return to the place you were damn near abducted from."

She smiled. "They aren't there. My father never stays in the same house but for a few months at the most, so I keep things that are important to me with me at all times. But I have an apartment—owned by my father—but it's not in my name. The building can't be traced back to him because it's registered to a company that doesn't exist, although a paper trail indicating they are indeed a thriving business was created. I doubt they know about my apartment, and if they do, then they would have had to have been watching me for a good while. Because I never drive straight from work to my apartment. I'm well versed in how to lose a tail and the habit is so ingrained in me, courtesy of my father, that I never deviate from it."

Beau shook his head, muttering, but he didn't look at all surprised by the meticulous fail-safes her father had put into place.

"Now when do we leave?" she asked eagerly.

Beau sighed, scrubbing a hand over his face in resignation. "We leave as soon as I alert the others of the change in plans, which will precipitate a whole new level of protection because we were *not* planning to bring you along. I would have felt much better if you and Ramie had remained here so we could be assured of your safety."

"You can adapt on the fly," she said cheerfully. "I've seen you in action. This should be a breeze for you."

He reached for her, framing her shoulders and looking di-

rectly into her eyes, a veritable storm of emotion swirling chaoti-
cally in his.

"You don't get it, Ari. If you were any other client, I'd be cool
under pressure, and yes, our motto is change, adapt and overcome at any cost. But you aren't just another client. And therein
lies the problem. Because if something happens to you, I can *not*
be held responsible for my actions. Because I'd unleash hell itself
if it meant getting you back. And if the unthinkable happened
and I *lost* you . . ."

He had to break off momentarily as emotion, so thick and
tangible, seemed to clog his throat, making it impossible to articulate the turbulence of his thoughts and his realization that it
was entirely possible he *could* lose her.

"I'd never survive, Ari. Do you understand that? *I* would
never survive losing you."

She stared at him in shocked realization. There was so much
unguarded vulnerability there for her to plainly see. There was
a physical, all too real ache in her heart almost to the point
of discomfort. She even lifted her hand to rub absently at her
chest, though the ache was deep. So deep that there was no way
to ease it.

There was no effort to hide the rawness of his feelings from
her. The tension—and sincerity—emanated from him in tangible
waves that she could feel, almost touch. They brushed over her
ears and rapidly absorbed into her very soul.

He may not have voiced those words, the words she so very
much wanted to hear. But in a moment of clarity, she realized he
didn't *have* to. Didn't need to in order for her to understand, to
believe. She *felt* his love, and that was infinitely more precious than
hearing words—just words. Words without actions—proof—were

meaningless. And his every action, reaction, his every word and his body language was not of a man who had only passing interest in a woman. Or considered her a temporary fling, one that he could walk away from with ease. Nor a woman that his heart, mind, his *soul* weren't solidly invested in.

He may not have said *I love you*. But he didn't *have* to. Not anymore. Her insecurity over those three words evaporated and simply lifted away. Because he'd said them in every other way *possible* without ever giving voice to the sentiment.

And that was more than enough proof—reassurance—that he felt for her absolutely everything she felt for him. That he, in fact, returned her love. Fiercely. Without hesitation, no second-guessing.

Two halves of an incomplete whole, empty and aimless, searching for that perfect match, had finally come together in a seamless, perfect, no longer separate heart and soul.

Because now they were complete, and their souls were merged, becoming one, never to bear the heartache of separation or experience that feeling of emptiness and hollowness.

Perfection. Sweet, utter perfection. And at last, it was hers—*theirs*.

She could wait for the words. In his own time, he would give them to her. But it didn't mean she wouldn't give them to him.

TWENTY-FOUR

THE atmosphere in the SUV carrying Beau, Ari, Zack, Eliza and Dane was silent and tense. Beau had insisted Ari be seated in the middle row so she wasn't a vulnerable target from the windshield or the panel of glass on the liftgate on the back of the SUV. His hand was gripping hers tight enough to make her wince, but she uttered no protest, realizing that he was truly terrified that something would happen to her despite the extensive planning and security measures that had been taken to prevent such a thing from occurring.

Another vehicle shadowed the vehicle bearing Beau and Ari, with five more highly skilled DSS operatives, whose acquaintance Ari hadn't made. But if they were indicative of the rest, she knew she was in good hands.

Caleb had remained behind with Ramie at Beau's insistence, though Caleb had been extremely reluctant to let his brother go off without him. Despite Caleb's intimidating demeanor, Ari could see the true love and concern reflected in Caleb's eyes when he looked at or spoke to his brother. For that alone, she could forgive any rudeness he had shown her in the past.

They pulled up in the private parking lot across the narrow street separating it from the skyscraper that jutted into the sky, seemingly piercing the stars. They'd pulled the building schematics and opted not to risk the elevators since it would be easy enough to shut them down, trapping the occupants between floors and making them sitting ducks.

Which meant a long-ass hike up twenty-three flights of stairs. She knew Beau was skeptical that she was physically capable of accomplishing such a feat, not because he didn't believe her strong or in shape, but simply because the events of the last couple of days, the multiple psychic bleeds and bouts of debilitating headaches had taken their toll.

She wasn't sure she was up to the task, but she was determined to push past any pain or exhaustion and in no way slow them down. She knew it was imperative that they got in and out as quickly as possible, avoiding detection. Ideally they wanted to slip in unnoticed and avoid any potential confrontation. The idea of them engaging the enemy and one of them—any of them, even the men she hadn't met—getting hurt or killed made her sick to her stomach. She didn't want to be responsible for yet more blood and violence. She'd had enough to last a lifetime, and if she never had to face it again, it would be too soon.

They'd all worn dark clothing, blending seamlessly into the night as they moved stealthily to the fire escape behind the building and the entrance to the stairs.

Dane issued a series of hand signals she didn't understand, but evidently his men did. And he must have stationed two men at the back entrance to stand guard and watch for any potential danger because the two men melted away into the darkness, rifles up, handguns at their side.

Dane posted another man at the door leading from the stairwell into the building. He locked it, preventing anyone from entering from the inside, but then took up a post to the side that the door opened up to so he would be obscured and would have the element of surprise.

Ari hadn't been nervous before. She was too excited over the possibility of Ramie being able to locate her parents. She had utter confidence in Ramie and her abilities. But now, as they rapidly ascended the stairs on soft feet, no sound emanating from the specialized military-issue boots that were specifically designed to be soundless, as Beau had explained when he'd laced up the pair he'd slid onto Ari's feet, her nerves began to make themselves known.

Unease skittered up her spine, wrapping around her chest, constricting and squeezing until her heart began to race under the restraint. She inhaled silently through her nose, sucking in deep, silent breaths and letting them out the same way so she risked no sound of her fear escaping her mouth.

She was protectively positioned between Zack in front and Beau behind her with Dane leading the way and Eliza taking position behind Beau, bringing up the rear. The operatives that had taken the other vehicle had been strategically positioned at various points, every angle carefully considered from the eyes of someone wanting to penetrate and gain access to the group.

She knew they would have no care for the men risking their lives to protect her. Their sole focus was *her*. An incessant prayer quickly became a mental chant, repeating in an endless cycle in her mind, as she pleaded with God to protect them all. To side with good so they prevailed over evil.

She prayed that they would be successful and would return—every one of them, not a *single* man sacrificed in their bid to aid her—safe and sound, that they'd encounter no resistance so they could get back to Ramie with haste so that she could attempt a miracle.

Her fingers curled into determined fists as they reached the eighteenth floor and she felt the first sign of fatigue and the beginnings of a burning sensation on the stitched wound on her side. Her ribs, which until now had not given her a single twinge of discomfort after the second day of taking it easy, suddenly made it known that they were in fact bruised and tender and that she was working them way too hard.

She would not slow them down. She would not be the reason for any delay. A delay that could prove fatal.

Gritting her teeth and mentally blocking the pain, she increased her pace, keeping her head bent so no one would be able to see her fatigue and distress. Thank God no one present was psychic and could pick up her thoughts or she'd be totally busted, though Beau did have an uncanny way of picking up on her *slightest* discomfort or worry.

Shit. The warm slide of blood registered but before she could hurriedly wipe it away with the back of her sleeve—thank God it was black—it dripped onto the step below her in a large circle. Worse, it dribbled in a line to the next step. She hastily wiped the blood and then used her cuff to do a more thorough clean so she didn't miss a spot.

She should have known that Beau wouldn't miss it. For once,

could he just not be so damn observant? He should be focused on their objective. Not *her*.

But when he jumped a step so he was no longer behind her but on the same step, keeping pace with her, he reached over, jerking her head around even as they climbed, and stared hard at her features with eyes full of concern.

The only thing working in her favor was the strict need for silence and she could tell it was killing Beau to have to remain quiet and not reprimand her for not schooling her thoughts more. But it was hard when her mind was a veritable beehive of activity. Terror—not only confined to her parents—occupied and consumed her every thought. Particularly when they were sneaking up to her apartment, not knowing if they'd be ambushed at any time. Or what awaited them in her apartment.

Finally they reached her floor and not a moment too soon because Ari was ready to wilt. She was grateful that Dane directed them all to flatten themselves against the wall on the same side as the door and she was granted a short reprieve to catch her breath and try to block the pain.

Dane and Eliza took point, Eliza carefully sliding the keycard into the slot to open her door while Dane stood directly to the right of the door. He would be the first in, Zack directly on his heels and Eliza on his. It was a coordinated entrance with each of them clearing separate areas so there was no possibility of being caught off guard.

When and only when Dane gave the all-clear would Beau come in with Ari. Since the lovies were, fortunately, in her living room on a shelf containing photos and other memorabilia, it meant not having to chance going beyond that room. It would be a quick in and out and then they'd haul ass down the stairs as fast as possible.

Eliza was directly in the middle, in the sight path of Beau, but not Ari, since he had her securely behind him, one arm behind him, wrapped around her slight body, anchoring her to his. His other hand held a wicked-looking handgun and it was up and his entire body was rigid against her, a sign he was at full attention.

When she felt him begin to move forward, still holding her securely to his body, she assumed they'd been giving the all-clear. He stopped inside the door only long enough to put Ari in front of him instead of behind him since there was no longer a chance of danger coming from in front of them, but behind was still a possibility.

"Go get the stuffed animals," Beau whispered. "Be quick. We're remaining at attention and you'll be covered so don't worry about looking around you. Just get the items and then we're getting the hell out of here."

She all but ran across the room to where the large shelving unit was anchored to the wall, and she snatched the two lovies from their places of honor and held them close to her chest, knowing that as silly as it sounded, these two beloved stuffed animals could very well be the key to finding her mother and father.

TWENTY-FIVE

"I don't like this," Zack muttered as they drove back to Beau's home.

Dane was driving, as before, but Eliza was riding shotgun, and Ari was in the middle row seat, Beau and Zack on either side of her.

Maybe it was because from the beginning, Zack had been there. And he'd been kind to her when her welcome by others hadn't been the warmest of introductions. But she felt completely safe and secure with Zack on one side and Beau on the other, although she was more on Beau's side instead of the true "middle," because she was leaned into him, his arm wrapped solidly around her, and her head rested comfortably on his shoulder.

When retrieving the lovies had been met with no obstacles, no barriers, no danger, she'd been elated. As soon as they were back in the vehicle driving away, she'd wanted to do an honest-to-God fist pump. Hope, excitement, a sense of victory . . . faith.

Complete and utter faith in these men—and Ramie, especially Ramie—that they would find her parents and bring them home.

She wanted them to meet Beau. As rigid and hard to please as her father was, she knew Beau would pass muster with him. When he looked at Beau, he'd see a kindred spirit and more important—to her father—he would see a man who would protect Ari with his life, protect her every bit as fiercely as he had.

But Zack's words quickly jolted her back to the grim reality of her situation.

"What's bothering you?" Dane asked, not sounding at all skeptical. His question was calm and it reflected his trust in Zack's instincts.

"It was too easy," Zack said grimly. "I don't buy for a minute that they didn't have every possible place Ari could run to or return to under close surveillance. And yet we were in and out in a matter of minutes and it was so smooth that it immediately made my what-the-fuck alarm start going off and I got a knot in my gut I only get when I *know* something's all wrong."

Ari went rigid against Beau, and he immediately gathered her closer, even as his complete attention was focused on his man. His hand ran up and down her arm in a caress meant to soothe, but it only agitated Ari because now she had a knot in her stomach the size of a softball.

"So the question is why?" Eliza said, half turning in her seat to look at Zack. "Why lay off when they've been balls to the wall in their effort to get to Ari. They have her parents, and the sooner they bring her in, the sooner they can use her parents to manipulate her into doing whatever they want. Because they *know*, just like we all know, that there is nothing Ari wouldn't do to protect her parents."

Ari's mouth popped open at Eliza's very calm, matter-of-fact assessment of Ari's character. She didn't know the other woman. Her association had been limited to only a few minutes here and there and they'd certainly never even spoken directly to each other.

Eliza picked up on Ari's surprise and she smiled warmly at Ari. "Girl, it's obvious how much you love them. It's equally obvious that you're intensely loyal to the people you love. It's not a stretch to think you'd do anything in the world if it meant keeping them safe. I'm a people watcher, Ari. I sit back and I observe. And I pride myself on being absolutely correct in my first impression and my assessment of a person's character. The only thing I see when I look at you is a woman with strong convictions. Perhaps a bit naïve and too trusting. Who sees or rather *chooses* to see only the good in people. And when it comes to the people you love, you can be a fierce badass, powers or no."

Heat crept into Ari's cheeks and she ducked her head, flattered and a little floored by the admiration she heard in the other woman's recitation of her impression of Ari. Well, and she was one hundred percent accurate. So what could Ari say? Thank you? It seemed an absurd response given the woman wasn't giving her a compliment but rather a simple report on her assessment.

But she did lift her head and gift Eliza with a smile and a nod of acknowledgment.

Beau's arm tightened around her, and he smiled at her obvious befuddlement. He leaned in close to her ear, so only she would hear.

"She's right you know. She only left out a few things. Like how beautiful you are when your eyes are glazed with passion.

How perfect your breasts and the ultra-soft petals that surround your pussy opening. A pussy that belongs to me. Do you know what it does to me to know that I'm the only man who's ever touched you deep inside your body? That I and only I am the one you gave such a very precious gift to?".

She blushed to the roots of her hair, heat singeing her cheeks and neck. God, she hoped no one was looking her way at this very moment, because they'd know exactly the kinds of things Beau was whispering in her ear.

Damn the fact that her face always broadcasted her thoughts, her feelings, her mood and her emotions. She was, for all practical purposes, a walking billboard.

She elbowed him fiercely in the ribs even if she was absurdly thrilled with his words. "Stop it," she hissed. "You're embarrassing me!"

He chuckled low. "Later, I'll show you. Remind you with my body instead of my words."

Her breathing sped up and heat traveled to other parts of her body, most especially her breasts, now heavy and aching, and between her legs where her clit pulsed and throbbed painfully.

"You are so going to pay for this," she vowed.

His grin was slow and an example of pure male arrogance and utter satisfaction. "I look forward to every minute of your revenge."

She breathed an audible sigh of relief when they pulled into the driveway of Beau's home. Her thoughts immediately shifted and focused on the two lovies in her lap. She absently stroked the tattered and worn fur. They showed their age, but she'd always taken care to ensure they didn't fall apart. They simply meant too much to her. Why she connected so deeply to these two items when she was a mere baby she never knew. But even now, when she saw them, touched them or even just thought about them, she was filled with instant warmth and love.

She scrambled out of the vehicle on Zack's side since he was the first out, ignoring Beau's outstretched hand to assist her out. She was simmering with impatience, eager to get the objects to Ramie as quickly as possible so she could glean whatever information she was able.

She set a brisk pace, even keeping up with Dane's long, determined stride, leaving the others to follow. Beau didn't bother issuing a protest, because he had to know how important this was to her. To finally take a proactive step in finding her parents.

Excitement burst over her when she saw Ramie and Caleb in the living room, obviously waiting, and they'd likely received a call to let them know they were on their way back. Caleb looked ill, sick with worry, and while Ari sympathized with him, understood his reluctance and even shared it to a degree, she wasn't hypocritical enough to be truly regretful over what this could well do to Ramie.

She prayed that it wouldn't be horrifying for her because that meant her parents were undergoing the same horror. She hoped with all her heart that they'd incurred no injury since they were essentially bargaining tools for a higher purpose.

Ari walked over to Ramie, standing back a short distance to give the other woman space. Then she held up the stuffed animals that had been lovingly cradled in her arms.

"These have been handled by both my parents for many years. Their imprint, aura, or whatever you want to call it, should be all over it, as well as mine. What do you need me to do? Is there any way I can help?"

When it looked as though Caleb would respond, Ramie silenced him with a mere look. His lips settled into a grim line but he sat back and remained quiet.

"I usually prefer to do this away from others," Ramie said softly. "It can be bad. Horrifying even. But in this case, I think everyone needs to be present. Sometimes I say things that come from the victims, things I don't always remember. Or perhaps there is an action that I mimic that you would recognize. The things I may say may make more sense to you than to anyone else. All I ask for is space. Don't crowd me. And above all else, do not interfere in any way, no matter what happens. It can be very dangerous to me if anyone does anything other than observe."

Ari nodded vigorously. "Whatever you want. Whatever you need. I won't interfere. I swear."

Ramie looked to the others, her gaze bypassing Dane and Eliza as though they were well acquainted with the process, but it settled on Beau and then Zack, lingering as though she were gaining their promise as well.

"I'll stay with Ari," Beau said quietly.

Zack merely acknowledged Ramie's request with a nod and then took position on the far side of the room where he had a clear line of sight and was still within hearing distance but was well enough away that there was no way he would be a nuisance.

Ramie took a deep breath. "Okay then. Please give the toys to Caleb. I prefer for him to be the one who gives them to me. Then back away to give me several feet of space, and again, remain completely silent and don't do anything that could possibly distract me."

Ari nervously held out the animals to Caleb, her hands shaking slightly, her gaze refusing to meet his.

To her surprise, Caleb didn't merely pluck the animals from her grasp. Instead he curled his hand around hers and gave her a gentle squeeze. "I hate that I've made you afraid of me," he said in a low, regret-filled tone. "I swear to you I'm not the person I showed you that day. I fully admit that I tend to get irrational when it comes to my wife."

Ramie issued a snort that caused Caleb to shoot her a dark scowl. She merely laughed in response.

"I hope you'll accept my apology, Ari. And for what it's worth, I hope that Ramie will be able to help you find your parents."

"Thank you," Ari said sincerely. "I hope so too."

He let go of her hand and she backed away several feet to give Ramie the space she'd requested. Beau's arm immediately went around her for support, giving her shoulders a squeeze.

Ramie took a deep breath and then reached for the toys Caleb held in his hands. He slowly extended them, placing one in each of her hands at the exact same time. For a moment she simply stared down at them, and then her eyelids flickered erratically and when she reopened her eyes, it was an eerie thing indeed.

It was almost as if her eyes changed color. Her pupils were enormous and her stare was vacant as if she had no knowledge of her current surroundings. She immediately began to rock back and forth as if in great distress. Caleb looked as though it were killing him not to be able to pull his wife into his arms and comfort her. But he adhered to the "rules" and sat there, his jaw rigid.

"How can we do this?" Ramie asked, a tearful voice that wasn't her own.

"How can we not," she said, this time clearly speaking from a different person's point of view.

"Look at her. She's beautiful. So innocent. How can we simply abandon her?"

"Because we don't have the means to protect her. Franklin Devereaux has promised to help us. He knows someone. Someone who can protect our baby. It's our only choice to have a normal life. You know if they take her back, she'll be treated like an animal. Caged, poked at, prodded, forced to do God only knows what. We can't allow that to happen."

At the mention of Franklin Devereaux both Caleb and Beau froze. They stared at one another, their eyes glittering. Beau had even dropped his arm from Ari, seeming to forget all about her for one brief moment.

"What did she say?" Caleb whispered in a choked voice.

Beau held a finger to his lips. He hadn't wanted this to come out, damn it. Hadn't wanted to give Caleb even more reason to despise or disdain Ari. He raked a hand through his hair, wishing to hell that that particular piece of information hadn't come through Ramie's connection. A connection that evidently extended beyond Ari's adopted parents. But it made sense if the stuffed animals were left with Ari, items her birth parents had provided for her.

Then Ramie hunched over, shaking violently, her lips actually blue as though she were exposed to freezing temperatures.

"It's so cold," she said in the feminine voice of the first person she'd transmitted from. "What if she freezes to death? We can't leave her here! What if they don't even want her?"

"They'll want her." There was certainty in the voice Ramie now spoke in. "Franklin told me Ginger Rochester has suffered countless miscarriages and all evidence points to her being unable to have a child. Our daughter will be the blessing to them that she deserves. She'll never want for anything. And most importantly, she'll be safe."

Ari let out a choked cry, unable to comprehend what she was hearing. She slid to her knees, her legs no longer able to bear her weight. She buried her face in her hands as the implications of what Ramie was experiencing—saying—hit her hard, denial sharp and instant. She shook her head irrationally, shutting out the voices. It was a mistake. It couldn't be true. Ramie was *wrong*.

Beau sank down beside her, and though his face was a wreath of regret, he didn't seem surprised. Even amid her confusion and heartbreak, that fact registered. Just how much had he kept from her?

He tried to comfort her, wrapping his arms around her, pulling her into his arms, but Ari fought him off, nearly hysterical. She didn't want to be touched. Didn't want to be comforted. There *was* no comfort, no salve, no bandage big enough to ever cover this wound.

"Goodbye, my love," Ramie whispered. She mimicked holding an infant in her arms and kissing the air where a child's head would be.

There was brief silence, though Ramie remained as if in a distant place, not here, lost in some other time, captive to the secrets the stuffed animals were relating.

"Oh dear God, Gavin! Someone left a baby out here to *freeze*?"

Ari went utterly motionless as Ramie's voice changed once

more to one that so eerily resembled her mother's that it sent chill bumps racing over her entire body. Instant cold settled into her bones. Dread had invaded her heart as it was confirmed—through Ramie—that the unthinkable . . . was *true*. No. No! It *couldn't* be. She was loved, not unwanted and abandoned by the people who'd given birth to her.

Ari's entire life was a lie. She was well and truly alone. Adrift. Utterly lost.

She encased herself in an icy bubble, surrounding herself, hoping to shut out the truth. The reality. But she could still hear Ramie's haunting voice, now her *father's*.

"We're leaving the country and we'll be gone for a while."

And then her mother's again, only *not* her mother. "What are we going to do, Gavin?"

Ramie's voice became gruff, just like when her father was serious, implacable. And decisive. "We're going to do as we were asked and raise her as our daughter."

Ramie went silent, her eyes flickering in rapid-fire succession as if processing at the speed of a computer. Her hands curled and uncurled in her lap as if in agitation. She was clearly not here, still firmly ensconced in the past. But what about the present?

Not matter that Ari's entire world had been turned upside down in the space of a few minutes, she still loved her . . . parents. Or whoever they were. She wanted them safe now more than ever because she wanted answers. She wanted the truth! A truth she should have been given when she reached an age where she would be able to understand. And coming from her adoptive parents, the information wouldn't have been so shocking because she could have been privy to their motives. Whether they truly wanted her or if they just couldn't bear the thought of an orphan child being taken into child protective services and shuffled through the system, never truly having a stable home and people she could rely on.

She needed that reassurance and it could only come from them. No one else. If she'd been desperate to save them before, that desperation had multiplied tenfold. Because if they died before she could have answers to the questions that swirled in her mind at supersonic speed, making her dizzy and light-headed, her life would forever be incomplete. An important part of herself would always be out of reach. How could she expect Beau to accept her when even she didn't know who she was anymore?

She'd been fully aware that her father hadn't always been on the straight and narrow, that he had a murky, questionable past, but that when her mother swept into his life, his future had been irrevocably altered and he'd made a concerted effort to be the man she deserved.

But now, for the first time, she questioned whether he'd truly left his old life behind. Whether the "good" man she'd always considered her father to be was yet another lie in an ever growing list of lies and untruths. Lies of omission were even worse than outright lies in Ari's opinion. Because lies of omission were blatant attempts to *hide* the truth. To keep a person from ever *discovering* the truth. It was sheer manipulation and it wasn't honorable, nor did it speak to a person's integrity.

It hurt to think that a man Ari had always looked up to, idolized and worshipped, was capable of such deception. Because now she was forced to question every other aspect of her past. What else had he kept from her? What else had he outright lied to her about? Was it all a lie? Every part of her existence?

Through the fog of her grief and utter despair, she saw

Ramie suddenly sag, listing in the opposite direction from Caleb. He immediately made a grab for her though his hands were infinitely gentle. He guided her back toward him and then simply pulled her onto his lap, cradling her tenderly, his lips pressed against her brow.

There was profound relief in his eyes that she hadn't endured the unthinkable. But Ari was sick with worry. What did it *mean* that she seemed to only see the *past*?

Ari couldn't stand. Her legs were so rubbery and she was so utterly devastated that her strength was completely gone. So she half crawled, half dragged her numb extremities toward the couch where Ramie lay in Caleb's arms, awake but drowsy and lethargic.

Apology was in Ari's eyes and on her face as she met Caleb's gaze. Once again he surprised her because she was met with tenderness and sympathy.

"I know she's tired. I know what a toll this takes on her. But please. I need to talk to her before she goes under. I have to know."

Ramie stirred and directed her cloudy gaze at Ari. "I'm okay, Ari. Much better than the other times. I'm only tired because of the mental strain of maintaining links, in this case, four separate entities. I'll try to answer your questions if I know the answer. Just be patient with me. I'm a bit slow when I come out of a session and my thoughts are unfocused."

"You trying is all I ask," Ari murmured

She leaned her elbows on Caleb's knees, hoping he didn't mind the extra burden, but it was the only way Ari herself would be able to support herself and keep from sliding to the floor in a useless heap.

"Everything you talked about was in the past. A long time in the past," Ari said hoarsely. "But what about now? Did you pick up on anything that would help us find them?"

Sorry and apology swamped Ramie's eyes. She weakly reached for Ari's hand and drew it into her grasp, squeezing in a show of comfort and support.

"Nothing," Ramie admitted. "I'm so sorry, Ari. I would have gladly endured *anything* if it helped you. The impressions I did get were *strong*, despite the events being from years ago. There were flashes after the passages I related aloud. But they were random. You as a baby. Then as a toddler. A young girl. A preteen and then a teenager blossoming into a woman. The lovies, as you call them, were like silent observers of events that transpired over the years. Almost like a history, the history of you and your family. They are very special items. I hope you can keep them for many years to come."

Ari rocked back on her heels, wrenching her arms from Caleb's legs, not wanting anyone to touch her, to see her, to witness the horrible, gut-wrenching agony that consumed her. It was all for nothing. Instead of being able to find her "parents" and bring them home safely, all she'd received was life-altering news that flayed her heart open, leaving it bleeding.

"No!" she cried out, shaking her head, refusing the truth that stared her right in the eye.

She stumbled upward, weaving, unsteady, again warding off Beau's hands when he tried to help her. He backed off, at least giving her that. She couldn't bear to be touched. She felt dirty. Rejected. *Unworthy*. When for her entire life she'd felt assured of her place in the world. Assured of her parents' love. She felt . . . betrayed . . . in the worst possible manner. The kind that went soul deep and ripped her to shreds, leaving her with . . . nothing.

And no one.

The sudden feeling of being utterly alone in an unfamiliar, dark and cold world, where she had no safe harbor and nothing was as it seemed, filled her with despair to her very soul. In a single moment, she'd been stripped of everything. And she no longer even knew *who* she was.

TWENTY-SIX

BEAU watched helplessly as Ari fell apart right in front of his eyes. And there wasn't a damn thing he could do to help her. No one could. Some hurts—betrayals—were simply too deep. Unable to be forgotten, forgiven or even understood.

"No," Ari said again, the sound of a wounded animal.

She wrapped her arms protectively around herself as if somehow she could shield herself from the painful truth. She bent over, pain rippling across her face, the objects in the room reacting to the obvious devastation in her mind.

Objects, even large pieces of furniture, vibrated as though an earthquake were occurring. A lamp fell over, shattering, the sound cracking sharply in the otherwise silent room.

"I was *not* unloved," she said brokenly. "I was *not* abandoned. I was *not* left to die in the cold, at the mercy of someone who may or may not find me on their doorstep."

Tears streamed unchecked down her cheeks, her eyes so utterly desolate that Beau's throat swelled with emotion and his eyes stung with answering tears. Not a single person in the room was unaffected by Ari's grief.

Eliza turned her face away, but not before Beau saw her wiping her own cheeks. Sympathy brimmed in Dane's eyes and he shifted, shoving his hands in his pockets, clearly at a loss as to what to say or do, and just as uncomfortable witnessing Ari's complete breakdown.

There was a bleak expression on Zack's face, his eyes desolate and far away as if remembering something equally painful.

Tears slid down Ramie's face and she shook off Caleb's comforting hold, no doubt thinking that she wasn't the one most in need.

Every time Beau tried to get near Ari, to touch her, simply hold her and be her rock, let her cry in his arms and on his shoulders, she reacted violently, almost as if she feared her taint would somehow spread to him.

He swore low and viciously, in that moment hating his father, Gavin Rochester and the bastards currently making Ari's life hell. She'd been manipulated at birth. How could they have done it? From what he could glean from the bits of information, dialogue that Ramie had repeated in her stupor, it would seem that Ari was little more than a transaction.

A pacification offered to Gavin and Ginger Rochester to ease their devastating losses. A token baby, as if any child would do, and Ari had just happened to be a convenient solution for everyone.

Why were her birth parents so adamant that they couldn't keep Ari? And what the ever-loving fuck did his father have to do with any of it? Was it possible that he'd truly "sent" Ari to Gavin? Did he owe Gavin in some way? And was it why Gavin had told Ari to seek out Caleb or Beau Devereaux if she was ever in need? Almost as if he'd been preparing for the eventuality.

The fact that Gavin had been the last person to see Franklin Devereaux alive, given the new information that had just come to light, made Beau more convinced than ever that Ari's adopted father had something to do with his father's death. Directly, indirectly. Who knew?

He doubted Gavin was the type of man to do the job himself. Not when he had plenty of hired muscle and bought loyalty. For the right price, one could have loyalty from damn near anyone.

Ramie rose from the couch, shaky, unsteady, Caleb's hand flying out in case she fell, but she falteringly made her way over to where Ari was hunched over, arms solidly around her middle, her sobs heartbreaking to hear.

Ramie lightly touched Ari's back and then when Ari didn't protest the gesture, Ramie gently pulled her into a hug. Ari buried her face in the other woman's shoulder, her entire body heaving with the force of her sobs.

"I'm so sorry, Ari," Ramie said, regret lining every word. "But, honey, listen to me. Look at me, Ari," she said in a firmer voice.

Ramie waited, patient, understanding, until finally Ari lifted tear-drenched eyes to meet the other woman's gaze. Beau's stomach clenched at the raw agony so very evident in Ari's face and expressive eyes.

"You *were* loved. Absolutely. Unwaveringly. Unconditionally. *That* is the truth. You were loved from the very moment Gavin and Ginger Rochester found you on their doorstep. They took great precautions to ensure that you would never be taken from them. That you would be able to lead a normal life. Of course that changed with the discovery of your abilities, but that only made them more determined to give you everything that was within their power."

Tears slid faster down Ari's face, glimmering brightly in her eyes, making them even more vibrant than usual. Electric. Nearly neon.

"And here is another truth, Ari," Ramie said softly. "One I want you to listen to and pay heed to. Because it *is* the truth. I would not lie about something so important, nor would I offer you token words just to comfort you when you're clearly devastated. You were dearly loved by your *birth* parents as well."

Ari automatically shook her head in denial, her eyes going cloudy with hurt once more.

Ramie sent her a fierce look. "I was there, Ari. I felt everything they felt. I knew everything they knew. Do you doubt my powers? Do you think that somehow this would be the only instance in my entire life where I'm wrong?"

"Then why?" Ari choked out. "I don't understand *why*."

"Because the same people who are after you now were after you even then. And your parents were terrified. Always on the run. With your mother pregnant, it wasn't as easy for them to hide. To disguise themselves. They were constantly looking over their shoulder, fearing the worst. And then you were born, and they loved you so very much. Thought you were a miracle. Something good and special in the midst of evil. They tried to keep you—wanted to keep you. But the people after you caught up to them. They escaped through sheer dumb luck and someone being in the right place at the right time. And that was when they knew they couldn't continue like this. That it was no way to raise a child. That your life would be hell. You'd never have the things children need the most. Stability. A home. Security. To be able to go to school, have friends, play sports or take up ballet."

Ramie paused, clearly exhausted by her ordeal, but she seemed determined to get through to Ari before she succumbed to the mental—and physical—toll it took on her.

"They wanted you to have all that. So they went to someone they thought would help them. Perhaps even take you in themselves. Caleb and Beau's parents, Franklin and Missy Devereaux."

Caleb and Beau flinched and Beau curled his hands into tight balls wondering at the staggering coincidence that he was tied to Ari and her family in more ways than just his love for her. Any doubt that the call from her "birth father" had been a hoax fell away as Ramie's words hit him squarely in the chest.

Ramie sent Caleb and Beau a grimacing look of sorrow. "You may not want to hear this. Ari and I can continue in private."

Beau surged forward, as did Caleb, standing from the couch. Whether intentional or not, the two brothers stood a mere foot apart, in solidarity.

Caleb spoke before Beau could muster a reply.

"There is nothing you can say about my father—or mother— that will shock either of us. We're well acquainted with exactly who and what they are—and what they weren't," he said in an icy voice.

Beau merely nodded, unable to add anything more that Caleb hadn't succinctly stated himself.

Ramie sighed and turned back to Ari. "Franklin complained to your birth father that he already had three brats and his stupid wife had gotten herself knocked up again—that they'd just discovered that fact a mere week earlier, and he couldn't possibly take on another child when he could barely tolerate the three he had with a fourth now on the way."

Even knowing what a complete bastard his father was, Beau couldn't control the flinch of hearing his father's words spoken baldly.

"It was then that he recommended Gavin Rochester, saying he was a business associate and as luck would have it, he and his wife were desperate to have a baby, but had thus far been unsuccessful. He even provided money and the use of his private jet so their movements wouldn't be traceable."

Ramie cupped Ari's damp face in her palms, forcing Ari to look at her.

"Ari, I want you to listen to me. I *need* you to hear this."

Ari blinked and then trained her unfocused stare at Ramie, blinking to clear away some of the obvious confusion.

"Your mother and father—your real mother and father—and by that I mean the people who raised you as your daughter, who loved you and protected you your entire life, didn't know about any of what transpired between your birth parents and their pursuers nor did they have any idea of Franklin Devereaux's involvement and the fact that he in effect sent you to them until two years after they adopted you.

"They answered a doorbell on a snowy Christmas night and found . . . you. A beautiful little angel girl. And a note. Begging them to take you in and raise you as their own. That they were unable to provide for you and that you would always be in danger. Gavin and Ginger loved you instantly. And so Gavin took you and his wife out of the country where he began a systematic paper trail that documented a pregnancy, your delivery in a foreign country and your subsequent return to the United States.

"He sold off everything he owned prior to you, except one oil company, here in Houston. And they moved here, to begin their lives with you. That is the truth and the only one that matters. You were loved. You were wanted. You matter."

Ari slipped her arms around Ramie this time and fiercely hugged the other woman. "Thank you," Ari whispered. "You can't know what that means to me."

"I can well imagine," Ramie said softly.

Ramie cast Beau a look, her eyes softening as she took Ari's hand in hers, twining their fingers tightly. Then she held out Ari's hand in Beau's direction before looking back at Ari.

"I think there is someone who would very much like to hold you right now. This has been hard on him too, Ari. He found out some very difficult information as well. You should lean on each other."

Beau watched the myriad of emotions flash across Ari's face as she looked up at Beau. Then with an inarticulate cry, she ran across the room and threw herself into his outstretched arms, wrapping her own around his waist and hugging him for dear life.

"I'm sorry," she whispered brokenly. "I'm so sorry, Beau. You didn't deserve how I treated you. You're the last person who deserved it. Please forgive me. You are the only one true thing in my life right now. The only person I have complete faith in. The only person I trust. Please, please don't be angry with me."

He gathered her to him, crushing her, holding as tightly as he dared without breaking her bones. He buried his face in her sweet-smelling hair and simply held her in silence, his chest heaving with unshed emotion.

He wouldn't break down. Not here. Not in front of the others. Not when Ari desperately needed him to be strong for her.

When he finally pulled back, he framed her beautiful face and stared intently into her eyes, drowning, losing his very soul in her. He never wanted to be found. He was lost in her and he planned to stay lost for the rest of his life.

He kissed her. Just a gentle brush, the tenderest of kisses. Meant to comfort, soothe and reassure her that he was here. He was real. Solid. And he wasn't going anywhere.

She leaned her forehead in, resting it against the hollow of his throat so that his chin rested atop her silky hair. He could feel the fatigue emanating from her in waves. Knew she'd reached her absolute breaking point.

He reached down and gathered her hands in his. "Let's go to bed, honey. Tomorrow we'll launch a full-scale attack. We'll draw the fuckers to us and then we'll extract the information we need no matter what it takes."

She shivered against him, and he knew that she was imagining the implications of his words. But she didn't react in horror or disgust. She simply drew her head away and looked up at him as if he was her entire world. And damn it, he wanted to be. When all of this was over, he was going to pour out his entire goddamn heart. He was going to cut it out of his chest and lay it before her. Make himself completely vulnerable to her and bare his very soul.

He could only hope that when he did that she wouldn't reject the only gifts he had to give her. His heart. His soul. His body.

His love.

TWENTY-SEVEN

BEAU sat straight up in bed, Ari literally falling from his arms back onto the mattress below. She murmured a sleepy protest but promptly snuggled into the pillow, never once opening her eyes.

"What the fuck?" Beau demanded, blinking his eyes as the room was suddenly flooded with light.

When he could see, Zack was standing there, rifle over one shoulder, two pistols in a shoulder holster, several flash bangs as well as grenades circling his waist. Another gun was strapped to the inside of his thigh, while the other leg had one strapped on the outside of his thigh so the pistols didn't bang against each other when he walked. If that weren't enough, he had at least three knives strapped at convenient, easily accessible areas on his body and yet another, smaller pistol secured around his ankle. He looked like he was fucking going to war.

Beau was instantly alert, out of bed before Zack could even open his mouth.

"Sitrep," Beau barked, already reaching for his own arsenal. He didn't reach for a shirt yet, only pausing long enough to pull on fatigues that were specially designed for *his* weapon preferences. He quickly secured a Kevlar vest around his torso and then yanked a black long-sleeved shirt that was invisible at night.

"They're coming at us on our own turf. They're mounting a major assault. They've already breached the perimeter and are just past outlying security and moving fast. I've already alerted the others but you need to get Ari to the safe room. Caleb is bringing Ramie there now."

"Fuck!"

After securing all his weapons and adding some perfectly illegal C4 to one of the pouches on his fatigues in easy reach, he ran to the bed, not even bothering to wake Ari up or even try to explain the situation. Time was of the essence and his first priority was to ensure her safety.

He hauled her up more roughly than he'd like and Zack preceded him from the room, providing cover, though by all accounts, the intruders were still at least four minutes out. Four very precious minutes in which they had to stash the women and decide the best course of defense.

"Beau?" Ari asked in a sleepy puzzled voice.

"Shhh, honey. I don't have time to explain. Just trust me."

To her credit she went utterly still, though he could see the instant fright in her eyes. She closed her mouth, though he knew it had to be hard for her to just blindly accept his dictate without having at least a hint of what was happening.

He hit the hallway at a full run, covering the distance to the safe room in record time, even bearing Ari's slight weight. Zack got there first, punched in the security code so the door swooshed open just as Beau arrived and rushed through the door.

Ramie was already there, huddled in one of the chairs, looking utterly terrified, eyes wide, all color leached from her face. But when she saw Ari, she seemed relieved not to be alone any longer.

Beau deposited Ari into the chair next to Ramie and then swiftly went to the gun cabinet housed inside the safe room. He grabbed four handguns and two extra clips for each, in addition to the clips already loaded in the pistols.

He thrust two in Ramie's direction, ensuring she had a firm grip before he relinquished his. Then he did the same with Ari. A bewildered look crossed her face as she stared at the gun as though it were a completely alien object.

He cursed under his breath. She'd obviously never so much as touched a gun, which surprised him given her father's overzealousness when it came to personal protection. He'd assumed when she'd so calmly taken the gun from Brent that very first day and climbed out of the wrecked vehicle and then later tossed it to him that she had knowledge of weapons. Now he realized she'd just acted on instinct, her driving force to protect others.

"Listen to me, Ari," Beau said in a tone that brooked no interruption. "This is a Glock. It doesn't have a safety so be damn careful about where you point it and keep your finger off the trigger unless you intend to shoot. If anyone and I mean *anyone* but one of us manages to gain access to this room, you just point and shoot and you keep shooting until you take the fucker out. Understand?"

He turned to Ramie to ensure she'd heard his curt instruction. She nodded her acknowledgment.

"Let's go," Beau barked at Zack. "Give me the rundown on where the others are and what positions they've taken and if we have any backup that will arrive in time to do us any good."

TWENTY-EIGHT

"WHAT'S happening, Ramie?" Ari asked.

Terror had its unyielding grip around her neck, nearly choking her. She could barely draw breath and had to concentrate on every single inhale and exhale so she didn't do something really stupid like faint.

"I don't know," Ramie said faintly, her eyes reflecting the same terror Ari felt. "We're under attack. Caleb didn't say more. There wasn't time. He dumped me here and ran."

"How safe are we here?" Ari asked fearfully.

"I don't know all of the logistics," Ramie admitted. "I do know it would take a bigger than normal dose of explosives to penetrate the door. The walls are triple-layered, reinforced steel, the middle being bulletproof and blastproof. But it's never been tested. I always thought it overly paranoid for them to have a room like this, but right now I'm pretty damn grateful for it."

Ari nodded her fervent agreement. And then voiced her other paralyzing fear.

"What about . . . them . . . though?" she asked in a shaky voice. "How do we know what's happening? What if something happens to them? Why would they lock me in here when I could be of great use to them?"

Ramie looked down at the guns, her hands trembling, and she repositioned her finger so it was nowhere near the trigger. "Beau would never put you in the line of fire. It doesn't matter what you can or can't do. They're trained for this. You aren't. You would be a distraction, because Beau—all of them—would be more worried about you than protecting themselves and taking out any potential threat."

"God, I hate just sitting here. Completely helpless," Ari said fiercely.

"I know," Ramie agreed in a low, trembling voice. "I'm scared too, Ari. I'm petrified. I don't want to lose Caleb."

Pain slashed wickedly through Ari's chest and she was momentarily incapable of breathing. "They can't die," she said fiercely, when she regained the ability to speak. "They can't. They won't. They have to come back to us. They *will* come back to us. We can't allow ourselves to entertain any other possibility."

Silence fell between the two women as they both sat in contemplation, each tortured by their thoughts as they imagined everything that could go wrong.

Ari watched the digital clock on the wall, each minute changing seemingly in hours, not sixty seconds. The time dragged into eternity until Ari was on the verge of going mad with worry, fear and uncertainty. What was going on out there? Was Beau lying out there injured? Unable to protect himself?

She closed her eyes, biting hard into her lip, the next logical step in her stairway to doom hovering on the fringes of her mind.

Was he even alive?

Oh God, she couldn't do this. She couldn't simply sit still. The silence, the walls that seemed to close in around her, making the room smaller and smaller until she felt as though she'd suffocate. She was going to go crazy.

She carefully laid the guns aside and then dug her palms into her eyes, pressing inward, rocking back and forth as a vile ache began in her head.

"Ari, are you okay?" Ramie asked anxiously, breaking the silence for the first time in what seemed like hours.

Ari glanced at the clock to see, that in actuality, fifty-three minutes had elapsed. A lifetime. That had to be bad, right? If they'd gone out, kicked ass and eliminated the bad guys, they should be back by now, shouldn't they?

Bullets were fast and efficient.

The room shook curiously and for a moment, Ari thought it was just her reaction to the claustrophobic sensation that was becoming more prevalent by the minute. Ramie must have felt it too, because her gaze immediately flew to the door and Ari's breath caught.

Were they back? Were they coming in? Or was someone who shouldn't be trying to gain access to the door? Maybe the room vibrated when an incorrect code has been entered. If an explosive had been attempted, they would have certainly felt more than the subtle vibration they felt.

"What was that?" Ari whispered.

"I don't know," Ramie whispered back. "Do you still hear it? I don't."

Ari strained her ears, wondering if they'd both imagined it, but surely they wouldn't have both had the same delusion.

And suddenly a deafening explosion sounded, a light flashing that was so blinding that Ari was rendered just that. Blind. The force of the explosion hurled her across the room and she hit the wall with a resounding thud before sliding slowly down to a sagging, sitting position on the floor, only remaining upright because the wall was propping her up.

She couldn't see or hear a damn thing. Her mind was in utter chaos and it had nothing to do with her powers, not that she could focus enough to use them, nor would she know how to direct them at an unseen attacker when she was utterly blinded. What the hell had just happened and how?

The door hadn't opened. She and Ramie had both been staring at it when the explosion occurred.

Rough hands hauled her up, and she knew instantly that this was not Beau. Nor was it someone who was in any way protecting her. Fear and adrenaline jolted through her body, giving her a much-needed boost to ward off the effects of the stunning explosive.

Ramie cried out, a shrill sound of fear.

"Ramie!" Ari shouted. "Are you all right?"

A hand clamped over her mouth and a rough voice whispered next to her ear. "Shut up and keep quiet and listen up or your friend will suffer a very unpleasant death."

Ari went completely still, terror forming ice in her veins. If the intruders had somehow gained access to the safe room, it meant they'd gone through the DSS operatives. No way, if Beau was alive, would he fail to protect her. Tears burned her eyelids and trailed down her cheeks, colliding with the hand still clamped over her mouth.

"Now, here's how it's going to play out," he said against her ear that was still ringing from the deafening explosion. She realized with sudden clarity that he was, in fact, shouting the words.

"We only want you. We have no need for the others, nor do we want to kill unnecessarily, unless you force our hand."

Her heart pounded furiously. Did that mean Beau and the others weren't dead?

"You have two choices. You leave quietly with us, or we kill everyone, beginning with the female you're currently sharing quarters with. Right now, my men are merely delaying the others, waiting for your extrication. So it's up to you. You refuse and I issue the order to kill everyone and we still take you, so your fate is inevitable. It's just a matter of whether you want to spare some lives in the process."

"I'll go," she croaked. "Don't kill them. I'll go. I'll cooperate. I swear. Just please don't hurt her and don't kill the others."

Her vision had started to clear just enough to bring her fuzzy surroundings into focus. It was then she saw how the safe room had been breached. Through the roof, into the attic and then a wide hole, large enough for two people to fit through easily, had been cut out.

She instinctively jumped, startled when a drop-down ladder fell through the hole and into the room. She glanced Ramie's way, wondering if the woman had heard the bargain Ari had just made for her life. For all their lives.

Judging by the tears in her eyes and the way she stared helplessly at Ari, she drew her own conclusion that Ramie was well aware of what was going on. She was being held in the not so gentle grasp of another man who looked military. Like a killer. His eyes were dead and cold. Like little mattered to him. She shivered, knowing that had she not complied with their wishes, they wouldn't have hesitated to murder Ramie right in front of her.

She sent Ramie a look, a plea to understand. The man holding her maneuvered over to where the ladder dangled and Ari's stomach plunged at the idea of having to climb the damn thing.

She needn't have worried. She felt a sudden sting, like that of a wasp, in her neck and the room went even fuzzier. The last thing she registered were the tears streaking down Ramie's face, and her utter look of devastation.

TWENTY-NINE

ADORNED with night vision goggles, protective gear and enough firepower to rival a small country's military, Beau and Zack sprinted across the courtyard clearing, keeping low so they didn't present an easy target.

They needed to catch up with the others fast because they stood a hell of a lot better chance of taking down the intruders together than if they were scattered over the entire perimeter.

Suddenly Dane and Eliza emerged from the shadows, blending seamlessly into the night. With a nod in Beau's direction, Dane spoke quietly into his mic and instructed the others of their coordinates so they could group up and blow the hell out of everyone who didn't belong here.

In a matter of seconds, they were joined by the remaining men, Caleb, Isaac and Capshaw, and they moved out, separating just enough that they didn't present an easy target for someone seeking to take them out with a single blast.

There was a drop-off halfway between the house and the heavily wooded area surrounding the property on all sides. Here, the ground sloped sharply downward before leveling off again the farther they got from the house.

Beau was heading the group and was so focused on his immediate surroundings and keeping a watchful eye toward the woods and any other potential ambush spot that he tripped over something large and bulky, nearly sprawling to the ground.

What the fuck? That felt like . . . a *body*.

Beau scrambled for his footing before backing away and motioning the others to do the same. Zack and Dane leveled their weapons at the downed figure while Beau moved in closer.

The man lay perfectly still, no detectable respirations. Eliza knelt beside Beau and quickly shone her small flashlight over the man's face and Beau recoiled. Holy hell. The man had been beaten to death.

"Shit," Eliza breathed. "I've never seen anyone beaten this badly. Who the hell do you think it is?"

To their complete and utter shock, the man's lips moved the barest of centimeters. But enough for them to realize he was alive. The entire group exchanged baffled looks. How someone this badly beaten was even semiconscious was flabbergasting.

"Ari," the man said with a gasp, wincing in pain at just the one word that whispered past his lips.

Beau surged to attention and leaned down to stare in the man's battered, swollen and bloodied face. God, he was utterly unrecognizable as a human being. He looked more a monster than a man.

"What about Ari?" Beau demanded. "What happened to you? Who did this to you? And what do you know about Ari?"

"Daughter," he rasped out.

A chill went up Beau's spine and he glanced back at the others in disbelief.

"Need . . . you . . . tell something."

His voice was growing weaker by the second and Beau had to lean even farther down to hear what he was saying.

The man's hand fluttered weakly upward, flailing, as if reaching for something to anchor himself with. Beau's response was automatic. No matter who this man was or what he had done, no one deserved to be savaged this way.

Once Beau's hand gripped his, his fingers tightened around Beau's and his eyes slitted open, determination flagging in their depths.

"Tell Ari . . . I loved her. Mother loved too . . ." His voice trailed off and he suddenly choked and then coughed convulsively, blood dribbling profusely from his mouth.

Oh man, this was bad. This was really bad. There was no way an ambulance would reach him in time. And they had to take out the threat to Ramie and Ari as well as to themselves.

"P-p-promise me," he stuttered, blood bubbling and foaming down his chin. "Loved her always. Tell her. Never forgot her. Wanted her to be . . . happy. Have . . . good life."

Ari's biological father closed his eyes and sagged heavily, seeming to wilt right into the ground. Beau followed him down so their faces weren't far apart and so he could hear Beau's vow.

"I promise," he said, still gripping the man's hand. "Do you hear me? I swear I'll give her your message. Rest easy now."

His eyes opened one last time and then a peaceful smile settled over his face, softening some of the brutality wrought by extreme violence.

"Thank you," he whispered. "Means the world."

And then his head lolled to the side and his hand went completely slack in Beau's grasp.

"Son of a bitch," Beau swore. "These people are animals and they want Ari!"

"Easy, brother," Caleb said, putting his hand on Beau's shoulder. "We'll just have to make sure that doesn't happen."

"Jesus, they put a toe tag on him like they do at the fucking morgue," Zack said in disgust.

And sure enough. When Eliza shone her light down the man's legs, a notecard was affixed to his toe with a string.

"What does it say?" Dane demanded.

Zack shook his head, disgust evident in his features as he slipped the tag off and took out his own flashlight to shine on the words.

"Jesus," Zack muttered. "This is goddamn unreal."

"What for God's sake?" Beau said through his teeth. "We don't have time to be fucking around here."

Zack's voice trembled with anger as he read what was scrawled on the card in small lettering.

We were much more merciful with him than we were with his wife, but only because we were on a tight timeline. We won't show you any mercy. This is what happens to people who interfere with our cause in any way. Arial Rochester is ours. We created her. We are her blood. Back off before your entire organization is wiped out. We have more resources and power than you can ever imagine.

"Oh *hell* no," Eliza said in a rage-induced, pissed-off voice. "Those assholes are taunting us? I'd like to tell them exactly what they can do with their *resources*."

Beau ran a hand over his face, closing his eyes, regret for Ari so strong. His heart ached for her. For all the hurt this would cause her. Her life would never be the same again. She'd know too much to ever live with the naïve innocence she once enjoyed. He didn't normally advocate willful, ignorant bliss, but in this case, Ari would be so much better off if she had never known the truth. Because now that she had part of it—the most important part, that the Rochesters weren't her biological parents—she'd want—demand—the rest of the story and she was entitled to it. She deserved the truth, no matter how much it hurt her. No matter how much it hurt *him* to have to be the one to give her all the damning evidence. But at the same time, he didn't want it coming from anyone else. He wanted to tell her when he could hold her and offer comfort. Damn it. If he had his way he'd always be there to comfort her when she needed it.

Who the hell wanted to exist knowing they were merely an experiment? Meant to be a freak of nature. Molded and fashioned to be just that, so her powers could be utilized in a manner not of her choosing. Her life would have never been her own had her blood parents not reached out to his father in desperation.

He hated to give his father credit for anything. He was a selfish bastard who thought only of himself, and yet he'd done

Ari a great kindness by sending her to Gavin and Ginger Rochester, because at least there, she was loved. Truly and deeply adored. Had his own father agreed to raise her, she would have grown up isolated and lonely, always an outsider.

"Our father has so much blood on his hands," Caleb said in a flat voice. "I'm ashamed to share *his* blood—the blood of others. I'd give anything not to."

Beau nodded grimly, unsure that he could put to voice his own thoughts without becoming utterly enraged, and right now he needed a clear head if they were going to ward off an outright attack on his home. Ari's home. Her place was with him, whether she realized it or accepted it yet or not.

"His sins are not your own, Caleb," Eliza said gently. "You've done much to atone for his crimes. No one can fault you for what *he* did. The choices he made when you were just a *child*. It's what you did later that counts. And you did the right thing. You and Beau chose the right path, not only for yourselves, but for your younger siblings as well."

She directed her statement as much toward Beau as she did to Caleb, but Beau was too lost in his own agonizing thoughts and realizations to pay any heed to her words.

How much more of this shit could Ari take?

Her parents who weren't exactly her parents had been kidnapped, her birth mother had been tortured and eventually murdered and now her biological father had met the same fate. No doubt because he'd called to warn Beau, and the men responsible for Ari's surrogacy had retaliated swiftly and viciously the instant her biological father had risked discovery by contacting Beau.

Who were these people to have such a vast, all-knowing network? The kind of technology they possessed was not civilian. Hell, it wasn't even recognized military for that matter. They knew too much. They were too patient. Too exacting. And they hadn't acted blindly the moment they wrested information on her whereabouts from her biological mother.

No, they'd waited, biding their time for the right moment to strike, and Beau would bet everything he owned that the video leaking was the very last thing the people hunting her had wanted. With her powers going public, or at least speculation about her powers, the men plotting to get their hands on Ari had been forced to speed up their timeline.

Beau doubted her parents would have even been targeted, because the more people involved, the more room for error. It would have far better suited their purposes to simply take Ari when she—and her parents—least expected, leaving Gavin powerless to help her. And to ensure her cooperation, they would have simply pulled a few surveillance feeds showing her they knew who her parents were and how to find them and that if she didn't cooperate they'd die.

Ari would have given in without hesitation.

"Why leave him here?" Isaac asked, a worried expression tugging on his face. "I don't get it. They're sending a message but why? They're here. We're outnumbered. Why not just take us all out, grab Ari and make a run for it."

Everyone exchanged instant looks of "oh shit."

Beau broke into a run before anyone could say anything further. "Get back to the house. *Now!*"

A thunderous boom sounded and echoed through the night air. Everyone dropped to the ground, instinctively covering themselves as the earth shook and rumbled beneath them.

"Fuck this shit," Zack said, fury lacing his voice. "I've goddamn had about enough of this BS. It's time to take those assholes out and cover them up with six feet of dirt. Pansy-ass motherfuckers preying on women."

"It's like fucking Armageddon," Capshaw muttered. "I'm ready to cap these bastards. Light them up and send them straight to hell."

Yeah, well, so was Beau, though he didn't even make the effort to say anything. His sole focus was on Ari and the fact that the explosives had gone off directly in the vicinity of the house.

Fuck!

Ari and Ramie were alone and vulnerable in that house, safe room or no.

"It was a goddamn diversion," Beau yelled as he scrambled back to his feet. "They knew the body would distract us momentarily. The note was just intended to let us know what they're capable of. Or maybe they thought we'd be scared and actually back off."

"What they're capable of is fucking themselves," Eliza snarled. "And I'll back off when I have their goddamn balls."

"Down girl," Dane murmured, though Beau noticed his lips were in a thin line, suppressing his chuckle.

Eliza was one vicious woman when on a mission. Beau admired that about her.

Their plan, though hastily put together in light of the fact they'd had less than five minutes to come up with one, had been to fan out from the house and then come back together from different directions so they could take out as many targets as possible before launching a full-scale frontal attack.

But the single most and *only* important directive the entire team had been given was to keep intruders away from the house. Take the fight to *them*. Protect Ramie and Ari at all costs.

"We *don't* split up," Beau commanded as they ran for the back entrance to the house. "For God's sake, don't get separated from the group and make it even easier to pick you off."

Always cool under fire. Unwavering. Solid. Stony and rigid. Yeah, right. He was a hot *mess* because he knew this was *bad*. The worst possible outcome, one they clearly hadn't seen coming. Goddamn it!

There was no gunfire. No ducking for cover. The night had gone eerily silent where before it had been ablaze with gunfire and explosions and yet not a single shot had come close to them.

It had been nothing more than a fucking distraction.

He was at full sprint when he hit the veranda and nearly tore the door off its hinges in his haste to get inside. To Ari.

They pounded into the house, guns up, spreading out as they cleared each room in a direct route to the safe room. The only place they could be assured the women were safe because they sure as hell couldn't risk allowing them out of the house. But now Beau knew that somehow, the safe room *had* been breached and the unthinkable had occurred.

When they reached the still closed door of the safe room, Caleb's face drew into an expression of confusion. With shaking hands, he punched in the security code, cursing when, in his haste, he failed to enter the correct code on the first attempt.

Zack merely shoved him out of the way and punched in the right code. The door slid open and they rushed straight into the bowels of hell.

The entire room was in disarray. There was a huge hole in

the ceiling, which meant the bastards had gained entry from the attic, through the goddamn *roof*. The room was hazy from dust and the remnants of smoke swirling erratically. The gaping hole was large enough for a damn elephant to fit through. They would be lucky if the explosion hadn't killed one or both women, because to force entry into the safe room, regardless of direction, it would take a hell of a lot of explosives.

"Ramie!" Caleb shouted hoarsely. "Ari!"

Caleb's cry was echoed by Beau's own as he yelled for Ari.

And then they saw Ramie, huddled in the far corner, her knees drawn to her chest, a vacant look in her eyes. Her pupils were dilated and her stare fixed forward unseeingly as she rocked back and forth in obvious distress.

"Dear God," Caleb whispered as he rushed to kneel beside his wife.

Beau searched the room furiously as the smoke and haze began to clear through the now-open door, his gaze catching the rope ladder dangling through the opening in the ceiling. Already, Zack was nimbly scaling upward, pistol in one hand, rifle slung over one shoulder from a strap, securely holding it in place. Dane scrambled up behind him to provide cover, and all Beau could do was stare numbly at the wreckage of the safe room, absorbing the knowledge that he'd utterly failed to protect the woman he loved with his entire heart and soul.

Rage. Sorrow. Horror so paralyzing that he literally couldn't breathe. He was bombarded by pain. So much pain. Terrified for Ari and what she was enduring even now. Knowing she'd trusted him. Had put her faith in him. And how frightened and alone she must feel, realizing he'd *failed* her.

Slowly he turned, knowing the only answers lay with Ramie, who was clearly in a stupor as Caleb touched her, talking to her in urgent tones, trying to bring her back from whatever hell she had descended into.

Tears streaked silently down her face, and like Caleb, Beau knelt on her other side, biting his lip to keep from demanding the answers he so desperately wanted—*needed*.

"Ramie, baby, talk to me," Caleb pleaded. "What happened? Are you all right? You're scaring me. Please, *please*, come *back* to me."

Slowly her head turned in his direction, eyes dull and lifeless as yet more tears slid in endless streaks down her cheeks.

"He touched me," she whispered, then looked away from Caleb, resuming her rocking. He *touched* me."

She chanted it over and over, and cold rage froze Caleb's eyes into hard ice chips. His jaw was locked in fury, and gently, as though she were the most precious, fragile thing in the world, he pulled her toward him, carefully wrapping his arms around her. He closed his eyes, seemingly losing the battle over his own emotions. Tears of rage, fury . . . grief . . . trailed down his face, carving raw, anguished trails.

"What did they *do*?" Caleb choked out. "Talk to me, baby. Please. I have to know how to help you."

Ramie lifted her head but she didn't look at her husband. Her gaze found Beau, and Beau was gutted by the grief reflected in her gray eyes. Sorrow. Regret. Guilt? Beau's brow furrowed, and he leaned in closer, seeking to offer his sister-in-law comfort when she seemed on the verge of shattering into a million pieces. A feeling he fully shared and was currently experiencing himself. Only the knowledge that he had to keep it together for Ari quelled the overwhelming despair clutching at his heart.

She seemed to come back from whatever faraway place she'd sheltered herself in, a self-protective measure to escape her horrific reality. God only knew what had happened in this room. The safe room. Beau wanted to level the entire goddamn house. It was cursed. He never should have rebuilt it. It had seen nothing but pain, devastation and loss. And now, yet again, it had failed to be the impenetrable fortress he'd intended. *Safe room.* He wanted to choke on the irony that the one place Ramie and Ari should have been the safest was in fact where they'd been the most vulnerable.

In his and Caleb's arrogance—hell, the arrogance of the entire DSS cooperative—they'd assumed that they could leave Ramie and Ari here, untouched. Safe from whatever evil lurked in the shadows that was coming for them. There was simply no such thing as a safe room. It was a naïve, stupid belief to think, no matter the measures they'd taken in its construction, that it would prove indestructible and impossible to compromise. It was a mistake he could well pay for and have to live with the rest of his life.

Ramie's soulful eyes connected with Beau's, and he flinched at the stark pain reflected in those stormy eyes.

"They *took* her. I'm so *sorry*, Beau. I couldn't do *anything*. He *touched* me. Had his hands on me. And the evil. Oh God, the *evil*. It was so overpowering. It flooded every part of my soul, and there was nothing I could do to ward it off. I was defenseless," she said in a broken voice. "And then . . ." She closed her eyes, her face contorted with abject misery. "They told her that she had two choices. Go peacefully with them and they'd spare me and everyone else, or they'd slaughter everyone and take her anyway. But the end result would be the same so it was a matter of whether she wanted to spare our lives. Not her own. *Ours.*"

Ramie began to weep in earnest, huge, gulping sobs, where before her tears had been silent in her daze. She buried her face in her hands even as Caleb drew her in even closer, nearly crushing her with his strength. Caleb was pale, and he too looked at Beau with so much remorse and . . . pity. It made Beau want to vomit.

"She willingly went so they wouldn't kill *me*," Ramie choked out between heaving sobs. "And there wasn't a single thing I could do to help her. I was utterly helpless!"

She beat her fisted hand down on her leg, repeating the action until Caleb finally wrapped his hand protectively around hers and brought it to his chest so she wouldn't harm herself further.

Ramie's gaze was haunted, a lifetime of regret simmering in her stormy, sorrowful eyes.

"She sacrificed herself for all of us."

Zack and Dane dropped softly from the ladder, in time to hear Ramie's whispered statement. Silence fell over the room as everyone absorbed the sheer selflessness of Ari's act. Discomfort and grim determination were reflected in every single DSS operative. Eliza's eyes were ablaze with fury. Zack's features had grown so cold that Beau felt the prickle of chill bumps cascade down his arms.

"They hopped a chopper and were already in the air by the time we got to them," Dane said quietly. "We couldn't stop them. We weren't in time."

Right that instant the grim reality of just what had occurred hit Beau square in the chest. His knees buckled, and he found himself right back on the floor after rising just seconds earlier when Zack and Dane had reappeared.

A roar shook the room, the sound terrible, much like a wounded, enraged animal who'd lost his mate. Beau dimly registered that it had come from *him*. An emphatic denial, though he knew every word Ramie had related was truth. Pain like he'd never experienced welled from the depths of his soul, filling his heart with such despair that it overwhelmed him. He couldn't find his footing and so he knelt there on the floor, numb with terror. Grief. And love so staggering that he was awed that he had the capacity to feel such depth of emotion for another human being.

Love? He fucking *adored* her. Worshipped the ground she fucking walked on. Love was a paltry, inadequate word to describe his feelings for Ari. Maybe he'd *never* truly find the words. But he would *not* lose her. *Couldn't* lose her. Because, even if he could never convey with words all that he held inside him, he would show her. Every single day for the rest of their lives. But his vow was empty, meaningless, because the woman who should be hearing it wasn't *here*.

Ramie broke away from Caleb's hold, though how, Beau wasn't certain because Caleb had what amounted to a death grip on his wife, as if by merely holding her, he formed a barrier between her and the rest of the world. A barrier to the pain and grief she was experiencing even now.

But Ramie crawled the short distance to where Beau knelt on the floor, his face buried in his hands, shoulders shaking as though . . . He scrubbed at his face, shocked to feel dampness covering his cheeks. He stared down at the wetness on his palms in bewilderment just as Ramie's much smaller fingers slid over and curled around his.

"I'm so sorry, Beau," she said in a tortured voice. "I let them take her. I wish I had her powers. God, I wish I had anything but this wretched curse to feel the kind of evil that took her."

Beau roused himself from his agonizing suffering because this was in *no way* Ramie's fault, and he would *not* allow her to torture herself one second longer. Even as Caleb's lips pursed to form a protest, Beau held up his hand to his brother, sending him a look that instantly quelled his response.

"This is *not* your fault," Beau said fiercely. "It's mine and *only* mine. We spoke of moving her, of keeping her on the move constantly, never at one place for too long a time. I had yet to set that into motion. I was arrogant and careless. But maybe . . ." He cast a look of despair in Caleb's direction, knowing he had no other choice. "Maybe you could help us locate her."

Ramie was nodding vehemently when Zack broke in.

"No need, man. We injected her with the tracking device, remember? Dane's already working on getting a bead on her location. I vote we go in, wherever she is, with some serious shock and awe and lay waste to the entire fucking lot of them."

"Fuck me," Beau said in frustration as he glanced over to where Dane was booting up one of computers. He just hoped to fuck it worked after the utter chaos that had occurred. "I can't even goddamn think straight! Of course! Jesus, how could I have forgotten the one thing I was the most adamant about? The one thing that would give us a chance if exactly what happened tonight occurred."

"Keep it together, man," Zack said softly, his eyes brimming with sympathy. "I know well the frustration in not knowing where someone important to you is. I've lived it over a decade. But we'll get your girl back. You can take that to the bank."

THIRTY

ARI'S eyes slitted open and bright fluorescent lights stabbed her pupils like shards of glass. Wincing, she slammed her eyelids shut once more and emitted a soft moan. Where was she? What had happened?

Her brain was effectively scrambled. Maybe she'd finally had the big one. The super psychic bleed Beau had feared. Or maybe she'd simply had a stroke. But weren't they essentially one and the same? A stroke was a bleed in the brain, right? Hers just wasn't the normal kind of bleed most stroke victims incurred. Her mind was so fuzzy that she strained to remember anything at all.

The ache in her head intensified as she tried to focus. To concentrate enough to make sense of her surroundings. Because something wasn't right.

She couldn't move.

Her arms and legs were restrained and cold *metal* surrounded her neck.

Her neck?

Her eyes flew open in alarm and this time she ignored the splintering pain the action caused, and she forced her gaze to her surroundings, panic billowing like a thunderstorm. Oh God, where *was* she? Was she ensconced in her worst nightmare? And if so, why couldn't she awaken and seek comfort in Beau's arms? Her shield against all hurts and fears.

And then the events of the night crashed into her, staggering her and leaving her breathless. Tears stung her eyelids. Were the others even alive? Was *Beau* alive? Oh God, he couldn't be dead. No! The men who'd taken her were completely without honor. But she'd known *her* fate was inevitable once the safe room had been breached. Her only choice was to take a shot that they actually *would* leave Ramie and the others alone. Content themselves with finally achieving their primary objective. *Her*.

Now she would finally know what these . . . fanatics . . . wanted, and honestly, she was terrified to have that question answered. But if these people had her parents, would she finally see them? At least know they were safe? Alive?

Her pulse ratcheted upward until her breaths came in shallow bursts.

"Ah, you're awake."

The sound speared through her skull like someone pounding a pickaxe through her head. Nausea boiled in her stomach, and she swallowed convulsively even as she knew that swallowing the accumulating saliva would only nauseate her more.

"What do you want?" she rasped, shocked at the effort it took to even speak.

"We have a few tests we want to perform," the man said as calmly as if he were discussing something as mundane as the

IN HIS KEEPING 317

weather. "You have a higher purpose, Arial. It's time to embrace your destiny."

Destiny? She didn't want to embrace this freak's idea of her destiny. Her destiny lay with Beau. And finding her parents so she could have her family back. So she could start her own. Share her new family with her mother and father. She just wanted a normal life!

The disembodied voice was seriously freaking her out, so she twisted left and right, craning her neck until her gaze finally found the source of the voice. Her heart leapt. Not at the sight of the gaunt medical-looking person wearing a lab coat, but rather the two men who flanked him.

Heavily muscled, tall. Towering over the much smaller-framed man. Both were expressionless but their eyes spoke of ruthlessness. They were hard and cold as they stared dispassion-ately at her. Her eyes narrowed in recognition of one of them. The asshole who'd been employed by her father. The man who'd attacked her. Tried to drug her. Unsuccessfully.

But they didn't scare her. Once they would have. She would have scurried under the nearest table like a frightened mouse and covered her head and ears, shutting out everything around her. Now that she knew exactly what she was capable of and armed with the knowledge that there was likely a whole lot more she didn't know she could do but possessed the necessary powers for, these assholes could easily be dealt with.

Did they think simply restraining her would prevent her from unleashing hell on them all?

Some of what she was thinking must have been reflected in her ever-expressive eyes and face because without speaking a single word, one of the goons simply turned, pointing a remote at a monitor mounted on the wall.

It flickered once and then came immediately into focus. Ari's breath caught in her throat and stuck there. Her chest constricted and burned, robbed of air as she simply stopped breathing.

Her parents were in what looked to be a jail cell. Like common criminals, or worse, hostages subjected to deplorable conditions. Her father was seated on a flimsy-looking cot with her mother curled into his arms as he tried to comfort her. Judging by the look of distress—and defeat—on her mother's face, even her father couldn't manage something he'd never failed to do before. Reassure his wife that everything would be all right.

Bile rose in her throat and hatred burned a hole in her stomach. She, who had never truly hated anyone. She, who balked at the mere idea of inflicting violence on or hurting anyone. In this moment, she knew she was absolutely capable of, not only hurting, but killing these bastards for what they'd put her parents through. And she'd suffer no remorse whatsoever.

She embraced her powers, finally realizing she *did* serve a higher purpose, but it sure as hell wasn't what these bastards imagined. If they knew that she was imagining in exacting detail their deaths, they'd likely flee like the complete cowards they were.

Around her objects began trembling, shaking, as if in the throes of an earthquake. Frames fell from the walls. Glass vials flew from their resting spots to shatter against the far wall. And she stared at the worm in the lab coat who'd calmly announced he wanted to run tests on her. Like she was some kind of an animal. Her parents were already—had been for days—being treated with less regard than animals. Caged in filthy quarters. Only each other to lean on while worry for their daughter tortured them every bit as much as their disappearance and not knowing their fate tortured Ari every single hour since their abduction.

Goon B's lips curled into a sneer, and he spoke for the first time, seemingly undaunted by her show of strength. Not that it had been an impressive feat by any stretch. She was still weak from the powerful sedative they'd administered. She didn't even know how much time had elapsed since she'd been taken from the safe room, where she prayed to God Ramie was still safe and sound.

"Cease your tantrum," he bit out.

"Or else?" she taunted, her eyes narrowing on the focus of her ire.

Immediately his face turned red, and he grasped his neck with both hands as if fighting off an unseen attacker. He pried uselessly at the invisible hand wrapped around his neck, slowing squeezing the life right out of him. Ari *wanted* to kill him. She was pissed enough to take every single one of these assholes out and damn the consequences.

"Enough!" Goon A barked, yanking her attention momentarily from Goon B.

Goon B coughed and sputtered, holding his neck as he gasped for breath.

"You're going to pay for that, you little bitch," he snapped, his face red either from the pressure she'd exerted or sheer fury. She didn't care one way or another. Never had she felt such a pervading desire for vengeance. Violence. She wanted to hurt these people, whereas a month ago, the mere thought of her unleashing violence on another human being was abhorrent, against her very nature. Now? She was anticipating with every breath just how she would exact her revenge on these people for upending her life, for threatening her parents—adopted or not—and for bringing their fight to Beau and his family's doorstep.

God help them all if Beau was dead. God may have mercy, but Ari would have none.

"Maybe you should have a look at dear mommy and daddy again," Goon A said in a mocking tone that grated on her nerves enough to make her want to squeeze a different part of the anatomy than she'd attacked on Goon B. Walking around ball-less and singing soprano would certainly take his ego down a notch or three.

But when she tracked back to the monitor, unable to resist the urge to see her parents after hearing the underlying threat in Goon A's voice, she froze.

Four men burst into the cell and erupted into a flurry of action. One of them snatched her mother and wrapped a beefy arm over her breasts, curling around to the back, where he fisted a handful of her hair to yank her head upward to bare her vulnerable neck.

It took the combined efforts of all three of the other men—huge men—to subdue her father when the fourth put his hands on Ari's mother. His rage was a terrible and awing thing to behold, and she couldn't help but feel a surge of pride that it took three impossibly large men, with the aid of weapons, to subdue her father, and even then it took every bit of their combined efforts to keep him pinned to the floor, although they made certain his face was pointed in his wife's direction so he could see exactly what was being done to her.

His face was harsh with rage and agony. And suddenly sound

burst through the room where Ari was helpless to do anything but watch. Her father's voice was hoarse, desperate, *pleading*.

"Leave her alone, damn it. Take me. Do whatever you want with me but leave her alone. She's done nothing wrong. Take *me*, goddamn it!"

Tears burned Ari's eyelids but she furiously blinked them away, determined for these assholes watching her closely not to see how affected she was by the sight of her parents. How relieved she was they were alive even as terror snaked through her body when the man holding her mother's head at an uncomfortable angle slowly drew a knife and placed it against the front of her neck.

Ari could see the stark fear in her eyes even as she visibly tried to prevent her husband from seeing just how terrified she was. Again, Ari felt a burst of pride, this time for her mother, because she didn't want her husband to know just how scared she was. Her expression was defiant, a definite *fuck you* look stamped on her delicate features. Even her eyes, after that first flash of fear, eyes that had never held anything but warmth, love and tenderness, were cold with hatred and defiance. She stared the men down holding her husband as if to tell them *you can't win. He'll kill you. He'll find a way and he'll kill you.*

Not if Ari had anything to do with it. She was going to take these bastards out herself or die trying.

Some causes were noble and just, even when steeped in violence, blood and . . . murder. Some fights, regardless of impossible odds, were still meant to be fought because unless you fought back there really *was* no hope. And Ari had to believe that somehow, someway, she would prevail and save her parents. Even if she herself was forfeit in the process.

Some things were simply worth fighting for. Worth it to the bitter end, with the very last breath. And Ari could think of no better reason than . . . *love*. Love for her parents. Love for Beau.

Defeat was merely the absence of hope. And until she'd exhausted every last avenue of hope then she would not—would *never*—concede. It was a vow echoing through her mind, shutting all else out.

Until her mother's pained scream broke through the dark shadow of Ari's thoughts. Through plans for death and retribution. She froze when a thin trickle of blood slithered down her mother's neck as the asshole holding her sliced a shallow cut through her delicate skin.

Her father went crazy, his bellows of rage, his promises of retribution echoing her own thoughts. He managed to break free from his captors, and he flung himself across the cell, prepared to take apart with his bare hands the man hurting his wife.

And then her father's body arced, bowing backward, his face contorted with pain as his extremities shook and twitched violently.

The cowardly bastards had tased him from behind. For one brief moment Ari thought her father would actually fight through the devastating effects of the stun gun, his determination to safeguard his wife overriding all else. But then another shot from one of the other guards dropped him like a stone and Ginger cried out, her movements causing more blood to flow from the cut that was now deeper because she'd instinctively lunged forward in a desperate attempt to shield her husband.

"Stop!" Ari cried. "Don't kill her! For God's sake, you've done enough! You've incapacitated my father, and if the bastard holding a knife to her throat makes one wrong move, he'll kill her!"

"Then perhaps you should reconsider your rejection of our plans," Goon A said coolly. "Because I have no compunction whatsoever about slicing her throat and letting you watch her bleed out, seeing her take her last breath and then letting her husband wake up in a pool of her blood next to her lifeless body."

Ari shivered at the emotionless threat. But no, it wasn't a threat. She could see his absolute resolve. Knew he'd carry out his *promise* if she offered any further resistance. Could she hold it together? Endure whatever they meted out so as not to be completely crippled afterward, so she would be able to destroy this awful place and every single person inside it except her parents.

Without knowing whether Beau was alive, she had to operate under the assumption he was so she made the right choices. This was no time to allow emotion to interfere with cold logic and what she knew to be absolutely true.

This man would order her mother's death and suffer not one iota of remorse. And God only knew what they'd then do to her father when they no longer had her mother to force her compliance with.

"I'll do whatever you want," she said with calm she had no idea could be summoned in a situation that would normally have her paralyzed with fear, helpless to do anything but be some damn shrinking violet.

Fuck violets. She'd never liked them anyway. And the use of the F-word just strengthened her resolve to be the warrior Beau was. The warrior her parents needed. The warrior she must *become*.

Hardening herself for the ordeal ahead so she wouldn't be incapacitated afterward would be the toughest test of her endurance yet. Beau wasn't here to pick up the pieces, to coddle and comfort her.

But for her parents. For herself. For Beau. She could and would endure. And God help them all when she finally unleashed the full fury of her powers. Her gift. One, that for the first time in her life, she was grateful for and that she wholly embraced.

THIRTY-ONE

GAVIN Rochester flinched when he heard the telltale sound of the door leading into the hallway where the cells were aligned open. Then the thump of booted feet. More than one set.

His entire body was still on fire, but this time . . . he'd kill the bastards with his bare hands. Rip out their spinal cords and force them down their throats.

They'd put their filthy hands on his *wife*. They'd made her bleed. Worse, they'd terrified her, and he'd been rendered incapable of stopping any of it. He'd been stripped of power. Any decisions or choices. Not since he was a child eking out a living in squalor had he had his choices taken away and no say-so in his future.

Since the day he'd killed the monster—his sperm donor, because he would not give such a man the honor or respect of ever naming him father, biological or not—he'd taken control of his own destiny. His mother, too far gone into the murky world of drugs and addiction, had been grateful to Gavin for ridding them of the man who abused them both. Grateful, for fuck's sake. A polite thank-you rendered unemotionally as though she were thanking a stranger for a small act of kindness.

When he'd begged her to leave with him. To seek out better. A better life. A better *existence*, panic had swirled in her eyes, and he knew the source of her panic was being cut off from her drug supply, something more precious than even her own child.

After that, Gavin had left his old life behind. Every single aspect of it. Not even Ginger knew the whole of it. Only that his parents had been the worst sort of people. People who should have never been allowed to procreate. But he'd never confessed to her that he'd killed his own father in cold blood.

She knew much about his past. Knew he was steeped in gray and that he'd crossed a lot of lines, or blurred them at the very least. But she didn't know he was a murderer, and until now, until that little selfish, spoiled rich brat bastard had gone after his daughter, until a man had drawn his wife's blood, he'd never considered descending into the world of cold-blooded killing again.

But now he craved it with every part of his heart and soul. He burned with rage and the need to shed the blood of the men who'd made his wife and daughter—the two people he loved most in the world, the *only* people he loved—hurt and afraid.

He knew the point had come when he had to act. Had to take a calculated risk and escape as quickly as possible. Because God, somewhere out there, scared and alone, was his precious daughter. Who likely thought her mother and father had simply abandoned her. At a time when she needed them the most.

He couldn't even think about what circumstances Ari might presently be in without going insane. He had to focus on only what he could control. His and his beloved wife's escape so they could see to their daughter. And when this was over, he was moving his family as far away as possible. Never to return here. Complete identity changes. Completely new lives. In a place where he could be certain they'd never be touched by violence again. He should have never returned to the States. But it was useless to indulge in regret for actions already taken. But he *could* ensure he never made the same mistake again.

When Ginger cried out, Gavin soared to his feet, his head coming up, searching for what threat was posed, what had made his wife cry out in anguish. But no one was even in the cell at this moment and yet Ginger's face was writhing with pain, stress and fear radiating from her in tangible waves. He could *feel* her utter panic, see her body tremble in extreme agitation.

Tears streaked down her cheeks and her gaze was fastened down the hallway, down a sight line Gavin wasn't privy to because he'd put Ginger in the far corner and instructed her to remain there, as far from the entrance and where the men would force their way in and where Gavin intended to kill them.

Failure simply wasn't an option. Earlier, they hadn't been treated badly. In fact, they been treated with indifference, viewed with simmering impatience as if they awaited something else entirely and Gavin and Ginger were mere obstacles in their way.

So why keep them? Why kidnap them at all? If it was a demand for ransom, Ari wouldn't know how to liquidate enough assets to pay what would likely be an outrageous sum, nor would he want her to. The very last thing he wanted was his daughter remotely connected to any danger.

But with the sudden shift in the tide earlier and the menace he'd seen in their captor's eyes. The way they'd terrorized Ginger, tased him, as if the entire thing was a carefully orchestrated play. Everything had changed on a dime. But for whose benefit came the sudden shift in urgency? What was happening, even now, behind the scenes? Circumstances he wasn't privy to.

Gavin swiftly moved in front of Ginger, obscuring her view so he could see what she was reacting to and so he could protect her from whatever threat loomed. To his surprise, Ginger shoved hard at him, causing him to stumble forward and she raced to the bars, fingers curling around them, gripping until the tips were completely white and bloodless.

"Ari!" she screamed. "Don't touch her, you bastards!"

Gavin's blood went ice cold as dread filled his heart. No. Oh God, *no*. Not Ari. Goddamn it! Not his daughter, too! Wasn't it enough that his wife suffered? Did their only child have to be terrorized as well?

He yanked Ginger back, all but tossing her onto the cot, and then he pinned her with a stare that brooked no argument. "Do *not* fucking *move*," he said harshly. "You stay here, and do *not* interfere, not matter what happens. Do you understand me?"

"But—!"

Gavin held up a hand to his wife, something he never did, though God knew he'd never raise his hand to her in violence. He'd never before given her the disrespect of cutting off anything she chose to say by being so dismissive as to reject her words with his body language or to so abruptly call a halt to her words or argument.

In this moment, he didn't care. He wanted compliance. Instant and unquestioning obedience. He locked his fierce gaze with his wife's equally fierce stare. Because if by forcing her compliance, she stayed alive—unharmed—she could be pissed at him for the next twenty years and he'd be more than happy to grovel every single day of those two decades.

"I can't lose you both," Gavin said hoarsely, his voice cracking with emotion. "Stay where you are, Ginger! Let *me* see to Ari. I can't afford to have my concentration split between you and our daughter. I need to know you are out of harm's way. Do this for me. *Please*."

Some of the stark, vulnerable fear that weakened him to his knees must have shone in his face because Ginger's eyes softened, and she simply nodded, though her gaze immediately flitted beyond Gavin, her eyes anxious and seeking now as they awaited their daughter.

For one brief moment, he leaned in and pressed his lips against her forehead, closing his eyes. His sweet, loving and forgiving wife. It was bad enough that she'd endured such torment over the last days. But now these fuckers had Ari? The only solace they'd found was in the fact that Ari hadn't been taken. Despair shoved aside the hope that she was someplace safe. Out of harm's way. Because she wasn't. She was here. In this hell with him and her mother and he'd never felt so goddamn helpless in his life at his inability to protect the people who mattered the most to him.

He reluctantly broke away from his wife, but he had to see what had been done to his daughter. He rushed back to the bars, straining forward to better see in the dimly lit hallway. The cell was lit by only a single bulb, one he purposely turned off at night when he slept, Ginger between him and the wall so he was a barrier between her and anyone coming into the cell.

His reason was twofold. One, in the darkness, holding, touching his wife, he—they—could forget for the space of a few stolen moments that they were being held captive by un-known people for an equally unknown reason. And two, darkness bothered Ginger immensely, except for at night when she slept, curled into his protective embrace. If he left it lit all the time, it would eventually burn out and it was doubtful it would be re-placed, especially if Ginger displayed any sign of distress over the loss of the single source of illumination.

He strained his eyes, only seeing what Ginger had seen. The unmistakable color of Ari's hair, though her head was downcast, only the crown of her hair visible. He tensed, realizing she was being *dragged* between two men and neither was taking the slightest bit of care in their handling of her.

He bit back a string of oaths, knowing that they would de-rive great pleasure in giving him even more reason to protest, and the last thing he wanted was more hurt for his daughter.

He watched for any sign of . . . life. Movement. His chest burned, oxygen trapped in his lungs as they compressed and squeezed even tighter in sheer, gut-wrenching panic.

She was listless. Unmoving on her own. She was jerked along like a puppet or rather a doll being dragged behind a child by a single arm. Her hair was tousled, strands going in a dozen different directions. It looked tangled and in complete disarray.

His gut clenched even harder as he imagined all the possible reasons for a woman to look as she did. He turned, ensuring Ginger was heeding his order, something he never gave his wife unless it had to do with her or Ari's safety.

Her gaze leapt to his in question, her entire body surging forward, though she gripped the edge of the cot with her fingers as though to prevent herself from flying forward to see for her-self. God, if he could only shield her from this. If he could have only shielded her and Ari both. The weight of his mistakes, his failures, weighed heavily on his heart and mind, but for now he had to push past his guilt and overwhelming sense of helplessness and figure out a way to get his family out.

Finally the long path down the hallway brought Ari close enough for Gavin to look closer. Still unmoving, hair in disarray, *bruises* . . . He bit back a savage oath as he took in the purple blotches, the size of fingerprints, on her arms and shoulders. She was wearing only a thin tank top and then he froze when one of the guards jerked her in his direction so the other could unlock the cell.

The movement sent the hair that tumbled forward over her shoulders, covering most of her chest, to the side and he saw the white tank top turn scarlet before his very eyes. His heart seized, terror slamming his airway shut.

It—and she—were bathed in blood.

"Back up!" the guard with the key barked at Gavin.

As if reinforcing the other guard's demand, the man holding Ari hauled her more upright, shaking her like the rag doll Gavin had likened her to as she'd been dragged down the hall. Behind him, Ginger gasped in horror and then cried out in utter despair, "Ari!"

His wife's agonized cry shook Gavin from his momentary stupor and torment. He lunged for the bars, hitting them so hard they shook and rattled as he roared his rage, forgetting all about his worry that his reaction would incite them to further malice.

Desperately, he thrust his arms through the thick bars, straining forward, trying to reach his daughter. Trying to get his hands on the men responsible.

"Get back!" one of the men snarled, though he took a hasty step backward even as he uttered the command, ensuring he was well out of Gavin's reach.

The one not holding Ari brandished a stun gun, the same one he'd used on Gavin before. This time he aimed it not at Gavin, but at Ginger, who now stood upright beside the cot, her face sheet-white as she stared at her bloodied daughter.

"Perhaps you forgot what happened last time you forgot your place," the guard said in a menacing voice. "Get back or I'll shock your wife, and you can forget seeing your precious daughter."

It took every ounce of Gavin's discipline to simply stand down, to slowly back away, ensuring his body once more stood between Ginger and the guard holding the Taser. He wanted to go after them both as soon as the door was opened, wanted to take them apart, piece by bloody piece. Spill their blood as they'd spilled Ari's.

When the guard was satisfied that Gavin was a sufficient distance back, he inserted the key into the lock, but his gaze never left Gavin and Ginger, and the hand holding the gun was steady, never lowering.

With a groan, the cell door strained to open, years of rust and neglect eating away at it. Gavin had spent the entire first forty-eight hours of confinement ruthlessly and tirelessly testing every square inch of the cell, looking for any deficit, any weakness to exploit. Anything that could prove a possible escape route. Only to come up empty-handed.

Not even entering the cell, perhaps rightfully wary of Gavin's savage rage that Gavin knew was clearly outlined on his face and in his eyes, and evidently not wanting to afford Gavin any opportunity to lash out, the guard holding Ari stopped just shy of the open doorway while his partner took position between them, the Taser pointed in Gavin and Ginger's direction.

Then the guard simply propelled Ari forward, her slight weight momentarily becoming airborne at his vicious shove. She hit the floor with a resounding thud that made Ginger cry out again, and Gavin flinched at his daughter's motionless body lying on the floor like a broken doll.

She lay there, eyes open, but completely unaware. Blood streamed from her nose, her mouth. God, it looked like it was coming from her ears and even her eyes.

The guards beat a hasty retreat, closing and locking the cell door before hurrying away, disappearing from sight.

Gavin rushed the few feet over to Ari, sinking to his knees, his hands automatically running over her body, afraid of what he'd find. Ginger joined him, her eyes red and swollen, so much worry reflected in her tormented gaze.

"There's so much blood!" Ginger choked out around a sob. "Oh God, Gavin, is she . . . Is she even alive?"

Gavin's eyes briefly closed even as he carefully smoothed Ari's hair from her neck so he could check for a pulse. His own heart was about to beat out of his chest. His hands were shaking so badly that his fingers kept glancing off her skin before he could ascertain the strength of her pulse. Or if she even had one.

Finally he forced himself to calm enough that his hand steadied, and he pressed the area over her carotid artery. He sagged, nearly toppling over with relief when he felt the erratic flutter against his fingertips.

"She's alive," he said quietly.

"Oh thank God," Ginger whispered brokenly. Then she touched his arm to get his attention, her terrified gaze finding his. "How can we know how badly she's injured? What if we do her more harm by moving her?"

Gavin had the same fear but he'd be damned if he left his daughter on the cold, hard floor of the dank cell. He would certainly handle her more carefully than the guards in their brutal treatment of her.

"Let me lay her down on the cot, darling," Gavin said, forcing calm into his voice he neither believed nor felt.

Just as much as he didn't want to panic Ginger, neither did he want her to see how precariously close he was to becoming utterly unhinged and losing any semblance of control.

He cursed softly as he began to shake again when he slid his arms underneath her body with frustrating slowness. His instincts screamed at him to gather her in his arms, hold her close and never let go, never let her back into the hands of monsters.

He was genuinely worried that his legs simply wouldn't support Ari's slight weight, much less his own. He sucked in several steadying breaths, trying valiantly to calm the raging fury storming through his veins.

Gently, he lifted, still crouched in a kneeling position. He drew her up and into his arms, cradling her against his chest. For a moment he paused, praying he wouldn't falter when he tried to stand. Never had he had a more important reason to be so patient and careful.

"Here, let me help you," Ginger said anxiously, anchoring her entire body, stiffening with all her might as she attempted to help haul him to his feet as he held Ari the entire time.

Though his petite, delicate wife, so much like Ari, despite not being her biological mother, hardly had the strength to accomplish such a task, he didn't deny her aid because he sensed she was on the verge of completely falling apart and needed to do something—anything—to remain stalwart. A feat he admired since he was just as close to breaking down himself as he stared down at his bruised and bloodied daughter.

Tears burned the corners of his eyes as he ever so carefully placed her on the cot, inching his arms from underneath her. Though her eyes were fixed and glassy, she didn't seem remotely aware of anything, almost as if she were unconscious despite her eyes being wide. But still, he didn't want to do anything that would inadvertently cause her more pain, which was why he moved with extreme slowness, careful not to jostle her.

"Oh Gavin," Gingerly said tearfully as she settled just above Ari's head. "What did they do to her?" She shifted her pleading gaze to her husband, anger, fury and utter despair burning brightly in her brown eyes, which that were now nearly black. "What did they *do*?"

Sorrow was a heavy, suffocating blanket over the entire cell. Gavin couldn't even form the words to offer his wife comfort when he had none to give. He couldn't give her an answer that would appease her because he was afraid he would be telling her a complete lie.

There was so much blood. It soaked the entire front of her shirt, streaked from her ears down the sides of her neck, where it collected in large splattered spots atop the ridge between her shoulders and base of her neck. More blood covered her mouth, was drying in her nostrils and now that he was studying her closer he was able to confirm his earlier suspicion that she'd even bled from her *eyes*.

Had they beaten her so badly?

Despite the fact he'd already checked her pulse, his hand

found its way to her neck again, seeking reassurance that he hadn't imagined feeling the soft flutter of life beneath his fingertips. As before it was erratic, but it was strong against his touch. But his fear was of internal injuries, things he couldn't see.

Despite his fear that she'd been badly beaten, he couldn't find evidence of swelling or bruising on her face or head. The blood seemed inexplicable because the only bruises he found were those on her arms, as if she'd been grasped roughly. Ari had always bruised easily, and these somewhat small bruises looked to be fingertips. Nothing that would account for the blood so stark against her skin.

Ginger's hand hovered over Ari's face, her features rigid with consternation as she sought somewhere—anywhere—she could safely touch her daughter. Finally she laid her hand over Ari's forehead, gently stroking up and over her scalp in a soothing motion.

Ari immediately flinched as though Ginger had struck her. It was the first time Ari had made any sort of movement or signaled any awareness of what was going on around her.

"Ari?" Gavin said urgently. "Ari, can you hear me? Are you awake? Please, sweetheart, open your eyes so your mother and I know you're all right."

To both their surprises, Ari brushed away her mother's hand and then rolled away from them both to face the opposite direction. She pulled her legs up—a protective measure—to her chest and wrapped both arms solidly around them, seeming to pull herself into as small a ball as possible.

An agonized moan escaped her lips, and Gavin's position was such that he could still see her face, even though she'd turned away from him and Ginger. Her eyes briefly closed as though she were battling ... agony? Fear? Awareness? Or perhaps she merely wanted to escape her present reality. Maybe she was in so much pain that she simply wanted to slip away to someplace where it wasn't so sharp and unbearable. Gavin hastily wiped the corner of one eye and blinked rapidly to maintain his tenuous grip on his composure.

"Ari?" Ginger started to touch her again but stilled her hand and let it drop away, anguish flashing in her eyes.

"Don't," Ari begged. "Oh God, please don't."

"Don't what?" Gavin asked urgently. "Ari, can you talk to us? Can you tell us what happened? What did those bastards do to you?"

He choked off, unable to go on any further. Tears clogged his throat, rendering him temporarily incapable of speech. Ginger thrust her fingers through his, curling them around his hand, holding tightly, so much tension radiating through her body.

"Don't touch," Ari said, another moan escaping, her words so low, Gavin could barely make them out. "No noise. Please. I can't bear it. Hurts. Hurts so much. Please, just don't touch me. Don't say anything."

Ginger's hand flew to her mouth and tears slipped from her eyes, more appearing as soon as the others slithered down her cheeks.

Ari reached up to cover her ears and then began slowly rocking herself back and forth, locked in her own private hell that Gavin and Ginger were helpless to soothe, calm or take away.

Ginger stood, honoring her daughter's broken request, her eyes grief-stricken in a manner Gavin hadn't seen in nearly twenty-five years. Not since the last child they'd lost had she looked so heartbroken.

Gavin jerkily rose, his fury mounting with every passing moment. Rage smoldered through his veins like a potent drug, his vision growing dim and hazy. He turned his back to both his wife and daughter, not wanting either of them to see the terrible thoughts reflected in his eyes. The thirst for vengeance. For violence. To destroy every last person involved in this whole sordid mess.

He let out a rumbling sound of pure male fury, one he instantly tried to quell when he saw Ari stiffen.

"The light," Ginger said suddenly. "The light probably hurts her too."

Ginger hurried toward where the single bulb hung from an electrical wire and fiddled with it a moment, loosening it just enough so that it flickered off.

Gavin turned, closing his eyes as grief and helplessness washed over him like a tidal wave. He hit the iron bars caging him, needing an outlet for his savage rage. Pain didn't even register as he rammed his fist over and over into the groaning metal. The acrid smell of blood arose and it slid warmly over his fingers, dripping onto the floor below him.

Ginger threw her arms around his side and then slid around him until she separated him from the bars he'd been pummeling. Reverently she took his now-swollen hand in hers and pressed a kiss to the torn knuckles.

Then she buried her face in his chest so her sobs were stifled. Her entire body shook, and Gavin wrapped his arms around her in response, anchoring her. Then he buried his face in his wife's hair, his own tears dampening the silken strands, as his heart, like his wife's, simply broke in two.

They held on to one another for a long moment before Ginger's muffled voice rose. "What did they do to our baby, Gavin? What do they want?"

Gavin ran his hands up and down the length of her spine, trying to offer her comfort when there was none to be had. "I don't know," he said in a low voice. "Damn it, I don't know!"

"How can we protect her when we're helpless?" Ginger asked, her distress becoming more pronounced.

"We aren't helpless."

Gavin and Ginger both whipped around in shock as Ari's dull, toneless voice reached them. She sounded almost... robotic.

"What, baby?" Gavin asked softly, though he'd heard her clearly. He just wasn't sure what she had meant.

"I'll bring down the entire house," she said softly, turning over so she faced her parents willingly for the first time.

Power snapped and sparkled around them, electrifying the very air in the damp cell. Where before the air had always been stuffy, hard to breathe, now it seemed charged, particles shimmering, a breeze suddenly shifting, restless, blowing a chill through as if a window had been opened to allow fresh air in.

The bars began to rattle ominously. The cot shook beneath Ari. The concrete floor trembled beneath their feet. Outside the cell, in neighboring ones, pillows, blankets, even an old, discarded shoe rose into the air, spinning rapidly before slamming against the iron bars caging the small interiors.

Ginger glanced at Gavin, worry and unease dark in her eyes.

He knew his expression wasn't likely any different. Something was very wrong here. In the distance, the sound of breaking glass could be heard, the shattering of a window. The wind whistled down the hallway, howling ominously, like a wind tunnel.

"Gavin!" Ginger whispered, her horrified gaze locked on Ari.

Gavin pulled his gaze from the objects whirling freely through the air and focused on his daughter and immediately saw what concerned Ginger. Blood was seeping from Ari's nose, dripping onto the worn sheet of the cot.

"Ari, baby," Ginger said in an aching voice. She hurried over to her daughter and carefully slid onto the edge of the bed, careful not to touch her. "Is that where all the blood came from? Did they make you use your powers?"

But Ari's eyes were distant. Vacant, as though she were miles away. Here, but *not* here.

"I'll kill them all," Ari said, her eyes coming to life, glowing eerily where before they'd been utterly lifeless. Then she leveled a stare at her parents, for the first time seemingly aware of her surroundings. "And Beau will come," she said simply.

THIRTY-TWO

AFTER Ari's cryptic statement, she'd immediately drifted into sleep, her features contorted at first and then finally easing as she slid deeper into rest. Ginger lay beside Ari while Gavin paced the confines of the cell restlessly, like a caged lion.

He wanted to know what the hell had been done to Ari, but she'd been unable to provide answers, and he wasn't about to push her when she was seemingly so fragile. But then she'd made that chilling vow that he was still turning over in his mind.

She'd sounded, not only determined, but resolved. Confident. Fearless. And that scared him to death. What the hell was she planning to do? And how could he stand by and do nothing? How could he stop her from whatever it was that put that implacable expression on her face? One that told him she would not be swayed from her objective.

He closed his eyes, whispering a prayer to an entity he'd never believed in before Ginger and Ari had entered his life. He truly believed they were a gift from the angels. God. A higher being. It didn't matter what He was called. Gavin believed—truly believed—when he'd never believed in anything but what he himself had the power to accomplish in his life.

Now he prayed a sincere, fervent prayer for God to watch over and protect his wife and daughter. What happened to him was inconsequential. He'd give his life for the two women he loved so dearly and never hesitate. But he wasn't willing to allow either of them to do the same for him.

He shook his head at the ridiculous turn of his thoughts. Ari had been insensible. Catatonic. Deeply traumatized. He doubted she'd even remember her words when she next awoke. Even as he prayed she'd awaken soon so he could have the answers he so desperately wanted.

Though Ginger was lying on the cot with Ari, she wasn't asleep. She was as wide-awake as Gavin. Ari had sensed her mother's presence even at rest and had snuggled closer to her as she'd settled more firmly into the grasp of sleep. Healing sleep, Gavin hoped.

Ginger ran her fingers through Ari's long hair, something Ari had always enjoyed from an early age. She loved having her hair played with, her head rubbed. It had often comforted her when she'd wake crying in the night. Or when she wasn't feeling well.

"Mama?"

Ari's soft voice reached Gavin's ears and he whipped around, his gaze immediately seeking his daughter. Her back was still to him. Ginger had crawled between Ari and the wall of the cell so she could lie down with her daughter without disturbing her rest.

"Yes, darling," Ginger said quietly, in deference to Ari's earlier sound sensitivity.

"Where's Dad?" Ari whispered back. "Is he here?"

Gavin started to respond, and he was just about to rush over so he could see her for himself and vice versa, but Ari's next words stopped him cold.

"They have monitors in here. They can't see that I'm awake so don't give it away that I am," Ari said in the same whisper. "Look at Dad, so I know where he is, but don't do or say anything to suggest I'm awake."

Gavin controlled his frown. Barely. To Ginger's credit, her expression remained worried and thoughtful just as it had in the last two hours Ari had slept. No betraying emotion or flicker of worry, excitement or anticipation reflected in her carefully controlled features.

Ginger glanced up at Gavin and held his gaze long enough for Ari to ascertain his whereabouts.

"Tell him not to move or rather continue doing whatever he was doing," Ari continued to whisper so Gavin had to strain to hear. "Well, don't say that," she hastily amended. "They can hear you."

"He can hear you, darling," Ginger said without even moving her lips as she continued stroking Ari's hair and holding Gavin's gaze, just as she'd done the entire time Ari had slept.

Gavin saw Ari visibly relax. He hadn't realized just how much tension was contained in her small frame until he saw her sink further into the bed.

"There are things you need to prepare yourselves for," Ari continued.

Gavin walked over to the bed, just as he'd done several times over the past hours and peered down at her as if checking on her. Her words worried him and he needed reassurance. Just to look at her, touch her so he knew she was okay.

"Has she awakened at all?"

He directed the question to Ginger and reached down to lightly stroke Ari's cheek with his finger, another thing he'd done many times in his worry since she'd fallen into sleep.

Tears glittered on Ari's eyelashes, and Gavin's chest tightened in emotion. Damn it! There was so much he wanted to ask. So much he needed to know and his hands were tied. He simmered with impatience, but forced himself to remain in character, not deviating from the pattern he'd established as he and Ginger had watched over their sleeping daughter.

"Not yet," Ginger said in a louder tone. "I'm worried, Gavin. What if they did something terrible to her?"

His clever, clever girl. Finding a way to ask Ari the questions he was dying to ask without anyone being able to pick up on what they were doing.

"I had to let them," Ari said, not moving or reacting to her father's touch, though the tears he'd seen just seconds earlier told him a wealth of information. "It's complicated."

Ari took in a steadying breath, careful not to allow her body language to signal she was anything but deeply asleep. Everything hinged on their captors not picking up on her deception. The havoc she intended to wreak, the vengeance she planned to bring down on them like the wrath of God, had to be unexpected.

Her parents wouldn't like what she had to say. Her father especially wouldn't at all like that he would have to take no active part in her plan. That only Ari would face down their enemies. Alone.

"They want to use my powers. And they're strong. My powers, I mean. So much more than we ever dreamed. In just a short time, I've managed feats I would have never believed myself capable of and yet I know I can do so much more."

"Do you think she was experimented on?" her mother asked her husband, still playing her role to perfection. "Is that where the blood came from?"

"I don't know," Gavin murmured, injecting fatherly outrage and anger into his voice.

"Yes," Ari whispered, slowly reaching for her mother's hand. The one lying in the space between them. With her father standing behind her and her mother so close to her on the narrow cot, there was no way for the camera to pick up on the subtle movement.

She squeezed her mother's hand, tears pricking her eyelids. These were her parents. Biological or not. These were the people who loved her, protected her, stood by her always.

"But I allowed them to," Ari continued. "What I have to say, what you must hear from me will be very hard for you to hear. And even harder to accept. But I'm asking you to trust me. If you've ever loved me, as I know you do. If you've ever had faith in me, as you always have. Then trust me now and listen to what I must tell you." Ari sucked in a shallow breath so her body wouldn't betray a larger motion. "And accept what I must do."

Worry flickered in her father's eyes, raw emotion etched in his features. His back was to the cameras and he stood there a long moment before visibly composing himself and then straightening as if he'd simply shared a private, intimate moment with his wife and shared his worry for their daughter with her for the briefest of moments.

"I allowed them to overload me," Ari said. "So much has happened since you went missing. So much I've learned about myself. My powers. Still so much untapped. Undiscovered. And yet I know there is so much I can do. More than I ever would have thought possible."

Though her mother didn't voice her question aloud, Ari could see it clearly in her eyes.

"I went through a series of tests that were in fact very easy," she explained. "But I purposely thought of things that would put unbearable strain on me so they would see me in psychic overload. So they would see me experiencing a psychic bleed. I needed them to be disgusted or perhaps disappointed or even believe I was worthless to them. At least until I could find you and Dad. Because when they come for me again—and they will—you have to be ready. And you must do exactly as I tell you. It's the only way I can keep you both safe when I bring the rest of this place down and reduce it to rubble, taking every sadistic son of a bitch with it."

Shock registered in her mother's eyes, and she quickly dropped her gaze to hide her response. Though Ari could no longer see her father, she could feel him close, could feel the instant coil and snap of tension within him. It went against his every instinct to willingly allow his daughter to go into a dangerous situation while he hung back waiting to be "saved."

He would be the one hardest to convince and this is where she had to win her mother over so she could rein him in.

She sent her mother a pleading look, begging her to understand. Begging her to trust Ari. To have faith in Ari's abilities.

Her mother's hand tightened around Ari's, squeezing just a little.

"Go on," her mom said without moving her lips.

"I am very powerful," Ari said honestly. "These men are no match for me and I need you to trust in that. To know I'll be safe and to understand that the way I came to you was my *choice*. I had to know where you were. That you were still alive. Because when the time comes, I'll be able to provide a protective barrier around you, but you *must* stay. No matter what you see, what you hear, what you think. You have to stay here while the house is destroyed around you."

She could hear her father's sudden expulsion of breath and then the acceleration of his respirations. Again, she glanced pleadingly up at her mother, asking for her help in convincing her dad.

Once more her mother squeezed her hand, this time with no hesitation. And what Ari saw reflected in her mom's eyes staggered her. Love—of course. But also trust. And . . . *pride*. It shone like a beacon in her mother's eyes. It lit her face, etched into every facet of her expression.

Ari blinked back tears, squeezing her mother's hand and holding on. Simply holding on to that tangible link between mother and daughter. A bond like no other. Irreplaceable. Unwavering. Old as time itself. There truly was nothing like the love of a mother. Unconditional. Solid. Indefinable and limitless. Capable of surviving anything. Able to triumph over the impossible.

And Ari *would* triumph. She believed in herself, just as her mother believed in her. She wasn't a freak of nature. Some accident of birth to be studied, examined or controlled. She did have a purpose. She *was* special.

It had taken her twenty-four years to understand her purpose. To accept it and embrace it. Not to shy away from it, duck it, or suppress or ignore it. Never again. It was an integral part of who and what she was.

And now it would save the people she loved and the people who loved her more than anything in the world.

Blood didn't make a family.

Love did.

"Dad," she called softly, not loud enough to be heard but enough that her mother would somehow let him know to get within hearing range.

"Gavin, come here, please," Ginger said in concern. "Did you see she bled from her ears? Why on earth would something like this happen?"

Ari wanted to smile. And then she felt the warmth seep into her chilled body as both mother and father flanked her once more.

"Dad," she whispered again.

"I'm here," he murmured.

"You have to protect Mom."

It was a manipulative, dirty trick, but she knew by appealing to the protector in her father that while he might be forced to stand down and not take an active role in his daughter's protection, he certainly wouldn't do anything that would bring her mother harm.

Her mom's lips twitched suspiciously as though she knew exactly what Ari was doing. But then her mom had given her useful information over the years on how to handle a male. Particularly his ego.

"You have to make sure she doesn't move once I leave," Ari continued, driving her point home to her father. "If she were to move even a little, if a gap formed between the two of you, then she could very well end up outside the barrier and she could be killed."

Though she was certainly trying to do anything she could to convince her father of the necessity of his remaining behind, she was not lying about his need to protect her mother.

Her mother was fierce when it came to the defense of her only child, and God help them all if she thought Ari was in need or danger, or worse . . . hurt and defenseless.

She felt rather than heard the soft expulsion of his breath in a resigned sigh.

"It was never an issue of me not trusting you," her father said gruffly, emotion thick in his voice.

And there was something else in his tone. Something that warmed her to the bone, warding off the aching chill that seemed a permanent part of her now.

Pride.

She could hear how proud of her he was just by those few words he spoke. It was often the way he spoke of her mother, talked to others about her mother, though God knew, they didn't exactly cultivate any social acquaintances.

"No matter what happens, know I love you both. There is no one in the world I'd rather have as my parents—my family."

She swallowed back further words before she exposed what she knew to be true.

They shared something far more precious than blood. Something she'd never take for granted again.

They shared love. And family. More than anything she wanted Beau to become a part of her family. Her dad would hate him on sight—of course. He wouldn't be doing his fatherly duty if he didn't scowl, threaten and try to intimidate the man he'd swear wasn't good enough for her.

"And there is no one other than you we'd love more as our child," her mother said fiercely.

Once more, her father leaned down to brush his lips over Ari's cheek. And then he whispered as he pulled away.

"We are not going to say our goodbyes and our I love yous like one or all of us is going to die," he reprimanded. "By all that's holy, Ari, if you don't get your ass back to this cell and let me and your mother out so we can escape this place together I'll follow you to heaven and fight God himself for you. He'll get his time later. But for my lifetime, you belong to me."

Ari closed her eyes, peace settling over her like the warmest, most soothing blanket.

"When they come for me, be ready," she whispered, her heart thumping, not in fear, but in anticipation of what was to come. "When they take me, you must stand together and remain in the exact spot you are when I last see you. It's the only way I can save you. Trust me. Have faith in me. I *won't* let you down."

THIRTY-THREE

THEY came sooner than Ari expected, but she was glad for it. She'd rested against her mother, surrounded by her warmth and love, and then she'd roused from sleep, but she had remained stoic and silent, not wanting to give anything away to the silent observers she knew were there.

The only concession she'd made was to tell her parents she was fine. Just a little tired. But that was for the benefit of her observers. Because she was *ready*.

Not even a half an hour later, they came for her.

The same two guards came striding down the hall, stopping at the cell door, both holding guns again, but these were real. Or at least they looked real to her. Holding real bullets capable of killing in a matter of seconds. She knew it was a silent message to her not to resist. A not so silent message to her father when one of the guards simply held a gun to her mother's head and coldly told her father that unless he wanted his wife's gray matter splattered all over the walls he'd stand down and not make any trouble.

As Ari had requested, as soon as Ari "surrendered" herself to the guards and went without a fight, her father gathered her mother to his side and stood directly in front of the cot, his arms firmly around her.

Ari stared back at them as she was roughly shoved through the cell door. She memorized every marker, every detail, taking mental measurements of as much of a barrier she'd need to encompass them both and keep them from harm.

Then she smiled and mouthed "I love you" just before one of the guards yanked on her arm and hauled her out of view of her parents.

It was hard for Ari to act resigned, afraid, and tentative. Like she *feared* these bastards. When what she wanted to do was rain hell down on them with a fury they'd never experienced in their life. What life they had left, that is.

But she forced herself to be patient, knowing she needed this to go off without a hitch. She needed to be far enough away from her parents so that the most devastation would occur in the center of the compound and not the periphery where the cells were positioned and where her parents were being held.

She focused on and anticipated seeing the shock and the eventual realization that they'd seriously underestimated her. That they had fucked with the wrong woman. Revenge was thick in her mouth, a coating on her very soul. Not a taint. Not a scourge. Nothing she would ever be remorseful over.

It was *sweet*. Or so the saying went.

Because the world was a better place without people like these. People who thought nothing of death, intimidation, hurt and fear to achieve their twisted objectives. The hell of it was she still didn't know what their primary goal was. Only that they wanted to use her—her powers—in a way she *knew* was evil.

It could be said she was as twisted and as evil as they were, and she supposed there was some truth to that sentiment. But at the end of the day, her actions, her conscience, the *consequences* for her choices were between her and God. And she was okay with answering to the higher power who'd gifted her with her own "higher power."

She was once again shoved into the sterile, blindingly white laboratory with the same two goons—this time she was going with Pete and Repete—and the smarmy "medical professional" who no more had a medical degree than she did.

"So what now," she said tiredly, purposely injecting extreme weariness—and resignation—into her voice.

The lab rat rubbed his chin in an exaggerated fashion and studied her intently, his eyes flashing with irritation.

"So far you've proven to be a major disappointment," he said in disgust. "And considering the time and money that have gone into the careful cultivation of gaining access to you, disappointment is an understatement."

"Gee," she said with heavy sarcasm. "I feel so insulted that a lab rat and his goons find me a major disappointment. What's the matter? Were you expecting me to be able to achieve world peace? Or maybe fix the ozone issue. Oh wait, there's also the issue of all the starving children in Africa."

She began to press each digit of her hand to count down each point.

"Or maybe you wanted me to find a cure for Ebola. There've been at least ten cases reported in the U.S. over the last month or so. Want me to annihilate all the African nations on the Ebola watch list for you?"

"For someone who seemed willing to do anything to save your parents, you show none now," "Pete," aka Goon A, said in an icy tone.

She sent him a mocking smile that had him furrowing his brow in brief confusion.

"You can't touch my parents," she said softly, satisfaction forming her smile.

"Clearly the brain bleeds leeched most of your intelligence," the lab rat said, shaking his head. "Perhaps a demonstration is in order."

He turned to Repete, Goon B, and issued an order that would have made Ari's blood freeze in her veins if she wasn't *certain* that she was capable of pulling this off. Now more than ever, as much as she'd asked her parents to believe in her, she had to have absolute faith in *herself*. There was no room for error or a breach in her concentration. This was the most important stand she'd ever take in her life. She'd *die* before failing her family.

They turned on the monitor, and to Ari's relief, her parents were still standing in the exact spot, in the same position as when she'd left them. She breathed a silent thank-you that they'd trusted her and prayed that they wouldn't react to whatever this asshole had up his sleeve. Because shit was about to get real.

Goon A barked an order to execute her mother through his radio and mere seconds later, without even opening the cell door, two minions appeared on the periphery of the monitor and opened fire.

Three mouths dropped open when the bullets bounced

harmlessly off an invisible barrier surrounding her parents. Her father had instinctively wrapped himself around her mother, turning so he would take the bullets if Ari had failed, but they hadn't moved from the boundary she'd set. Thank God for her father's rigid discipline.

The lab rat turned his seething glare on her and began advancing, a syringe in his hand. His two goons also began to close in around her and she let her powers fly.

Every single thing she'd dreamed up while lying in the cell with her parents unrolled with ease. She didn't dare close her eyes to concentrate on what she was attempting to achieve over a much longer distance because she faced the very real threat of being drugged, which would render her ineffective. The barrier around her parents would simply disappear and they would die.

So one problem at a time. Her parents were safe. She still had faith that Beau would come to the rescue. All she had to do was wreak some serious havoc in the meantime. And right now? After all these bastards had put her and her family through?

She was thinking this was going to be a lot of *fun*.

Resolve and determination settled over her, cloaking her with confidence she hadn't imagined ever possessing. And she set about unleashing the hounds of hell on the three men who posed the most immediate threat to her.

"You have no idea what you're dealing with," she said in a soft, menacing voice that didn't so much as tremble with fear.

Gone was the meek, shrinking violet *weak* Arial Rochester. Yeah, that's right. *Rochester*. Her name. Her heritage. Blood meant nothing. After all, look where it had gotten Caleb and Beau and their siblings.

Really shitty parents who didn't one damn about them. Yet

her adoptive parents had given her more love in twenty-four years than most people were blessed with in a lifetime.

"That's my line," Goon A said coolly. "I have a score to settle with you, little bitch. And don't think I'm not going to enjoy every second. The people who pay me may want you alive, and now that we've confirmed your powers, your price just skyrocketed, but there's nothing to say I can't make you *wish* you were dead."

Before she could react, taunt him back or make a wickedly sarcastic remark, he pulled out a pistol and put a bullet in the back of lab rat's head. Before Goon B could respond to that shocker, he also received a bullet. In the forehead. Right between the eyes.

Holy shit!

Oh God, oh God. Okay the little fucker had completely stolen her thunder and had temporarily scrambled her brains, and now she was at a loss as to what the hell to do next.

Play it cool, Ari. Never mind you've never been a cool kind of girl. You freak at the slightest fright. You've always been frightened by your own shadow. Get over it. You're not that girl anymore.

"Well, thanks," she said cheerfully, her mind racing as she ran through the possibilities. For once, her photographic memory came through in spades. Yes, it was helpful in her profession as a teacher, not that she'd likely ever have that job again. But now it was going to save her ass because her mind was processing each scenario at the speed of a computer, discarding ones with the least likelihood of succeeding, latching on to the ones with more merit.

His eyes narrowed at her quirky response.

"What?" she asked. "You not used to being thanked? My mama did teach me manners. You just took out two of the guys on my hit list. Now if you'd be so kind as to shoot yourself then I could move on down the list and call it a day."

She was doing a miserable job of covering her panic and hysteria and the bastard realized it. He actually smiled at her. It was a perfectly evil smile, worthy of any movie villain. But then they could be the lead roles in a sci-fi movie. Hell, they were living a damn movie because who would ever believe this shit?

Her mom was so going to wash her mouth out with soap. Apparently being around Beau and his co-workers had lowered her verbal acuity by more than a few points. She'd never cursed so much in her life, despite her father's own propensity for F-bombs.

"What I think is that you're scared shitless, Arial," he said in a mocking tone. "Not so brave now that you have blood on your hands. Were you playing pretend? Or were you really going to kill us all in cold blood?"

"Damn straight," she said, anger injecting a bite to her words. "And I'll suffer not one iota of remorse when I send you straight back to hell, where you crawled from. This time I hope you stay there and rot for eternity."

He clapped, the sound jarring, startling her, his eyes laughing, mocking her at every turn.

"Watch and learn a lesson," she hissed. "Never piss off a woman who has the power to take your balls and feed them to you on a plate."

She caught his look of surprise just as he lifted straight up into the air and hurtled backward, slamming into the wall several feet away. The force with which she sent him flying through the room made the sound of his impact loud and forceful. Satisfaction gripped her and it was her turn to openly mock him.

"Amazing how much of a pussy men become when you threaten their wee little manhood," she drawled. "Bet you don't have that much to work with anyway, so I don't imagine it'll take much effort on my part to separate you from your smaller head."

She donned a thoughtful expression and cocked her head to the side just before she sent him straight upward, crashing into the ceiling. She held him suspended, pinned against the ceiling as though he were caught in a spider's web.

"Although there *are* limits to my powers," she said in amusement. "I have to be able to imagine it in order to manipulate it and if there's not much to work with . . . Well, you understand my problem."

His eyes glittered with fury and then, strangely, *triumph*. A chill went up her spine just as the overwhelming urge to duck and react defensively overtook all else. She dropped like a rock and then performed a powerful leg sweep, rotating blindly behind her.

She connected with something hard and solid, pain shooting up her leg at the contact. Judging by the muffled oath, her assailant hurt worse than she did, though. Splitting her concentration between two objects, or rather people, was more difficult than she'd imagined it would be.

Goon A, still suspended from the ceiling, dropped about a foot before she shot him upward again, but the lapse in concentration cost her dearly. A fist connected with her chin, sending her reeling back several feet. The damn man had *bricks* for hands.

She grasped her jaw, massaging as she focused on keeping the man who scared her the most where he could cause her no harm while planning her offense against her newest assailant.

Her gaze lighted on the pistol the goon trapped on the

ceiling had shot the lab rat and Goon B with. Evidently, he'd dropped it when she slammed him into the wall. Remembering what Beau had told her about Glocks she whispered a prayer that this was a Glock as well and she didn't have to figure out how to mentally turn a safety off. But then surely the goon wouldn't have engaged the safety after killing two men.

Now that she was effectively splitting her mental energy between three things, she found it a lot harder to summon the pistol from across the room. It went skittering erratically over the floor, bumping and knocking. She winced hoping to hell it didn't arbitrarily go off because if she had to ward off a speeding bullet, she could kiss all her other focus goodbye.

Finally the gun lifted into the air and floated toward her, unseen by her newest assailant. The damn goon shouted a warning though, and the man turned just in time to see the gun dangling in front of his face.

Shit!

He reached for it and her instincts, or self-preservation, kicked in. She pictured the gun leveling itself, aiming for the man's shoulder, because damn it, she just couldn't bring herself to be the cold-blooded killer she'd *almost* convinced herself that she could be.

The gun went off and the man went down, holding his left shoulder as blood rapidly spread, seeping through his fingers, coating them red.

She flipped the goon off and then sprinted from the room, knowing she had a hell of a lot more to do before she could call it a day. She squared the ceiling goon away, compartmentalizing him in a section of her mind, issuing a firm command for him to stay.

Then she realized, to her utter horror, that she'd been thinking she was having to split her focus on *three* things when, in fact, she had *four* things going on simultaneously.

Her parents!

Oh God. What if the barrier had slipped? What if she'd killed *them* because she'd spent too much time focusing on *not* killing someone who actually deserved it? She and her conscience were going to have a serious come-to-Jesus meeting when this was all over. Because clearly, having a conscience didn't get one ahead in life. If anything it put her at a major disadvantage in the evolutionary chain.

Her plan would have to change on the fly. She couldn't very well bring the building down and reduce it and everyone in it to rubble if her parents were vulnerable. Damn it all. She wasn't an on-her-feet thinker!

She'd committed the winding passageways to memory— again, thank you, eidetic memory—on her way out today with the guard dogs because her first trip through them wasn't exactly under the best circumstances.

It took her three of the longest minutes of her life before she finally entered the long hallway that housed the ancient jail cells. Where the hell were they, anyway? What kind of creepy place had a lab and prison cells?

She was at full sprint, counting the cells, until she skidded to a halt outside the one that housed her parents. The door was wide open and not only was there no invisible protective bubble. There was absolutely no sign of her parents.

What she *did* see froze her heart to the very core and fear blazed like a wildfire through her veins.

There were multiple puddles of blood—a mortal amount of

scarlet liquid pooled on the floor exactly where she'd instructed her parents to stand. *Fresh* blood. Worse, there were smears of blood that ran from the spot in front of the cot all the way to the door, and as she looked down, she realized it had continued into the hallway. What the hell had they done to her parents? Had they shot them and then dragged them off to parts unknown?

While she was being snarky and sarcastic, indulging in taunts with her enemies, her parents had been left unprotected because she wasn't adept at multitasking with her newly tapped powers.

Utter despair, grief and . . . rage flooded her mind, swamping her in wave upon wave of agony. She'd failed. She'd vowed to them she could do this. Had made them *swear* they'd trust her.

And she'd failed.

Desolation and vast emptiness invading her soul, she slowly turned, her eyes glowing so that she felt the warmth emanating from them. Robotically, she stalked back through the passageways, the twists and turns that would take her back to the center.

God help whoever crossed her path. Gone was her conscience, her squeamishness over killing quickly and efficiently. Revenge and retribution consumed her. She could taste it, feel it. Wrapped herself in its cold and soulless embrace.

A sound alerted her to the presence of men in the passageway with her. They stepped in front of her, an ambush.

She lifted her frigid gaze, completely unruffled by the fact that they were spraying the entire hallway with bullets. They bounced off her, off the barrier that had formed without her even needing to focus on its construction. She saw fear in their eyes, the realization that she was untouchable. It was the last cognizant thought they'd have.

She simply snapped their necks—a quick mental flick of her powers and they collapsed onto the floor. She kicked one aside as she pushed past them, not giving them any more attention than they deserved.

They would pay. They would all pay. Starting with the bastard still suspended from the ceiling where she'd left him minutes before.

THIRTY-FOUR

"WE'RE going in hot," Beau said grimly as the highly classified stealth chopper prototype that did *not* officially exist zoomed over the land, hugging the treetops and traveling at a dizzying rate of speed. "This has to be fast, as clean as possible, *until* we retrieve Ari and her parents. Once they're accounted for and safe then I vote we level the entire goddamn place."

"Fuckin' A," Zack muttered.

"That gets my vote," Eliza said, a scowl darkening her pretty features.

Dane simply nodded his own agreement while the other two operatives, Isaac and Capshaw, gave a thumbs-up, something that amounted to eagerness reflected in their eyes.

They were all looking forward to some serious payback after the breach that resulted in Ari's abduction. It was a black mark and a blow to their pride that they'd been fucked on their own turf. For a second time.

When this was all over with, Beau was going to take great

satisfaction in leveling the fucking house that had proved nothing more than a means of hurting the people he loved. And if he was lucky enough to have a future that included Ari—God he hoped he wasn't setting himself up for major disappointment—then he'd build a fucking fortress that would make security at Fort Knox look like child's play.

Ari would always need protection from the public eye and fanatics wanting to harness and use her powers for their own twisted agenda. Oh *hell* no. Not while he breathed.

Just as Caleb had closed ranks around Ramie and was ruthless in his protection of her, so too would Beau do the exact same with Ari. He may not have understood his brother's overzealousness when it came to Ramie in the past, but he damn well understood it now. Identified with it. He'd spend the rest of his life keeping Ari safe, no matter the cost.

"Almost there," Dane said, his eyes sharp with readiness for the mission ahead. "Everyone needs to be ready to go on my count. This has to be fast because we're open targets when we descend the ropes from the chopper."

Dane, with his endless connections, half of which still managed to bewilder Beau, had gotten his hands on a fucking military stealth helicopter that was invisible to radar and looked like something out of a futuristic movie.

It always pays to have friends in low places.

That was Dane's pet phrase and one he frequently whipped out when asked how the ever loving fuck he managed to get his hands on something most civilians would never even know existed, much less actually *see*. Not that they'd know what the hell they were looking at if they ever did lay eyes on it.

Zach, who'd headed the recon of the partially underground

compound in the Mojave Desert, had uploaded scanned schematics from ground and air surveillance. Using a high-tech classified heat-seeking device, they'd been able to identify three heat signatures just hours before on the periphery of the compound where old jail cells were housed. And Beau had been able to confirm that Ari was one of those heat sources by pinpointing her location with the implanted tracking device. Thank God they'd at least gotten that accomplished before everything went to hell or they truly would be uncovering a needle in a haystack, and he shuddered to think of Ari being out there and him not having the first clue where to start their search for her.

The building used to be a sanitarium in the 1800s. The prison cells were later added in the early 1900s when the hospital had turned into a maximum-security prison for the criminals clinically insane and exceedingly dangerous to society.

The place was creepy as hell and had been deserted for decades. Or so the records stated. It was owned by a corporation not publicly traded and there were zero public records on file for the company that pointed to yet another dummy corporation. Things got interesting, however, when Eliza uncovered a link between PRI and the fictitious corporation that owned the facility.

PRI, or Psychic Research Incorporated, leased the main holding as well as half a dozen outbuildings on the sprawling thousand-acre parcel. Coincidence much?

Apparently some nut research foundation was not only active in cultivating and exploring psychic phenomena, but had invested a mind-boggling amount of money into an actual breeding program disguised as a surrogacy foundation called Creative Adoption Solutions.

Beau had a sickening dread that Ari was a product of that

breeding program; and worse, courtesy of Eliza's mad hacking skills, further digging had uncovered a complicated and well-disguised record of substantial "investments" to the foundation by none other than Franklin Devereaux.

How to explain to Ari that not only was she the product of an experimental birth, but that his own father had a significant role in funding its "research"? Suddenly Gavin Rochester's association—and subsequent visit to Beau's father a mere day before his parents' suspicious deaths—seemed not only plausible but in fact highly probable.

Neither Beau's nor Ari's fathers was a shining example of the founding principles of capitalism and success the old-fashioned way—working your ass off and earning it. No, these two men were so steeped in shadowy dealings that they'd never hold up under concentrated scrutiny no matter how well they covered their tracks.

The question was whether Ari's father had had a hand in Beau's father's—and mother's—untimely deaths. The "coincidences" were mounting and were quite staggering. He was disgusted by his father's participation in something so completely fucked-up and wrong. But then it seemed, the more he discovered the kind of man his father was, the more he realized that he was likely only uncovering the tip of the iceberg, and God only knew what other nefarious acts his father was involved in.

Beau sighed because it was one giant clusterfuck of epic proportions. If Ari's parents were recovered alive, the bombshell of the true circumstances of her birth and his father's role in the whole sordid affair was going to be one big-ass hurdle for Beau and Ari to overcome in their relationship.

Ari could only be expected to forgive so much, and she was

already reeling from the shock of finding out she wasn't Gavin and Ginger Rochester's biological daughter. The additional information could simply prove too much for a woman already on the verge of breaking.

"I only have two heat signatures now," Zack said grimly. "They haven't moved in half an hour. Same spot. Completely still. Seems suspicious as hell."

Beau swore because he didn't have time to check Ari's position within the compound because they were seconds away from go time. His only choice was to go in and turn the entire building upside down to locate her.

The others readied themselves for the helo drop just yards from where the cells were located. It was the most likely place to stash prisoners, though now there were only two visible heat sources, where before there'd been three.

Beau should have known it wouldn't be that easy. His pulse had accelerated upon learning there were three people housed in a single cell. It sounded too good to be true. But Ari had been there along with two others, and their heat signatures signaled that they were all alive. Heat meant life. They'd planned to go in guns blazing, using some serious shock and awe, cause as much confusion as possible, set up explosive diversions so the fuckers wouldn't know which way was up or down and would have no idea where Beau and the others were coming at them from.

He forced himself to calm. One thing at a time. If Ari's parents were in the cell, they'd go in, secure the two prisoners and stash them so they were out of the line of fire, and then Beau was going to take the entire compound apart piece by piece until he recovered Ari. Once he was assured of her safety, he didn't give two fucks what happened to the rest. As far as he was concerned, this entire facility was evil and twisted and the world would be a better place without its existence. Because if Ari had indeed been a part of some fucked-up program disguised as a surrogacy organization then it stood to reason others had been as well, and if taking out the building and the assholes responsible for so much pain and grief saved others the same, then all the more reason to bring it down and reduce it to rubble.

With the helicopter now in position, Beau and the others rapidly descended the ropes, dropping to the ground below while the chopper hovered in place. As soon as they were in position, the helicopter streaked away to the designated rendezvous point, a designated "safe zone" that was easily defendable and where they could be assured of the safety of Ari and her parents.

In full military gear, they raced to the outer wall of a cell two down from where the heat signatures had registered. Dane and Zack quickly set the explosive that would create a large enough entry point into the facility so they could get in and hopefully out with at least Ari's parents.

In thirty seconds, the explosive was set and Dane motioned for them all to take cover. As soon as everyone had ducked from sight, Zack triggered the explosion and a loud boom shook the ground. A large chunk of the stone wall simply disappeared in a cloud of dust and rubble and even before it cleared, Beau was on the move, the others falling into position as they one by one ducked through the opening and inside the gloomy, dank, dungeonlike building.

The first thing Beau registered as they surged out of the cell and into the long hallway was the sound of gunfire. Close.

Fuck!

A female cry arose, sharp in the ensuing silence. Then more gunfire. Beau's pulse exploded and he rapidly motioned the others to be on the ready.

They spread out, quickly pouring down the hallway in the direction of the sounds of shots fired and the feminine cry of fear. At least he *hoped* it was fear and not pain.

When they reached the open cell door, a gruesome sight greeted them. Gavin Rochester had taken down two armed men and was systematically taking apart the third and only remaining assailant.

When the man managed to break away from Gavin's enraged grasp and lunged for Ginger, Beau didn't hesitate. He put a bullet through her attacker's head and he dropped like a rock, mere inches from where Ginger stood, pale, frozen, eyes wide with shock and fear. In the attacker's hand was a wicked blade, one he clearly intended to use to take Ari's mother out, and if it weren't for Beau's sudden appearance, the man would likely have succeeded in his desperate attempt to lash out.

Gavin whirled, eyes cold, enraged, prepared to take on the new threat. He was an impressive sight even with blood dripping from multiple wounds.

"Stand down!" Dane barked. "We're on your side."

Beau took a step forward, careful not to trigger any violence from Gavin, who was clearly determined that no harm come to his wife.

"Ari came to us," Beau said in a calm voice. "I'm Beau Devereaux. These are my men. We need to get you out of here now."

Gavin visibly relaxed and now stark fear replaced his earlier fury. Ginger flew into his arms with a cry, burying her face in his chest as her body heaved with sobs. Gavin tenderly cradled his wife's head with his palm, holding her tightly. His gaze lifted to Beau's and the raw agony, fear and emotion in his eyes were stark. Beau nearly flinched from the very real pain in the older man's face.

"Ari," Gavin said hoarsely. "You have to find her. Save her. She let them take her. *Wanted* them to take her because she planned to destroy the entire damn building. She instructed me and her mother to remain in one spot so she could protect us and how she was able to do it I have no idea, but she erected some sort of force field around us. The bastards opened fire on us and the bullets just bounced *off*."

The incredulity in his voice was evident, but Beau only nodded because none of this information surprised him. He'd witnessed firsthand just how powerful Ari was. But fear skittered up Beau's spine, because the protective shield had obviously been *breached*, which meant that Ari had faltered at some point. He shook off the paralyzing, gut-wrenching thoughts of her being incapacitated. Hurt. *Dead*. He couldn't—wouldn't—go there.

"There's a lot you don't know about your daughter's power, sir," Beau said. "Now, we need to go and I need you to tell me every single thing you know so we can find Ari. But you and your wife have to be out of the way and safe."

When Gavin started to launch a protest, Beau immediately shut him down.

"With all due respect, sir, if you love your daughter, if you want her safe and alive, then you'll go with my men and you'll remain out of the way. We can't afford any distractions or hindrance and you would be both. Let us do our jobs. I will *not* rest until I have her back."

The last statement came out fierce. Not the words of a man

simply doing his job. There was a wealth of emotion in those words, but they slipped past his lips, heavy on his heart, determination beating as incessantly as his pulse.

Gavin's eyes flickered and he stared hard at Beau in response to Beau's choice of wording. His gaze narrowed, almost as if he were trying to discern Beau's interest and whether it was purely professional or if it was . . . personal.

Ginger too looked up, turning to face the man who'd just declared he'd save her daughter. She studied him even as Beau's men surrounded them and began herding them toward the door.

Ginger paused when they reached the point where Beau was standing, waving off the efforts of his men to get them on the move. She reached out and gently touched Beau's arm.

"What is my daughter to you, Mr. Devereaux?" she asked softly.

"She's *everything*," Beau said bluntly, not even trying to disguise his own vulnerability, the wealth of emotion he was sure shone in his own eyes.

It should have made him crawl right out of his skin to make such a personal, open declaration in front of two people who were strangers to him as well as his entire team of operatives. But he didn't give two fucks, because damn it, she *was* everything. *His* everything. Without her, his life would be incomplete and he didn't give a shit who knew it.

Ginger squeezed his arm and then to his surprise, she leaned up on tiptoe and brushed a kiss across his cheek.

"I think my daughter could be in no better hands," she whispered. "Bring her back to me, Mr. Devereaux. I'm begging you. Bring our baby back to us."

Beau gently touched her elbow, guiding her toward the hallway so they could be taken to safety.

"I *will* get her back," Beau vowed, including Ari's father in his sweeping gaze, one firm with resolve. "You have my word."

Just as they reached the cell where the explosives had carved out an exit through the wall, the ground beneath them quaked and rolled, nearly knocking Ginger off balance. Gavin made a grab for her, securing her against him as they all looked around in bewilderment.

The entire building began to shake. The walls vibrated. Dust kicked up and swirled. Objects began flying around the air in a vortex that resembled a tornado. In the distance, loud cracking and splintering sounds erupted. Harsh shouts of fear, muffled by even more quaking.

The sound of grown men screaming in fear and *pain* sent a bone-deep chill through Beau.

Again the floor literally rolled beneath their feet. A crack appeared in the concrete, rapidly snaking its way along the floor, opening up, widening. Then more. Like a spiderweb, smaller cracks burst through the floor and raced in all directions. It was like experiencing an honest-to-God *earthquake*. A *huge* one.

Unease crawled up Beau's spine even as he shot an urgent look in Zack's direction. Dane's expression was grim with the realization that had hit them all. Only Ari's parents seemed bewildered and uncertain of what was happening. But everyone else knew.

Ari's powers had been unleashed and this was only the beginning. Beau knew that the full extent of her powers had yet to be tested and that she was capable of so much more than that which she'd come into in a very short period of time.

"Oh fuck," Beau swore.

"What?" Gavin demanded.

"What's happening?" Ginger cried.

The desperation in both their eyes was evident. Fear. Worry for their daughter. They had no idea what Ari was capable of. They'd only gotten a taste of the full extent of her powers. Hell, Beau himself was certain he had seen only the tip of the iceberg and that now, unchecked, Ari's rage would be a terrible thing to behold.

With the threat of her parents' lives hanging in the balance, Ari's fury would know no bounds. There was nothing she wouldn't do to save the people she loved. And Beau was terrified for her. Because though Ari was steadily coming into her own and growing more adept at directing and focusing the awesome scope of her abilities, she was extremely vulnerable in the aftermath. She could die from a massive brain bleed or suffer a stroke she never recovered from. The probability of her incurring a debilitating injury was extremely high, and unless Beau got to her fast, there wasn't a damn thing he could do to save her.

"What the hell is going on?" Gavin barked. "Is my daughter in danger?"

Beau looked up at Gavin as they shoved out of the hole in the wall and stood outside the shaking building. Pieces of the roof, shards of glass from broken windows and even pieces of the stone exterior littered the landscape. Ari was taking down the building and everything in her path. With her *in* it.

"Sir, your daughter *is* the danger."

THIRTY-FIVE

IT took precious minutes—minutes they didn't have—for Beau to convince, or rather order Gavin Rochester to remain at the rendezvous point with his wife, the pilot and a very reluctant, displeased Eliza.

Dane had insisted Eliza remain behind and she was not chill with that at all. Her eyes had narrowed to glaring slits and Beau had heard more than a few curses tear past her lips. But when Dane had put it in the light of there needing to be at least two people on point to protect not only the Rochesters, but the helicopter as well, because if the helo was disabled, they were fucked in the middle of the desert, Eliza had grudgingly capitulated.

Still, Beau could feel the heat of her glare as he, Zack, Dane, Cap and Isaac rapidly made tracks back to the inner sanctum of the compound.

Zack walked ahead at Beau's side, pulling up Ari's position, as well as pinpointing the other heat signatures in the building.

Beau's eyes widened when he saw the screen flash and display the results.

"What the fuck?" Beau asked incredulously.

Dane caught up on Zack's other side to peer at the device and then whistled.

"I'd say you've got one pissed-off hellcat," Zack said.

Where before there were at least four dozen heat signals inside the building, there were now only a little over a dozen. As he'd noted before, heat meant life, and well, unless the device had malfunctioned, Ari had gone on a rampage and taken down three-fourths of the men responsible for holding her and her parents prisoner.

"Ari is here," Zack said, pointing to a blinking light at the end of a long corridor. "As you can see there are three heat sources there. But none between the cell where she and her parents were held and the room she currently occupies. Which means she mowed down anyone in her way."

"And none there," Dane murmured, gesturing toward one of the hallways that was bare of any heat source.

"The rest are here." Zack pointed to a concentrated area where ten dots overlapped one another on the screen. "If we get lucky, we can slip down that first hallway that is across the compound from where Ari is, take out whoever the two blips are in the room with her then take her, and get the hell out before the others decide to come looking for us."

"Sounds like a plan to me," Beau muttered.

Beau would normally be more proactive in planning missions down to the minutest detail. But he had no objectivity for this one and he knew it. He also knew he couldn't trust himself to make sound, unemotional decisions. Not when it came to Ari.

So he'd allowed Zack free rein, which probably didn't sit well with Dane, but if it bothered the other man he didn't show it. All he displayed was his usual determination to see a mission through successfully. Beau appreciated that particular trait, now more than ever. Because this mission was deeply personal and if it went to hell, Beau would go right to hell with it.

As they approached the wall of the prison cells, the pitched roof in the middle of the facility simply collapsed and flames roared upward, licking toward the sky. Smoke billowed in black clouds and the fire began to race across the rest of the roof.

Ash, cinder and burning debris blew hard over them, pelting down like a hailstorm.

"Your girl is wreaking some serious havoc," Zack said, awe in his voice. "I think I might be in love."

Beau merely stared, more worried than ever, as they closed the remaining distance, picking up speed until they were at full sprint.

They ducked inside the gaping hole in the wall and streamed one by one into the hallway. Dane and Capshaw took the others' sixes by turning so they walked backward, guns up, scanning the hallway behind.

When they got to the doorway that opened into a large circular room with a glassed-in dome, they paused only long enough to ensure Ari's position hadn't changed and that they weren't in for any unexpected surprises.

The mostly vacant area of the complex they were standing in was likely at one time either a nurses' station or a reception area with each of the corridors branching off housing different wings of the so-called hospital. Obviously the more serious threats to society were housed in the filthy, vermin-infested barred cells, and Beau was sickened that anyone would be treated with so little humanity. Even if the criminals were the worst sort of human beings.

Here they were reduced to the furthest thing from humanity one could get. Most animal shelters and, hell, modern prisons, for that matter, offered better accommodations.

But then the bastards who'd put their hands on Ari, who'd stuffed her parents into a tiny cell with deplorable conditions, deserved far worse, so Beau would reserve his judgment in the future before offering blanket sympathy to anyone.

"We got a problem," Zack said grimly. He turned halfway so he stared at the hallway to the far lower right. "Got movement in the northern wing. Headed this way."

Dane tensed, immediately shifted so his hands held a weapon in each. Then he nodded at Cap and Isaac.

To Beau and Zack he said, "Go and retrieve Ari. We'll provide cover here and make sure they don't get past us. Let us know when you're coming in, though, so neither of you gets your balls shot off."

"Thanks," Zack said dryly. "I'd rather not part ways with my dick."

Restless, Beau started down the hallway. Toward Ari. Toward his *life*, leaving Zack to catch up. Or not. He wasn't waiting another goddamn minute. He trusted Dane and the others to do their job and keep the men creeping toward them at bay long enough for them to tag Ari and get her the hell out.

No sooner had they taken two steps down the corridor than

the floors buckled and rolled like ocean waves beneath their feet. The walls shook, knocking already askew paintings down to clatter on the tile below. The ceiling and rafters creaked and groaned in protest, swaying until it felt as though the entire building was in motion. The sound was ominous, the signal of impending collapse.

Relying on Zack's techno recon, Beau ran toward the end. Toward the one closed door that Ari was behind, paying no heed to the barren rooms that lined either side of the hallway. Zack was hot on his heels, guns in both hands, arms up, his piercing gaze missing nothing. Beau knew he was being reckless, but he counted on his partner to cover his stupid ass. Zack had never failed him yet in their rather short acquaintance.

Beau slowed only enough to let Zack catch up so they could kick the door in. But before they made any motion to do so, the door splintered apart, breaking free from its hinges and sailing down the hallway in *pieces*.

Both men ducked, barely in time to prevent their heads from being taken off.

"Down!" Zack yelled, shoving at Beau as he started to get to his feet once more.

A *man* went flying down the hallway after the door, crashing into the far wall. He punched a hole straight through the Sheetrock, forming a cavernous opening.

"Holy *shit*," Beau said, his face a mask of shock. "She's kicking some serious ass!"

"Uh, yeah. What was your first clue? Three dozen heat signatures suddenly vanishing? Oh wait, make that one more in the 'ticked off the list' column. Ari thirty-eight. Bad guys ten. Or maybe it was the huge-ass hole in the roof with an inferno blazing and erupting like a fucking volcano. Or perhaps—"

"I get it," Beau muttered. "Smart-ass."

Zack snickered but cautiously rose, humor disappearing from his features when he stared inside the now-open doorway.

"Beau," Zack murmured. "You need to get in there. Now."

THIRTY-SIX

EVEN Goon A's smirk was now gone. Where before he'd been smugly assured that Ari didn't have the guts to actually kill someone, uncertainty now marked his features and fear was stark in her eyes.

Good.

Because she meant goddamn business. Gone was any squeamishness whatsoever over causing the deaths of the assholes who'd killed her parents and dragged their bodies off like discarded trash.

Fury sizzled and boiled, hissing through her veins until a warm throb reverberated through her entire body.

"What did you do with them?" she demanded, her tone so frigid that she could discern an actual temperature change in the room.

A puzzled look furrowed his brow and then pain rapidly took its place when she applied pressure to his throat, momentarily cutting off his airway. He was solidly plastered to the ceiling, incapable of moving. He was completely paralyzed and capable of doing her no harm whatsoever.

"Tell me what you did with them or I swear to God, you'll die an agonizing, long death and you'll beg me to kill you and end it all," she said in a dangerously soft voice.

She let off the pressure on his throat, but twisted his testicles painfully until his face was a mask of pain.

"I don't know what the fuck you're talking about," he ground out, his jaw clenched and bulging as he breathed through the agony she was inflicting on him. "You saw what I saw. Whatever the hell kind of voodoo you performed rendered bullets ineffective."

The mental strain she was under was fast sapping her strength and taking its toll. Blood seeped in a continuous stream from her nose and she could feel the warm slide of liquid down the sides of her neck.

She wiped her nose with the back of her arm, smearing some of the blood over her lips. It was a metallic, sickening taste in her mouth. The floor beneath her feet reacted to her psychic energy, vibrating and buckling, tiny cracks forming and then growing larger.

An ominous creaking sound filled the room as if the building were expressing its weariness and weakness. Lightbulbs popped, shattering and sending shards of glass in all directions. A few hit her, inflicting cuts, but she ignored everything, never wavering in her focus on the man above her.

The entire area was responding to the restless, wild energy flowing through her and around her. Her skin tingled as if the air was electrically charged and a continuous current flowed in a cycle.

She felt . . . otherworldly. Like someone in a fantasy movie. Magic or witchcraft. Whichever of the two fit. In this moment, she felt a rush of power so strong that she nearly fell to her knees. It filled her, consumed her, nearly overwhelming in its intensity.

Never had she felt so strong, capable of any feat no matter how impossible. Her spine stiffened and she straightened, resolve settling over her and instilling the will to do what she must.

Pain speared through her head, her body, making her feel as if her bones were shattering. Blood poured from her orifices and she could only imagine how horrifying she must look. She hoped to hell she scared the holy shit out of the little bastard pinned by the awesome force of her powers.

Some of what she was feeling had to be readily visible, because the goon's face went white as a sheet and he stared at her, realization—and doom—flashing in his eyes.

"Yeah, you little fucker," she whispered in an eerie voice. "Resign yourself to your fate and the embarrassment over being beat by a 'little bitch,' as you so succinctly put it. Well, this bitch is going to send you straight to hell."

"Ari!"

She flinched at the loud outburst and took an instinctive step back before she realized who it was calling her name. She turned, relief crushing down on her, when she saw Beau inside the doorway, his eyes bright with terror. Zack rushed in to stand beside him and immediately put the man on the ceiling in his gun sights.

"He's mine," Ari said, her voice like a whip cracking through the room.

"Ari, honey," Beau said in a soothing tone. "We need to

get you out of here before the entire place goes up in flames or comes down on our heads."

Tears burned her eyelids and she wasn't sure if it was blood or tears that now streamed from her eyes. Maybe both.

"He killed them," she said hoarsely. "He killed my parents! He ordered their executions while I stood here. And oh God, I had a barrier around them, but I let my focus waver and the shield slipped. I saw their blood!"

Beau's eyes widened. He and Zack exchanged quick glances and Beau cursed softly under his breath.

"Ari, they aren't dead."

"I *saw*!" she shouted. "Don't try to appease me. Don't lie to me to get me to come with you. I won't go until every last one of these assholes is dead."

"Ari, they are not dead," Zack said, his voice firm, not as soothing as Beau's. Utter seriousness was etched in his features as he stared at her. "We got them out of the cell. The blood you saw was from the two guards your father killed. Beau shot the third one when he went after your mother. They're fine. I swear to you. They're safe and waiting for you. They're worried sick about you. Afraid to their bones that something has happened to you. So let it go so we can take you to your parents. So you can see for yourself we aren't lying to you."

Ari blinked, her mouth drooping open, some of the horrifying thoughts of anger and violence diminishing as she gauged Zack's sincerity.

"They're *alive*?" she whispered.

Beau stepped closer, his movement tentative as though he were afraid to touch her. Afraid she'd shatter.

"Yes, honey, they're alive," Beau said quietly. "You protected them. Your barrier prevented the bullets from hitting them. And when it did fall, your father took out two of the men in quite an impressive manner. They're safe, and waiting for you, and as Zack said, they're out of their minds with worry. Because you sacrificed yourself for them. Don't do something now that will cause them to grieve the rest of their lives and feel guilt over the fact that you sacrificed your life for them. Don't make *me* grieve because I lost you."

He slid his hand up the length of her arm, over her shoulder and then around her nape, gently pulling her toward his body.

"Please, Ari. Come with me," he softly begged. "The building is destroyed. It won't stand much longer. What few you men you didn't take out, Dane, Capshaw and Isaac are taking care of now. It's over. You kicked their asses, and you made sure that no one will ever use this place for evil again."

She allowed herself only a brief, sweet moment in Beau's arm, in his strong, protective embrace, before reluctantly pulling herself away. Then she slanted a glance in the goon's direction.

"There's still one more," she said coldly. "And I have a personal score to settle with him anyway. He's the asshole who tried to drug me the morning after my parents disappeared."

Beau's eyes grew cold as he shifted his stare toward the man pinned helplessly on the ceiling.

Then another quake rolled through the entire complex, rattling chairs, furniture and the very foundation. Distant crashes sounded, drawing closer and closer. Indeed, Beau was right. The building was coming apart at the seams, guided by her overwhelming rage and psychic energy.

"Leave him," Beau said, slipping his fingers through hers.

"Let him die when the building comes down on him. He doesn't deserve a quick and merciful death."

Still, Ari hesitated because the taste for revenge was still strong in her mouth.

A deafening crash much closer this time and then a shout carried through the accumulating rubble. Beau's name.

"Let's roll," Zack barked out. "Do you want us all to die so you can have your revenge, Ari?"

Beau snarled at him and Ari could see the rebuke poised to fly. She squeezed Beau's hand. "He's right, Beau. I'm not thinking clearly. Forgive me. The last thing I want is for anyone to die because of my hatred and thirst for vengeance."

Beau wrapped a steadying arm around her and guided her toward the doorway. Or what was left of it. As the rush of adrenaline began to wear off, her knees started shaking. Her entire body shook. Her legs buckled and Beau had to haul her up against his side to keep her from sagging to the floor.

"I'm all right," she said through gritted teeth. "I can make it. You need both your hands."

"You are *not* all right," Beau bit back. "You don't see how bad you look, Ari. You scared the ever-loving shit out of me when I saw you back there. God. I thought I was too late. I can't believe you're still standing after bleeding so damn much. The very first thing we're doing when we get the hell out of this godforsaken place is take you to a hospital."

They hurried down the hall amid shouts from Dane to Beau to hurry his ass up. Ari knew she was slowing them down, but Beau refused to let go of her.

They were within sight of Dane and the two men flanking them when the walls on either side of them exploded outward, pelting them with debris and Sheetrock. An ominous cracking sound erupted and then Ari found herself flying backward, Beau cradling her to absorb her fall.

The entire ceiling and second floor had caved in, blocking their pathway to where the others waited.

"Zack?" Beau yelled, worry in his voice.

"I'm here. I'm okay."

Then Beau reached up to frame Ari's face in his hands. She was atop him, Beau having broken her fall. His worried gaze raked over her. "Are you all right? Do you hurt anywhere?"

She grimaced. "I hurt everywhere but it has nothing to do with this particular incident. I'm fine, Beau."

"We're going to have to get out another way," Zack said grimly.

"What?" Ari asked incredulously. "I can get through that. I've certainly done a lot more difficult things."

"No," both men said in unison.

She shook her head, sure she was misunderstanding something.

"You can't take much more, Ari. Any fool can see that. You're done. Finished. If you incur another bleed I can't even imagine what will happen and if it's all the same to you I'd rather not have you a vegetable for the rest of you life."

"Oh for God's sake," she muttered. "And how do you propose we get out this 'other' way if you won't let me use my powers."

"Because we'll blow a hole in one of the outer walls so it doesn't bring the interior structure down on our heads," Beau said patiently.

She sighed. "Whatever. Let's get on with it. I want to see my parents."

They picked themselves up from the floor and Zack led the way, Ari positioned between the two men. She should be in front. It made no sense for men who were vulnerable to bullets to be on the front line instead of a woman who wasn't vulnerable to attack to lead. But she didn't even waste her breath arguing because one, they'd never agree and she'd waste precious time beating her head against a brick wall. And two, she just wanted it over and done with so she could see for herself that her parents were okay.

At least Beau was letting her walk under her own steam this time, and she was determined not to hinder their progress in any way, so she powered past the agonizing pain and extreme exhaustion and stayed right on Zack's heels the entire way.

They veered left into the very last room before the one where the goon was playing Spider-Man and Zack immediately went to the far wall and began adhering plastic explosives at various spots.

"Won't this just blow a hole into the corridor of prison cells?" Beau asked with a frown.

Zack shook his head, never looking up from his task. "The last three rooms in this hallway extend farther than the outbuilding that houses the cells. When we bust a hole in this wall, we'll be on the outside."

"Works for me. Hurry," Beau urged.

"Get down and take cover," Zack directed.

Beau ducked behind an island cabinet that looked like solid steel construction, dragging Ari with him. Beau got down on his haunches, but Ari was much shorter, so she simply half squatted, just to the left side of Beau so her hand held his shoulder to steady herself.

An eerie prickling sensation caused every hair on her body to bristle and stand on end. A chill chased down her spine and around to her gut, tightening her stomach until it was a clenched ball.

Just as earlier, when she'd sensed an immediate threat to her and had dropped and lashed out, instinctively defending herself from an unseen attacker, she knew that danger was imminent.

She turned her head over her shoulder, because it was the only place there could be danger. The only place not readily in her sight line. She froze, the entire world moving in slow motion. Like she was in some bizarre dream where she watched but was helpless to do anything else.

The goon she'd left trapped on the ceiling to die when the building fell was standing in the doorway, gun in hand, pointing it directly at . . . *Beau*.

There was no spontaneous, instinctual self-preservation barrier that immediately formed without her having to build it in her mind because *she* wasn't the target. And she knew she didn't have time to erect one around Beau because she was simply too weak, too unfocused to form it in time.

A shot sounded, and she did the only thing she could do. The only thing she had time to do. She stepped in front of Beau, her back turned to the gunman. She grabbed Beau's head, yanking it protectively to the top of her thighs, covering him as best she could, and she closed her eyes.

THIRTY-SEVEN

BEAU'S head was suddenly yanked back and he let out a startled exclamation just as a gunshot sounded. It was all simultaneous and happened so quickly that he couldn't make sense of what had just occurred.

Ari had his head and neck in a death grip and held him rigidly against her legs. But then he felt her stiffen, and a harsh cry of pain pierced his heart, freezing him in abject fear.

Oh God. Gunfire. Ari stepping behind him. Ari cradling his head protectively in her arms. Ari crying out in pain. No. Oh God, no! It all added up to one thing and one thing only. She'd put herself between him and whoever fired the shot.

Zack reared as soon as the shot sounded, gun whipping up and aiming behind Beau. Before Beau could even turn to see the source of the gunshot, Zack fired two rounds in rapid succession and then immediately sprang to his feet.

"Ari's taken a hit," Zack said unnecessarily.

Beau *knew* Ari had taken the bullet meant for him, and he

was utterly sick to his soul. It seemed like it took an eternity to turn, catching her in his arms before she collapsed to the floor when in actuality it was a fraction of a second. The entire episode had taken two seconds at the most, but his reflexes were sluggish. Paralyzed with utter terror for what he'd discover when he managed to see the extent of the damage wrought by the bullet.

"Ari!"

His agonized cry shattered the eerie quiet that had descended after Zack took out the assailant.

Her face was stark white, bloodless, her eyes dull and lifeless as she listed to the side, going utterly limp in his arms.

"Oh God," he said brokenly. "Ari, honey, why? Why would you do this? *Why?*"

Not waiting for an answer. It wasn't important. He knew damn well *why*. Because it was her nature to put herself before others. To protect when she was the one in need of protection. If she died saving his life it would be for nothing because his life wasn't worth a damn thing without her in it.

He gently laid her down on the floor so he could find the source of all the blood spilling onto the floor. His heart was about to explode out of his chest. Never had he felt such a black wave of despair. Never had he felt so utterly alone as he did right now. He couldn't lose her. Couldn't live without her. He couldn't remember his life *before* her. Didn't want to imagine a future without her in it, by his side. Always in his heart, mind, soul, bed. Raising a family—their family—together, surrounded by love as bright as the sun. Love that outshone any star that ever shined. There was no brighter light than Ari. Not to him.

She had to live. For him, she had to survive, or he would be forever lost. He'd forever be bereft of her light. He'd live in total darkness, never to love—truly live—again.

"Jesus," Zack muttered as he knelt next to Beau. "I hope to hell it didn't nick her femoral artery. She'll bleed out long before we get her to a hospital."

"Shut the fuck up!" Beau said fiercely. "She's *not* going to die. I won't let her!"

He turned his attention back to Ari, who sluggishly blinked, her eyelids fluttering weakly.

"Beau?"

Her voice was quivery, and she sounded so weak that it struck terror to the depths of his soul.

"Yes, honey, I'm here," he said, trying to keep the sheer panic from his voice.

"Are you hurt?" she said in barely a whisper. "Did he shoot you?"

Tears burned like acid in his eyes. She lay there barely conscious and yet her only thought was whether *he* was okay or not. A thin rivulet slipped down his cheek. And then another.

He smoothed a shaky hand over her hair and then pressed a kiss to her forehead, letting his lips linger there for a long moment as he tried to collect himself. He inhaled deeply, trying to settle his seething emotions. So he could be strong for her. As strong as she was, as strong as she'd been for *him*. It shamed him to the depths of his soul that she'd been the one to save him. Not the other way around. Never again. He'd protect her with his dying breath for the rest of his days.

"I'm fine," he choked out. "Swear to God, Ari, if you ever pull this kind of stunt again I'll lock you in the goddamn bedroom and never let you out."

Her smile was crooked. And pained. She closed her eyes, her body seeming to fold inward.

"Ari!" he said in a panicked tone. "Don't go out on me. Stay with me. *Please* stay with me. Stay awake. Just a little longer and then you can rest. I promise."

He was begging, pleading with her and he didn't care. He had no pride when it came to her. There was nothing he wouldn't do to save her.

Zack was on the radio barking orders to the others, his tone harsh and urgent.

Without taking his anxious gaze from Ari even for a split second he said to Zack, "Blow the damn wall so we can get the fuck out of here. We have to get her to a hospital as soon as possible. I don't care about anything else. Just get us the hell *out*."

"The charges are set. All I have to do is pull the trigger. You got Ari covered?"

Even as Zack asked, he didn't wait for a response. Instead he moved over so that he and Caleb protectively flanked Ari. Zack took care to cover the parts of Ari Beau couldn't, and then he set off the explosion, ducking his head to protect his eyes from any debris.

Beau did the same and simply shoved Ari's face into his chest, his palm covering the back of her head and holding her in place so nothing touched her.

The explosion shook the room, the floor, the walls and the rafters.

"Shit!" Zack said in an urgent voice. "We have to get out *now*. The entire roof is coming down. Get Ari and go!"

Beau needed no such urging. He was already hoisting Ari

more securely into his arms and he rose, keeping her face against his chest so she didn't inhale any of the smoke or dust that blew through the room like a hurricane.

No sooner had they cleared the gaping hole in the wall than the roof caved, in collapsing like a cascade of dominos. Another cloud of dust and smoke kicked up and surrounded them until both men were coughing.

The air was fresher, cleaner, the farther they got from the building and was a welcome change from the stale, oppressive interior of the compound. Beau inhaled deeply in an effort to clear not only his lungs, but his mind as well. His heart was too heavy with worry and grief, but he needed his senses about him because, until he had Ari well away from there and in a hospital getting the care she required, he needed all the mental acuity he could muster.

"They're landing the helo here," Zack said. "No way Ari can make that trek to the rendezvous point. There isn't room for us all, so you, Ari and her parents will take the chopper. The rest of us will commandeer one of the vehicles here and get there as soon as we can."

"I want you with us," Beau said firmly.

Zack was, in Beau's mind, his right-hand man, just as Dane was Caleb's. He trusted Zack to watch his and Ari's six when Beau knew he wouldn't be as sharp as he normally was.

"Then I'll go," Zack said quietly.

Just like that. No questions. No hesitation. Just unwavering loyalty and resolve.

"Thanks," Beau said softly.

"Never have to ask, man."

"I know. Appreciate that."

To Beau's relief, the chopper appeared, only a slight hum to the air to signal its arrival. Beau was moving toward it before it even landed, waiting as it gently touched down.

Dane, Capshaw and Isaac quickly climbed out while Beau surged forward bearing Ari with him, Zack on his heels.

As soon as Beau climbed into the interior, Ari's mother cried out in alarm and her father let out a blistering round of curses.

"What the fuck happened to her?" Gavin roared.

Before Beau could respond, Ari stirred in his arms, opening eyes cloudy with pain and confusion. Then they cleared and frost entered the multicolored orbs.

"Beau, wait," she said, her voice stronger than it had been just moments earlier.

"No we will *not* wait," Beau said fiercely. "You have to get to a hospital now. In case you forgot, you've been shot!"

Ginger gasped. "What?"

Ari struggled to sit up, Beau's arm a barrier to her objective. When he realized she wouldn't rest and would only do herself more harm if he didn't allow her up, he reluctantly eased her upward, careful to keep a steadying hand at her back and around her waist.

Her eyes glowed as she stared at the building just yards away. Pain wrinkled her face and her concentration was fierce. It was then he realized what she was trying to do.

"Goddamn it, Ari, no!" Beau roared. "Enough! I refuse to let you kill yourself over this. You've bled far too much even before you were shot. You're going to have a stroke or an aneurism."

He turned his pleading gaze on her parents, silently asking for their support.

"Ari, whatever it is you think you're doing, please don't," her mother said softly. "Please, just come home with us."

Ari shook her head, eyes still glowing. Blood began to slowly creep from her nose and her ears as her brow furrowed even more.

The earth shook beneath the helicopter, making it shake too. Ari's parents glanced uneasily at their daughter and Gavin forcefully interjected himself.

"Ari, stop it," he demanded. "I won't let you do this. I won't let you do further harm to yourself. For your mother's sake—for my sake, *stop.*"

"I have to do this," Ari said softly. "I can't let them win. I made a vow. To myself. And I have to see it through. I can't let others endure what's been done to me and countless others."

Then she closed her eyes as if shutting them all out. Beau. Her parents. Everything but her objective.

Beau issued a sharp command to the pilot to take off, hoping that would deter Ari.

He should have known better.

Even as the helicopter rose, hovering a split second before zooming over the building and away, the entire complex went up in an explosion of flames, a mushroom cloud resembling an atomic blast hurling upward into the air.

Everyone in the helicopter stared down in awe as the building simply disintegrated before their very eyes.

But Beau was only looking at Ari. At the blood running like a river from her nose, ears and mouth. He tightened his hold around her even as he was careful not to move the leg that had taken the bullet meant for him.

Ari's eyes were dull and lifeless, the spark that powered the surge of mental energy necessary to bring down the entire compound was now nothing more than a dim light source in danger of being extinguished.

She stirred in Beau's arms, pushing weakly as if she wanted to sit up. But she couldn't even support her own weight. Beau carefully lifted so she could see her parents, but her gaze was empty. Blank. She stared beyond the occupants of the helicopter to the orange fireball erupting into the sky and the thick wall of smoke that blanketed the entire area.

Her unfocused gaze found Beau, her eyelids fluttering weakly, as though it were a struggle to merely remain conscious.

"Is it gone?" she asked hoarsely. "Is it destroyed?"

Beau's throat closed in, swelling with emotion until it was impossible for him to swallow.

"Yes, honey. It's gone. You destroyed it just like you swore you would."

"And my parents?" she whispered.

Beau exchanged quick worried glances with her mom and dad because they were sitting right next to her. They'd held her, talked to her. And she wasn't aware of their presence?

Beau pressed his lips to her forehead. "Your parents are okay. More than okay. You saved them. They're here now with you. Do you want to see them?"

Ari's eyes closed and she sagged limply against Beau.

"It's finished," she whispered.

Beau gathered her more tightly in his arms, fear knotting his insides. He held her fiercely as if by holding her tighter he could somehow hold her spirit with him in the here and now. Because he could see her fading away. As though she'd mustered just enough strength to achieve her objective and now was sliding away from him with each passing second.

"No, it's not finished," Beau choked out. "Not you and me, Ari. We're just beginning. You hang on. Don't you dare give up. Do you hear me? This isn't finished!"

He pressed his lips to the top of her head, hot tears sliding down his cheeks.

"Don't go, Ari. Don't leave me. I love you," he said brokenly.

He bowed his head, pulling her closer into his body even as his fingers stroked her neck, searching for a pulse. There'd been so much blood. So much mental strain. How could anyone survive something like this?

Her breath, so light and erratic puffed and then stuttered against his skin. And then she went utterly still. No rise and fall of her chest. No air exchange. No pulse. Nothing.

"No!" Beau roared in fury, denial raging in his mind, heart and soul. "Goddamn you. Come back to me, Ari! You can't leave me. You can never leave me!"

Zack and Gavin managed to pull Ari from Beau's grasp and they laid her on the floor of the helicopter so they could begin CPR. But it was all distant. Like it wasn't really happening. As though Beau was watching it happen to a complete stranger with mild curiosity.

Only this was no stranger. Ari was his entire world. Without her to share it with him, it simply wasn't worth getting up in the mornings.

She wasn't responding to Zack and her father's urgent attempts to bring her back. It was simply too much for Beau to handle any longer.

He dropped to the floor and gathered Ari's limp body in his arms and rocked back and forth, his face buried in her hair.

"Don't leave me," he whispered. "Please don't leave me, Ari. Stay. Fight this. Fight for us. Just please don't leave me when it took so long for me to find the other half of my soul."

THIRTY-EIGHT

BEAU paced the interior of the waiting room like a caged lion, edgy, raw, his nerves so jagged that any sound whatsoever set his teeth on edge. Every time one of the medical staff opened the door to the waiting room, he surged to attention, hoping it was someone bearing news about Ari.

He hadn't wanted to be separated from her, not even for a minute. But the nurses hadn't been swayed by his harsh demands, pleas or frustrated raging. Not even her parents had been allowed back while the doctor and other nurses worked rapidly to stabilize her. He'd drawn no comfort from that fact, because while he wanted to be with her, absolutely, he just didn't want her to regain consciousness alone and frightened.

And judging by the restless, worried expressions on her parents' faces, they weren't faring any better than he was.

He closed his eyes, remembering the warning from so long ago. Tori's dream. In reality, not that much time had passed, but so much had happened since then that it seemed a lifetime ago.

Him, covered in blood, on the floor. He'd been right about one thing. It wasn't his blood in his sister's dream. It had been Ari's. But Tori hadn't seen something that had already occurred. She had seen the future. Ari's fate.

Dane, Eliza, Capshaw and Isaac had arrived an hour and a half after the helicopter had touched down on the roof of the hospital. If the personnel had been taken aback by the strange aircraft, they hadn't let on. They'd set about briskly and efficiently doing their jobs. Saving Ari's life.

But Beau was worried about the amount of blood loss she'd incurred. It seemed she'd lost over half her volume. Just what she'd lost with the multiple and continuous psychic bleeds would be enough to fell anyone. Add a gunshot wound on top of that?

She had lost and regained a pulse numerous times on the helicopter flight to the hospital. Upon arrival they'd intubated her and began CPR again.

That was hours ago. What the fuck could be taking so long? Didn't they know there were people out here dying a slow, agonizing death waiting to know if Ari lived or died? Would it kill them to give some kind of update?

But then if she'd died, they would have already reported that, so he took comfort from the fact that not a single person had been out to give Ari's status.

Beau had been on the phone with Caleb and Ramie every hour since Ari's arrival at the hospital. Ramie had wanted to fly out in Caleb's plane immediately, but Beau had convinced her not to. There was little she could do and Beau would prefer they not leave Tori alone with only Quinn for protection. His little sister was still in a very fragile, vulnerable state, and subject to anxiety attacks if left alone for more than a few hours.

Quinn, too, had called, though his younger brother hadn't even met Ari. Apparently Caleb and Ramie had filled him in, though, because he was anxious over the condition of his "future sister-in-law."

Beau blew out his breath. If he was lucky, Ari would give him the time of day after he'd let her down so many times.

"Man, sit down for a while," Zack said in a low voice.

Beau looked up to see Zack standing beside him. He hadn't even noticed the other man's approach. Zack held a cup of coffee out to Beau and he took it gratefully. He was weary to his bones and needed any surge the caffeine would provide because he refused to even contemplate sleep until he'd seen for himself that Ari was out of the woods.

"You're wasted," Zack said bluntly. "You aren't doing anyone any good, especially not Ari, by stalking around here making the other people in the waiting room nervous as hell and you're certainly not helping to diminish Ari's mother's worry. You saw Ari. You were with her. Her parents weren't. So to see you so eaten alive like this only makes them think the worst."

Guilt surged over Beau and he glanced momentarily over to where Ari's parents sat. Ginger had her head laid on her husband's shoulder, his arm firmly wrapped around her. Her eyes were red and swollen from the tears she'd shed and worry was bright in both her and her husband's eyes.

Conceding that he wasn't helping matters any, Beau took a seat and leaned back, fatigue washing through his veins, nearly overwhelming him in the process. He sipped at the strong coffee and grimaced his distaste.

"I didn't say it was *good* coffee," Zack said in amusement. "But it should definitely give you a zap of caffeine. I think it qualifies as sludge more than actual coffee."

Beau peered down into the cup and frowned his agreement. Then he sighed and forced another sip down his throat.

The minutes ticked by with excruciating slowness, each one seemingly an hour. Beau watched the hand tick around the wall clock, counting each second. Silence had fallen over the small room, and no one seemed to want to change that.

There were half a dozen other people occupying the waiting room, but they'd all relocated to the far wall when Beau and the others had burst in. He couldn't say he blamed them. Beau was covered in Ari's blood, Gavin had dried blood in more than one place from his altercation with the two men he'd killed and the rest just looked pissed off.

Beau leaned back, cocking his head toward the ceiling, forcing his gaze from the clock and his frustration with how slowly time was passing. His eyes had just began to close when he heard the door to the waiting room open.

Bracing himself for disappointment—again—he surged to his feet, only this time the woman wearing scrubs called out Ari's name. He strode across the room, but Gavin and Ginger were closer and they eagerly approached the nurse.

The nurse frowned when she saw many people gathered at the mention of Ari's name.

"I'm sorry, but only immediate family is allowed back."

Beau stood there, stunned. They weren't going to let him back? What the fuck?

His fingers curled into tight fists at his sides, his desire to hit something—anything—a violent need boiling inside him. He was a simmering cauldron of fury, his impatience reaching its breaking point.

Before he could open his mouth to blast the nurse and dare her to keep him away from Ari, Gavin motioned to Beau with his hand, shocking him with his next words.

"Come on, son."

Ginger smiled up at the nurse. "He's her husband—our son-in-law."

Beau wanted to drop to the floor and kiss his "mother-in-law's" feet and he would have if he thought he could get back up. Embarrassing tears welled in his eyes at their unconditional acceptance of him. Was this what it was like to have parents who loved you? That behaved like real parents, or like they should?

He couldn't even choke out his thanks as he walked through the open door behind them because he wouldn't have been able to get the words past the knot in his throat. To his further surprise, Ginger curled her arm around his, walking beside him as the nurse led them down the hall to one of the rooms.

She gave him a little squeeze, almost as if she knew the weight of his emotions and the impact her words had on him. God, he wanted nothing more than to hug her.

The nurse hesitated at the door and Beau's stomach tightened.

"She's groggy from the pain medicine," the nurse said. "But she's comfortable for now. The doctor will be by in a few minutes to fully update you on her condition, but I knew you'd want to see her as soon as possible."

"Damn right," Beau said gruffly.

The nurse smiled. "Go in then. If she gets restless or agitated, push the nurse call button. Until a surgeon is consulted and a decision is made as to whether she requires surgery she needs to remain as still as possible because we haven't set her leg yet."

"Set?" Beau croaked. "As in it's broken?"

Ginger swallowed hard and Gavin's face went gray with worry.

"She sustained a femur fracture, but the fracture itself isn't too serious. The force of the bullet's entry dislocated her hip, and the orthopedic surgeon is being consulted to see whether the tear in the cartilage needs to be surgically repaired or if we can reset the dislocation and she'll heal on her own."

Beau winced. That sounded damn painful. But he nodded, only wanting her to get out of the way so he could see Ari. His heart thundered, his pulse loud in his ears when she finally moved, allowing them entrance inside. He pushed by quickly, in his haste going right by Ari's parents, who were every bit as eager to see her as he was, he knew.

But they hadn't been there when she'd been shot. When she'd taken a bullet meant for him. They hadn't held her while her blood poured all over him and onto the floor in a scarlet wave. They hadn't experienced the harrowing thought that she was . . . dead.

He breathed in, shaking the horrible memories from his head. And he went straight to Ari's bedside, curling his hand around her limp one. The other hand had an IV attached and she was hooked to an assortment of other machines. His blood chilled because there was a crash cart next to her. Had she *coded*? Surely they would have been notified. Or had they merely feared and prepared for the worst given the condition she'd been in when she arrived?

His gaze raked hungrily over her, taking in every detail, watching each and every breath, the soft rise and fall of her chest. This time tears didn't merely burn his eyes. They streaked down his cheeks, blurring his vision.

She was alive. It nearly brought him to his knees. The sheer gratitude that she was alive, breathing, that she would recover. And God willing, she'd recover with him every step of the way.

Her parents crowded in on the other side of her and her father leaned down to kiss her brow. Her mom carefully picked up the hand the IV was attached to, and in that moment, she was being touched by the three people who loved her most in the world.

"Beau?" Ari murmured, her voice cloudy with confusion. But thankfully no pain. At least it didn't sound pained.

"Yes, honey, I'm here," Beau said, wiping at his tears with his shoulder. Damn if he'd sob all over her like a child.

She licked her lips and then smacked them together as if ridding herself of a bad taste. But no, that wasn't what she was doing at all.

"Kiss me," she whispered.

Ah hell. She didn't realize, in her drug-induced fog, that her parents were standing right there. But he wasn't going to let that get in the way of complying with her wishes because it was what he wanted right now more than anything.

He leaned down, capturing her mouth gently with his. She sighed against his lips, and then he pulled away, though he'd love nothing more than to spend the next several hours simply touching and kissing her, reassuring himself that she was alive.

"Honey, there are two people here who want very much to see you," Beau said, brushing her soft cheek with the crook of his finger.

Her brow scrunched up as she looked at him. She hadn't even looked in her parents' direction yet, but they didn't seem bothered by that fact. Ginger was smiling through her tears, watching the interaction between Beau and her daughter. Her father wore a slight scowl, but that was to be expected. What self-respecting father ever liked the man his daughter hooked up with at first sight?

"Who? Where?" she asked in puzzlement.

"Here, baby." Her mom finally spoke.

Ari's head turned swiftly and she let out a small cry when she saw both her mother and her father there.

"You're all right," she breathed. "You're not dead!"

Gavin frowned. "Why on earth would you think a thing like that?"

Knowing it would be difficult, not to mention tiring, for Ari to explain it all, Beau explained what Ari had seen—and assumed—himself.

"Oh baby, I'm so sorry," Ginger said. "You didn't fail us and I won't have you saying so. You saved our lives. Because those men absolutely meant to kill us. They tried to kill us. But your power stopped them. And well, by the time they realized the barrier was gone, it was too late," she added ruefully. "Your father was pretty pissed by then."

Gavin's face darkened. "That's an understatement."

Ginger laughed and Ari smiled and Beau went weak at the knees. Man did she have a beautiful smile. It lit up the entire room. Warmed his entire body.

Then Ari sobered, her expression somber and utterly serious. "Mom, Dad, there's something you should know."

Knowing precisely what Ari wanted to tell them, Beau lifted her hand and pressed a kiss to her palm.

"Would you rather I left you alone to speak to your parents?" he asked softly.

Something flickered in her eyes, and then she shook her head. "I'd like you to stay. That is if you want to. If you'd rather—"

He put his finger to her lips, shushing her. Then he followed it with a kiss. "Wild horses couldn't drag me away. I'll always want to stay, Ari. But if you wanted privacy I'd certainly grant it."

Instead, she laced her fingers through his and turned nervously toward her parents.

"What is it, baby?" Ginger asked, her brow creased in concern.

Ari took a deep breath. "I know the truth. That you and Dad adopted me."

THIRTY-NINE

HER parents wore mirroring expressions of alarm. Fear leaped into her mom's eyes and her father actually paled. Ari lifted the hand with the IV attached to where her parents' hands rested, one atop the other, on her bedrail. And she covered it with her own.

"How?"

It seemed the only word her mother was able to speak. She looked so shocked—so terrified—that Ari wondered if they feared rejection. Her anger. Disappointment? She would give them none of those.

The only thing she'd ever give them was her love. Well, plenty of other things too. Loyalty. Laughter. Grandchildren . . . ? She snuck a quick peek at Beau as she thought the last. She could just imagine little dark-haired boys who looked like their father. A blond angelic baby girl. Or perhaps even a daughter with her father's dark hair. The possibilities were endless, and

Ari wanted a big family. She just hoped Beau felt half of what she felt in return.

"It's a complicated story," Ari said with a sigh. "And I'll tell you all the specific details sometime. The important thing is that I know."

"We're so sorry," her father began, but Ari cut him off rapidly, not even wanting him to venture in that direction.

"The other important thing—really the only important thing—is that I love you both so much. And you are my parents—my family. Blood doesn't make a family. Love does."

The words, the sentiment or epiphany—whatever she wanted to consider it—had come to her in the worst of circumstances and now, giving voice to them, made it all the more real.

Tears spilled down her mom's cheeks and her father turned his face away so she wouldn't see the emotion churning in his eyes. But she had glimpsed it. Just before he turned away.

Beau's hand tightened around hers in silent support. She waited for her parents to collect themselves before she said anything further. When they seemed more controlled, she continued.

"At first I was hurt—devastated," she admitted. "The idea that I was unwanted, unloved, left on someone's doorstep to die if no one came."

She broke off. Despite being at peace with her past, a knot had still formed when speaking of her birth parents.

"Oh baby," her mother whispered. "You are so very loved."

Beau cleared his throat, clearly wanting to say something, but he seemed to battle whether to do so or not. Then he sighed and ran his free hand over his head, a signal of his agitation.

"Ari, the night you were taken from the safe room, when we all left the house to engage the threat against us . . . I tripped over a body. It was a man who'd been badly beaten. In fact I didn't think he was even alive. But then he spoke and he made me promise to give his last words to you."

Her eyes rounded with shock and her parents gave him a look of equal bewilderment.

"Me?" she asked, flabbergasted over Beau's statement.

Beau took a deep breath and squeezed her hand, lacing and unlacing their fingers, hesitating a fraction of a second longer.

"He was your birth father."

"What?"

"Oh my word," her mother whispered.

Her father remained silent, his expression and features stoic. He'd frozen the moment Beau had dropped the words "birth father." At least he hadn't said *father*. Because that would have been an insult to the man who was her father in every way except blood.

"I have to back up a little," Beau admitted. "He called me a few days before. Not long after you came to me for help. And he warned me. He told me what they'd done to your birth mother in order to glean information about who your adopted parents were."

Ari's hand broke free of her parents' grasp and she brought it over her mouth as a gasp escaped.

"I won't go into the details," Beau said in disgust. "There's no need. These people are—were—animals. But then I neither heard from him again, nor did I ever see him in person until that night. When I found him outside. And he made me swear that I would give you his message."

"What was it?" Ari asked, her voice catching.

"That he loved you. That your birth mother loved you. And that when they discovered the true intentions of the surrogacy foundation who funded your birth mother's pregnancy, they ran. They had several close calls, so after you were born they went to ..."

He broke off and closed his eyes as if what he would say next hurt him more than it would her.

"They went to my father," he said hoarsely. "Because he was an active donor/participant in the foundation, and they begged him to take you in and raise you. So you'd be safe."

Her father closed his own eyes when Beau spoke the last and Ari frowned, realizing this hadn't come as a surprise to him.

"My *father*," he said, with bitter emphasis on the word, "refused and instead sent your birth parents to ... them."

Beau pointed at her parents as his words trailed off.

"I'm very glad that he did," Ari said softly.

She reached up to touch Beau's jaw, sliding her thumb over the hard cheekbone.

"I would hate to think of us as having been raised as siblings. That would put quite a kink in our relationship, don't you think?"

And then she groaned.

"Oh my God. Forget I said that. I did *not* mean it that way."

"Jesus," her father muttered, reaching to cover his ears. "There's only so much a father can take, Ari."

Her mother was battling a smile and Beau looked baffled, almost as if he'd fully expected her to think he was repugnant because of the kind of man his father was.

"It would indeed put a kink in it," her mother said with a completely straight face.

"Enough!" her father groaned.

Beau went tense again, and he was studying her father intently.

"There is one thing I'd like to know," Beau said in a quiet tone.

Since it was obviously directed at her father, he nodded in Beau's direction.

"You went to see my father the day before he died. Ari would have been around two years old then. Both my father and my mother died the next day. They were murdered."

Ari gasped because surely . . . No, he couldn't think . . . Did he think her father had anything to do with his parents' death?

Her father met Beau's gaze unblinkingly. "If you're asking me if I had anything to do with their deaths, the answer is no. I did, however, go to see your father. I went to warn him."

"About?" Beau prompted.

"About the fact that there were some very discreet inquiries into Franklin's business dealings. Particularly those involving his funding of CAS—Creative Adoption Solutions. And let me answer your next question before you ask. No, I had no idea at the time that Franklin had anything to do with Ari appearing on my doorstep. There was a note left in her car carrier begging us to take her in and raise her as our own daughter. So we did. It wasn't until Ari was several months old that we made the move to Houston. When Ari was a year old, Franklin came to see me. To tell me about his role in Ari becoming my daughter. And I'll be straight with you, son. The son of a bitch tried to blackmail me."

Beau flinched, but he didn't look at all surprised by her father's accusation.

"If he tried to blackmail you, then why would you later warn him?" Beau asked.

Her father signed. "Because he had you. And three other children. He had a family anyone would be proud to have and his children didn't deserve to suffer because of his sins. I'm just grateful that whoever did the job didn't also kill you and your brothers and sister."

"So am I," Beau murmured.

Ari squeezed Beau's hand this time, offering him reassurance and comfort. She knew his father wasn't Father of the Year material but she hadn't realized just how loathsome he was.

The two men talked a bit further, but the pain was starting to come back, and she drifted, trying to get comfortable on the narrow hospital bed. The doctor still hadn't come by, so she didn't know if she required surgery or not.

The idea of having to be off her feet for so long was irritating. But at least she could use her powers to float food and drinks to her. Or maybe Beau would sign up for the role as her personal assistant. The idea had merit. She'd make a very exacting job description for him.

She was about to hit the nurse call button, realizing her pain was only getting stronger, when she heard her name being called. Shaking herself, she looked up to see Beau's concerned face as well as her parents'.

"Do you need pain medicine, honey?" Beau asked gently.

She nodded.

Beau reached over for the controller that operated the TV as well as the call button and punched it. Her father leaned closer to Ari, placing his hand over her forehead and wiping up and over her hair in a soothing motion.

"Are you sure you're okay?" he asked gently.

She knew he wasn't acting about her physical hurts. He was asking if she was okay emotionally after having so many bombs dropped on her in such a short period of time.

She was silent for a moment and then she glanced up at her parents, love for them welling deep, so deep.

"Do you think it's stupid of me to grieve the deaths of two people I never knew?" she whispered.

Ginger lowered the bedrail and carefully slid onto the edge of the bed so she faced Ari.

"You've always had such a huge heart, Ari. I'd be more shocked if you didn't feel at least some sadness for the deaths of the people who gave you life. I owe them a debt I could never have hoped to repay. The only thing they asked in return for the blessing they gave us was for us to love you as our own daughter, and baby, that's the easiest promise I've ever had to keep. No promise was required because we fell in love with you the minute we laid eyes on you.

"So, no, I don't think it makes you stupid at all. It makes you human. It makes you the beautiful inside and out daughter we love with all our hearts."

"Thanks, Mom," Ari said, emotion thick in her voice. "I love you."

Her mom leaned over and kissed the top of Ari's head. "I love you, too, my baby. And you will always be my baby. I don't care how old you are."

"Same goes here," her dad said in a gruff tone.

The door opened and a nurse came striding in, pushing a portable cart that held the computerized record keeping as well as meds and instruments for checking vitals. Ari's mom and dad backed away from the bed to give the nurse access to Ari's IV port.

After checking all her vitals, the nurse drew out a syringe already filled with medication, swabbed the port site and then injected the pain medicine into the IV line.

Ari felt the uncomfortable burn of the medication as soon as it hit her bloodstream and continued up her arm until it reached her shoulder, at which point the burn dissipated and a nice, warm, floaty feeling assailed her.

She vaguely remembered her last encounter with pain medication and she hadn't lasted more than a few minutes before she'd sunk into oblivion. This time she wasn't ready to float away. She'd only just gotten her parents back. She'd only, just hours before, experienced the euphoria of knowing Beau was alive. She didn't want to give them up, even for a minute.

Blinking furiously, she fought the effects of the drug, frowning with concentration.

"Stop fighting it, honey," Beau said in a tender voice.

"Don't want you all to go," she fretted.

He kissed her forehead, placing his palm on top of her head.

"We'll be here. We're not going anywhere."

"Promise?"

He stroked his thumb down her cheek and then to the dimple in her chin.

"Promise."

FORTY

BEAU sat in the darkness of Ari's room, elbows propped on his knees, his hands wearily covering his face as he scrubbed his eyes to stay awake. He refused to go to sleep and miss the opportunity to speak to Ari—alone. Gavin had taken Ginger to a nearby hotel so Ginger could rest after her ordeal.

He couldn't go another day, hour or minute without knowing if he had a future with Ari or not. Whether she felt for him all that he felt for her.

He couldn't help but swell with pride, his male ego stroked that he'd been her first lover. And her last if he had anything to say on the matter.

His head shot up when he heard her stir and then emit a soft groan. Immediately sliding to the edge of the chair he'd positioned at the head of her bed, he lifted her hand and twined their fingers together.

"How are you feeling, honey?"

Another sigh.

"Hurts."

"Let me call the nurse."

"No," Ari protested. "Not yet. It just knocks me out and so all I've done is sleep. Between the anesthesia taking forever to wear off and the pain meds, I feel like a zombie."

Beau could understand, and if he were honest, he was glad she was refusing the medicine, at least until he got to have his say. Hopefully she'd put him out of his misery so he could start breathing again.

She'd been taken to surgery the morning after she'd been brought into the hospital and she'd been out of it that entire day and well into the next until dusk had descended, heralding the coming night.

For the next six weeks she'd wear an awkward cast that encased her hip and was completely inflexible. It was like wearing a block of cement. Or so she'd grumbled to him.

"I love you," he said starkly.

Ari's startled gaze found his and he groaned, lowering his head to smack his forehead repeatedly with his palm.

"Fuck," he muttered. More slapping. "That was smooth." More thudding his head against his palm. "Jesus, I've been waiting for this moment. I've *wanted* this moment. With you. I've imagined it in my head a million times. It's all I've thought of. And when I finally get to the big event, the one where I tell you that you're my entire fucking world and that I don't want to live my life without you I freeze up, and all I can manage is three words with no preamble, no context, no buildup."

He sighed, a mournful, disgusted sound.

"I'm so sorry, Ari. I completely fucked this up."

She smiled, her eyes lighting up like he'd just laid the world at her feet. Was it possible she returned his love? That she had the same dreams and desires he did?

"It may not have been the most eloquent declaration in the world, but it was utterly *perfect*," she said in a dreamy, satisfied voice. "I mean who can argue with phrases like 'You're my fucking world' and 'I don't want to live my life without you'?"

She patted the space beside her on the bed. "Come here."

He leaned farther toward her and then, as her mom had done that first visit, he carefully slid his ass onto the edge of the bed, ensuring he didn't jostle her in any way. And then his eyes narrowed, but not before she saw stark vulnerability reflected in them.

"Do you have something you'd like to say to me?" he asked pointedly.

She nearly laughed, but he looked too close to being sick for her to tease him. She could swear he was sweating.

She crooked her finger at him, making him lean farther and farther until their faces were mere inches apart. Then she slid her arms loosely around his neck and pulled him into her kiss.

"I love you too," she whispered

He immediately sagged, closing his eyes. He rested his forehead against hers, his breaths coming in ragged bursts over her chin. He lifted his hand to caress one side of her face, sliding his fingers around and then thrusting upward into the thick mass of her hair.

"Thank God," he whispered back. "*Thank God*. I thought I was flying solo on this one and it wasn't a pleasant thought at all."

He gave her a light smooch, peppering tiny kisses along the entire arch of her mouth.

"Will you marry me?"

"Hmm, that depends," she said, waiting for his reaction. He was going to kill her because he was sweating bullets and she was teasing him mercilessly.

"On what?" He sounded outraged.

She waggled her free hand at him. "The ring, of course."

He chuckled, shaking his head. "I think I can manage a ring. Now, if I promise to deliver the perfect ring, will you marry me? Please?"

"I'm a sucker for please," she grumbled.

"Wish I'd have known that sooner," he said dryly.

"Yes, I'll marry you, Beau," she said, suddenly growing more serious. "I can't imagine not being with you now. I don't want to imagine it or live it. I dearly love my parents, but I had already moved out on my own, even if I was more dependent on them than I liked."

"I'll build the most fucking amazing house you've ever seen," he vowed.

"How many kids, er-um, bedrooms will we need?"

His eyes narrowed for a moment, almost as if he were trying to ascertain whether she was yanking his chain again.

"How many do you want?" he asked, turning it around on her.

"At least four," she said, a contented smile on her face as she imagined a house full of children. Her parents visiting their grandchildren. Watching her children wrestle with their father on the floor.

He lifted his eyebrows. "Four, huh. Sounds like I have a lot of work to do."

Her mouth dropped open. "A lot of work *you* have to do?

What the heck does a guy do except get a really good orgasm? The woman carries the baby around for nine months and . . ."

She broke off and then glared at him when she realized he was merely dishing it back at her and yanking *her* chain. "Just for that, you draw diaper duty for the first nine months to offset the nine months I carry them around inside me."

She sent him a smug look that dared him to top that.

His features softened, and a warm smile lit his face. "When will you marry me? Or maybe I should ask how *soon* will you marry me?"

She could feel herself softening just as he'd done. Her heart contracting under his bone-melting smile.

"As soon as my cast comes off," she said, looking down in disgust at her plaster-covered hip and thigh. "I want a wedding, honeymoon, the entire shebang, and I can hardly enjoy any of that with my clunky cast on."

Joy flooded her heart, bursting like fireworks as the implications of their oh-so-casual conversation really hit her.

"You *love* me," she said in wonder. "*And* you want to *marry* me."

She stared at him in utter bewilderment. And then she promptly burst into tears.

Beau was horrified, frantically scrambling for tissue and then tilting her chin up so he could wipe the tears from her face.

"Ari, what's wrong?" he demanded.

"I'm happy," she said with a sob.

He scowled. "You have a damn funny way of showing it. You just scared about a decade off my life. Okay, we have to establish some ground rules for this relationship right now. Starting with you never being able to cry, because the sight of you crying, even happy tears, scares the ever-loving hell out of me. And manipulating me with them now that you know what they do to me."

She laughed and wiped at her tears, trying to keep more from falling. Then she gave up, facing him, her hands extended outward for his. He clasped them firmly in his warm, strong grasp and gently squeezed.

"I love you," she said, tears still glistening on her eyelashes.

He gazed at her, returning love glowing like a beacon in his eyes. "Promise me you'll never leave me," he said hoarsely. "Promise me you'll love me forever. Stay with me forever."

" 'Til death do us part," she murmured. "I've at least got that much down."

He smiled. "Yeah, believe it or not, I paid attention at Caleb and Ramie's wedding. Or at least to the good parts. 'Til death to us part' is right up there with 'to love and cherish.' Because, Ari, I will cherish you. All the days of my life. You'll be the most pampered, spoiled and adored woman in existence."

"Oh, I don't know," Ari said thoughtfully. "My dad may have the market cornered on pampering, cherishing, et cetera. It's kind of embarrassing to see my badass father make a complete wuss of himself over my mother."

He scowled again. "Is that a challenge I hear? When it comes to taking care of my woman, there is nothing remotely embarrassing about doing whatever it takes to make her happy—to make her smile."

"Glad you think so. I admit, watching my parents makes me jealous sometimes. I never dreamed I'd have what they have," she said softly.

"Just wait until our wedding," he vowed. "Then we'll see who does the most spoiling."

"I want my parents there," Ari said wistfully. "I want my father to give me away. I want my mother to see me in my dress. To help me with my hair and give me marriage and wedding night advice."

He looked horrified. "Of course they'll be there. What would make you think any differently? And really, Ari. Wedding night advice? Have I not shown you I'm more than capable in the wedding night department?"

She looked laughingly up at him. "Maybe I was thinking more about advice for me. And well, as far as the wedding goes, I wasn't at all certain you weren't going to haul me out of the hospital and to Vegas or something so we got married more quickly."

"It's tempting," he mused. "But your mother would kill me."

"And not my father?"

Beau laughed. "He's a man, honey. He'd probably buy our airline tickets if I even mentioned eloping. Hell, he might even buy us our own plane. We hate wearing suits and monkey tails, remember?"

She rolled her eyes. "Whatever."

Then her expression went soft and serious and she shifted as much as she was able to free up a small area beside her on the small bed. He knew without her saying what she wanted.

Gingerly, he maneuvered his big body against hers, carefully lifting her head so he could position one arm underneath her head, the other free to roam and caress the rest of her body.

"You think you can live with my powers?" she asked quietly.

He went still and then leaned back just enough that he could see her face. With his fingertips, he nudged her chin up so her gaze connected with his.

"I love you, Ari. Everything that makes you who you are.

Everything about you. And if you come equipped to ward off an entire third-world nation's army then I guess I won't ever have to worry about getting my ass handed to me."

Her eyes sparkled in the low light of the hospital room as she reached up to trace her fingers down his jawline.

"Having this cast on sucks," she said huskily. "But I guess it'll make our eventual wedding night all the more sweeter."

"Honey, I hate to be the one to break it to you, but after six weeks with you and no sex my balls will be so blue that I give myself thirty seconds tops inside you before I have the mother of all premature ejaculations."

She leaned up to nibble on his chin, eliciting a soft rumbling groan from his chest.

"My cast may knock me out of the orgasm game awhile, but I don't see why you should suffer. There's nothing wrong with my hands—or my mouth," she finished with a throaty purr.

"Have mercy," he rasped. "You're killing me here, honey."

"Mercy?" She laughed. "I can assure you, Beau. Mercy is the very last thing you'll want from me over the next several weeks."

Damn if she didn't prove to be right about that.

Don't miss SAFE AT LAST

The next Slow Burn novel by
#1 *New York Times* and *USA Today*
bestselling author Maya Banks.

Available April 2015 wherever books are sold.